THE
Secret
PAGE

A NOVEL BY

AL TURNER

The Secret Page

This novel is a work of fiction. Names, characters, places, and incidents either are the product of the author's imagination or are used fictitiously. Any resemblance to actual persons, living or dead, businesses, events, or locales is entirely coincidental.

Editing by Caroline Kaiser
www.carolinekaisereditor.com

Book cover design by The Book Design House
www.thebookdesignhouse.com

For the Ultimate Cyn, who believed and supported me throughout this process.

GULF OF MEXICO

Several hours out of New Orleans, the supply vessel emerged from a curtain of rain and proceeded southeast toward breaking skies. It was a typical Gulf storm, hardly worth writing home about, with some showers and wind. The *Dream Stream* pushed onward through seven- to eight-foot head seas that dissipated as she moved toward calmer waters.

Officially, she was listed as an offshore supply ship, about 230 feet from stem to stern. To the casual observer, she was a common vessel on a typical supply run —exactly what her crew and passengers preferred others to think.

The ship readjusted her course, as she was no longer required to skirt the edge of a Gulf storm, and headed south to her destination.

Her skipper, known only as Captain Albert to those aboard, stood on the bridge and surveyed both the sea and sky ahead. His ship was only a few years old, built in the mid-eighties in the US, flagged in Panama, and refitted for special duty. She had been rechristened with her new name only weeks before. Albert had only been her skipper for the past few days and wasn't privy to her prior name.

With his weathered skin and keen eyes, he looked the part of a man at sea. In all his years, though, he had never had a haul like the one that sat in the ship's hold. Not that he knew what it was; it was all hush-hush. There were the men in dark suits, the brass in uniforms, and the brainy ones in white coats.

Then there was this other guy, the real brains of the bunch, and just as interested in the weather as he. His hair was short and disheveled, while his wardrobe consisted of cargo pants and a Hawaiian shirt. He chewed away at his gum and blew the occasional bubble. The bubble first appeared, it seemed, as he was on the threshold of reaching a conclusion about whatever was on his mind. As it grew and popped, it signaled he was close to making some announcement. When the man spoke, everyone within earshot listened.

"So we made it through the first one. Moving forward, I'll assume clear skies," Dr. Albert Dasinger said.

The captain knew it was directed at him. "We've got another line coming up from the south, but it's light rain that should pass to our west."

"Let's hope your forecast is correct," he said curtly, his slight German accent barely noticeable. He added a thin smile as if to soften his words a bit.

"Beyond another quick shower, we should have mostly clear skies, Dr. Dasinger," Captain Albert assured him.

While the rest of the crew and passengers were under strict orders to use only first names, ranks, or titles, this scientist refused to be called by his first name. He had earned his degree, and the suits that were aft and below didn't seem to push the matter. The captain surmised correctly that he was the most important guest aboard.

"Good. Thank you, Albert," said Dr. Dasinger. "My colleague is counting on everything being ready." He blew another bubble, apparently contemplating something.

It was a mystery to the captain who the man was trying to coordinate with. At the same time, he wouldn't bother to ask questions that would surely go unanswered. "Of course," he replied, unsure of what he had agreed to. He was just the guy charged with getting men and supplies to what he understood to be an oil platform in the Gulf. No details given, just coordinates.

Captain Albert was glad to have work again. He had thought his career was over, but then his prayers had been answered when the call came in. Someone needed a replacement for another captain who had some sort of medical emergency. He felt they had made a mistake. He was, after all, under review, and the last thing he expected was a job offer to come his way.

The brush with a sandbar in a vessel owned by someone else had come at the worst time. It was what happened when a captain's mind was on his personal losses and not the river he was supposed to navigate. Two losses, his wife and his captaincy, occurred in as many weeks. The pain was almost more than he could bear.

When his only son had heard the news about the job offer, he didn't seem too surprised. Albert wondered if Cornelius had pulled some strings to make it happen. He wouldn't confirm it, though his lack of a denial did just that. Cornelius told him that the opportunity could go a long way to ensure he captained again—that is, if he could do the job without question or comment. He often wondered what his son actually did for a living.

Dr. Dasinger stood for a moment longer. "I do like your name, Albert," he said with a wink as he departed. He then retreated from the bridge, probably to check his equipment.

The man didn't quite fit the mold of his vision of a scientist. Then again, he had to ask himself what an old skipper would know of such things. "Thanks, doc," was his reply.

The ship carried on until she arrived at her destination. She pulled alongside the large platform floating in the sea. From a distance, it had at first resembled a spar oil platform. However, as they drew closer, the captain noted it was rather queer for what the oil companies typically built.

It rose higher above the sea, for one, and had more levels. At the top of the floating structure were several thin vertical masts that formed a circle around the center. Each of them rose several stories and were as black as night.

Captain Albert stayed on the bridge as the rest of the ship came alive with people and equipment being quickly unloaded. Cranes from high above hoisted equipment off his ship. Impressed by the efficiency of this medley of events, he watched for a while.

A half hour after they had arrived, everyone switched from unloading to setting things up. Groups of workers hastily moved to other areas, as if anticipating what was to come. The captain made a few rounds, stopping by the galley to grab a quick snack, then returned to the bridge. Even from his vantage point, he couldn't see what was happening on the higher levels of the platform. He was certain that was exactly the way his employers liked it, whoever they were.

His first mate, a man he had met on the voyage, paced behind him. He was a wiry, gray-bearded man called Geoffrey. The crew, however, had already nicknamed him Jitters. The captain swore he looked older than himself, although the man insisted he wasn't yet fifty. The drugs and booze must have aged him quicker than most, he thought.

How he was assigned first mate to any ship was beyond reason. Of course, the rumor mill had it that ol' Jitters had connections. Looking at the man, Captain Albert could only assume his former life was well behind him. Still, there must have been some value to the man.

"Shouldn't we be leavin' soon, Cap'n?" Jitters asked.

He nodded. "We'll leave when we're told."

The man went back to pacing. It wasn't exactly a nervous gesture—more of one that conveyed impatience. "Ya know I have plans back in N'Awlins."

The captain cringed as he glanced at him disapprovingly. He knew what the man wanted. By the time they made port, he would be in a fetal position, suffering from withdrawal symptoms. The captain imagined Jitters, like several of his motley crew, had probably been in and out of prison.

"I'm gettin' a bad feelin' about dis," Jitters moaned.

There it was again. The man constantly had to rattle on about his paranoia. At the beginning of their journey, he'd seemed a different person. Of course, that was before his vice had started to wear off.

"It'll be over soon enough," Captain Albert said, not making the effort to hide his annoyance. "You can get back to whatever plans you have at port, with a little more money in your pocket."

Jitters suddenly stopped his pacing and walked over to a window on the starboard side of the bridge. His stare became fixated just past the big platform they floated next to. "Wadn't da weather 'posed to clear up?"

Interested, the captain grabbed his glasses and studied the same area of sky. The low sun was obstructed from view by the platform to their starboard side, but its orange glow shimmered across the water and reflected off clouds that formed in the distance.

"There's supposed to be another shower passing close by," said Captain Albert.

"Looks more dan a showah," Jitters insisted.

"Perhaps you're right," the captain murmured. He watched as the so-called shower grew in intensity as it approached. Plenty of energy packed into that one, he thought. More than their forecast indicated.

On the platform, people moved toward the edge and hung over the rails as they pointed in the same direction. Initially, the approaching storm aroused curiosity, but this turned to distress as it drew closer.

An even more alarming situation had begun to unfold. The storm no longer appeared to be coming from just one direction but from all around. Directly above it was mostly clear, but misty gray mountains rose and encircled them. A strange energy in the air caused the hairs on the captain's arms to stand straight up.

Then something occurred on the platform. At first, it sounded like a low hum, but it grew louder. The sky above cast a greenish haze as lightning danced freely in all directions. The wind howled in the distance, but oddly a strange calm surrounded the platform. The sea, however, churned with anger.

"What da hell's goin' on?" Jitters cried. "We gotta get away from dis place."

That very thought had occurred to the captain, but he hadn't yet received clearance to depart. He ordered Jitters to get on the comm and confirm removing the moorings so they could get clear. The endeavor was pointless—all communication attempts returned nothing but static.

A command decision had to be made, and Captain Albert ordered the vessel under way. Even while his crew carried out the command, various individuals from the platform made their way over at the last second, apparently preferring their chances on the *Dream Stream*.

Once the ship was clear, the captain gave the order to put some distance between her and the rig. He intended to circle the platform and hope for the best. But as the storm grew, it was the worst he prepared for.

Just outside the ring of masts, at the highest platform of the rig, Dr. Dasinger desperately tried to determine what could have gone wrong so he could correct it. An unforeseen variable had been introduced, he thought as he glanced up at the sky.

Behind him, close to the edge of the upper platform, two men were engaged in intense conversation. Their voices were raised, whether out of anger or to be heard over the wind he couldn't tell.

Unwilling to just leave what he was doing, he waved to get their attention. The naval officer, in his khaki uniform, didn't notice. The other man, dressed in a gray sports jacket and fedora, glanced over and saw him but returned his gaze to the uniformed man. The officer pointed to something out at sea. Begrudgingly, Dr. Dasinger left his makeshift console and trotted over.

As he approached, the man in the fedora told the officer, in so many words, to go have sex with himself. He knew little of either man, except the fedora was some intelligence agent and the uniform a naval commander named McWilliams.

The object of their frustration was the departed vessel McWilliams had arrived in. The officer wanted the ship back, while the agent seemed content to let the vessel circle them. All things considered, it seemed a strange thing to argue about.

"Can I get some help?" Dr. Dasinger demanded.

Both men stopped the bickering long enough to give him their attention.

"How may I assist, sir?" Commander McWilliams asked stiffly.

"I need to get a hold of my colleague at Source."

Immediately, the officer shook his head. "No can do, sir. Orders are that all comm goes through a single secure channel."

"Well, then let me use that channel to indirectly contact my colleague at Source." He felt silly using the code word for the other location, but those government types had insisted.

Again the officer simply shook his head. "All comm comes from Source to Echo, not the other way around—unless there's an emergency."

Dr. Dasinger suspected his bewilderment would be obvious from his expression. "Let's just forget how stupid it would be to not realize this is an emergency. Something's gone terribly wrong. If I don't correct it, we'll all die on this platform."

The officer paused as if considering his words or, perhaps, what his own response should be. "I'm sorry. That's not within protocol, sir."

"Damn your protocol! I need to talk with my brother now."

Before the officer could answer, the other man said, "You're wasting your time, doc. He's a brainwashed military drone who can't take a dump without permission."

"Up yours, Shelby," McWilliams said and turned. "I've got orders, and better things to do."

"Orders? Where are you going?" Dr. Dasinger asked, stunned that his request was being ignored.

Shelby replaced the fedora upon his thinning blond hair. It was so windy, he had to hold it in place with one hand. "Probably to go play with himself one more time before he gets everyone killed on this lightning rod."

Dr. Dasinger was still in a state of disbelief. "Does he want to die?"

Shelby pointed to a ladder at the end of the platform. "C'mon, doc, there's no use joining 'em. Let's get to that ship over there. I bet we can find you a way to communicate on board. I like our chances better there than on this rig."

"It's a long way down to the sea. Do you plan to swim?"

"That ladder leads to life rafts," Shelby yelled back.

Dr. Dasinger felt deflated. "I must stay here and try to do whatever I can."

"Whatever you say, doc," Shelby called back as his attention turned to the strangest sky he had probably ever seen. Waiting around another minute wasn't an option. He started his journey down the ladder but only got about halfway before a thunderous boom shook the rig violently. Lightning struck multiple times above him. He tried to quicken his pace but lost his footing. His grip on the wet rung lasted only a second before he fell into the churning sea below.

Above, Dr. Dasinger had trotted back over to his equipment, hoping to find at least one terminal online. Damn, he thought, noticing nothing but error messages and DOS prompts. He tried to reboot again. "Lousy government equipment," he muttered.

The platform beneath him undulated so much, it should have been impossible to stay standing. The sky above opened and bloomed into a maelstrom of energy. The tall metallic masts became as reeds blowing in the wind as they bent and twisted to the will of the forces around them.

Within seconds, a new reality bled into his own world. He could no longer hear the screams of the others around him as he took one last look at what remained. Time seemed to cease—both the perception of it and in reality—for him and the others. He could only accept his fate.

Unseen forces drew the platform, sea, and sky together into another plane of existence. Several flashes from explosions occurred, but it was as if the void had swallowed all sound. An ethereal world expanded as it replaced the natural one.

Then the heavens sealed up.

Thousands of tons of seawater returned to the ocean, followed by what was left of the once-large rig. The distorted, smoldering wreckage slowly disappeared beneath the surface of the chaotic sea.

On the *Dream Stream*, the wind, energy, and waves hit hard on her starboard side. She listed dangerously to the port until she finally began to right herself. Battered, she bobbed silently as normalcy returned around her.

Captain Albert managed to get to his feet on the dark bridge and tried to assess things. He rubbed the shoulder that had absorbed most of the impact of their being tossed around. "Status," he called out.

"Sir, we dead in da watah," Jitters called back.

FAST FORWARD

2016

Summer nights in Florida were sultry, particularly when you factor in a jacket and a polyester fedora. Still, it was difficult to hide three pistols and a dagger without the cover. The steady, warm breeze that swept the patio helped, but the extreme humidity along the Emerald Coast was anything but exaggerated.

At least Shelby could take refuge in his cold drink. The combination of ice and booze was always an antidote to the warm, humid air. He lit a cigar, a Cuban, and watched the two men from a few tables away. They went about their conversation unaware that, among the crowd of late-night Friday patrons, they had an audience.

Both were somewhere in their thirties. The one was going on about everything from his exaggerated exploits in the military to how simple it was to land his recent bartender's position. Plenty of bars dotted the coast, but Shelby had picked out this particular one for a reason.

He felt the men were nearing the point in their conversation where he might actually learn something useful. At least he hoped so, since their banter was about as interesting as watching paint dry.

His phone's vibration indicated an incoming call, but he ignored it. About half a minute later, it notified him of the voice mail that awaited his attention. He retrieved the phone from his jacket and glanced at the name.

Wynona Troy, he thought. He would definitely want to listen to it later; now was hardly the time. He turned the phone on its face so he could focus on the task at hand.

He adjusted the small antenna dish, innocuous since it was shaped like a flower, to ensure he had the best reception of the conversation, which he listened to via a low-profile earbud. Another device in his pocket also recorded their words, in case his memory left out any details. It was tough getting older.

The one known as Matt, the braggart of the two, was quite proud of himself. Not only had he charmed some striking older woman, but he was also certain this easy mark would show up over the next few days. There was apparently a wager between him and the one he called Mark; Matt had a couple of more days to reel in his quarry in or lose a Ben Franklin.

Had Shelby not known who they referred to, the chatter might have just seemed like guy talk. However, he had been trailing Matt for the past several days. The woman he had set his sights on was an interesting choice, to say the least. She was quite a beauty, but her looks weren't the reason for the man's interest.

Mark, the more reserved one, shook Matt's hand and reminded him that time was of the essence, and that he had to be absolutely certain when his part of the mission went down since it involved some coordinated effort. The hundred-dollar bet would be the least of Matt's worries should he let his partner down. Clearly, a hefty payday was at stake.

Neither of their names, of course, were the ones they were born with. Such was the business that Shelby found himself in. Within his world were goals and the lies that supported them. The men he shadowed were hardly the professionals he had dealt with in the past. They were just pups by his standard. Still, even pups had teeth.

They parted ways, with Mark leaving the little bar while Matt headed back to his new, and temporary, bartending job. Neither had even looked his way.

Amateurs, Shelby thought. He finished his drink and left a nice tip for Matt. The bartender would earn his pay soon enough, albeit not in the way he probably envisioned. As Shelby placed the barely smoked Cuban in his glass, he turned the phone over and accessed the voice mail.

The message was hardly short but not overly long either. Wynona's frantic voice came alive in his ear. One of the best inventions, he thought, is the Bluetooth earpiece.

"Shelby, this is Wynona. We're at the location and have run into a problem. Can you believe these assholes are doing another experiment at Echo? They've spotted us, so I don't know how much time we have until that submarine overtakes us. Before you wonder, yes, there were some fireworks, but not the same as before. Still, you should know that these bastards are apparently still playing with fire. If you don't hear from us again, you know what happened. Make sure our kids are taken care of."

Damn, Shelby thought. The frantic update was something he had been waiting on for years. He played the voice mail again to ensure he had heard the part about the submarine correctly. He hated being right but knew something was on the horizon. Frankly, it surprised him it had taken this long to happen.

He gathered the fake flower that housed his listening device, glanced around one more time as he rose, and headed out. There would be several interested parties, but with the latest development, he knew where he needed to go first. He just had no idea what type of reception he would get.

CHURCH MEETING

Viridian Cove, a former fishing village-turned-unincorporated town in the mid-twentieth century, lay in close proximity to Pensacola, Florida. Home to roughly a couple of thousand people, a volunteer fire department, and a tiny police department, it was the tiniest of spots on the map. The town's plaza was named Viridian Cove Square, though the locals referred to it simply as Viridian Square.

Located to the east of Viridian Square, the small church wasn't much to look at on the outside and only slightly more pleasant on the inside. With its faded red carpet and worn, cushioned pews, it was the archetype of low-budget churches. Since it was Saturday, the normal congregation of around eighty-five members was mostly missing. The doors were open for those who wanted to come pray, practice choir, or speak with the pastor.

The pastor, however, was out of town visiting a dying friend. His associate pastor, Jack Page, a man barely into middle age, held down the fort. His mood seemed to sour as he spoke on his cell phone. Dressed casually in blue jeans and a tangerine button-front shirt, the dark-haired man with a sparse beard stood at around six foot. He ran his hand across his rugged salt-and-pepper chin as he contemplated his wife's sudden decision to cancel their lunch plans.

Jack had stepped away from a teens' discussion group to speak privately. His wife seemed to bounce around the reason she had to cancel their plans, but she did promise to make it up to him. He expressed his love, ended the call, and headed back to his young audience.

The five kids ranged in age from twelve to sixteen—three boys and two girls. The three were all brothers, the Miller boys, who regularly attended church with their parents. They didn't always show up on a Saturday, as that would be odd for teens who lived so close to sugary beaches. However, the eldest, Steven, was smitten with the associate pastor's daughter. Although she was several years older than he was, the lad seemed to crave the opportunity to flirt with the lovely young woman and hoped she would make an appearance.

Jack turned to the group sitting in the front pew when he noticed a figure entering the double glass doors that were the main entrance to the small building. The man didn't look up as he walked in, and his dark blue fedora obscured his round face. He wore a thin navy-blue jacket, which was a bit odd. Midsummer in Florida was hardly the jacket-wearing season and locale. The man grabbed a hymn book from the back of the pew in front of him and thumbed through it. As Jack watched, he replaced the book and pulled a newspaper from his jacket and studied it. Who really read newspapers anymore?

He had totally missed Steven's question. It soon became clear to the boy that he would need to repeat it.

"Are you sure Carson won't be here today, Mr. Page?" Steven asked again.

This time, Jack heard. He slowly drew his attention back to the teens but positioned himself so he could monitor the guest in the back of the church. "I don't think so, Steven," Jack replied. "I believe she and her brother are going on a boating excursion this morning."

One of the girls, a twelve-year-old named Sonja, giggled about something. Steven's youngest brother Ben elbowed her. Jack gave them both a suspicious eye, then glanced back at the man who continued to read his newspaper. He licked his finger each time before he turned a page. The action seemed for show.

After a moment, Jack tried to give the children his attention again. "Sorry for the interruption. What were we discussing?"

"Sex before marriage!" Ben blurted out. He was hushed by the others.

"No, I don't think we were having that particular discussion, Ben," Jack said, knowing the boy loved to be funny.

"Pastor Page," Sonja said as she held up her hand, "we were talking about forgiveness and how it helps the forgiver as much as the one forgiven."

"Oh, right," Jack said. "Very good, Sonja. Does anyone have an example of a time when you or someone you know chose to forgive?"

Ben jumped to his feet. "My dad forgave my mom for telling her friend that you were really hot," the boy said with a big grin. The girls giggled while both of Ben's older brothers took turns punching him in the shoulder, causing him to cry out in pain.

Jack held up a hand to the teens as he fought to hold back a laugh. It was true that several women in the church found him to be attractive, if not charming. Even though some of his features were hidden by facial hair, he seemed younger than his actual age. But he was the first to admit it was he who had married up. You only had to glimpse his beautiful wife to know there was truly a fountain of youth somewhere in Florida.

Jack tried to think of a way to move past the remark. "I'm glad to hear your dad is a forgiving man, Ben. Anyone else?"

At that very moment he noticed a movement in the back of the church. The man in the fedora stood up and started for the exit but took his time about opening one of the glass doors. He paused as if considering something, glanced back, and then departed.

Jack only caught a glimpse, but it was enough to confirm his suspicion. Shelby wanted his attention. He took a deep breath as he debated whether to follow him or not. Finally, he decided to excuse himself.

But Jack realized he had missed another question. "Sorry, what is it, Steven?" he asked hastily. He was already heading to the end of the pew to start his pursuit.

"Are you sure Carson isn't coming today?" Steven asked with a mischievous grin.

Jack fought off the irritation. "Steven, why do you keep asking me the same question?"

"Because she's standing right behind you," Steven said as he pointed.

Those in the front pew erupted in laughter as Jack realized his daughter, observed by the others, had quietly positioned herself right behind him. She must have been there for some time, hence the inside joke among the group of kids.

With her sandy-blonde hair, blue crystals for eyes, and a physique toned by life on the beach, Carson was every father's worst nightmare. His beautiful daughter was the fox every hormone-filled hound wanted to chase. Her Daisy Duke shorts and white cami only amplified the effect.

"Hi, Dad," she said with a snicker. "Does Mother know about your popularity with the ladies?"

For a moment, Jack forgot about the man in the fedora. "Oh, that," Jack said as he tried in vain to hide his embarrassment. "You know kids—they'll say anything."

"Especially the truth," Carson said and gave a quick wave to Steven. The boy's countenance brightened like the sun.

Jack hugged his daughter. "I thought you were with Tripp today."

"He'll be here shortly," she said. "You know how tardy my brother can be." Before he could ask how she had gotten there, she added, "I caught a Uber over here. I wanted to see you before we headed to Destin to meet a dude."

"A dude?"

"His name is Derrick."

"Is everything okay?"

"Oh yeah, things are fine," Carson said unconvincingly.

Jack eyed her, knowing it typically took her a moment to warm up to discussing things. She was quick to blurt out her opinion but less inclined to discuss her feelings.

"Well, I'm glad you stopped by," Jack said as he glanced back at the door, resigned to Shelby being long gone. "I'd invite you and Tripp to join me for lunch, but I'm sure you guys want to get started on your fun day."

"I was under the impression you and Mother were having lunch," Carson said suspiciously. "At least that's what she told me earlier."

Mother, Jack thought. She and her mom must be at odds again. "Your lovely mom had to cancel. Her friend needs to chat with her about something."

Carson's hands went to her hips as her face turned to a scowl. "You mean Lynn? The friend who's out of town this weekend?"

Jack noticed the teens all grew silent as they listened. The last thing he needed was a rumor floating around the church. "I'm not sure which friend," he lied, then decided to change the subject. "Where's this new fella taking you?"

Carson must have realized he was avoiding the subject, so she, in turn, ignored his question. "Maybe you should just join us today. You'd have fun, Dad. Not to mention you'd feel better knowing the dumbass I've charmed behaves himself."

Jack couldn't fight off the smile as the teens snickered behind him. His daughter was anything but filtered. "Thank you, sweetie, but I'm confident your brother will make a fine chaperone."

"Tripp?" Carson laughed at the thought of her twin brother actually intimidating someone. "I'm taking him simply to expand his horizons— sort of a late birthday present. He really needs to get out of Viridian Square more often—particularly that dingy room he and Daniel call an office." She was referring to his best friend, who was Asian. Tripp had formed a private investigation business, while Daniel was a computer consultant.

"Agreed, but don't you mean an early birthday present?"

"Oh, I still owe him for last year."

"I see."

"I'll go with you, Carson," Steven said with enthusiasm.

Carson turned and tried to pretend she was flattered. "That's very sweet, Steven, but they only allow people of drinking age on the boat."

The boy's expression reminded Jack of a tire deflating, if not a blowout.

"Daniel didn't want to go too?" he asked.

"I didn't ask."

"I see. At least having your brother tag along will send a subtle message to this guy that you're more interested in his boat." It was wishful thinking on his part.

Carson pointed a finger and winked at him. "He'll figure it out."

"You know you could've used the family boat, sweetie," Jack said. The Yamaha 242 jet drive was moored on the lift at his house.

"I know, but this guy Derrick says he has a large yacht."

"Of course he does. Just remember that young men tend to exaggerate," Jack said and patted his daughter on the shoulder. "Coffee is in the back if you need some."

"Let me worry about Derrick, Dad. I'm a big girl."

"Geez, I know. You're almost twenty-four years old. How time flies. Just be safe."

"I will," Carson promised. "Is Julia here?"

As if on cue, Julia, the church's secretary, walked from the back area with a cup of coffee. She was a kind woman but had questionable taste, as demonstrated by the matching pea-green blouse and slacks she wore.

"Hi, Julia!" she said, waving.

"Hi, darling," Julia said with a smile. She hugged Carson as she passed by on her way to the coffeepot.

"I'll give you a hug too before I leave," Carson called back to him and then headed to the church's tiny kitchen.

Jack waved at his daughter, then excused himself from the group of kids. He walked to the back of the church where the fedora-clad man had last been seen. As he reached the pew, he glanced around and saw the newspaper, neatly folded and purposely left behind. He spotted Julia watching him, wondering what he was up to. She was an excellent source of church gossip.

He ignored her and instead focused on the newspaper. Cautiously, he picked it up. The first thing he noticed was its yellowish-brown color, an indication it was old. It wasn't a local paper but one from Dallas. Then there was the date. A knot formed in his stomach as he read it.

October 17, 1991.

He could feel his skin crawl as he opened the paper to find the article. As if for convenience, it was circled in red. Although he knew the article by heart, he read the bold print again.

Local Man Dies in Fiery Crash

Jack winced as he thought back. It had been over two and a half decades, but it still haunted him. It had changed everything.

The article being left was a message in itself. The intended meaning, however, was unknown. Jack rolled up the newspaper and placed it in the back pocket of his jeans. He hid it from obvious view under his shirt. As he made his way back over to the group of teens, he pondered what Shelby's gesture meant. He started to make a phone call, then stopped.

Carson came from the back room with a Styrofoam cup full of steaming black coffee. She rarely cared for cream or sugar. She had just hung up her own phone as she approached him. "Tripp is outside," she said as she reached up for a hug and to kiss his cheek.

"Okay, be safe."

"Tripp wouldn't have it any other way." She started to leave but turned back to him. "Have you heard from Pops lately? He keeps promising to come visit, but then he's a no-show."

"You know your grandfather, sweetie. He's always busy doing something. He last mentioned heading to Key West."

"That's a place I wouldn't mind going back to," Carson said and held up the cup as she was leaving. "You know, paper would be better for the environment."

"I know. Julia bought so many that we just haven't run out yet. We'll do paper next time." Jack watched as his little girl opened the front door to leave. He called out before she stepped through, "Tell your brother it wouldn't hurt him to come in and visit sometime."

With a quick thumbs-up, Carson was gone.

Jack turned to the group. "I have some errands to run, kids. We'll chat next weekend."

With Carson gone, the boys had lost interest anyway. Jack informed Julia he had things to do and also left the building. He scanned the parking lot before using the key fob to remotely start his red Dodge 2500 4x4 pickup. The air conditioning would kick in and cool things enough to enter the sunbaked cab.

Jack carefully observed his surroundings as he walked to his truck. Before he drove off, he had to shake off the uneasy feeling that overshadowed an otherwise pleasant day.

A KEY ENCOUNTER

On the southern tip of the Sunshine State peninsula, the coral archipelago known as the Florida Keys stretched south-southwest, forming a natural barrier between the Atlantic Ocean and the Gulf of Mexico. With its shallow waters, green shorelines, and twisting canals, Key Largo had a character all its own among the keys.

Bradley "Pops" Page had previously been in Key West conducting business when the call came in from his longtime friend to meet in the more northern key, Key Largo. It was probably a blessing, as he tended to drink too much once he hit the bars along Duval Street.

A boat ride later, Pops arrived at the requested location. After a few passes along the perimeter of the Atlantic side, he throttled back to a slow cruise and watched a couple of fishing boats move around a nearby islet. One boat caught his attention. It didn't seem to have a destination but was circling around as if looking for something—or *someone*. He decided to set an intercept course.

The skipper of the other boat, a custom twenty-two-foot center console, noted the other closing in and adjusted course. Matching speed, the two vessels met somewhere in between and seemed poised to circle one another. Then the other boat straightened its course and headed back toward the eastern side of Key Largo.

Pops steered his vessel, a thirty-two-foot catamaran cruiser, in pursuit. As they throttled down their engines to accommodate the no-wake zone, they navigated toward the mouth of the channel. Twisting and winding through the narrow mangrove-lined waterway, both paused to allow space for a larger boat coming around the bend to pass.

The series of channels, sounds, and bays were all part of the Florida Keys National Marine Sanctuary. As Pops continued to follow the lead boat, he wondered where he would end up. He hoped not too far, as he had a schedule to keep. The boat guided him to a secluded branch of the channel that dead-ended off the main route. There, both vessels set anchor and were tied off to one another.

Pops cut the power to the twin outboard engines and tried to focus on the captain of the smaller boat. He thought the thin Asian, wearing aviator sunglasses and dressed in white pants and a polo shirt, belonged more on the golf course than the water. The man gave him a brief wave and hopped onto the multihull cruiser. Pops was impressed by the effortless leap across boats. As his guest drew closer, however, he realized he had made a mistake. The so-called man was a woman. He convinced himself her short hair and attire had tricked his aged vision—the closest he would come to admitting he needed to wear his glasses.

"Come aboard, Captain?" she asked and stepped over the front seats onto the bow.

"Aye, come aboard," Pops said. He waited for her to reach the back of the boat where he was standing. She walked through the opening of the dual console and made her way to the stern. The woman wiped sweat from her brow before offering a small but firm hand. Pops shook it and figured she wasn't acclimated to the Florida humidity. She also hadn't offered the normal greeting he was accustomed to. Pops was used to being escorted straight to the destination, not taking a detour. It was odd.

"I've been instructed to take you to the meeting place," she said as she looked him over. "Please follow me to the rendezvous point."

"Why did we stop here first?" asked Pops, frustrated by the delay. He noted her subtle accent was probably Korean, not the expected Chinese. He had spent enough time in the Orient to know one accent from another.

"I was told to ensure you came alone."

"Fumi knew I would. Do you see anyone else?" He gestured to the rest of the boat. "I'm Pops."

She studied him carefully. Pops was confident she'd see him as the fit old fart he was, a leathery tanned man of the outdoors.

"Of course you are," said the woman with a quick nod.

"And you are?"

"Suki."

He wondered what role she served for his friend. With Fumi, the possibilities could stretch the imagination. There was also something about her that bothered him. "Well, unless you want to frisk me too, I suggest we get going. I hope it's not far."

"It's not," Suki said and glanced around one more time.

She hopped back to her boat with cat-like ease and prepped it for departure. She was already maneuvering back around Pops's multihull as he fired up his outboards and pulled anchor. He followed her out to the main channel, around another curve, and soon veered off at another dead end. This time, however, they were not alone.

As they rounded the corner, Pops was unsure what the larger vessel was at first. He finally determined it was a custom trimaran, but it looked more like a spaceship. He gauged it at close to one hundred and forty feet in length and about sixty or so in beam, including the smaller outrigger hulls. Its silver curves were accented with black trim and a single red stripe that broke only to display the name of the big yacht, also in red letters. Both craft passed the length of the yacht and moored on the aft lower section.

"*Astute Gemini II.*" Pops read the name of the vessel aloud.

Suki had already disembarked from her boat and offered him assistance onto the yacht while a deckhand tied off the lines. Pops followed her into the aft entrance. The deck was teak, the railing solid stainless steel, and the hull a solid composite material. He half expected a robot butler to greet him as he reached the red-carpeted area. It was hardly far-fetched, considering Fumi's many investments included robotics research.

"Permission to come aboard?" Pops yelled.

"Permission granted," came the well-spoken voice with a distinctively Chinese accent. He followed the source of the voice into the saloon. There on a large settee, dressed in a purple satin robe and sipping a glass of red wine, was a familiar face. Fumi Yoshida set his drink down and stood up to greet him. "You don't look a day older, you old sea dog."

Pops appreciated the lie. "You're looking pretty relaxed yourself," he said. He surveyed the saloon. "She's nice." The vessel was a mixture of modern and classic design. The LED lighting from the ceiling cast a soothing glow upon what was best described as a Zen approach to decor.

"Would you like a tour?"

"Another time, perhaps. You called me here for a reason, Fumi."

"She's a lovely craft," said Fumi, as if not hearing Pops. "A state-of-the-art multihull. I find the ride quite pleasant in most sea conditions."

"I've also learned that two hulls can be better than one. What's going on?"

"A beverage, perhaps?"

"No thanks."

Fumi smiled and sat back down on the simple yet comfortable sofa. His name and taste for the finer things were inherited from the Japanese businessman who was his father. His determination and cleverness, however, were products of his Chinese mother. He offered a seat with a gesture of his hand. "Patience was never your virtue, Bradley," he said. While most called Pops by his nickname, Fumi preferred using his birth name.

Suki ushered the remaining servant out of the room, closed the entries on both sides, and exited. While it wasn't unusual for Fumi to want privacy, Pops knew the impromptu meeting was hardly related to one of his business opportunities. He wondered what his old friend had on his mind as he watched him retrieve his glass of wine.

Fumi took a drink and cleared his throat. "An old acquaintance has been busy. The shepherd is doing more than watching his flock these days."

"What the hell is that crazy bastard up to now?"

"Same thing he's been up to for years, except things aren't as quiet as they used to be." Fumi paused long enough for Pops to take in what he was saying.

"Go on."

"Cornelius Shelby believes someone's trying to speak to the dead."

Pops snorted a laugh. "What conspiracy theory has he cooked up this time? Better question . . . how did he gain your interest?"

"He's always had my ear. The man does have a gift for uncovering things others want left hidden."

Pops shifted his weight from one leg to another. "What did he learn?"

"First things first. I need you to understand something. Both you and I have existed on the outskirts of this system for some time. That recently changed for me, as much to my surprise I was appointed into a rotating role on the chamber."

The hoods over Pops's eyes lifted. "I'm surprised you'd want to wear such a shackle. As you know, the chamber trusts neither of us. The feeling is mutual."

"Yet things have changed, Bradley. The chamber no longer trusts itself. We have a new threat—one that requires new approaches."

"Which government is trying to get its foot in the door this time?"

"I'm afraid it's not a sovereign power this time—rather, a shadow of ourselves."

"You speak in riddles, my friend."

"If only that were true. We suspected a few years ago that another consortium had sprung up from seemingly nowhere. They have similar ties, influences, and are well funded, much like ourselves."

Pops wished he had taken Fumi up on that drink. "Someone's already infiltrated the Guild of Libra?"

"Not infiltrated," Fumi said. "I believe this new entity has roots that sprouted from within the guild itself."

Pops showed little surprise. "So the creature has begun to devour itself. Who?"

"A fine question. Resources were scrambled but were met with resistance."

"What type of resistance?"

"The type that causes the chamber to reach out to me, and in turn I reach out to you."

Pops walked over next to Fumi and sat down. "You must be desperate," he said as he pulled out a cell phone, dialed a number, and waited. "Ed, cancel the rest of my weekend plans." He hung up before the man could protest and then tossed the phone aside. It landed on the cushion next to him.

Suki appeared a moment later and moved the phone to the little table in front of Pops, then disappeared again. He watched as she left.

"She's not a fan of clutter," Fumi said with amusement.

"It seems she's not a fan of a private conversation either," Pops said dryly. "Where did you get her?"

"On loan from the guild's chamber."

"The type of loan you couldn't turn down, I'm sure. Mind if I shoot straight?"

"Of course not," Fumi said with a polite nod.

"So the chamber sent my old friend to investigate whether I'm friend or foe. An unorthodox approach, especially since I know how this is supposed to work—lest you forget."

"I could hardly forget," Fumi said with a hint of incredulity.

"Then let's stop playing games, shall we?" Pops snapped.

"No games, Bradley. You simply don't understand the magnitude of the guild's woes."

"You're about to enlighten me."

"Correct. As you very well know, Capricorn is our internal affairs. Gayla, your old protégée, would have been the ideal investigator. She did learn from the best." Fumi took a sip of wine and thought of his next words. "Before I get started, you should have that drink now."

"Sure," Pops replied uneasily. As if he had rubbed a magic lamp, Suki appeared behind him with a short crystal glass containing a single sphere of ice and amber liquid. Her appearance had changed; she had replaced her clothes, or possibly covered them, with a brown *yukata*. Pops was familiar with the oriental-style robe. As he took the drink, he wondered, Did she change so quickly, or are there twins? He nodded to her, impressed at her soft walk. "Not many can sneak up on the ol' man like that," he said. He detected a hint of a smile before she disappeared again.

"I hope twelve-year-old Scotch will suffice?" said Fumi.

While Pops knew he didn't look like a distinguished man, he was picky about his booze. "It'll do. So where's Capricorn in all of this?"

"Capricorn is gone."

Pops had just taken a drink and coughed some of it out. "Gone?"

"Gayla and many of her team were killed, one by one, while attempting to carry out their investigations," Fumi said. "Gayla was found recently. Both her eyes were gouged out."

The thought sickened Pops. Gayla was a friend and, at one time, a very attractive woman. "What the hell type of message does that send?"

"The message isn't clear. In ancient cultures gouging out the eyes was a form of punishment, while serial killers have been known to have a fascination with or fear of eyes."

Pops shifted to his detective mode. "I doubt it was merely a psycho or someone invoking Sharia law. It could have been torture—or a very personal message. Was Gayla the only one found with her eyes removed?"

"Yes."

"The others from her group?"

"Professionally assassinated, one way or another."

Pops thought about this. "Maybe the message was meant only for Gayla."

"Or someone close to her."

Pops's mind traveled down a road of possibility. "Yes, maybe business took a personal turn."

"You may be on to something." Fumi reached inside his robe, pulled out a manila envelope, and tossed it onto the small table in front of Pops.

Pops opened it and found several pictures of his family. He looked at each carefully and observed they were taken at various times and places. One showed his son standing in front of his church, another his granddaughter playing sand volleyball, two showed his grandson and friend walking in Viridian Square, and so on. After going through them all, he placed the pictures back in the envelope and set it down.

"Where did you get these?"

"They were found hidden in a hotel room in Hong Kong —the one Gayla was staying in at the time of her death."

Pops tried to make sense of it. "So, after wiping out most of her people, someone takes Gayla out and she's found with pictures of my family."

"Correct."

"Are you going to tell me why she had an interest in my family?"

"We don't believe Gayla was watching your family, but rather, on the trail of whoever was."

"It sounds like she caught up to them."

"An unfortunate event. They tore her hotel room apart, took her camera, phone, and laptop. But they missed the pictures. She hid them well."

"Good girl," Pops said softly. "Anything else?"

"Perhaps the most interesting piece. There was an SD chip found on her body. Her killer didn't think to look where she hid it. You'll find a picture pulled from that chip that's interesting." Fumi produced the photo from his robe pocket and handed it over.

Pops felt the blood drain from his face as he examined it. "Stella," he said softly.

"Yes, it appears your ex-wife was also in Hong Kong."

"That old crone lives like a hermit in Southeast Oklahoma now."

"She apparently had business abroad. Lest we forget, Bradley, she still has powerful connections to the guild."

"Tell me what you're thinking, Fumi."

"No. You should be the one to weave this tale."

Pops pondered it but was unable to come up with anything but far-fetched theories, none of which fit all the pieces. "She's crazy and dangerous, but not clever enough to pull off the type of things you mentioned. If the guild suspected her involvement, why haven't they brought her in?"

"We believe she serves as but a piece of the puzzle."

"You think she's the smaller fish that will lead you to the bigger catch."

"Your metaphor sums it up, Bradley."

The wheels had begun to turn in Pops's head. "There's only one obsession that crazy woman has had on her mind for the past twenty-five years. You know what I speak of."

"It was a tragic time for both of you. Her bitterness obviously drove her mad."

Pops sat for a moment silently, but then a realization struck him. "You test me, old friend. You don't need my help. What were you hoping to obtain by this visit?"

Fumi released a sigh as he placed his empty wine glass on the table. Suki showed up seconds later to refill it and disappeared again. "You've grown paranoid over the years, old friend. There's no secret agenda here. I do need your help."

"With?"

"We believe Stella is connected somehow, but there are still many missing pieces to the puzzle. The big picture is scattered, perhaps across the globe."

"You want me to find a piece or two in my own backyard, don't you?"

"No one has more resources in this hemisphere than you, Bradley."

"While that may be an exaggeration, I suppose I can poke around a bit. That said, I'm doing it for you, not the guild."

"Thus the reason I'm here."

Pops chuckled. "I guess I really should treat my friends differently than my enemies."

"I would encourage it. While we're on the subject, Fitzpatrick sends his regards." Fumi smiled mischievously.

Briefly, Pops turned his back to his friend. "Which part of my anatomy shall I stick Fitzpatrick's regards in?"

Fumi's head fell back as he laughed aloud. When he regained composure, he reached over and patted Pops's hand. "You are too funny, Bradley."

They enjoyed the humorous moment and then sat briefly in thought. After Pops downed his drink and absorbed what he had heard, he was ready to discuss the next topic. "So back to Shelby. What's his part in all of this?"

"Ah yes, Cornelius has an interesting theory. I dispatched him to the Gulf Coast to follow up."

"You dispatched him? What theory was so interesting?"

"It would be wiser if you went straight to the source."

The way Fumi said it told Pops it wasn't a matter to be discussed further. "Okay, but I'm not exactly thrilled about working with Shelby. The man has a tendency to leave messes in his wake."

"I understand, Bradley, but you'll need him on this one."

"You know I value your wisdom. Still, it would have been nice to have arranged a poker game. It's been too long since we had our regulars at the same table."

The term used for secret meetings was well known to Fumi. "Yes, it's been far too long. Unfortunately, the new collar I wear comes with a shorter leash."

"Understood. Don't let me cause you to take any undue risks."

Fumi lowered his voice. "I fear that bridge has already been crossed, my friend." He automatically resumed his normal tone, as if for some unseen audience. "I wish I had more for you, Bradley, but I was just passing through. As always, the chamber appreciates any assistance you can provide. Be sure to see Sammy on your way out. You know he loves to share his fishing stories."

Pops was surprised to hear the name of the grandson of one of the permanent chamber members. He hadn't seen Sammy since he was a boy but remembered he and his father didn't have much use for the family patriarch. He didn't care for the young man's grandfather either, but the rest of his family were good people. Still, it was odd for him to be on a journey with Fumi that took him so far from home. "I may just do that."

"You should hurry, though. Sammy's eager to get some fishing in before we depart."

Pops took the hint that it was time to leave. He stood, stretched, and returned the bow his friend gave him.

"Oh, one last item," Fumi said as Pops started to walk away. "Tell my nephew I'll be sending him something soon."

"Will do," Pops replied and then left.

FOLLOW THAT CAR

The faded blue muscle car cruised east on US Highway 98. It was over a decade old and showed signs that its previous owner had also driven it in an environment of moist, salty air. Tripp, the current owner and driver, attempted to have a conversation with Carson, who sat in the passenger seat. This proved difficult; the windows were down since the air conditioning was on the fritz.

For her part, Carson tried to listen while not making fun of how her brother's short, dark hair stood straight up from the hot wind. She glanced into the vanity mirror a couple of times to confirm that her own sandy hair looked sexy as it blew around her small face. Still, she wished she had pinned it back.

They had left the church in Viridian Cove and headed toward Destin. At that time of day during summer, it wasn't unusual for traffic to slow to a crawl. Tourist season on the Emerald Coast made for tedious travel along the barrier islands.

"We're going to have a great time," Carson said. "I just wish I hadn't wasted so much of my life yesterday convincing you of that."

"As usual, you hardly needed to exert yourself," Tripp replied.

It was late morning but still early for two adults in their twenties who had stayed up late into the night. Tripp had been at his apartment with Daniel, trying to finish a quest they had started online. Carson had spent her evening at Navarre Beach, playing volleyball, drinking, and being pursued by young men—both locals and vacationers. In a game she played, she typically hung out with whoever could put up with her the longest—a task she never made easy. She didn't go home with the winner that night, since it might have interfered with Derrick's offer to take her on his so-called yacht the next day.

"Daniel was a bit hurt at the lack of an invitation," Tripp said.

His sister scoffed at the thought. Although Daniel was an attractive man, Carson couldn't see him as anything more than her geeky friend. Even at that, she tended to be mean-spirited toward him. All part of the experience, she told herself. "He'll get over it."

"If only he would," Tripp muttered, mostly to himself.

Carson figured her brother never understood what Daniel saw in her. It was obvious she had good genes, but in spite of that, few mortals seemed willing to spend any length of time with her. Daniel was an exception.

"What?" asked Carson.

"Never mind. Tell me again why it was so important I tag along?"

"Because I love my lil' brother, and you need to get out and mingle." She felt entitled to tell him what to do; she was, after all, technically the older of the two by a good eight minutes. She often reminded him of that fact. Tripp, in turn, would counter that she was out of the womb first because she was the impatient one. She could hardly disagree.

"I do socialize, though I'm hardly as gregarious as you."

"That's an understatement."

"Say again?"

"Well, if you'd roll up the damn windows," Carson said.

Tripp rolled them up and turned up the fan. The muggy air filled the cabin as the wind noise dissipated. "Is that better?"

"For hearing, yes. Why didn't you have Daniel fix the air in this thing? I thought he loved doing that sort of stuff."

"He does love to try and invent things, or at least make them better—the key word being 'try.' As you've observed, on more than one occasion, his success rate is less than impressive."

"The damn thing's already broken. What's the worst that could happen?"

"You do remember the microwave that used to be in my office?"

Carson giggled at the memory. "You survived it."

"I still worry about the possibility of cancer. You missed what happened to his new Smartwatch."

"Yeah, about that . . . sorry we haven't hung out much lately, with my being out of town storm chasing and all."

"You *have* been back from Oklahoma for almost two months, you know."

"I had to catch up on my life."

"We live in the same building."

Carson quickly changed the subject. "This car smells. I wish now you'd kept the Bimmer."

"And listen to your perpetual disdain for it?" He glanced at her to catch her expression.

She simply snorted. "I only pointed out the fact that the asshole loved you more than me."

"Grandpa also bought you a Jeep that you seem to have gotten a lot of mileage out of. Case in point, this past spring's extended tornado hunt in Oklahoma and Kansas."

She knew Tripp would never understand the level of venom she had for their mother's father. He tried to make eye contact with her, but she looked away.

"So? He got me a used Jeep and you a new BMW. You were always his favorite."

"I know he can be biased. But have you thought about trying to be more pleasant toward him? It may change how he, and possibly the rest of the planet, treats you."

"I'm not going to kiss anyone's ass, particularly his wrinkled buttock. My Poppy treats me fairly regardless of how I act. I guess we know which side of the family has good grandparent genes."

Tripp snickered. "Good grandparent genes are an important trait."

She ignored his sarcastic comment. "You know Dad's side of the family is way cooler."

"It shouldn't surprise me you'd feel that way."

"Oh?"

"Mom has said you have a personality that rivals Pops's."

Carson rolled her eyes and turned her attention to outside her window. Something caught her eye. She scanned the white Mercedes for the pink license plate cover with little black paw prints all over it. She had bought it with her own money many years before. It was also attached to the car up ahead.

"Nothing witty to say?" Tripp asked.

"No, I'm done with that conversation. Follow that car."

"Why?" he asked, apparently trying to determine which one she referred to. Traffic had become dense and there were several possibilities.

"Really, detective? You haven't spotted it?"

"Mom's car? Why should I follow her?"

She gave him that look, the one that would make him feel stupid for not knowing what was on her mind. "Because I want to know where she's going. Please keep your eye on the SUV in front of you."

Tripp applied the brakes and glanced over at their mom's car, about three spots ahead, still in the right lane. "It's not like she is having an extramarital affair."

Compared to the many other parents they had heard about, their parents were the epitome of the perfect couple—or so Tripp seemed to think. They hardly ever fought and, with few exceptions, they always showed one another respect. More importantly, the couple that prayed together stayed together. At least, that's what their mom always said. Carson realized that Tripp found no reason to doubt this and considered their long relationship itself empirical evidence.

"In your eyes, Mother can do no wrong. Now follow that car!"

"You always call her *Mother* when you're upset. Now what did she do?"

"Just drive."

With a sigh of surrender, Tripp made his way to the next lane, behind his mom's car. They followed her to the next turnoff.

Carson ensured he duplicated the turn, knowing her mother wouldn't notice them behind her. *Amateur*, she thought, smirking. She, on the other hand, was always aware of her surroundings.

They tailed the car as it headed south toward the barrier islands. As they drew closer to the destination, Carson recognized the place. That sneak, she thought. It was far enough away from their town to reduce the chance of running into the church folks but still close enough to get back from quickly if she was missed.

It was also where her mother's friend Lynn liked to go, and this may have been a good cover story except for one problem: Carson knew her son, and he had already mentioned his parents would be out of town for the weekend. Since they had a pool, plans were already afoot for a party at their place.

After their mom had pulled into a parking space, Tripp found a spot not far from her car. It was close enough to monitor her without giving them away. Carson decided those private eye classes—or whatever he had hired that grubby skip tracer to teach him—might actually have proven useful. They both watched as their mom got out of her car, finished a quick call on her phone, and headed into the little bar and grill.

Her long dark hair was pinned back in a French twist, and she wore faded blue jeans with a white blouse. Nothing special for someone allegedly having a secret rendezvous. Still a very attractive forty-something, she made simple attire look sexy.

"She must've forgotten to shave her legs," Carson said as she noticed the jeans instead of shorts or a skirt. "That old lady still has a nice ass," she added as her mother disappeared inside the bar.

"That's hardly something I'd notice or comment on," Tripp said with a scowl.

The Brine Barnacle wasn't as nice as the place where Carson bartended, but still not bad. The beer selection was paltry, but the appetizers were reasonable. The view of Santa Rosa Sound from the back patio was the best part. That said, it was hardly a place their mother would venture off to without either her friend or her husband.

Carson got out of the car and motioned to her brother.

"I'll stay with the getaway vehicle," Tripp said.

Carson walked over, stood by the entrance, and silently debated if she really wanted to go in.

Finally, she forced herself to enter the Brine Barnacle and scanned for a sign of her mother. The place had a small inner bar, along with a coastal decor, and a larger outside back patio for enjoying the view. Most of the patrons were outside. Sitting at the bar was a very unattractive woman in an equally unflattering sundress.

Through the open door that led to the patio, she spotted the back of her mom's head. Slowly, she wound her way to the bar, where she could get a better look.

The day outside was lovely, with blue skies and little whitecaps in the bay. A kite surfer a few hundred yards away caught Carson's attention and she wished she were out there instead. First things first, she thought.

She hovered around the bar near the entryway to the outside patio. Waiting to see who sat at her mother's table, she suddenly felt she too was being watched. Off to her left the ugly woman was staring at her. It took a second look to realize it was a man dressed in drag.

"How are you today, young lady?" The voice was unmistakably masculine.

"Good, I suppose."

"Enjoying the view?" The man had a terrible blonde wig and even worse makeup. He nodded toward the patio and lifted his glass in a toast before he drank.

A drink sounded good, but there had been no sign of a bartender since she arrived. A waitress meandered around the back and checked on tables but never even looked her way. Not exactly a well-run bar, she thought.

"The bartender stepped out for the view," said the man in drag, as if he read her mind. He motioned to the outside again.

Carson had been distracted just long enough to almost miss the bartender take a seat at her mother's table. His white shorts and half-buttoned Hawaiian shirt might have seemed sexy to her mom, but he seemed like a throwback from the old *Magnum, P.I.* episodes she used to watch with her dad.

The man had to be at least a decade younger than her mother. "Cougar," she said in a low growl. The drag queen to her left must have heard her because he chuckled. Carson couldn't have cared less and decided to go crash the party.

As she was about to leave, the man spoke to her. "What's your name?"

"Forgive me," she replied with obvious irritation. "I'm not really in the mood for niceties."

"I can see that," he said. "You seem a woman on a mission."

"You've very perceptive. Now excuse me while I go start a fight."

The man leaned back in the bar stool and stretched. "I'm Shelby," he said. "Before you go out there, do me a favor, kiddo."

"What's that?"

"Remember my name."

An odd request, Carson thought. She hesitated before she exited to the patio.

LUNCH TO DIE FOR

The light, salty breeze coming from across the sound was a welcome visitor. It didn't completely offset the heat of the summer day, but it was better than the small fans in the corners of the patio of the Brine Barnacle. The breeze also gently swept a loose lock of Kate Page's dark hair across her angular face, and it dangled over one of her dark, almond-shaped eyes.

As she considered the sweltering day, Kate wondered why she hadn't taken the time to shave her legs that morning. It would have allowed her to put on something a bit cooler than jeans. A better question was this: Why had she even bothered to show up? She tried to look past the younger man seated across from her and get a better look at a boat, the blue water . . . anything but the eyes that were undressing her. His stare made her uncomfortable.

Of course she was flattered by the invitation to have a drink sometime. It wasn't as if it was the first time someone had made a pass at her, although it had become increasingly rare after she hit forty. She reminded herself she was happily married, for the most part, and loved her family. Her husband was still the most attractive creature in the world to her, although she wondered if he felt the same way about her.

She snapped herself back to the moment. Something about this man piqued her curiosity. It was more than just his flattery. Her gut was telling her it was something else. She needed to know. If she had learned anything from the family she married into, it was to look beyond the surface. Still, lying to her husband and meeting a stranger wasn't her style.

That said, she had assumed the invitation meant he would serve her a drink, not have one with her. It was a bit presumptuous of him. It wouldn't look right. She had a reputation to uphold.

The man looked at her curiously. Kate wondered if she had been doing that thing where her hands moved in the air as she was thinking. For the first time, she noticed his attire. It had taken her years to get Jack to quit wearing stuff like that, although he still did on occasion. But she wasn't in any position to be judgmental.

"You sure you're okay with me sitting here?" the man asked.

He had dropped in a week ago at the hair salon she owned and operated on Viridian Square. He had made a point of speaking with her while also making it clear he wasn't interested in a haircut.

"No, you're fine," she replied with a forced smile.

Kate was certain he could tell she was uncomfortable. He had the type of gaze that looked through someone, not at them. She knew at least a couple of other people, her husband included, whose gaze had that quality.

"I just stopped in for a quick drink—then I'm off again," she said with a nervous laugh.

"Well, I'm glad you dropped in," he said. "A new guy in town like me doesn't usually get to chat with someone as interesting as you."

It was clearly just a line. She wondered if he hoped she was a cougar. "I'd think a bartender would talk to a lot of interesting people," she said.

He seemed briefly taken aback but recovered. "Yes, a lot of people, but not very interesting ones." A charming smile followed. "I'm usually bad with names, but I believe you are Kate?"

"Very good," she said, trying to remember if she had told him or if he'd simply read the sign at her shop, Kate's Place. "And you are?"

"My mother calls me Matthew, but to everyone else, it's just Matt."

"As a mother myself, perhaps I should go with Matthew." She laughed but immediately felt awkward and regretted more than ever that she had shown up. "I come here often with my friend Lynn," she said quickly. It wasn't a complete lie, since she had been there a handful of times over the last year. "Maybe you've met her. She has short blonde hair—"

"Let me grab you a drink. A beer? Cocktail?" He obviously wasn't interested in talking about her friend.

"Vodka and soda, with a lime, please."

"Be right back," he said as he headed for the bar. He slowly walked back inside, as if to give her a moment to study him. She decided to aimlessly go through the contents of her purse and check her phone.

As he entered the bar, Matt noticed the man in the ugly dress was still sitting there, as well as a hot young blonde. She simply glared at him, no doubt because she had to wait for service. She looked familiar. The queen had a silly grin that made him want to punch him. He and the girl had apparently been engaged in conversation. He ignored the man and nodded to the young woman.

"I'll come get your orders right after I tend to this lady outside," he said. He didn't hear a response, but the girl's expression was far from pleasant.

As he started to make her mother's drink behind the bar, Carson graded him as painfully slow. A newbie at best, she thought. She noticed Shelby had taken an interest in what the bartender was doing too.

Matt turned his back to them tentatively as he added the final ingredients of the drink. Carson wondered if he sensed he was being watched.

She hoped the man hadn't slipped her mom a roofie. "What's your name, bartender?"

"Uh, Matt."

"Uh? You're not sure, *Matt*?" She watched as he grew irritated. She figured he was probably calling her a bitch in his mind and wished he would say it out loud. That way, she could justify decking him.

"It's Matt." He finished the drink, turned to head out from behind the bar, and ran right into the wall covered in floral fabric.

Shelby got up and stumbled into Matt, and the drink the bartender had been carrying flew back into himself. Initially, Matt jumped backwards. From his shirt to his white shorts, he was covered in the cold liquid. After the shock of it wore off, he raised his head and his temper flared.

"What the hell!" Matt clenched his fists. He threw the glass to the floor, shattering it and causing a couple at the table behind them to stop and watch. As if perfectly timed, the song on the jukebox ended, leaving an uneasy silence.

"Oh sir," said Shelby. "I'm not sure which of us was the clumsy one, but let me apologize first." The angry, wet bartender started to push past Shelby, who stopped him. "You should probably go to the bathroom and dry off, sir. You wouldn't want the lady outside to think you peed yourself."

Matt fumed even more as Carson laughed. He paused as if debating his next move, then carefully maneuvered around the beefier man and headed to the bathroom.

Carson decided that was her signal to join her mother out on the patio.

Kate almost leapt from her seat. She was expecting the figure that came up from behind her to be the flirtatious bartender carrying her drink. Instead, she saw the piercing blue daggers of her baby girl staring down at her. She instinctively glanced around to see who else might be there.

"Hello, Mother," Carson said loudly. She slapped both her palms down on the table. She took the seat Matt had recently vacated, folded her arms, and glared.

"Mother," Kate was aware, meant Carson was upset. How had she found her? She still hoped Carson hadn't seen her sitting with the bartender.

"So who was the guy you were drooling over?"

Damn was the first thought that entered Kate's mind. She really didn't have a good story about why she was there. Of all the people to approach her now, she could hardly think of anyone worse than her daughter.

"How are you, my sunshine?" Answering a question with a question was the best she could manage.

"The guy?" demanded Carson.

"Oh honey, that was just the bartender." Kate fumbled around to put the contents of her purse, tossed around when she was startled, back in their rightful places.

Carson leaned over the table to watch her fidget with the small Coach bag. "Is that a new purse?"

There is a Lord in Heaven, Kate thought, more than happy to change the subject. She placed it on the table to display to her daughter. "Like it?" she asked with a smile.

Carson's eyes narrowed. "You showed me it two weeks ago, when you first bought it."

"Oh, okay. Well, where's your purse?"

"It's in the car with Tripp."

"Tripp is here too?" Kate looked around, wishing she had never even met the bartender.

"Why yes, Mother, but the momma's boy was too chicken to come in. He wanted to keep that perfect image of you in his pretty lil' head."

Kate hoped nobody had heard the last statement. A couple eating nearby were staring straight at her. From the absence of smiles, she assumed they were from the northeast.

"You know," said Carson, "it looked like the dude slipped something in your drink. Good thing he's wearing it or you might've woken up with your legs spread, a bad headache, and no good cover story."

"Carson!" her mother exclaimed. "Really!" She was both angry and embarrassed, as she noticed people at a couple of the other tables had started to watch the show. "You threw a drink on him?"

"No, that was the dude in drag," she said, pointing toward the bar. "Hard to explain that story, so I won't even try." Kate felt perplexed. "Anyway, I need to go. Places to be," she said, standing. "Besides, I don't want to see any more. I might be asked to testify at your divorce."

Carson walked away, ignoring her mother's plea to sit and talk. She took the quickest route out the door, and Kate figured she probably didn't even realize the drag queen and the bartender were gone. She was obviously in a hurry to retreat to her brother's car.

The guy in drag casually walked into the men's bathroom and scanned the area in front of him: two urinals, a single stall, and one sink. Matt wasn't in the stall but waiting to ambush him from behind the door. It was time to play the game.

Matt meant to grab the sundress-wearing man around the throat and jab the knife into a rib. However, things didn't go as planned. To his surprise, the man was quick and skillfully twisted Matt's wrist behind his back while sweeping his leg out from under him. With grace and subtlety, he was disarmed, his face in the sink and the click of a small caliber, silenced weapon in his left ear. The bartender froze with the knowledge he had been set up. He waited, nervously, for the man who had bested him to speak.

"Where's your partner?" his attacker asked in a calm yet firm tone.

Matt's mind raced with questions. Who is this guy? How long has he been watching me? What does he know? He tried to remember his training and searched for a way out. There was no way he would talk to the guy.

"Look, man, I don't know what you're talking about. You have me confused with someone else."

His forehead struck the porcelain sink with a thud. He tried to shake off the pain, but his head was again forced into the sink.

"The first one was for effect, the second for fun. Do you want to see what I do when I stop having fun?" the man asked sternly.

"No," was all Matt could muster, his head ringing. But stalling further seemed pointless. "I don't know where he is."

The deep sigh let him know the man didn't believe him. Whatever he did or said going forward, there was probably a bullet in his future. Matt wasn't keen on the idea. He had plans. It wasn't going to go that way, not without a fight. He just needed a bit of luck, like someone walking in at the right time. One tiny little distraction is all I need, he thought.

Unfortunately, he didn't have the luxury of waiting. The man painfully pinned his right hand behind him. Matt tried to move his left hand toward his own gun, tucked behind him and under the jacket. As soon as he tried to make the slightest move, his head once again met the sink. The last blow resonated through his head like a bell. He was barely aware of being dragged into the only stall in the bathroom and being sat on the throne. He stared up, still dazed, at the small black pistol with a silencer attached. Matt heard the man speak but didn't quite catch what he asked this time.

His attacker drew a bit closer. "I said, do you like my dress?"

It was hardly the question he expected. The guy was toying with him.

"It's ugly—like you, man."

The man's smile suggested he admired Matt's spunk. "Well, I wore it just for you, little man. At least we're making progress. Let's try another one, shall we? Why are you here?"

"The woman," Matt muttered.

"Wowsers, she's a hottie," he said with a whistle. "She's also married to a preacher. Did you know there are special levels in hell dedicated to assholes who try to poke a preacher's wife?"

"I wouldn't know."

"You don't really want to find out, do you?"

"No, I don't," Matt said, staring up at the man to see if there was any possibility of getting out of the stall alive.

"Then tell me where your partner is," he said as he drew even closer to Matt.

"Waiting on me," he began, "to bring the woman. Can I move my hands, man? They're killing me." He had been tossed on the toilet seat, his hands tucked under him, beneath the seat. It was painful.

"No."

Matt tried to ignore the pain and focus on how to get out of the stall. He felt a glimmer of hope when someone else entered the bathroom. That hope faded when his captor pressed the gun to the other man's forehead and dared him to make a peep. The patron did his business and exited as quickly as he had arrived.

Matt's hopes were further dashed when he realized the man was twirling his .40 caliber pistol, which he thought was concealed, in his free hand. He didn't realize he had grabbed it.

"So you were supposed to hurt her? Rape? Kill?" asked the man, still twirling Matt's gun.

"No, just hold on to her."

He drew Matt's pistol back as if to strike him with it.

"Okay, jeez. Not kill—just hurt her."

"And?"

"Anything else I wanted, as long as she was in good health when I returned her."

The man made a tsk-tsk sound as he shook his head. "Go on."

"That part was very specific—not that I'd want to kill a woman."

His attacker took a deep breath. "And the twins? When and where is your boy supposed to grab them?"

"I—I don't know. My job only involved the woman." The moment he said it, he knew the man didn't buy it. He braced as the man clubbed him in the chin with the gun's barrel. He shook it off. "I'm a dead man if I tell you any more," Matt said, spitting blood.

"You're already a dead man, soldier boy. Who else do you want to take with you?"

"Why should I talk if you're just going to kill me?"

He stepped back, as if it were some revelation, and put away Matt's gun. He produced a small syringe from another pocket. "I've got a better question, Matt. Why should you talk when this shit will make you sing?" He held the syringe in front of Matt's face.

"What's that?"

"Just a little happy juice," he said, sticking it in Matt's arm.

Matt felt the burning sensation travel through his body. After a moment, he started to relax. After a few more minutes, he no longer felt the pain in his head or hands. His vision had started to blur. He tried to move, but his body resisted.

"What's your real name?" the voice asked, echoing in his head.

"Kevin. My employer gave me the name 'Matthew' to use."

"Who's your employer?"

Matt tried to resist, but the drug's effects overwhelmed him. "Lloyd Tactical Forces."

"What were your plans for the Page twins?"

"We were just going to grab the girl and hold her. Mama was the one I was looking forward to."

"I bet. Now, if you weren't such an amateur, you just might've noticed that the daughter was the little blonde you were eyeing at the bar."

The realization hit Matt. "Oh shit," he said, slurring his words. "The hot one? I have to go get her." He tried to stand but only moved a couple of inches before realizing he wasn't able to do more.

"I don't think you have it in you," the man said and patted his leg. "You really are a rookie." He pulled the dress off. Underneath, his jacket was wrapped around his waist to make him look bigger, as well as keep it for later use. He removed his wig and grabbed a wipe, making quick work of removing the bad makeup job. Afterward, he stuffed everything in the dress, wadded it up, and placed it on Matt's lap.

"Are you going to kill me?" Matt struggled to focus on the liquid the man was dousing the dress and him with.

"Yep." He continued to squirt gasoline all over Matt and the surrounding area.

"You're a sick prick," Matt said, his head slouching.

"Says the lil' bastard who was going to rape a preacher's wife and steal his daughter." He grabbed a cigarette, stuck it in Matt's drooling mouth, and lit it. He quickly backed up. Matt tried to raise his head but couldn't.

"Don't worry, Matt," the man said as he put his fedora back on. "The drug may kill ya first. The fire will cover my tracks." He started to leave, then paused. Leaning back into the stall, he added, "Let me know if I was right about that special place in hell."

He left the bathroom, whistling as he walked away.

CASTING OFF

Carson hadn't said much since they had left the Brine Barnacle—that is, except words like "drive" and "faster." She was angry and didn't bother to hide it. At the same time, she wasn't yet ready to talk about it.

They approached the bridge to Okaloosa Island in the seaside town of Fort Walton Beach. As expected, traffic slowed them down. She studied the blue water in the bay but preferred the emerald of the beaches. That's where she looked for treasures in the form of seashells, sand dollars, or old coins— anything to make some jewelry to wear or sell. That's where she sculpted her athletic build and dark tan. Like her Poppy, Carson loved the sea. She was ready to get back to the water, but the traffic was sluggish and patience wasn't her virtue. Of course, she had many attributes folks didn't find virtuous, but she was fine with that.

Carson's phone vibrated again, but she refused to answer it. Afterward, Tripp's phone rang once, but she threatened him if he touched it.

"You know she'll worry if we ignore her," he said.

"Good."

Tripp allowed her to vent at times and get past whatever consumed her, just not at their mother's expense. Carson figured he had decided to avoid a confrontation and would check in with his mother later when she wasn't around. "Sorry."

It took her a moment to acknowledge him. "For what?"

"For whatever happened between you and Mom."

"You've done nothing wrong. Stop apologizing for things you didn't do. I'll be just fine." In her mind, as soon as she boarded a boat and hit the water, her world would normalize again. If the boat they were heading toward was even half as nice as that blowhard had made it out to be, she would soon be enjoying ocean spray and cold drinks.

"I've found that your responses tend to exceed what is appropriate for a given scenario," Tripp said.

"Did you just say I tend to overreact?"

"Yes."

"Next time, simply say that instead of the crap you just spewed. I swear you love to sound more intelligent than anyone else around you."

"Aside from my delivery, would you disagree with what I said?"

"You're right. I do tend to overreact. As I said before, I'll be fine."

"Do you feel it's wise to join a complete stranger on his vessel when you're upset? We can always find something else to do."

"We talked about this. If a dude can spend more than two hours putting up with my ass, then I don't consider him a stranger anymore." She knew even her brother could hardly argue that point. "If you're worried, I told him we have a relative who's a cop. And if he turned out to be a creep, I'd send the cop his picture and he'd be hunted down and castrated."

"He didn't rescind the invitation after that?"

Carson let out a big laugh and grinned. "I know, a real idiot, right? No worries—I'll have you with me."

"I'm hardly a foreboding presence, sis."

"You're tougher than you think. I remember a certain bully you picked up and tossed into the lockers when we were in high school."

"Well, he did push you down and call you the b-word."

"You can say *bitch*. It's okay. I won't tell anyone." She grinned. His disdain for profanity was just more evidence that he must have been switched with her real brother at birth. But just as she thought it, she could see in Tripp's face her mother's eyes mixed with a hint of their dad's rugged looks. Such a waste, she thought. Her brother could break many hearts if he weren't such a geek.

"Glad you're smiling again," Tripp said.

"All is well. I'm through being a whiny bitch for the day."

"Then enough said."

The rest of their journey was mostly silent, except for the radio and the wind from the open windows. They finally reached their destination, parked, and made their way down the pier.

Destin Harbor Boardwalk sat on the beautiful blue waters of Destin Bay. It had a nice marina, several bars, and various eateries. Assorted fishing trawlers, pleasure craft, and other boats traveled to and from the connecting bay.

Carson led them to a local hangout to grab a beer at the far end of the quarter-mile waterfront. They passed by a custom twenty-six-foot cruiser with dual outboards, moored nearby. Three people were sitting in the bow settee. A muscular man stood up and waved to get Carson's attention. She pretended not to see Derrick and he slowly sat back down.

Carson approached the open bar and motioned to the bearded bartender, who, in turn, promptly filled a glass with cold, dark beer from one of several taps. He nodded as he handed it to her.

"On my tab, darling," she said and walked back to where Tripp had stopped.

"You have a tab?" he asked.

"You would too, if you got out more."

"Were I not, as you previously stated, such an introvert."

"That and if you could stay off the damn computer games long enough to enjoy life. You want a beer?" Carson displayed her own drink to encourage him. She knew before asking that he was turned off by any liquid some measure of light couldn't pass through.

Tripp examined it with disdain. "That looks more like coffee with a head than beer."

"Then go order a watered-down lager or wheat ale." She nudged him with an elbow as she passed.

"I'm fine," Tripp replied. "One of us needs to keep our wits about us."

Carson circled back to the sports cruiser they had passed earlier. As she approached, Derrick stood up again from the U-shaped bench seat in the bow and greeted her. He towered over her five-foot-five-inch frame. He leaned in, as if for a kiss, but she handed him the beer instead and climbed aboard.

Tripp stood and waited for an invitation, as he felt was customary. He watched as Carson retrieved her beer and greeted the man with a warm hug. His well-defined big arms swallowed her thin frame.

After receiving no invitation, he simply asked, "Permission to come aboard, Captain?"

The man said nothing as he studied Tripp standing on the pier. Suddenly, Tripp was conscious of his khaki shorts and button-up green bamboo shirt. He must have seemed out of place to the others. It was clear he wasn't welcome.

"You're being a lousy host, Derrick," Carson said.

"Who's your friend?" Derrick asked.

"That would be my brother. I'm sure I mentioned him."

"The nerdy one?" he asked with a snort.

"Yes, the one who swims in the deep end of the gene pool, where you'd drown." She reached up and patted his cheek. "Derrick, this is Tripp. Tripp, this is Derrick. Welcome aboard, brother. "

Tripp climbed aboard and surveyed the boat, as well as the two other people aboard. A smaller yet fit guy in denim shorts and a loose black shirt sat beside a well-endowed brunette in a hot-pink bikini partially covered with a white crop top. Both looked amused by Carson's commanding presence.

Tripp introduced himself and learned that the other couple were Mark and Nikki. They seemed to barely know one another, much like Carson and Derrick.

Nikki instantly tried to strike up a conversation with him. She was an attractive woman, perhaps barely twenty. Although she seemed nice, he expected her to lose interest after they had spoken for more than a few minutes. He had that effect on women.

Mark, on the other hand, appeared out of place. His five o'clock shadow seemed appropriate, but something about him suggested he didn't belong with the others. That honor, Tripp thought, is typically mine.

"What do you think of my yacht?" Derrick asked Carson, who was already surveying it with disinterest.

Tripp figured his sister wanted to be brutally honest, but she held back and was polite. "It's a cute boat," Carson finally said. She decided to help with the mooring line.

"Boat?" Derrick asked. His square jaw hung open as if he was offended.

"Boat," Carson repeated.

Tripp hoped he would close his mouth before a flying insect found its way in there. "It's a nice vessel, Derrick," he said.

Derrick didn't even bother to acknowledge Tripp's words.

"If you're trying to impress me, you should know that my grandfather has a fleet of vessels much bigger than this fiberglass tub," Carson said. "That's okay, though—I do understand that boys tend to exaggerate size." Her gesture indicated how small it really was.

The others laughed aloud. Nikki in particular was tickled at how tough Carson was. Tripp, on the other hand, silently hoped the guy wasn't so juiced on steroids that he went into a rage and threw them all overboard.

Carson grinned, then added, "But don't let it bother ya, darlin'. Size isn't everything." She winked, tossed the mooring line down, and recovered her beer.

Derrick simply shook his head and continued to guide the vessel from its berth. The twins watched him. How much time had he actually spent on this boat that was allegedly his? His every move seemed to indicate he was a novice. Hopefully, he had at least completed the state-required safety course.

"Dude, your sister's a real ball buster." Mark took a seat next to Tripp on the settee and clapped him on the shoulder a couple of times.

"She's been called worse," Tripp said with a polite smile. "Do you go out on the water much?"

"No, man. I just thought it would be fun for me and my bro, Derrick, to take two hot ladies out for a pleasure cruise."

Tripp tried to read the man. Derrick was fairly simple to assess, but there was something phony about Mark. He resembled someone from a reality show or perhaps even a soap opera.

"Would you like a beer, Tripp?" asked Nikki as she leaned over Mark to touch his shoulder.

Tripp took it as a sign of attraction. "No, thank you, Nikki. I tend to avoid alcohol consumption while on a boat. A bottled water would be nice, though."

Nikki promptly hopped up and fetched it from the ice chest. She bounced on her way back, which made it even harder for Tripp not to keep his focus above her shoulders. She handed the bottle to him. He thanked her and took a much-needed drink. The humid summer heat could zap the body of fluids in no time, particularly if that someone had no working air conditioning in his car.

Nikki reclaimed her seat on the other side of Mark but continued to lean over him to talk with Tripp. "You have a cool name," she said, trying to keep the conversation going. "Like an acid trip?"

Tripp found this amusing. "No, it's a nickname that means I'm the third generation with the name 'Bradley Jack Page.' My mom started calling me Tripp, for short, and the name stuck."

"Oh," Nikki said with some embarrassment.

Tripp wondered if the man they were talking over, Mark, would get upset if they continued to invade his space. However, he seemed totally disinterested and instead stayed on Carson's every move, except when glancing down at his phone.

Nikki, being the curious one, tried to see who Mark was texting. He noticed her and left his seat to move a few paces away. Without missing a beat, she moved into his spot next to Tripp and smiled as her brown eyes looked him over.

"Where are we heading?" asked Tripp.

Nikki just shrugged as she kept her gaze locked onto him. He lost any doubt she was interested.

"There's a little-known islet in the bay we wanted to check out," Mark answered from a few steps away.

"I bet Carson would be familiar with it," Tripp said as he forced himself to pull away from Nikki's gaze. "Where exactly?"

Mark glanced up from his phone for a moment but returned to texting. "You'll see. It's a surprise."

Derrick sluggishly guided the twin outboard vessel out of the harbor, and they edged through the narrow channel that led to the larger bay. The engines powered up and they accelerated underneath the bridge Carson and Tripp had driven in on. They soon entered the bay.

WATER HAZARD

The cruiser made its way around the heavy bay traffic just off Crab Island. As the locals well knew, Crab Island wasn't really an island at all—that is, not anymore. Years of storms and erosion had turned it into little more than a sandbar, one that allowed visitors to walk around in waist-deep water.

It being a Saturday, there was no shortage of boats out and about. Located just north of the highway bridge that lead into Destin, Crab Island drew flocks of people of all ages who traveled to the emerald waters to socialize, swim, and drink. Floating platforms were set up to serve those who wanted to gather at the center of the famous hangout.

Carson watched as they navigated around the crowd of various sea vessels anchored, moored to one another, or puttering around. They had left Destin Harbor and were passing through the channel of Choctawhatchee Bay. She hated surprises and so wasn't keen on having to wait to discover where their hosts were taking them. Her efforts to get this information out of Derrick were in vain, as he was still pouting over her abrupt treatment of him earlier. She informed him he was a brooding jerk and took a seat in the back of the boat, arms folded, and glared.

Tripp and Nikki sat comfortably in the bow settee and chatted away. Mark had taken a place at the console across from Derrick, who steered them toward their prearranged destination. The dual console separated the two passenger sections fore and aft of their location, with a walkway between the two captain's chairs. Mark didn't seem to mind at all that Nikki sat so close to Tripp. The man seemed more inclined to keep watching either his phone or the navigational equipment in front of their skipper.

Carson began chewing on her pinkie nail, a nervous habit she'd had ever since she could remember. Like most young women, she liked to get her nails done. Unlike some, however, she tended to mangle hers before they were due for their next touch-up. She was mentally reviewing the various parts of the bay she knew of. As she did so, the fun group of boats around Crab Island gradually disappeared behind them. Finally, she couldn't take it anymore.

Carson rose quickly from her seat and headed to the walk-through of the dual console. She passed between both men sitting there and felt their eyes follow her. At the bow, she awkwardly forced herself between her brother and Nikki. They parted and made room for her. While impressed the woman could keep a conversation going with her brother, she had other things on her mind.

Carson glanced at Tripp to her left, then Nikki to her right. "Okay, what the hell is going on?"

Nikki seemed taken aback by the question and stammered, "We—we're just talking."

"I'm describing my day-to-day routine as a private investigator," Tripp explained.

"It's very interesting—"

"No," said Carson, "I'm not talking about what's going on between you two. The answer to that mystery will have to wait. I'm talking about those two bozos up there." She pointed at them. "Where are they taking us?"

"You're actually concerned about something that I'm not," said Tripp with amusement. He was usually the one who was a bit anxious in unfamiliar settings. Carson paused briefly, digesting the idea that she was probably acting more like her brother than he was.

"There's something not right about those two. I'm beginning to wonder if they even know one another." She glanced at Nikki. "How long have you known Mark?"

"Oh, I just met him today, on the walk. He was sweet and bought me another beer when I spilled mine." Nikki smiled as if it were a perfectly natural thing.

"And you just jumped in a boat with the dude?"

"Really, Carson, I can't believe we're having this conversation," Tripp said, incredulous. "How long have you known the poster boy for juicing? Less than twenty-four hours?"

"That's different," Carson said, trying to dismiss the similarities. "Besides, I sent you his picture in case anything happened."

"Was that before or after you invited me to join you on this boat with Darwin's missing link?"

"I don't remember," Carson said and realized how ridiculous she must have sounded. It wasn't a good feeling. "Okay, you got me there. At least I told Derrick that I sent his picture to our cop relative. Besides, I'm a big girl who's been in dangerous situations before."

"I'm a big girl," Nikki said in protest.

"I'm not talking about bra size, dear."

Carson didn't hear Nikki's rebuttal, as Derrick had kicked up the boat's speed from a slow cruise to almost full throttle. The three of them, facing the stern, lurched forward. The wind and engine noise made having a normal conversation difficult. They began to feel the spray as the bow bounced off waves. Normally, that would have been a good thing, but Carson was no longer in the mood.

"I'm telling you guys, I've getting a bad feeling." She had to raise her voice to be heard.

Nikki turned to Tripp for some reassurance. Strangely, he seemed the least concerned. He simply pulled out his phone, brought up a GPS map, and sent it in a text.

"There," he said.

"There what?" yelled Carson.

"I sent Daniel a text," Tripp said.

"And that helps how?"

"Helps what?" Mark asked. He stood right over them and stared straight at Carson.

She felt uncomfortable. "What?" Carson pretended she hadn't heard him. She pointed to her ear for effect. But before Mark could continue, the cruiser suddenly slowed down again as they neared a cove.

Mark straightened up and turned toward Derrick in frustration. "Why are we slowing down?"

"No-wake zone," said Derrick.

Carson practically leaped up from where she sat, taking advantage of their slow speed to speak. "Where are we going?" Mark ignored the question and pulled out his phone to send another text. Derrick also ignored her, but she would have none of it. "Okay, we're leaving."

"You plan on swimming back to shore?" asked Derrick, smirking.

"I'm an excellent swimmer."

"Hold on," said Mark and put his phone down. "Nobody's going anywhere."

"Exactly my point," said Carson. "There's no secret islet, or whatever you want to call it, in this direction. I know this bay. You, obviously, do not."

"Did I say islet? I meant hidden inlet. Cool hangout."

"And the bullshit continues. Take us back to Destin," she said. Tripp and Nikki had joined her at the center of the boat.

"Mark, she obviously doesn't want to go to this cool hangout. Let's just head back to Crab Island. We can hook up with some folks and just hang out," suggested Nikki.

At this, a peeved Derrick cut the engines. "Fine."

"Why did you do that?" demanded Mark.

"What's the point, dude? She's obviously freakin' out and not in the mood to play."

"Just get us moving again," said Mark sternly.

"Piss off, man. This wasn't the deal. This bitch was supposed to be drunk and ready for anything. Does she look ready?"

"Deal?" Carson and the other two said almost in unison. Tripp pulled out his Smartphone and started to tap another text. Carson put her hands to her hips and glared. Nikki just stood there, her mouth agape.

"What's going on here?" Carson demanded.

"Nothing. We're going to have a good time. Go sit down," Mark said, trying to soften his demeanor. Carson raised a defiant brow.

"Hey, man, I don't want this crazy chick flippin' out and filing charges on me. I'm already on probation," said Derrick.

"Oh wonderful," said Tripp. "Any other revelations we need to know about?"

Derrick, to everyone's surprise, did have more to say. "It's not my boat."

Tripp didn't look surprised, but Carson scowled. "What?" Her glare could have burned through the man. "Anything else you want to share?"

Derrick thought about this. "No, but I still think you're hot."

"Of course, that just makes up for everything else," Carson said. Even Derrick knew this was sarcasm.

"Exactly whose boat are we traversing the bay in?" asked Tripp suspiciously. It occurred to Carson he was concerned they might be on a stolen ride.

"I don't know. Mark told me he'd secure a ride if he could tag along with his lady. He said she'd always wanted to go out on a boat. It sounded good to me. We'd both take a ride on a nice yacht with our ladies."

"This is no yacht and I'm not your lady, Derrick," Carson said.

"I've been on lots of boats before," said Nikki, confused.

Mark became noticeably more frustrated and headed to Derrick to take control of the boat. He studied the controls, apparently inexperienced with the vessel he had acquired for their excursion.

"Wait," said Carson. "Nikki, you met Mark when?"

"This morning."

"And Derrick, you made this deal when?"

"Last night," Derrick said and thought about it for a while. He looked confused. It would be up to someone else to explain what was wrong with the story.

"It's strange that Mark wanted his lady, who he hadn't even met yet, to go out for a little water excursion. Isn't that odd, Mark?" asked Carson.

Mark reappeared from behind Derrick, not looking happy about the unraveling of his story. He made his way to the stern and stood up on the rear seat, creating a stage for himself. He scanned his audience and then clapped his hands together loudly to get their full attention.

"Listen up. Derrick will be piloting this boat to our destination. The rest of you will sit down and keep your mouths shut for the rest of the journey."

"Mark, I don't believe this is your call to make," Tripp said as he glanced up from his texting. "We should head back to Destin Harbor."

"I'm with this dude," said Derrick as he went back to the helm.

"Unless you plan on following my GPS course, don't touch that," said Mark.

Immediately, Derrick's chest puffed out and his muscles flexed as he turned to the smaller man who stood on his makeshift stage. He drew closer, but Mark didn't seem fazed. He looked more interested in who Tripp was texting.

Mark produced a small semiautomatic pistol, rapidly attached a silencer, and pulled back the weapon's slide. The click of the round chambering made everyone freeze. Sweat formed on Mark's face; not just his story had unraveled. "Everyone, stop what you're doing."

Carson and Nikki froze as Tripp slowly lowered his phone. Derrick lost his desire for confrontation and held his hands up, chest level and palms outward. He watched in horror as the angry man leveled the weapon at him.

"I-I-I'll just get the boat moving again," he said, but he didn't dare move without Mark's approval.

"Who else knows how to pilot one of these?" asked Mark. The question was met with an eerie silence, which prompted him to repeat it.

Reluctantly, Tripp raised his hand.

"Good."

The sound of a silenced pistol going off made everyone jump. Derrick's back was to the rest of them. He realized he had been shot and stumbled backward. After one final step, he dropped against the captain's chair and slid down it. The gurgling sound he made as he choked on his own blood was gruesome.

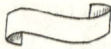

Tripp quickly assessed the situation. He wanted to assist the dying man, but he served as a barrier between the gunman and his sister. Carson was pale and petrified, while Nikki had dived into the bow near the seats and assumed a fetal position.

"Now that I have your attention, throw your phones overboard," said Mark, motioning with the pistol.

One by one they complied. Nikki's was the first in the bay; she tossed it like a hot potato and returned to her fetal state. Tripp tossed his carefully over the starboard side and reached over to retrieve Carson's from the purse wrapped around her body. She was unable to look away from their captor. With the final plop of a phone hitting the water, Mark stepped down from where he'd been standing. He motioned for Tripp to take control.

As Tripp made his way to start the engines back up, he heard something. Mark heard it too, and he swiveled in the direction of the noise. It was the unmistakable sound of a jet-propulsion watercraft closing in.

"Start us up," he said and lowered his pistol, so as not to garner attention. "Everyone find a seat and act natural."

Tripp reached over and sat his shaken sister in the starboard side console seat. He'd never seen her quite like this; she was in shock. He glanced down at the motionless body right behind him. He started to reach down to check on the man but was stopped by Mark.

"Leave him."

"He needs help."

"You will too if you don't do as I tell you," Mark said, glancing at the approaching wave rider, who was almost upon them. He held the gun closely to his body as he sat, trying to give the appearance that all was fine, though his discomfort was obvious. Had the rider seen him shoot Derrick? Had he heard the muffled shot? Mark seemed ready to shoot again, if need be.

Tripp pushed forward on the throttle and they started to move again. He kept one eye on the red watercraft, which bounced along the bay's small waves, spraying water around. Judging by its speed and direction, it would pass behind them, probably no more than twenty yards away. It was a two-seater but had only one rider.

As the rider drew closer, Tripp saw he was well tanned and had dark hair, and a white shirt flapping in the wind. His choice of khaki pants certainly seemed odd, as they were soaked from the spray. If only it was who he hoped it was.

Tripp continued to track the small vessel as it passed behind them. He noticed that Mark took a brief interest but seemed convinced it was just someone joyriding and turned his attention back to the others.

"Turn around and watch where you're going," Mark yelled.

Tripp had to adjust course to avoid getting too close to the shallows. "What's our destination?"

"It's around that point."

Tripp did as he was instructed and glanced over at his sister. She seemed understandably tense but not physically harmed. The sight of someone being murdered was traumatic.

"You okay?" he asked.

Carson nodded. She glanced up and shifted her attention toward Mark, who sat at the stern. She motioned something, but he didn't understand what she was trying to convey. Then he realized her right hand had formed into a gun.

"Yes," Tripp said. "He's still holding it."

She promptly shook her head and pointed to him. He realized then what she was asking. Tripp had his concealed carry license. As a private investigator, he thought it was the right thing to do. However, he hardly carried it and that day was no exception.

"No," he said and immediately saw hope fade further from her face.

Mark glanced over and barely had time to react before the wave rider broadsided them. He brought the pistol up with one hand and held the other one up in a defensive posture.

With well-timed precision, the rider leaped from the vessel as it slammed into the larger craft. He sailed over, foot extended, and caught Mark square in the chest, who immediately fell backward into the water.

The other man bounced off the backseat and hit the floor. The rest of the occupants were jolted as the cruiser listed back and forth from the impact. The boat's tethered kill switch, which should have cut the engines when Tripp fell from the captain's chair, hung unattached to its driver. The vessel continued to propel itself forward until Tripp got up and stopped it manually.

A familiar head popped up from the stern. Daniel's dark feathered bangs hung over his brow. He swept the hair aside and looked straight at Tripp. "Why are you stopping, dude?"

"After a collision like that, we need to check structural integrity."

"Forget that. Put some distance between us and that other guy."

"Good call." Tripp started the engines back up and pushed the throttle forward cautiously.

"Daniel!" yelled Carson, both surprised and thankful to see him. She tried to calm herself before she grabbed and hugged him. But her joy turned to horror as Mark's hand came over the transom and he lifted himself into the moving vessel.

Daniel turned to see the man rise to his feet. He rushed him and tried to kick him back in the water, but this time Mark was ready. He blocked the kick with his left hand and reached behind to pull out a white-handled dagger. He must have lost his pistol when he went overboard.

Mark swiped at him with the blade, but Daniel hopped backward and held a defensive stance. The two fought, with Daniel, to his friends' amazement, easily matching the other man's martial arts skills.

Tripp throttled down and tried to determine how to assist his friend. The two men were all over the boat, using better hand fighting skills than he possessed. They made their way toward the bow.

Daniel was too quick for Mark and caught the wrist of the hand that held the dagger. With his other hand, Daniel fluidly twisted the man's arm behind his back by controlling his wrist and elbow. With another quick motion, something popped in Mark's arm and the weapon dropped into the water. For good measure, Daniel swept Mark's knee in a painful motion.

With a groan, Mark went headfirst into the boat's deck. He tried to struggle, but with a bruised knee, dislocated shoulder, and an arm pinned behind him, it was useless. Ultimately, it was the metal fire extinguisher that met his skull with a dull thud that brought things to a conclusion.

Carson stood over the man, still holding the old extinguisher. She raised it to bring it down for another strike, but Daniel stopped her.

"He's had enough." He lifted the unconscious man and let him drop back to the deck.

Carson, convinced Mark was no longer a threat, lowered her newfound weapon. Her breathing was so heavy, Tripp feared she was hyperventilating. He tried to comfort her, but she brushed past him and grabbed Daniel in a tight embrace. Daniel must have been in heaven.

Carson released him and studied his face, as though ensuring he was real. He was slightly taller than she was, perhaps a couple inches. "What are you doing here?"

"Saving your butts," replied Daniel. "I guess next time you'll invite me."

"You have an open invitation from now on," said Carson and hugged him again.

Afterward, Tripp, Carson, and Daniel decided to go through Derrick's pockets. They found another knife, a thin wallet, a wad of money, and—after searching the boat—Mark's cell phone.

With a unanimous vote, they decided Mark was too dangerous to remain aboard. Without fanfare, they tossed him into the bay. The boat started her journey again and left him floating in the distance, faceup.

"Should we have given him a life preserver?" asked Tripp as he continued to pilot the vessel.

"That prick tried to kill us," Carson said, pointing at him. He bobbed like a human cork. "What do you think?"

"An emphatic no, it seems." Tripp turned the boat over to Daniel while he checked on Nikki, who was still too scared to move from her huddled position in the bow. After he calmed her down, he took on the morbid task of confirming what he already feared.

Derrick was dead. He had bled out from being shot in the heart. Tripp shut the man's eyelids, found a tarp in one of the storage compartments, and covered his body.

"Now what?" asked Carson.

"We should call the authorities," said Tripp as he took over piloting the boat again.

"With what, genius? Our phones are in the water and that bunghole's phone is locked."

"I have a phone," said Daniel. "Tripp's Smartwatch also has its own number. In fact, I used the GPS to find you guys."

"Oh," said Carson. "Wait . . . you tracked us?"

"Of course," Daniel said as he fiddled with Mark's phone.

She seemed to be the only one surprised that their whereabouts could be tracked. "You knew about this?"

"I counted on it," Tripp replied. "Daniel gave me the watch as a security measure in case I was ever injured on a case. To get here so quickly, however, he had to already be trailing us."

"What prompted you to do that?" asked Carson.

"I follow you all the time when I'm not invited," Daniel said with a shrug.

Carson seemed confused. "Why? And how the hell did you do all that other crap? Since when did you become our personal Bruce Lee?"

"Long story."

"Oh, I see. You go from nagging friend who always flirts with me to mysterious hero. Do I really know you?"

"You've known me for years."

"Okay," Carson said. She looked unconvinced she had gotten a real answer and turned to Tripp.

"I'm just as surprised as you," he said. "I was aware Daniel knew martial arts, but that was completely unexpected."

"Guys, I'll explain everything later. For now, we have to all agree on a few things," said Daniel. "One, we don't go to the police. Two, we ditch this boat and the body. And three, we all stick together from this point forward."

"We can't exactly hide what just happened," Tripp said. "Someone might think we killed Derrick. Also, we need to get Nikki to safety."

"I don't want you guys to leave me alone," Nikki said with panic in her voice. She walked over to the helm where Tripp was. He placed a reassuring arm around her, which seemed to help.

Carson looked critically at them, and Tripp realized she considered them an odd pairing. Perhaps she thought Nikki didn't measure up to him. "Okay, number four, we get Nikki safely to shore and she can explain to the Coast Guard what happened."

"I want to stay with you guys," Nikki said.

"You don't get a vote," Carson said dismissively and then addressed Daniel. "Just where do you think we're going?"

"A safe place, for starters," said Daniel.

"Why shouldn't we call the Coast Guard ourselves?" asked Tripp.

"Because this wasn't a random attempted kidnapping. That guy's a professional. There are more like him, possibly close by. When Mark doesn't show up with you, they'll come looking. We need to disappear."

Obviously, the idea was absurd to Carson. "Why would anyone come looking for us? It's not like we're rich or famous. Ever try to get ransom from a family on a preacher's salary?"

Daniel stopped what he was doing and faced her. "You ever bother to ask how a guy like your dad, on a small-town preacher's salary, owns several buildings, a bar, a boat, and who knows what else?"

Carson knew about these assets from an earlier conversation with Tripp. "Dad inherited money and made some good investments. Why? Are you implying he's involved in some type of shady business? If so, you don't know him as well as I thought you did."

"Your dad is a good man," said Daniel. "I don't have all the answers, but trust me when I tell you there's far more to the Page family than what's on the surface. This was no mistake. Whoever tried to grab you wanted leverage."

"That sounds like a conspiracy theory, Daniel," said Tripp. "I tend to agree with Carson. I can think of no reason why someone would want to harass our family. If you have something to share, then do so, but don't retreat to saying it's a long story."

Daniel looked disappointed, as if his line had been stolen. "Okay, listen. I'll tell you everything I know once we get to a safe place."

"Then let's be on our way."

Daniel directed them to an inlet outside of a residential area. Tripp started to tie off the boat but Daniel stopped him. Instead, he pointed the vessel back into the bay and rigged it to throttle away from the shore.

As Daniel leaped back onto the short pier, Tripp confronted him. "Why did you do that?"

"We need to buy time," Daniel said. "Let's go."

"You owe us an explanation," Tripp reminded him.

"We'll talk in the car."

"What car?" asked Carson, just before she spotted a blue sedan arriving on the street behind them.

"That one," said Daniel. "I used the Uber app. We need to keep moving."

"What about Derrick?" Tripp asked.

"He's dead. His condition won't change."

They all climbed into the waiting vehicle. The car drove away while the boat carrying Derrick's corpse continued its slow journey back out into the bay.

BUMP AND GUN

As Jack drove home, the ten-inch monitor on his truck's dash switched from soothing landscape images to an alert to an incoming Skype call. The image of his lovely yet upset wife appeared as he accepted it.

"Hello, Mrs. Page," he answered cheerfully.

Kate seemed anything but pleased. "Jack, I've been trying to get a hold of you. I ended up calling the church, and Julia said you'd been gone for a while."

"Sorry, my love," Jack said as he searched for his phone. "I must have muted it. I had to run an errand. What's wrong?" He could tell she had been crying.

"Carson's upset at me. She took off, and neither she nor Tripp will answer their phones. It's so unlike Tripp not to answer. I'm used to Carson ignoring me—"

"Whoa," said Jack. He had absolutely no idea what his wife was rattling on about. "So Carson's upset. How is this an emergency?"

"I'm sorry," Kate said as she wiped her tears. She sobbed briefly and tried to collect her thoughts.

"Okay, Kate," he said with forced calm. "I'll be home in a few. Where are you?"

It took a moment for her to collect herself. "I just closed up my shop and am heading home too."

"We'll talk soon."

"Please hurry."

"I'm on my way. Love ya," Jack said. With a bleep, the image of Kate disappeared, without the customary "Love ya." The only time that occurred was when his wife was upset at him. Thankfully, that wasn't often. He concluded she and their daughter must have had quite the disagreement.

Jack thought about how terrible Kate was at trying to explain something when angry or tearful. Like the time she was involved in a minor fender-bender several years back. It took him forever to figure out that she and everyone else was alive and well. Kate had lost her temper when the other driver, who had caused the accident, had the audacity to yell obscenities at her.

She was typically a very even tempered, lovely woman—that is, until she became upset. The day of the accident, Jack hadn't been sure if half of her words were even part of the English language. In retrospect, the story made him smile, though he would never let his wife know he found it amusing.

But today, with Shelby's sudden appearance at the church and his wife being upset, there was little humor to be found. He decided to try to give the twins a call. He used voice commands via his truck's Bluetooth to call Carson, then Tripp. Both times, it went to voice mail.

Carson's voice mail was an old recording she had used while on her grandfather's ship a few years ago. It was such an exciting experience, she continued to use it. Her voice could barely be heard over the howling wind and pounding waves. She had proudly recorded it while watching the waterspout, from a "safe" distance, off the Gulf Coast of Florida.

Tripp's recorded message, on the other hand, was a simple one. The only thing that gave it any character was Daniel yelling, "Voice mail bomb," in the background before the prompt to leave a message.

Daniel, he thought. Jack brought up the custom application on the touchscreen console of his truck. He pushed the question mark icon and waited as a map materialized on the screen. Daniel had mentioned the app a few months before and Jack liked the idea, so the young man installed it for him. It tied into the twins' Smartwatches and Kate's fitness bracelet. It was loosely based on other applications in existence but had customized benefits. While not all of Daniel's ideas worked out, this one had been built on already-proven technology. Jack had copied the app and used it in other devices.

A menu popped up with icons representing his wife and two kids. They were pictures Daniel had picked out, not ones he would have chosen himself.

He decided to select Tripp, since he was the more likely of the twins to be wearing his device.

A blue screen appeared, with nothing but a flashing dot. Jack watched it momentarily before he realized he needed to keep his eye on the traffic in front of him. Ahead, a white utility van with no windows was going slower than the speed limit. If he hadn't been on a winding two-lane road that led to his hometown, he would have passed it already. He glanced back at the screen and tried to zoom out.

He could see it was a body of water, a bay. So Tripp was on the water. "What bay?" he said. Jack studied the map a moment longer—it was Choctawhatchee Bay. He went back and chose Carson's picture. The flashing dot on the screen showed the same location; they were together and close to shore. He adjusted the map, trying to determine where they were heading.

The red brake lights caught his attention. Unable to maneuver defensively because of a low shoulder and an oncoming car in the other lane, Jack slammed on the brakes. With a jolt, his truck came to a stop—mostly from the brakes but also thanks to a mild collision with the van's back bumper.

"Just great." Jack swore. He sat another moment and stared at the van's windowless backside. There was no obvious reason for the driver's sudden stop. He set the truck's flashers, retrieved his insurance info, and exited the pickup.

After a couple of steps, Jack's phone rang. A picture of Daniel appeared on the Smartphone screen. "Hey Daniel," he answered. "I was just thinking of you. I used your app to track Carson and Tripp."

"That's cool, Mr. Page. Just wanted to tell you we're all fine. We've got a story to share later. Bye."

"Wait. You're with the twins?"

The silence told him the conversation was over. At least he knew they were okay. Jack wondered what story they would tell as he continued toward the van he had run into.

The driver's hairless, muscled arm hung out the window. For some reason, the guy hadn't even bothered to check his vehicle. Jack could see a light-colored cowboy hat in the driver's-side mirror.

He called out, "Sorry about that. I wasn't expecting you to suddenly stop."

The man spoke with a thick Texas accent. "No worries, partner," he said as Jack approached his window. "I'm sure you had other things on your mind."

Jack immediately recognized him and took a step backward. "Shelby, what the hell are you doing?"

"Getting rear-ended by a preacher," said Shelby with a chuckle, still using the fake accent. He even wore a red Western shirt for effect. "Get in, partner. We need to talk."

"You should stick with your natural Cajun. Your Texan sucks, and I need to get home."

"As you know, I lost the Cajun accent years ago. You looking for your kiddos?"

Jack lost interest in departing just yet. "What do you know about my kids? Why did you leave the subtle message on my church pew?"

"Get in and we'll discuss some family issues," Shelby said, minus the accent.

Jack stood firm. "What about my family?"

"I'm not gonna talk to you in the middle of the road."

"Well, why did you start the conversation by causing an accident, then?"

Shelby's signature snicker started quietly and grew to an asthmatic-sounding wheeze. "You got me there. I couldn't resist when I saw you looking down at your radio."

"I was checking my map."

"You've lived here for how many years and you still need a map? You really have changed."

Jack didn't try to hide his irritation. "I was trying to track my kids using GPS."

"Sounds high-tech. They're out on the bay, preacher man. They might be in trouble. We should get going in that direction."

"I just spoke to their friend, who indicated they were fine."

"Fumi's nephew? What's his name again?"

"I've little doubt you know Daniel's name, as well as too many personal details about me."

"It's my job. Look, preacher, they may be fine right now, but someone has an interest in 'em."

"I'm not clear what your stake in this is, but I'm going to go park my truck at home. After I check in with the wife, we can find a place to chat on Viridian Square." Jack turned and headed to his truck. He inspected his custom chrome bumper and noted the thick metal hadn't been damaged by the impact.

"Let's do it," Shelby said as he giddily rubbed his hands together.

Jack entered his truck, drove to Viridian Square, and parked close to the bar he and his best friend Rick Sanchez owned. He walked across the plaza and then around the brick building on the end, which he also owned, and proceeded to the area behind the square. He crossed the street and stopped by Shelby's van, which was in the private parking lot he and his family used.

Behind him were his kids' apartments. Before him, just across the small wooden bridge, was a line of three houses on the little canal that led to the sound. His home was all the way down—the last one. Rick's house was the first one, while the middle home was rented by a nice couple who knew Pops.

"I need to check in with the wife." Jack headed for the walkway bridge.

"Better to leave her out of this."

"That's a little hard to do when she's already involved. Not to mention, she called me earlier, upset over some argument she and the daughter had gotten into."

"Right, the exchange in the bar." He glanced over at Jack, whose interest was piqued.

Jack stopped halfway across the little bridge and waited for Shelby to catch up. "And?"

"Well, let's just say your lady was having a little rendezvous with a certain bartender several years her junior. This bartender—we'll call him Matt—had nefarious plans for Mrs. Page. Instead, your daughter showed up, got angry at Momma's flirtation, and had some words with her. Then Daddy's little girl left."

Jack was bothered that his wife wanted to meet with a younger man, but it was hardly a priority — and he didn't want to discuss it with Shelby. "How does this story end?"

"Let's just say the bartender's efforts went down in flames. He was allegedly hired to violate your lady and return her to you in some humiliating manner."

Jack tried to process what he had heard. "Why?"

"To send a message, of course. I imagine that after receiving your battered wife back, you would've been contacted with instructions on how to get your kids back. You see how that works? They do terrible things to your wife so you know they're serious."

Jack tried to shake off the images that formed in his mind. "Again, why?"

Shelby gave him a concerned look. "You've been a saint too long. Okay, let's just say they want something from you."

"Who are these people?"

"The immediate employers are a security company out of Atlanta, but who hired them is a bit of a mystery. I can tell you only what I know. You remember Alan Lloyd?"

"Sure, he and Pops used to do some business together until they had a falling-out."

"A 'falling-out' is a bit of an understatement. Alan cursed Pops for what he perceived as betrayal," said Shelby. "Alan took that venom to his grave. His son, Victor, runs the company."

"Victor? I thought Alan's boy was Christopher, or something like that."

"Nah, that's the actor."

"Well, Victor wasn't the man I remembered hearing about," Jack said, his thoughts wandering back in time. "Charles was his name."

"Correct. Victor was Alan's bastard child. I guess he figured ol' Charlie wasn't up to continuing his legacy. They say Victor's a much bigger prick than his old man ever was."

"That says a lot. So what does Victor want with me?"

"I'd be a rooster's great-grandnephew if I could tell you that."

"I won't even pretend to know what that means," Jack said. "I've kept a low profile for over two decades. I find it hard to believe this Victor person would come gunning for me over an ancient feud between our fathers."

"Agreed," Shelby said. "There's something else going on here. I received recent word from one of my scouts that someone's tickling the sky over Echo."

Jack knew he must've turned pale. "Who was it, and what were they doing?"

"Well, I don't know that. My contacts disappeared after leaving me a voice mail. Their last message was sent from their boat in the Gulf of Mexico. It's too bad—they were a nice couple. "

"So they spotted another boat doing experiments at the old Echo location?"

"Right, except replace the word 'boat' with 'submarine.'"

"A sub? Wouldn't that indicate a foreign power messing around that area?"

"Possibly, or someone who got their hands on a decommissioned sub. There are organizations out there with a lot of resources, including the people we're up against."

"So Victor's working with some large organization that wants something from me?"

"In case you don't know, preacher, we have our work cut out for us. Something big is on the horizon."

Jack felt irritated. He finished his walk across the small bridge but stopped abruptly after he stepped off onto the sidewalk. He looked past Rick's place and focused on his neighbor's home. Someone peeked through the blinds of one of the side windows.

Shelby saw it too. "Your neighbors the nosy type?"

"They're in Kansas, visiting their son and grandchildren."

"They have someone watching their house, then?"

Jack started to head cautiously toward their home. "That would be me."

They quietly walked around the back of the home where the boat dock and patio were. It was laid out similarly to Jack's backyard, minus the iron fence that separated Jack's patio from his private boat dock.

He noted that his neighbor's boat was secured on its lift. However, he didn't recognize the two-man dinghy that was tied off. He walked over to investigate the small craft while Shelby poked around the back of the house.

As Shelby moved from window to window, peeking in, the back door flew open and two men armed with silenced machine pistols appeared. One went straight for Shelby, while the other targeted Jack.

Shelby dove behind the brick grill station as a spray of bullets followed him. The rounds shattered brick and ricocheted off the cast iron grill lid; the man seemed to be trying to shoot his way through the solid structure. His magazine emptied fast. It only took a moment to slap in another and pull back the slide to his weapon, but that was too much time.

Shelby raised himself up, leveled his own silenced weapon, and fired several rounds into the man's chest. He put one in his head for good measure. The thug instantly fell against the back of the house and slid down the wall.

Jack disappeared into the water as his assailant approached and also opened fire. The man's broad aim produced about thirty water splashes as he closed in on Jack, but he failed to hit him.

The second mercenary stood on the wall at the water's edge and slapped another banana clip in, ready to empty it into the canal. He happened to glance back and notice his partner's lifeless body slumped against the house.

As the thug turned to locate Shelby, Jack grabbed his ankles and pulled him in. The water churned with the struggle beneath its surface. Just when things calmed, bubbles rose and Jack surfaced with his assailant in a headlock. He dragged the unconscious man behind him as he climbed ashore.

He checked for vital signs and then turned, only to be met by the barrel of a pistol. "He's out," he told Shelby, who lowered the gun.

"So's my guy."

"Mine is still alive."

Shelby glanced back at the dead man and the red stripe his body had painted on the house. "I don't think my guy's going to make it."

"I guess we'll be questioning this one," Jack said. He dragged the unconscious man onto the patio and secured his hands behind his back with his belt.

"Sounds like a plan. Let's wake 'em up, interrogate 'em, and make it look like both died when the house was caught in a blaze."

Jack paused to make sure he had heard correctly. "You're not burning down my neighbor's house."

"I prefer to think of it as cleansing the place with fire. You don't really think your neighbors want to come home to two dead guys in their yard, do you?"

"I bet the Smiths would hate it even more if they came back to a burned-out frame that used to be their home. Besides, Pops owns this place and I doubt he'd appreciate you torching it. Oh, and there's only one dead person, Shelby –just one."

"I meant one," Shelby said. "You do know the name 'Smith' sounds bogus, right?"

"Well, they *are* friends of Pops."

Their prisoner stirred and began to cough. It took him a moment to get the rest of the water out of his lungs. He came to his senses and realized his hands were bound behind him.

"You had that guy underwater for quite a while," Shelby said.

"When I was younger, I could hold my breath for almost two minutes."

"Who knew that would actually come in handy? Allow me to address our guest." Shelby turned his attention to the thug, who had quietly sat up. "Hey, asshole, who hired ya?"

The man's thick neck pivoted his head slightly as he spat on the ground near Shelby's left foot. The heel of Shelby's boot sent his square head backward onto the patio. His feet in the air, the man took another moment to sit up again.

"Look, I've already done this once today. Want to know how that one ended?"

The man spat again as he straightened himself.

"A man of few words," Jack said.

Shelby pulled a syringe out of his jacket pocket. "Time for a cocktail."

The man lunged at him but was caught by surprise when Jack grabbed him and thrust him down onto a patio chair. Jack held him down as Shelby injected him.

"We make a good team, preacher."

"Let's just get this over with."

"Soon we won't be able to shut this guy up. Give it a few minutes to take effect. Cigarette while we wait?"

"Don't smoke," said Jack but took one anyway. Shelby lit it for him and then his own. "Going to be one of those days, though," he added and took a deep drag.

They waited for the cocktail Shelby had administered to kick in. Jack paced briefly before his phone rang. It was a Skype call from Daniel.

As he answered, a smooth forehead appeared before Carson moved the phone back to bring her entire face into focus. "Hi, Dad."

"Oh, sweetie, I'm so glad to see you."

"We had a crazy day!" his daughter exclaimed.

"That makes two of us. Are you guys okay?"

"Thanks to Daniel. This guy tried to take us hostage and Derrick got killed!"

"What? The guy you were with is dead?"

"It's been a surreal experience. Anyway, I'll tell you about it when we get home. Love ya!"

"Okay, see you soon. Love ya."

"Love ya too, Mr. Page," Daniel said, laughing as his face replaced Carson's. "They're in good hands."

The video call ended before Jack could respond. He walked back over to where Shelby stood over their assailant. "Anything yet?"

"He's already babbling something about a mission gone wrong. They've been watching your wife and were trying to decide what to do next. I'll finish up, kill the bastard, and we'll move on."

"Just confirm who he works for while I give Pops a call." Jack turned and sighed deeply. "Let's not kill a helpless man, please."

"Sure thing, holy man."

"I'm serious."

"Gotcha," Shelby said with a nod and then grumbled, "Softie," as Jack walked away. He looked down at the man whose gaze had gone from defiant to inebriated. "Preacher doesn't want me to kill you."

The man bobbed his head and grinned.

"Stop smiling, you dopey bastard. I might still do it."

FISH TALE

Pops waited in his boat, still moored near the transom of Fumi's large yacht, for Sammy to meet him. He had just placed his earpiece in when his phone rang.

"Dad," came Jack's voice, "we need to talk."

"I was just thinking the same thing. You wouldn't happen to be near the keys, would you?"

"No, I'm close to home. There's been a series of unexpected incidents. I believe my family is being targeted."

"Targeted? Is everyone okay?" Pops felt it was hardly a coincidence that Fumi had summoned him right before his son called, needing assistance.

"Yes, but I need to get Kate and the kids away from here until I figure out what's going on."

"It sounds like you need more than advice. Where do you want to meet?"

"How about my place tonight?"

"Viridian Square?"

"Right, my bar, to be exact. I'll keep it open late for a private event, if you can join me there."

Pops scratched his chin hairs and thought of the quickest way there. "All right, son, I'll be there," he said and hung up.

Sammy had silently waited for the call to end. The young man had to be close to thirty, but his mannerisms and smile—not to mention that freckled face—still reminded Pops of the young boy he once knew.

Sammy walked up with a string of fish and heard the concern in Pops's voice. "Is everything okay, sir?"

"Hey there, Sammy. Aye, but I need to get going."

Sammy held up his string of fish. "Just a quick look, if you wouldn't mind, sir."

Pops was no longer in the mood, but Sammy's expression told him his fish tale was important. "That's a nice catch."

"Thanks. Most of 'em are mangrove snappers that I caught near shore, but this one's a yellowtail snapper that gave me a fight farther out near the reefs."

Pops admired the collection. "You always were quite the fisherman."

Sammy removed the yellowtail from his line. "You know it, Pops. I'd like you to have this one. Every fish has its story, and this one should interest you. Just be sure to remove the hook it swallowed."

Pops thought the gesture curious but placed the gift in his boat's live well and thanked him. As soon as he did, Sammy retreated to a Jet Ski tied on the other side of the yacht and was soon gone on his next adventure.

Suki approached and untied Pops's catamaran. She had apparently been waiting nearby. She stood on the aft deck and watched as he too departed.

Pops returned to the main channel and headed deeper into the twisting mangrove-lined waterway until he arrived in Largo Sound. He cut across the shallow sound and searched for another waterway that he knew led into Blackwater Bay. Once he spotted it, he navigated his twin-hulled boat through the narrow passage lined with canal homes. He moored in front of a two-story gray house that looked as if it hadn't been occupied for some time.

"I really need to take better care of my investments," he said. He had bought the house years before and planned to use it. But like many of his possessions, he allowed someone else to enjoy it. It appeared his friend hadn't used it in some time, though.

Pops called the skipper of the *Abril*, Captain Ed, and ordered his seaplane to be sent to some coordinates nearby. He had to argue with the man initially because the plane had already been scheduled out. As usual, however, he won the debate with his point that he owned the damn thing.

Pops informed Captain Ed that he needed transport to the Pensacola area. He also wanted a sea vessel with men properly attired for the occasion standing by when he arrived.

Typically, Captain Ed complained he wasn't the Almighty and Pops expected too much in too little time. Also typically, the response was, "Just make it happen, Ed."

Upon ending the call, Pops turned his attention to the yellowtail. It was well over the state-required twelve-inch length for keeping. He examined it but couldn't see a hook down the thing's mouth. Some quick work with a fillet knife still didn't produce a hook—not that he expected to really find one.

But as he continued to clean the fish, he discovered a small glass tube that contained something rolled up inside. Pops removed the lid from the tube and tipped it to one side. After some effort, he freed the rolled-up paper.

The note was handwritten. On one side was a series of numbers. On the other side, a single word. "Doppelgänger," Pops said.

He knew the general definition of the word. Beyond that, the word and the series of numbers were a mystery. He spent some time thinking about it but came to no conclusion; the meaning wasn't obvious so he put it away for later. He decided to travel back up the canal, dock at his place, and take a nap.

JUST BUSINESS

Victor Lloyd sat in his high black leather chair at the end of the large mahogany table, pondering. If the devil had a cousin, Victor's employees would have sworn it was their long-faced, beady-eyed boss. While a goatee might have accented the look, the man preferred to be clean-shaven. Still, the red silk shirt he wore did nothing to hurt his long-standing devilish reputation.

On his thirty-inch hi-res screen, the image hadn't changed, yet he stayed focused on it, as if memorizing every feature. The image was almost thirty years old, but it backed up the old saying that a picture is worth a thousand words.

There were two men in the photo. One was his late father, Alan Lloyd. He was a proud man who had built his company from scratch. The other man was Pops Page, a former friend and business partner of his father's. Page had managed to build a small empire, mostly under the radar. He had also betrayed and almost ruined Victor's father.

The five others at the table, Victor's personal staff, were silent as he sat going over various images on his personal monitor screen. They also had monitors in front of them, which were dark. While the content was related to the reason they were all there, he would decide when and what to share.

Victor wasn't concerned that he had called in his executive team on a Saturday. He had given no thought to their personal lives when he allowed them all one hour to report in. His reputation for being a bastard was secure, if not legendary. He hadn't earned the right to be CEO of his own company;

it had been given to him when his father had died. Regardless, he exercised absolute power over his company.

Neither the president, Victor's half-brother, nor the VP were invited. Neither would ever approve of the questionable project that was worth millions, and this was the sole reason they would never hear of it.

"You have a call from a Dr. Maynard." It was the voice of Victor's lovely assistant June coming over the intercom. He wished she had done a vid call on the monitor in front of him. He might have chastised or berated her for doing so, but he also would have enjoyed seeing the low-cut blouse she wore. She had been his personal assistant for years, mainly because she was so good at what she did. There was a time when the strawberry blonde was also an afternoon treat on the leather sectional in his office, but he'd moved on to younger and more hard-bodied women over the years. June still has her uses, he thought.

"I'm busy," he said without looking up. He knew the others in the room were probably disappointed they wouldn't get a break while he took the call. He could hardly have cared less. "When he finishes whatever he has to say, take notes and hang up."

There was a low chuckle at the table. Victor however, was well aware that June knew him too well to find anything he said humorous. He had expected her to quit years ago when she first found him being serviced by his new interest while he sat, of all places, at her desk. It was his way of letting her know she was nothing special to him. He spotted her and requested a cup of coffee once he was done with his "meeting," which of course added insult to injury. She was furious but refused to quit. Was it the money, or did she know he would have gone out of his way to punish her for leaving? She, like many others, loathed him. He suspected she'd spat in his coffee that day.

"Okay," June answered and, with a click, left the executive team to themselves.

Victor flipped through a few more photos. His eyes narrowed as he came across a more recent picture of Pops. The old man stood on the bow of his personal ship, unaware of being watched or having his picture being taken. His squinting eyes looked elsewhere, as if surveying the sea kingdom he probably thought was his.

"Pops Page," he said. The eyes in the room shifted upward at him. Maybe they hoped he was ready to include them in something. Soon they seemed to realize he was just talking to himself and returned to their phones and tablets. Conscious the others were listening, Victor lowered his voice to a soft hiss. "Your legacy is coming to an end, old man."

He doubted the old man even remembered who he was. That alone bothered him. Pops certainly remembered his father and even knew his half-brother Charlie, but Victor was always an afterthought known simply as Alan Lloyd's bastard. That would soon change.

He had been tapping the touchpad on his desk rather loudly. He wasn't quite ready for the attention of the room, but they were all staring as if they thought he wanted to say something. He had just come across a picture of Pops's son and his family. Everyone seemed happy in it. A middle-aged man put his arm around his wife. She was a looker, but a bit too old for Victor's taste. The two children, probably in their late teens at the time the picture was taken, were squatting in front. The fraternal twins, as he understood them to be, held hands. His attention focused on the lovely wife and Daddy's lil' girl.

Victor's smile faded as he thought about the events that hadn't gone as planned. He should have handled it personally instead of allowing fools to run the operation. It was just another example of how hard it was to find good help, people willing to bend the rules.

His thought was interrupted by someone at the table. At first, the man cleared his throat, as if finding the courage to speak. He finally heard the word "sir" and glanced up. It was his director of special operations. "Yes, Ron."

"Sir, I have an important conference call in thirty minutes. If we can—"

"On a Saturday night?"

"Yes, sir."

"You really are a workaholic, Ron. That is, assuming this is a business call."

Ron paused as if worried his words might trap him. "Of course it is."

"Then it's my business, is it not? It can wait until I'm ready for you to leave. Right?"

"Of course," Ron said and went back to looking at his phone.

Weak idiots, thought Victor. All except Carl, of course. In his hideous brown sports jacket, his chief operating officer was long past his prime. Still, the old fart spoke his mind and gave good counsel. As a show of respect, Carl would always wait until he and Victor were alone before challenging him.

"Another call for you, Mr. Lloyd," came June's voice suddenly over the intercom. It was unusual for her to just break in without good reason. And only one caller would likely cause her to show such urgency.

"I'm busy," he said and hoped he was wrong about who was calling.

"He said he tried to call your personal cell, sir. You did tell me this was the one call you'd take. I'll let him know to try your cell phone again," June said and disconnected. Victor could almost picture her smiling with the knowledge that he would soon be made uncomfortable.

With a loud sigh, Victor reached for the pocket he had placed the switched-off cell phone in. He turned it on and put an earpiece in to keep things private. He wanted to retreat to his office, but the phone rang almost immediately. As he answered, he walked over to the window and looked out at the view of the stadium in the distance. Victor was neither a fan of football nor views of a stadium--nor anything else for that matter. He preferred dark, windowless areas.

"This is Victor," he finally said. He tried to ensure the others in the room couldn't see his face.

From the corner of his eye, he noticed the others in the room trying to pretend they were paying no attention, but obviously the desire to get even a hint of what had made him jump on the phone—and cause a small bead of sweat to appear on his forehead right before he turned away from them—was too much to miss. Still, they tried to act discreet and appear not to listen.

Victor heard the man's voice say his name. It was not menacing but had a commanding quality to it. He had never actually met him in person, but they had spoken by phone on several occasions. Victor had no idea where he fit into the hierarchy of his client, but he seemed to be their voice.

"Yes, hello, Joshua. I was going to call you back," Victor said.

"I'm hearing some disturbing news come out of Florida, Victor. You were supposed to do one simple task."

"Right, I did that little task—"

"Your people failed miserably on the one task you were given and even botched the one you decided to go off and do yourself. My superior is quite displeased," said Joshua, obviously upset — but irritatingly calm.

"I was very disappointed as well with the results," said Victor.

"We pay you for results, not making the situation worse," Joshua said, his tone effectively conveying the threat.

Victor tried to keep up his confidence, but it quickly faded. "No, I completely understand. There was no excuse for such sloppiness." The pause was long as Victor listened and said nothing.

"We thought you were the right resource to handle this little project," said Joshua. "If you are not, then let us quit wasting one another's time. There is no further room for these type of mistakes."

Victor gazed out the window, conscious that the others probably enjoyed seeing the arrogant man uncomfortable and frightened—and from a phone call, no less. Maybe they had even decided that this Joshua person was their new hero.

"That won't be necessary," Victor said. "I promise to rectify the situation. Let's forget the little mishaps and move forward, shall we?"

He noticed Carl watching him pace as he listened to the call. The man probably wished he had taken the call somewhere else, as it was always a little embarrassing seeing someone squirm.

"Perhaps I should come meet you in person— to satisfy the burning question as to whether you are the right man for the job." Joshua was obviously quite good at subtly getting a point across.

Victor knew a visit only meant one thing. He had no intention of meeting the man. "While I'd love the chance to meet you in person, your presence here is hardly necessary."

"Then we understand one another?" asked Joshua. "If so, you will welcome some resources I send your way. These people will make your job more efficient."

"Yes, completely clear. I'll, of course, cooperate with anyone you send."

While he was used to being the one to abruptly end a conversation, it was Joshua who hung up. Victor stood momentarily in silence and collected himself. He took his seat again. The others at the long table watched him as he sat and tapped the table with a finger.

Finally, he cleared his throat, signaling he was about to speak to the group. "So things didn't go exactly as planned today." He tapped the pad in front of him and everyone's monitors came alive. A PowerPoint presentation filled their screens.

"You can thank Carl and June for quickly putting together this deck," he said as he advanced to the first slide. "I know you're probably familiar with these people, some more than others. That said, I want to ensure we're all on the same page moving forward."

The group reviewed the first slide.

"This is Bradley Jack Page Sr., also known as Pops Page. He owns several businesses under an umbrella corporation known as the Seven Seas but spelled out as 'Ccccccc.' I know, it's stupid."

There was a brief chuckle he ignored.

"His son, Bradley Jack Page Jr., goes by Jack. He's a small-town preacher who also happens to own a bar. We should probably sit in on one of his sermons someday."

The employees laughed out loud.

Victor continued. "The grandson, Bradley Jack Page III, seems to simply be called Tripp. He's apparently some kind of private investigator."

"Didn't we recently try hire this kid?" asked Agnes, his projects administrator. She was an older woman with jet-black hair and spectacles that perched low on her nose.

"I believe Carl reached out to him with an offer," Victor said and shot a glance toward the man.

Carl took a drink and cleared his throat. Before he could speak, however, Ron spoke up.

"He can't be older than his mid-twenties," said Ron. "I see nothing we'd want in a potential prospect. Why actually try to recruit him?"

"On the surface, you're correct, Ron. Fortunately, I go beyond the surface," Carl said as a mild slight to the man. "Months ago the idea was to gain access to the Page family. The young man is a bit of an enigma. He had tested for both college and the military. His scores were off the charts. He chose neither path. I'm not sure if that was his choice or his family's. Regardless, he showed little interest beyond talking with one of our recruiters."

"The boy is nothing," said Victor and waved Carl away. "Merely a link to the grandfather. Moving on, the next slide is of the preacher's wife, Katherine Page. She owns a beauty salon and typically stays close to Viridian Square, their home."

"Is that the one Steve's team missed?" Ron blurted out.

Steve, a former marine and special projects director, was the youngest of the group at barely thirty-five. He shot Ron a dirty look but said nothing.

Victor was irritated by the interruption. "Try to save your questions until after the presentation," he said dryly. "That said, yes. She alone was our client's target. Take a good look, people. She got away."

Victor's gaze locked onto Steve as he said it, and the man shifted uncomfortably in his seat.

"Let's just skip forward to a group photo of who wasn't today's target," Victor continued. A slide with Jack, Tripp, and Carson Page appeared on the screen. "Now Pops Page currently isn't a target either, but I chose not to include him here because I do eventually plan to get the son of a bitch."

A brief chuckle broke the tense mood. The next slide came up—another picture of Jack Page.

"Oh look, another pic of the preacher. I wonder why?" said Victor. "I know—it's because our client made it extremely clear from the beginning that this man was not to be approached in any way, shape, or form." He walked around the table and stopped directly behind Steve. "Yet I'm hearing he was almost shot by someone's team today."

The room grew so quiet that Victor could hear himself breathe. Steve, looking anxious with his boss standing directly behind him, tried to turn before he spoke.

"I made it crystal clear to my team leader that Jack Page was to be avoided like the plague. I'll investigate what happened." Steve paused to swallow. "As for the girl . . . in all fairness, she was added as an alternate target in case we missed the mom. She, of course, wouldn't have been harmed. You approved of this alternate plan, sir."

Victor abruptly grabbed the back of Steve's chair, which caused him to jump. "You're right. I did tentatively approve of the daughter as a plan B, but only if we missed her mommy."

Steve seemed to resume his normal breathing pattern again.

"But Steve, had you allocated all resources on the mother and not divided them, there would have been no need for an alternate plan. Let's also not forget the most important detail: not getting the preacher killed."

"Again, sir, I'll make sure my team knows there are consequences for this screwup."

"That's good. Shit should, after all, roll downhill. I like that saying much better than 'The buck stops here.'"

Steve allowed himself a smile. "I do too, sir."

"I hired you, Steve, to get me quality people. Instead, I got mindless drones who can't think for themselves when no one's there to hold their hand."

Steve's smile rapidly faded. "They were recommended, sir. I'll deal with the one who made the recommendations."

Victor wasn't impressed. He strolled back toward his chair and stretched before he spoke again. "This whole day has been one folly after another. We all find ourselves working late on a Saturday instead of having drinks and getting laid." He scanned the table, staring down each person. Only Carl didn't flinch. "Of course, Carl drinks more than he gets laid."

They chuckled again, and even Carl found humor in the remark. Steve looked relieved that the focus had shifted from him.

Victor paced for a moment, then stopped. "This company survives on its reputation alone. If we don't deliver to our customers, they'll go elsewhere. Or worse. As you all witnessed, my best-paying client isn't pleased at all. While I could take some of the blame myself, we did just discuss how shit tends to roll downhill. You're fired, Steve. Clear out your office."

"What?" exclaimed Steve as he leapt to his feet. "That's bullshit. How can I be responsible for everything that went wrong today? This was thrown at me with virtually no planning budget—not to mention the targets were obviously well connected."

"All true. A professional would have improvised. I guess that's what I get for putting a rookie in a pro lineup," Victor said calmly as he pressed a button. A large monitor was lowered from the ceiling, showing another image of Jack Page for everyone to see.

"I can fix this," Steve pleaded.

"Ultimately, this man is the mission, and he must be alive," Victor said, raising his voice. "Thankfully, Steve's stooges missed. Two idiots got themselves killed, one during the botched surveillance and the other when we were forced to clean up the mess. Another died mysteriously during a bathroom fire, while his partner is still missing. Steve, you will report directly to Carl when your people find him."

"I'm not fired?" Steve asked hopefully.

"No, you're definitely fired, but only from your current position. You need to go back to the minor leagues and practice your swing. I'll fill your vacant position with someone who doesn't make my company look like a junior varsity squad. You will report as new special projects lead. No, let's just call you a projects lead. There's nothing special about you."

"So I'm being demoted to my old job?"

"I thought that was clear."

Steve grumbled something under his breath before he said, "And the current projects lead?"

"You can bounce his ass to the curb for all I care. He did cost you a nice plush office and that hot assistant you had. Be more selective of your people next time and you may rise back up through the ranks—though I seriously doubt it. You may leave the room now—it's for major league players only."

Angrily, but without another word, Steve left the room. Victor turned his attention to the remaining audience as the door abruptly shut. "It looks like we'll need a new special projects director. Ron, you'll take over Steve's duties until you find a more competent replacement for him. Agnes, you'll assist with that."

Both simply nodded. Victor turned his attention to Carl. He could tell the man had something to say. Carl was usually a man of few words, unless he had something worth saying. He did have what Victor considered a "tell" in poker terms. When something was on his mind, he would run his hand through what thinning gray hair was left on his head.

"Yes, Carl?"

The man's baritone voice filled the room. "It can wait, Victor."

"So we wait for our client to make the next call?" Agnes asked.

"Yes, now we must wait. I need everyone to remain focused. This account is worth a lot of money to this company. There's no room for failure." Victor adjourned the meeting.

Everyone left rapidly—that is, except Carl. The old iron horse of the company walked over and sat in the chair adjacent to where Victor had been sitting. He ran his hand through his hair.

"Spit it out, Carl. It's getting late."

The older man let out a deep sigh. He glanced around to ensure everyone else had gone before he spoke. "Victor, we now have a powerful, pissed-off client to add to our woes. You know who's coming next. When that hurricane comes ashore, we're the barrier island between him and our client. Can we absorb that kind of pounding?"

Victor sat and leaned back in his chair. He had pondered this same question. He had probably made the situation worse by expanding the original plans beyond just grabbing the wife. What's done is done, he kept telling himself. He wanted to sound confident in his response but knew it was a roll of the dice. "If we can, I'll be rid of my family's old ghost and our client will reward us handsomely."

"I have my doubts, Victor."

Victor shook his head in frustration and was ready to unload on his old mentor. Coming to some understanding of the man's words, he stopped. "Look, Carl, if you're worried about your stake in the company, don't be. If you think our guys weren't up to the task, then I hear you. We'll bring in better people. Also, I'm told by our client that assets are being sent our way to assist."

"To assist? That can be interpreted different ways. Hell, they may assist in making Steve and his team disappear for the mess they made."

"Hardly a loss," Victor quipped. "As long as shit rolls downhill."

"That may work for now, but let me remind you of the type of people we're dealing with," Carl said. "Our client will require their pound of flesh. Pops will come as well."

"Your concerns are noted."

"Good," Carl said but remained seated.

"What?" Victor asked impatiently.

Carl leaned in closer and spoke in low tones. "Don't let your pride get in the way of your success. Your father made that mistake a long time ago. This company almost never recovered."

"Anything else, Carl?"

"Consider allowing me to take the reins on this one. At least until things simmer down."

Victor eyed him suspiciously at first, but then a grin slowly spread across his face. "That's exactly what we'll do." He stood up and slapped his old mentor on the shoulder. "Carl, you take the reins. We'll fulfill our requirements to our client, then I'll get my bonus. Keep me posted on all activity. After today, it's just business."

SECRETS AMONG FRIENDS

Daniel insisted that the cab driver drop off Nikki at her car in Destin. They asked her to call in an anonymous tip but not give out any of their names. Tripp handed her one of his business cards. Her goodbye hug lasted longer than they had time for. He eventually had to pry her loose but promised they would reconnect later.

They passed several residential streets on their way to Viridian Square, where Carson and Tripp had loft apartments. Daniel typically stayed either at Tripp's place or in their shared office space one floor below. The twins' parents had a home conveniently located one block south of the square along the canal that connected to Santa Rosa Sound.

Along the way, Daniel tried to explain that, although he'd been tasked to be their guardian for years, their friendship was real. Carson accepted it, though she clearly thought it was an insane revelation. Tripp, however, grappled with the validity of their friendship. Even with Daniel's insistence, Tripp seemed to have his doubts.

"Okay, I have to know how this came about," said Carson.

Daniel was happy to finally share the story. "Pops saved my uncle Fumi from a boating accident many years ago. He's considered family now."

"What kinda business do Poppy and your uncle do?" Carson asked.

"Officially?" Daniel tried to think of the best way to explain it. "Pops owns many small businesses incorporated under a larger one—fishing, oil surveillance, salvage, and some others. My uncle Fumi has a shipping business."

"And?" Carson asked suspiciously.

"I suspect they both dabble in the black market," Daniel admitted.

"I knew it had to be something like that!" Carson exclaimed. "Isn't that cool, Tripp?"

Tripp looked skeptical. "It certainly is. There's more to the story, is there not?"

Daniel caught the hostility in his tone. "There is," he said. "This is just through my, uh, own observations, but I believe they're also part of some organization."

"As in a cartel or syndicate?" asked Tripp.

"Something like that. I don't have the details," replied Daniel.

Carson's mouth fell open at this. "I remember traveling around the world as missionaries. Before I was even a teen, our parents were always on the move. They were very protective and always looking over their shoulders. They didn't chill out until we all moved to Viridian Cove. Do you think these creeps are after us because of something Poppy did?"

"I have no idea," Daniel said. "Most of my information comes from stories I overheard on my uncle's yacht in Singapore."

"I find it unlikely you obtained the lion's share of your information from the banter of seafarers," Tripp said dryly.

Daniel was known for using his computer skills to pry into things he shouldn't, and he tried to steer around the indictment. "Well, I did hear a story years ago about a tragedy involving two brothers. One died, while the other had to flee. I often wondered if it was about your family."

Carson looked puzzled. "You mean the story was about our dad and uncle?"

Daniel paused as he glanced over at Tripp, who in turn raised a brow, anticipating his response. "Well, I only assumed the story could be about your dad and deceased uncle."

"What happened?"

"It was a long time ago, but one detail puzzled me. One brother was trying to stop a disaster the other brother had caused. He died in the process, while the other fled in shame."

Tripp hardly looked receptive to the story. "Please enlighten us . . . how exactly did you draw a connection between this story and our uncle's car accident?"

"I believe it was a cover-up for how your uncle really died," Daniel said.

"You base this on what facts?"

"Just stories I've heard. I wasn't privy to all the details, Tripp."

"So this theory is based on hearsay, your imagination, and not much else?"

Daniel felt the ice forming between Tripp and himself. "You're right—the two accounts may not be connected at all."

"I would think not."

"And if they are connected?" Carson asked.

"That would indicate that our dad, the preacher, was a lousy brother," Tripp said glaring at Daniel. "Maybe he was just paid to be our uncle's sibling?"

Daniel sighed deeply. "I was told to watch over you. I would have been compensated whether we were friends or not."

"Yet, the convenience of friendship can make one's job easier."

Tripp had moved the conversation away from the conspiracy theory and back to his own hurt feelings, and Carson looked irked. "Really, Tripp? I'd love someone to pay me to hang out with some of the losers I've called friends."

Daniel groaned at her attempt to make things better. "It wasn't like that."

"I believe that puts things in perspective. Thank you, Carson, for clarifying. We're here," Tripp said as the car pulled into Viridian Square.

The driver was a pasty older man who likely received most of his daily sunshine through the windows of his car. He had been silent the entire time and undoubtedly had been listening in on their conversation. They had been completely oblivious to him.

Daniel took out two one hundred-dollar bills and handed them to the man. "Keep the change and what you've heard to yourself."

The man simply nodded as he admired the nice tip. He would have heard many a story in his years, but he probably thought this latest one was a doozy and was already wondering what the guys at the bar that night would think about it.

Carson had a bounce to her step as they walked away from the cab. "So Uncle Conner was some sort of badass hero?"

"I believe so," Daniel said, happy to steer the conversation away from himself. "Your uncle Conner was a naval officer and might have even been special forces trained." He hoped what he said next wouldn't spark an argument. "Whoever the story was about, it also involved killing some government agent."

"That's crazy," said Carson.

"A cloak-and-dagger tale of action and betrayal—it gets better and better," Tripp added with more than a hint of sarcasm.

Carson ignored the comment. "You said your uncle sent you here. How did that come about?"

"I was raised by my mother, but it was Uncle Fumi who arranged for me to learn certain skills. When Pops approached my uncle for assistance in protecting his family, he suggested I'd be an ideal solution."

"Why?" Carson asked.

"I guess because he trusted my family and I could blend in," Daniel said with a shrug.

"And blend in well you did," Tripp said, indignant. "You certainly had me fooled."

Carson looked weary of her brother being the difficult one, a job that was usually hers. She pulled Tripp aside, jabbed a finger in his chest, and glared up at him. "Listen, I may give Daniel a lot of shit, but he expects it from me. So if anyone's going to be the bitch around here, it's me. Got that? Oh, and try not to forget that he saved both our asses today." She poked him again for good measure.

Tripp's attitude changed completely. "You're right, of course. I apologize for my behavior."

Daniel nodded but said nothing.

Carson patted Tripp's cheek and walked on.

As they made their way up to Tripp's and Daniel's office, Daniel looked around to ensure they weren't being followed. He was hastily entering the code to the door when a voice startled them.

"You kids okay?"

They all turned, relieved to see Rick Sanchez in his normal uniform of blue jeans and a brown button-up shirt. Carson grabbed his hand and squeezed it.

Ricardo Sanchez, known to his friends as either Rick or just Sanchez, was the local detective in Viridian Cove. Of Cuban heritage, his family had come to the US before he was born. He and Jack Page had met back in their high school days in Texas.

"Mr. Sanchez!" Carson exclaimed, before finally releasing the man's hand. "We're so glad to see you. It's been a crazy day."

It was obvious Sanchez had been waiting for them to show up—at the behest of the twins' mom, no doubt. He studied them before he spoke. "A crazy day? Something happen on the bay?"

Carson started to answer, but Daniel cut her off. "Carson means crazy people, Detective Sanchez. You know how goofy it can get around Crab Island this time of year."

Sanchez eyed them with suspicion. "In fact, I did hear things got strange on the water. A body was just discovered in Choctawhatchee Bay. You guys hear anything about that?"

"Yes," said Tripp.

"No," said Daniel, elbowing his friend.

Carson stood between him and Tripp, looking back and forth, as if trying to determine which story to go with. "We might've heard a rumor. So the guy was just floating in the bay, Mr. Sanchez?" Perhaps she had learned from her mother that it was sometimes a good tactic to answer a question with a question.

Sanchez looked uneasy, as if something wasn't right. He was used to them getting into a little mischief—after all, they were a preacher's kids. But this was something totally different. "I never mentioned the gender, Carson, but the deceased *was* a male. My buddy at the Coast Guard station on Okaloosa Island says an anonymous caller tipped them off to a dead guy in a boat. This female caller also mentioned another potential body floating around, but nothing so far. Strangely, she went on about her tall, handsome rescuer and his Mexican sidekick."

Tripp glanced over at Daniel and allowed a slight grin to form. "I'll wager that Mexican sidekicks are nice to have around."

"Second only to Asian ones," Daniel said through gritted teeth. What a lousy anonymous caller Nikki was.

Carson seemed more concerned by a lack of a second body. "You mean the other guy is probably still alive?"

Daniel nudged her. "Assuming it was also a guy."

Carson tried to recover. "It sounds tragic. How are you?"

Sanchez was trying not to chuckle at their feeble attempts at pretending they knew nothing. "You guys have always been lousy liars. You should know that forensics will tell us who was on that boat with the dead man. And the anonymous caller used her own phone to call in, so the authorities will catch up to her soon."

"What a dumbass," Carson muttered under her breath.

Sanchez shook his head. "We'll discuss it further after you've had time to reflect on what happened. Come on, let's go see your mom."

Daniel froze. It wasn't a request but a polite way of saying they must accompany the man. However, he really wanted to get into his office, so he stood and pointed silently at the glass door.

Sanchez wasn't interested in any delays. "Whatever it is, Daniel, it can wait. Let's go."

That was that. They climbed into the back of Sanchez's black sedan. At the last minute, however, the detective had Tripp move to the passenger seat next to him. The front and backseats were segregated by a glass and steel cage for protection when he transported potentially dangerous people. A sliding glass window was usually open, so those in the two sections of the car could talk freely. But before they pulled away, Sanchez closed off the glass.

Forced to sit back and watch the two up front speak privately, Carson grew frustrated. "Just great," she said. "Sanchez has always known how to get the truth out of Tripp. You remember the time we borrowed that Jet Ski?"

"Borrowed? That's a nice way of putting it," said Daniel.

"If we hadn't been caught by Sanchez, we would've returned it."

"After Tripp admitted everything, I had to buy it to keep the guy from pressing charges. I ended up storing it near Destin," Daniel said.

"You bought the thing?"

Daniel shrugged. "For more than it was worth. Back then, I was just trying to protect my girl and my best buddy."

Carson looked mildly surprised at "my girl." It was ancient history to her, but Daniel had a hard time letting it go. She ignored the reference. "Where is it now?"

"Floating around the bay, I suppose," Daniel said. The Jet Ski was the vehicle he had ridden to the rescue on.

"Well, we got busted for that back then, and now, after Tripp gets done, we'll be screwed again."

"Carson, it's not like you asked to be kidnapped. Besides, Tripp can be tough when he needs to be."

Sanchez put the vehicle in drive and started the short but slow journey to the Page home. "So Tripp . . ."

"So, Mr. Sanchez," Tripp replied nervously. The vehicle was moving at a virtual crawl, ensuring plenty of time to talk. The worst part was that Sanchez had chosen him. He was a terrible liar.

"How are your parents?" Sanchez started, apparently wanting to break the ice before the interrogation began. The question at first disarmed Tripp, but well aware of what his dad's friend was up to, he still managed to relax a bit in his seat.

"They're well," he said but then added, "but you already know this."

"And that PI business is going good for ya?"

"Not as well as I'd hoped, but that's not exactly news to you either, sir."

Sanchez laughed, making Tripp aware of his own naïveté. "True, buddy. I sure hope all those conversations about investigative work came in handy."

"You know I appreciate everything you've taught me."

"I know you do. There is, however, something I don't know."

Tripp already knew what was coming but wanted to wait for the actual question. "What would that be, sir?"

"What happened to the dude in the bay?"

Carson and Daniel watched helplessly as Tripp's lips moved a mile a minute. They couldn't make out what he said but knew he would continue until he had provided the full narrative.

Carson felt the car would go backward in time if it went any slower. She tried to get Tripp's attention, but he was too busy spilling the beans.

"Okay, I was wrong," said Daniel. "I may need another plan to get to my office."

"After Tripp gets done talking, you may need a plan to leave the country."

"Oh goody."

Carson hoped Tripp would glance back and see the angry face she had prepared just for him. Instead, he continued to animate his tale with gestures. She could almost figure out what part of the story he had reached by watching his movements.

Sanchez glanced between him and the road. Finally, they arrived at the private parking area for those who lived on the canal. Carson held her breath and waited.

"We're going to jail." Daniel whimpered.

"No, Tripp and I aren't, moron," Carson said. "Sanchez is my dad's best friend. *You*, however, might want to practice not bending down for the soap."

"Oh, that's a nice thought. And moron? I just saved your life, remember?"

"Right. Sorry," Carson said. It was a rare apology. "Look, it's not like we killed Derrick. That creep Mark did."

"Right, but we might've killed the killer."

"We can only hope," Carson replied with a shudder. "I don't want that bastard coming after me again." She sank into the backseat farther and continued to watch the exchange between her brother and Sanchez.

Something strange happened as the conversation wrapped up. Sanchez put his hand on an exasperated Tripp's shoulder and hugged him. Briefly, Tripp seemed misty-eyed as he and Sanchez embraced before they both stepped out of the car.

He can be such a softie, Carson thought. She waited for her door to unlock but was disappointed to find she still couldn't open it. "Hello?" she said loudly, still trying to open it. "What just happened?"

Carson and Daniel could only watch as Sanchez spoke to Tripp in front of the car. The conversation ended and the two, almost in unison, turned their attention to them. Sanchez pointed a key fob their way that unlocked the back doors. Relieved, they exited and followed the others over the walkway bridge.

As they were about to pass Sanchez's home, the door opened and his wife Maria stepped out onto the raised porch and motioned to her husband. They stopped. At first, Sanchez thought she was waving but then realized she wanted his attention. "I better go see what the missus wants. You guys head straight home and I'll join you shortly."

Daniel and Carson turned around and walked the other way, while Tripp stood, unsure where they were going.

Soon Sanchez realized what they were doing. "I meant go straight to your parents' house."

Carson and Daniel rejoined Tripp and they continued to the last home on the canal. It, like the other homes, was built on stilts. They climbed the stairs to the little porch. Tripp didn't hesitate to open the heavy oak door and step inside. Daniel wasn't far behind him.

Carson, however, paused to take another look at the world around her. The sun continued its descent to the west. She inhaled the thick, humid air deeply and held it in her lungs for a few seconds. With her eyes closed, she exhaled slowly. A smile grew across her face before she too disappeared inside.

AN INCOMPLETE TRUTH

Shelby had wanted to kill the man once they finished questioning him, but Jack refused to condone an execution. Instead, they left him tied up for the authorities. Shelby bet Jack the man would be dead before the day was over anyway.

Jack rubbed his right shoulder. With all the action and adrenaline, he hadn't noticed that a bullet had grazed his upper left arm near his shoulder. It was bruised terribly, but he could also feel wetness where the bullet had opened his skin. A blood spot had formed on his short tangerine-colored sleeve. Just a scratch, he thought and ignored the pain.

His wife and Maria Sanchez were standing warily in front of their homes as Jack and Shelby reached the front of the Smith place. Shelby informed Jack he had other things to attend to and answered an incoming call. He meandered toward his van.

Jack continued home and met Kate. She grabbed and hugged him tightly. He returned the hug and kissed her softly on the mouth. Together, as she hung onto his sore arm, they headed up their steps and to their front door. He shifted her to the other arm, as the pain was making his head pound.

Kate noticed the blood spot. "Jack, you're bleeding."

"I'm fine, my love. I was more concerned for you. There were men watching our home. I'm glad you were the first thing I saw as I came around our neighbor's place."

"What happened?"

"Let's talk inside."

Kate had him sit on their brown leather couch next to her while she doctored him. She had volunteered as a nurse's aide when she was a teen, something her wealthy father had disapproved of as a waste of her talents and beneath her. Jack knew the experience had come in handy on more than one occasion, though. She rolled his sleeve up and noted the small wound was directly above an old scar high on his arm.

Jack told her about how he had run into Shelby, literally, and then about the altercation at the neighbor's place. He explained that the bartender she had met allegedly had ill intentions for her. Shelby had also warned him that someone might come after their kids.

Kate turned pale and it seemed to take her a moment to process what she had heard. "I just needed a drink," she said.

Jack knew it was a lie. "Why would you go meet another man?"

Kate's eyes narrowed. "You know why. I have to wonder if I'm even attractive to you anymore."

"That's silly. I lose my breath every time you walk into the room."

"Actions speak louder than words, Jack," Kate said. "You're always gone on church business or — only God knows what. You keep me in the dark and have little time for us. That wasn't our agreement."

Jack knew it was true. "Fair enough, but come to me — not some stranger," he said. "Once we get past whatever is happening, I promise to do better."

"If you say so," Kate finally said.

Jack knew Kate wanted to see some semblance of jealousy from him. However, it was too easy for him to turn off that emotion. He did so without even trying. "We need to focus on what's in front of us, Kate."

"Okay. Have you warned the kids? Carson wouldn't answer my calls. Then Rick told me a body had been found in the bay. He tried to call the kids but only received voice mail." Kate appeared to realize she was rattling on and took a deep breath. "Jack, what the hell is going on?"

"I don't know yet. Carson did mention they had a crazy day, but they're okay. They should be here soon." As if on cue, the front door opened. In walked Daniel and Tripp, with Carson a few steps behind them.

Kate sprang up from her seat and embraced Tripp and then caught Carson as she tried to walk past. "I'm so glad you're both okay. Thank you for bringing them home safely, Daniel." She grabbed and hugged him as well.

"You owe him more than a thanks for the ride," Carson said. "We wouldn't be here if he hadn't come to our rescue."

"Rescue? What happened?" Kate asked and kissed Daniel on his cheek.

"I'll let those two tell you," Daniel replied.

"Someone's already told the story once." Carson shoved her brother and walked past him. She spotted Jack on the couch and headed that way.

Everyone trickled into the living room. Kate reclaimed her seat next to Jack. Tripp nestled beside his mom on one side of the big couch, while Carson took up position next to her dad on the other end. Kate held her son's hand as he told her his version of the tale. Although Jack didn't hear much of what Tripp was saying, he noticed that Carson relayed her story to him much faster, and with more passion, than her brother did.

Daniel paced silently near the fireplace and stopped when Jack asked if he was okay. Rick had snuck in during the chatter and found a spot in the corner, not far from Daniel, so he could survey the entire room. His posture denoted his readiness for action.

The living room was a mixture of old world meets traditional with its combination of distressed, dark furniture and peach hues. On the walls were several oil paintings and a single tapestry that hung above the fireplace mantel. The rest of the home was similar, except for Jack's study, which closely matched the Caribbean motif of the patio it connected to.

When Carson ended her story, she looked ready for Jack to answer some questions. Everyone stopped their private conversations and gave him their full attention.

Jack surveyed the room in an attempt to gauge his audience's expectations. "I'm very thankful you're all okay."

"Tripp was extremely brave, while Daniel was a total badass," Carson said.

Jack smiled. "I'm proud of you all."

Carson went straight to the point. "Dad, why are people trying to kill us? Does this have something to do with Poppy's shady dealings?"

Jack's mind raced as he thought of what he should say. Uncertain of what was going on, he still wanted to convey a sense that everything would be okay. His wife seemed particularly interested in his next words.

After he cleared his throat for the umpteenth time, Jack fumbled for an answer. "Let me start by saying I'm perplexed about what brought about today's events. And I plan to do some digging into this. If it was an isolated incident, I might think it was a coincidence. After all, what beef would someone have with a preacher and his family?"

The others seemed to agree. Someone even voiced a hesitant "Right." But he had to do better.

"However, it would be unfair of me not to warn you of another possibility," Jack continued. "As you've probably suspected over the years, your grandfather was hardly a simple businessman. He rubbed shoulders with some powerful people in both government and industry."

"So he's a spy," Carson blurted out.

"Carson, please," Kate said. "Let your dad finish."

"Not exactly," Jack said. He wanted to be careful in his approach to the subject. "He did some work for an organization that monitored world governments."

"Like a human rights organization?" Tripp asked.

"In a roundabout sorta way," Jack replied, searching for the best words. "Let's just say they took more than a passive role."

"So they used some form of litigation or partnered with another entity like the UN?" Tripp asked.

"Close enough," Jack said. He didn't want to get stuck on the details. "The primary role of this organization was to keep any entity—government or otherwise—from dragging the human race to the brink of extinction."

"Well, with the number of nukes in the world, I'd say they're doing a lousy job," Carson said.

"As with any intelligence community, you never really hear of the times disaster was avoided," Jack explained.

"Okay, Dad, but why would these people want to come after us?"

"I don't believe they would, sweetie. I was merely pointing out that Pops belonged to a group that had powerful allies around the globe. But there are two sides of the coin. Certainly he also made many enemies along the way." Jack paused to glance around. "Have any of you ever heard of a company called Lloyd Tactical Forces?"

"That sounds familiar," Tripp said. "Yes, I was approached by someone who said they were recruiting for that company. I gave them sparse information but later said I wasn't interested when they called again. Daniel, do you remember that guy who came into the office a few months ago? You checked into it because you were suspicious."

"Oh, right," Daniel said. "They appeared legit, but I didn't understand why they were trying to recruit someone like Tripp."

"That is odd," Jack said.

At first Tripp looked slightly offended but said, "I felt the same way at the time. Am I to assume that someone from a security firm has been watching us for at least several months?"

The thought concerned Jack. "It's certainly possible."

"We should have 'em arrested," Carson said.

Rick had been standing by silently and listening. "Jack, how did you learn Lloyd's company was involved?"

"Right," Jack said, realizing he had left that part out. "We ran into some unpleasant fellas who had broken into the Smiths' house. One survived their attack on us and Shelby questioned him."

"Shelby? When did he resurface?"

"Long story."

"You know, partner, I should call someone to pick that guy up before someone comes looking for him."

"You're right, Rick. It may be wise to get the sheriff's office involved on this one."

While Rick walked off to make his call, Kate found her moment to interrupt. "Jack, I don't want that man Shelby anywhere near my family. How many people has he already killed?"

"Today?" Jack said and then realized it probably wasn't the best question to have asked.

"That's exactly what I'm talking about," Kate said. "We don't need that back in our lives."

"Whoa," Carson said, holding up a hand. "What are you talking about, Mother? How has that guy ever been in our lives?"

"Your dad can explain that one," Kate said and folded her arms.

"Thank you, dear," Jack said, feeling as if a bus had run him over. "He's someone I met long ago, during a more complicated time in my life. As you've probably figured out, he's also been watching the people who were watching us."

"Is he a spy?" Carson asked.

"What's this fascination with spies, sis?" Tripp asked. "This is hardly a page from a thriller."

"He once worked for the CIA," Jack said quickly before the two could start arguing.

Tripp looked surprised as Carson walked over and silently gloated. "Point for Carson," he said.

"Mr. Page, how did you get involved with the CIA?" Daniel asked anxiously.

"I wasn't involved with them per se, Daniel. Circumstances brought Shelby and me together. We found we had a common goal at the time."

"Did it have anything to do with your brother dying?"

Jack knew his discomfort was obvious. "That's not a subject I wish to discuss."

"I'd assume it did," Daniel said.

"Let's not assume anything, shall we?"

"I think we have a right to know, sir."

Jack's eyes narrowed at the young man. "No, Daniel—you weren't paid to pry into my personal life," he snapped. As soon as the words left his mouth, he realized his mistake.

Shocked, both the twins' mouths dropped. "Dad?" they said in unison.

"You knew?" Carson asked.

Jack realized the cat must have been let out of the bag recently. "Yes," he admitted.

Tripp seemed to accept the logic of the revelation. "If Pops was aware, it would make sense you were as well."

"It was your grandfather's idea, guys. It allowed Pops to watch over you from a distance. It also gave Daniel a fresh start, something he needed. As the saying goes, it killed two birds with one stone."

Carson turned her attention to Daniel, who looked as though he wished he had kept his mouth shut. "So you were running from something too?"

Kate let out a deep sigh that told everyone they were going in the wrong direction with the conversation. "We're not here to discuss Daniel."

"I'm sure you knew as well, Mother. You seem good at keeping secrets," Carson shot back.

The room erupted into argument as Carson and Kate went back and forth, while Tripp and Daniel got into a verbal sparring match. Jack tried several times to quiet everyone. It was Rick's sudden return, along with his worried face, that made everyone cease what they were doing.

"Jack, about that guy you left tied up . . . I just walked next door to check on him while I called the county folks. Know what?"

"He's gone?"

"No, he's still there. He has a new smile where his throat used to be."

Kate clapped her hands over her mouth in horror as the others cringed. Jack stood up and paced, deep in thought.

"Oh shit, the cops won't think Dad did it, will they?" Carson asked.

"They won't know your dad was even over there, at least not yet," Rick said. "But someone could eventually place him near the scene."

"I have little doubt," Jack said softly. "We'll worry about that later. For now, I want everyone packed and ready to leave."

"Jack, we need to deal with this now," Rick said.

Jack walked over and placed a hand on his shoulder. "Rick, you've been my faithful friend since our youth, but you don't need to get involved with this. Who did you speak with over at county?"

"I hung up when I noticed we no longer had a live prisoner. I'll need to do my job at the crime scene and then call this in with county. Is there anything I need to clean up?"

"Not unless my DNA is on the guy I tied up. As for Shelby, he usually covers his own tracks."

A thought struck Rick. "You don't suppose Shelby came back and did this?"

"Not after being specifically told not to. Besides, slitting throats isn't his thing."

"I'll head back over there."

"Be careful, Rick. Whoever killed him may still be nearby to clean up any evidence pointing to Lloyd's. I can go with you."

Rick shot him an incredulous look. "No thanks, buddy. You're the last person who needs to be anywhere near there. Besides, whoever silenced that guy is likely long gone. Dead men tell no tales, Jack."

"You're probably right. Go home and check on your wife first."

"Been there, done that. Anything else before I head over?"

Jack thought briefly. "No, but you may want to relay to whatever county resources show up that shots were fired and you found dead men. We may be able to steer them toward believing it's some drug-related rendezvous gone wrong. When Pops arrives, he can get some things in motion."

Kate had sat quietly fuming but could stay silent no longer. "Really, Jack? That's it? That's all you're going to tell them?" She got up and stomped toward the hallway that led to their bedroom. She stopped suddenly and tossed her head, a lock of dark hair flowed over the right side of her face. It might have been alluring had she not been so angry. "I'll be in my room packing. We obviously can't stay in our home." The door slammed behind her.

Jack turned to the others. The twins and Daniel were still trying to absorb the things they had just heard Jack say. Rick appeared to think it was a bad time to leave and retreated to his corner to call his wife.

"Okay, guys, let's start working on an exit plan," Jack said.

"Really, Dad?" Carson finally said, echoing her mother's tone. "That's it?"

"C'mon, Mr. Page, we can't leave just yet. There has to be more," said Daniel.

"You should probably go check on Mom," Tripp said, causing the others to glare at him. "She seems upset."

Carson groaned at her brother's words. "What you just said is more evidence we couldn't possibly be related, Tripp, much less twins. She's mad at Dad. What else is new? I want to hear more tales from our family tree."

"Yeah, Mr. Page—you hardly told me more than I already knew," Daniel said.

Tripp was irritable. "You're certainly not one to preach about being forthcoming."

"Hey, I'm on your side." Daniel looked oblivious as to why his friend was so hostile.

"Oh? Who paid for that privilege?"

Carson jumped to her feet and faced the two men. She pointed her index finger at one, then the other. "Oh no you don't. We're not getting distracted from the important stuff. You two can have your lover's quarrel later."

Jack noted the rift that had formed between the two young men and felt even worse about his earlier remark about what Daniel was or wasn't paid to do. "I should go check on your mom. Rick, if you insist on sticking around, take the kids' statements about what happened at the bay earlier. We'll at least have something to pass along to the authorities when the time comes."

"Oh, that was already done—thank you, Tripp," said Carson. "Where are you going, Dad? I have questions."

"Carson, people are dead. Please cooperate with Mr. Sanchez," Jack said and then headed to his bedroom. He knew he was in trouble with his wife.

The others stood around and grumbled in disappointment. Carson still insisted their dad knew far more than he gave up. Tripp didn't disagree but pointed out there were probably more important things to worry about. Daniel and Carson rejected this and attempted to pry information out of Sanchez, but he merely held up his hands and claimed ignorance.

Carson suggested they all march down the hallway and demand answers. Daniel agreed, while Tripp was resistant to the idea. Quiet conversation turned into noisy chatter, with Carson—naturally—the loudest of the three. Sanchez came over to quiet them down a bit.

"Look, guys, your parents have had a rough day too. Let's give them some privacy while we go over to your places and get some things packed. I'm sure your dad has a plan."

"Good idea," said Daniel, still wanting to get back to his and Tripp's office. He tugged at Carson's shirt, hoping to get her agreement.

Instead she pulled away and separated herself from the others. She stood defiantly, intent on pursuing something. "I've got a better idea."

Tripp shook his head as she strode down the hallway anyway. He and Daniel reluctantly followed.

TWO ROADS

The bedroom was spacious, with similar decoration to the rest of the house. Jack moved at a deliberate pace, passing the tall captain's chest and making his way around the poster bed. There Kate sat with her head in her hands. An open suitcase sat on the bed with only a few items loosely thrown into it.

He sat beside her and placed a hand on her leg. "I really don't know what you expected me to say."

She looked up, her dark eyes glaring, and gave him an astonished look. She raised both little hands in frustration. "How about the important stuff?"

Jack brushed aside a lock of her soft hair that hung over one of her lovely eyes, and she flinched slightly. "The truth is a bitter pill we've been protecting them from for years. I just wanted them to have a normal life."

"And you think I didn't?" Kate moved his hand abruptly and stood at the edge of the bed. "We were overprotective, paranoid parents for the first half of their lives. Why do you think they turned out the way they did?"

"We made some mistakes and adjusted, Kate. The kids turned out fine."

"They turned out fine in spite of those mistakes."

"What do you want me to do? Go out there and tell them everything we've kept hidden from them all of their lives? What good can possibly come from that?"

Kate's frustration turned to anger. "I didn't say to tell them everything, but they deserved more than that."

"I agree, but what parts do we tell them? After we open Pandora's box, how do we shut the lid again?"

"I don't know—maybe we don't. You always taught others that the truth will set them free. Well, preacher, you need to practice what you preach for a change. Time to go out there and give them more than that weak performance I just witnessed."

"The truth may set us free, Kate, but it can also condemn those we love. Have you forgotten the type of people who were involved? And those were the good guys. We left that behind us for a reason."

"No, it's always been chasing you, Jack. You only pretend to be outrunning it, and I'm tired of running with you. What happened today proves that a real danger still exists, and our children know nothing about it." She continued her packing.

"*We* don't even know what these events mean."

Kate's stare became stone and then she got things off her chest. "You live in denial, Jack. You've stored up all this knowledge and would dump it on our children only upon passing to the next life. The man I fell in love with was never paralyzed with indecision—nor would he ever take the coward's way out. I guess that man died long ago."

The words stung Jack. The hurt turned into anger, and he felt the urge to return an equally painful volley. Why not run home to your rich daddy, then? he thought. Maybe you should find yourself a charming young bartender. If I'm as good as dead, why must I put up with this crap? He almost said all this but instead chose to say nothing and allow the indignation to dissipate.

Jack decided not to give his wife the fight she so wanted. He rose from their bed, walked into the closet, removed his bloody shirt and replaced it with a clean blue button-up. He tossed his own suitcase onto the bed next to hers. It was efficiently packed and ready to go.

Kate noticed what had materialized before her. Jack wondered what she was thinking. Did she want to scream in frustration or settle into acceptance? Maybe a bit of both. "You're not coming with us, are you?" Her tone had a new placidity to it.

Jack let the suitcase drop to the floor with a thud. He turned to his wife and kissed her on the cheek. "Nope, I've a different road to travel. I'll have Pops get you and the kids somewhere safe."

"What are you going to do?" She looked concerned, perhaps thinking she had pushed him too far. She held her breath and awaited his response.

"You wanted me to do the right thing, Kate. Your wish is granted." He opened the door but didn't walk out just yet. "You think the children have the right to know more, but I think what you really mean is you want someone else to share the burden. I hope both you and they are prepared for what that means."

Jack walked out, turned left, and headed toward his study. He barely noticed the three young adults to his right as they retreated to the living area. As he entered his private room, the last of the day's sunlight came through the glass back door and drenched the vibrant Caribbean hues. The door led to an enclosed patio that in turn led down to the boat dock in the canal.

He still had things to do before he could leave. At his bamboo desk, Jack sat in the wicker chair and typed on the iMac's keyboard. He fired off an email before pulling up a map on the screen. He made some calculations and sent it to the printer in the corner of the room. After retrieving the output, he walked over to a picture of a palm tree on the wall and effortlessly swung it open to reveal a safe. To open it, he waved his hand in a pattern before the optical eye in the corner, then retrieved an envelope and a small caliber pistol. He put the envelope in his suitcase and stuffed the gun under his shirt in the waistband of his slacks.

From the same vault, he also retrieved a phone and a wad of cash. Jack hesitated for only a second as he examined the money. The funds weren't originally intended for this use and would fall short of his needs. That meant a quick detour. Leaving his suitcase behind, he exited his home through the back patio.

IT'S COMPLICATED

Carson casually headed back down the hall again. She stood by her parents' door until she heard the boat's engines fire up. As she entered the room, she already knew only one person was left. This bothered her more than the angry words that had come from the bedroom earlier. Throughout her entire childhood, her parents had hardly ever fought.

When they did fight, it was hardly earthshaking. Her dad, usually the calmer of the two, would go into some long lecture. Mom, on the other hand, was the passionate one—not unlike Carson. The face her mom typically presented to the world appeared calm and conservative. Behind closed doors, however, she could be totally different. What Carson had eavesdropped on earlier was something new.

As Carson peered into the room, she found her mother on the bed, her face buried in a pillow to drown out the noise. "Momma," she said softly.

Tripp and Daniel were close behind, but she knew they'd prefer not to venture into the bedroom uninvited. Her mom sat up at the sound of her voice. She tried to collect herself as Carson climbed into the tall bed beside her.

Her mother wiped her red eyes, pulled back her hair, and sat for a moment. "I'm sorry, sunshine," was all she could manage.

Carson glanced around the room, noting her mom's suitcase on the bed and her dad's shirt tossed on the closet floor. Some of the drawers on the captain's chest were still half open. "Where did Dad go?"

"He's gone," her mom said and started to sob again.

"I got that part. Why did he take off in the boat?"

Her mother grabbed her hand and just held it. Carson was afraid of the silence. She fought off the panic as it crept up on her. The day was supposed to get better after all the hell they had been through, not worse. Her father wouldn't just abandon them now. There had to be a reason.

"Mother," Carson said, beginning to tear up. "Where's Dad?" She moved her hand under her mother's chin and raised it to make eye contact.

"It's my fault," her mother said softly. The rest of what came from her mouth was inaudible.

Carson finally determined she had no idea. She fought the panic off with the best weapon she had—her anger. Fists clenched, she told herself to remain calm and think. "Why do things have to be so complicated, Mother?"

Her mom shook her head. "I don't know, sunshine."

"Mom," said Tripp as he cautiously entered the room. He sat down and placed an arm around her. "We've been adults for a few years now. I think we deserve to know what you know."

Daniel moved into the doorway. Her mother nodded and laid her head against her son's shoulder, grabbed his hand, and patted it. She had a captive audience.

"I was in high school when I met your father. He was so brash and sure of himself. I was dating someone else at the time but fell instantly in love with him. It wasn't long before we were dating. My father, however, wasn't happy with my choice. Your grandfather could be an overbearing man, and your dad was hardly his pick."

"I seem to remember something about Dad not being your pick either," Carson said.

Her mother frowned. "You only think you know what you speak of, young lady."

"Well, I'd know more if you'd let me finish what I started."

Her mother looked as if she wanted to respond but then noticed the other two were confused. Carson knew that only she and her mother knew about the stupid diary entries — the ones that Carson had been caught reading.

Tripp, looking unsure of the reference, decided to move the conversation along. "To be clear, Dad's avoided our other grandparents over the years because he wasn't considered the ideal suitor? That seems a bit excessive."

Their mother thought about her answer. "Like Carson, your dad never cared for my father. He can be a difficult man to warm up to. Still, I suppose I could've helped things more than I did." She started to sob again but quickly contained herself. "There were things that happened."

"It sounds like things started off rough for you two," Tripp said.

"I made some mistakes too."

Carson wondered if they were about to get some type of confession. "What are you talking about, Mother?"

"Your dad and uncle were as different as night and day, much like you twins are. Still, your dad was very close to his brother. When he died, your dad made some mistakes."

"What kind of mistakes?"

"The kind you can't take back."

Carson stepped closer to her. "That doesn't tell us a lot."

"I believe your dad suffered from some sort of survivor's guilt."

"It must be more than that," said Tripp.

Carson nodded.

"Your dad had harsh words for your uncle before he died," Kate finally said. "When he couldn't save him, it tore him up inside."

Tripp had a curious look about him. "I read an old newspaper article from that day. It said the blaze was so hot, it practically cremated the man on the scene. Saving him wouldn't have been an option."

"Better question—what the hell does this have to do with what happened to us today?" Carson asked.

"Perhaps nothing," her mom said. "We need to pack our things. We can go to Texas and stay with your grandparents for a while."

Carson took a step back. "Hell no," she said. "I am not going to Texas. I will not be patronized by that old bastard."

Her mother looked astonished. "I know you two don't get along, but he's still family."

Carson turned from her mother and calculated something in her head. She took a deep breath and came to her conclusion. When she spoke, she did so with her back to her mom. "You were so cruel to Dad earlier, but you've kept these same secrets. You're a hypocrite, Mother. Go to Texas. I'd rather join Pops at sea than run to my other grandfather, begging for shelter."

"If you prefer, we can do that. We just need to get somewhere safe."

"No, Mother, I will not run from anything. I'm tired of being smothered by your protectiveness. I'll start my own search for the truth. If it turns out Dad needs my help, I'll be there for him."

Distraught, her mom and Tripp tried to reason to her. But Carson had made up her mind. They all followed her to the living room, where Sanchez was. Before he could intervene, however, she was out the door.

Kate sent Rick to bring Carson back, while Tripp and Daniel spoke among themselves, reaching a quick conclusion.

Tripp kissed his mother and told her he loved her. "I have to go where Carson goes, Mom. We'll be fine." He stepped through the doorway as she shook her head.

Daniel paused before he followed. "I've got their backs, Mrs. Page."

Once again, Kate was alone. She immediately tried to call Jack to let him know what had transpired, but she got his voice mail. She left a brief message for him to call her back. Emotionally exhausted, she leaned back against the doorframe and slowly slid down to the floor. The house became a quiet theater for the ticking of her mantel clock.

Kate absolutely loved antique clocks, but as it ticked away, it only reminded her how empty the house was. As she began to think she might just slip into madness, her phone rang. She jumped at its sound and fumbled to answer it. It wasn't who she had expected.

"Kate," came the voice that could only belong to Pops.

She leapt to her feet and juggled the phone before she brought it back up to her ear. "Pops, thank God!" she exclaimed. The man was someone she both loved and loathed at the same time. He was also who she really needed to talk to. "Things are getting crazy. We need your help."

"I know," the calm voice said. "I'm already here. Prepare to be boarded. We have some things to talk about."

Kate knew he would approach from the canal. She locked her front door and headed to the back, where Jack had left only minutes before. As she stepped out onto the patio, she could see the lights from the vessel coming up the waterway. With a sense of some hope, she stood there and waited for it to dock.

CHOICES

Carson was almost at her apartment by the time Sanchez caught up to her. He grabbed for her arm, but she spun, fists ready for action. He stepped back, hands up, and quickly pointed to the badge on his shirt. "Whoa, *chica*—badge," he sputtered.

"Love ya, Mr. Sanchez, so please don't make me commit a felony." Carson continued toward the stairs to her loft apartment. He followed her again but at a distance.

"Love ya too, crazy girl," he called to her as she climbed the stairs. She waved a hand without looking back.

Sanchez was relieved when Tripp and Daniel arrived. He patted Tripp on the shoulder and pointed to his sister stomping up her stairwell. Her loft was on the top floor, just above the apartment Tripp and Daniel shared on the second floor.

"Carson is more like her mama than she cares to admit," Sanchez said as he tried to catch his breath. "Go talk some sense into her, son."

"I'll try," said Tripp, and then looked thoughtful. "You meant to say she's more like Pops, right?"

"No, son, your mama can be a tiger when you get on her bad side. Your dad can bear witness to that."

Sanchez and Daniel stayed back and allowed Tripp the space to calm his sister. Daniel had other plans; he tapped Sanchez on the shoulder and pointed to his office. Sanchez just nodded as he stayed in position and waited for Carson to return. As Daniel disappeared behind the glass door, Sanchez scanned the square.

Viridian Square was really more of a circular plaza, with the old brick building that served as both the city hall and police department in the middle of it. The perimeter was lined with local shops, including Kate's salon and the bar he and Jack co-owned. Once a fishing village, it had grown up gradually over the decades. It was typically quiet, just as the locals preferred it—at least until the sun went down. Then it became a popular hangout for the younger crowds that drifted in from the surrounding areas.

That suited Sanchez just fine. One of the main establishments to benefit was his and Jack's bar, the Viridian Gem, on the other side of the square. Saturday nights were busy, so he really wanted to wrap things up and see the twins and Daniel off safely. He still had a crime scene to process and his part-time job was managing the bar on the weekends — where he made more money in one night than he brought in the rest of the week. As he thought about it, he saw Daniel disappear into his office.

Daniel instantly began to open drawers and cabinets around his cluttered desk. Tripp was always giving him grief about how disorganized he was. He glanced over at Tripp's desk, across the room from his own, noting how pristine it always was.

No papers out of place, pens gathered neatly in a cup, and his computer monitor always wiped clean. The man even had two wastebaskets: one for trash, which was emptied every day, and the other for recyclables. Looking back at his own desk, he found last weekend's half-eaten donut where he had left it, slowly petrifying.

After opening the last drawer it could possibly have been in, he dove into a pool of various wires and cables from mostly obsolete devices. Finally, with a victory cry similar to the one he had made when he won a modest jackpot at a casino along the Mississippi coast, he found what he was seeking. He still had to free it from the spaghetti-like mess of wires before he could put it to use.

Once it was freed, he held the special connector in his hand. It was something he had cooked up himself, just for such an occasion. It would come in handy if Tripp ever needed to break into someone's phone while working a case.

At least, that was the idea. The connector was hexagonal with several different cables attached, one protruding from each side. It was the hardware needed for his task. The rest he would handle with special software he had written on the PC that sat in front of him.

He plugged in the standard end of the USB connection into his machine and fired it up. Tapping away with feverish speed on his keyboard, he brought up the application he would need and typed into a command-line interface. This particular iteration was version 2.0 of his software, the prior version being less user-friendly. After he had entered the last commands, a graphical user interface appeared on the screen.

Daniel searched for the correct connector among the cables and hooked up the phone he had retrieved from their kidnapper. A green progress bar moved slowly across the screen. After it finished, a prompt asked to initiate a subroutine that would start the cracking algorithms. Once this was executed, he watched a red progress bar as it appeared. This one moved even more slowly as his encryption breaker did its magic. Magic was probably what it would require—Daniel had yet to get it to work beyond the limited testing he had done on his own phone.

Upstairs, Carson peered out her back bedroom window from the third floor. She looked south toward her parents' home, with the backdrop of the cove that was a part of Santa Rosa Sound. Off to the west, the setting sun lit the waters ablaze with brilliant hues of orange and yellow. As she trembled, she had to remind herself she was tough.

She practiced her deep breathing, something she had done as a child when she used to get panic attacks. Perhaps, she thought, those attacks were what toughened her up to embrace the dangers of the world. But for some reason those old feelings of terror crept back. She absolutely refused to give in to them.

Carson didn't know how long Tripp had been behind her. How long had he been waiting for her to acknowledge him? When she realized he was there, she didn't turn around right away. Instead, she continued to gaze at the setting sun.

Tripp, although known for his patience, seemed to know she was waiting on him. He cleared his throat to get her attention.

"Speak," she said.

"What happened today wasn't Mom's fault." He gave her a moment to respond, but when she didn't, he said, "Your choosing to focus your anger on her is a sign of unresolved issues."

"Oh? So she pushes the one man who can protect the family out the door. It doesn't sound like I'm being unfair." Carson still fixed her gaze on the disappearing sun.

Tripp hesitated, trying to find the correct words. "While I'm certain she didn't intend to drive him away, I wasn't privy to their conversation."

Carson's snort was her only reply.

"Look, Dad left for a reason. He probably wants to avoid putting us at further risk." Tripp didn't exactly look convinced of this, but it seemed to make him feel better.

His words triggered Carson to spin around to face him. "Then why didn't he just tell us that?" she asked angrily.

"Did you try calling him?"

"No, my cell phone is in the bay, remember?"

"You do have a landline, sis," Tripp said as he pointed to the phone on her nightstand.

"I'd rather not," Carson said. "Can you call him?"

"I'm not sure what to say."

"Ask him if we can join him wherever he is," Carson said.

Tripp's first response was a deep sigh. Knowing Carson could only focus her anger in one direction at a time, he finally said, "You're just as upset at Dad as you are at Mom."

Carson retreated a step, stunned by his words. She hadn't really considered that possibility and pondered it. "You're right—probably more so."

"That's okay," Tripp said quickly, not losing his momentum. "Let's get our stuff packed and get ready to head somewhere safe. I have no doubt whatsoever that Dad has a plan—" He suddenly stopped as something outside grabbed his attention. Carson peered out the window.

The sun had disappeared, but even in the dusk they could clearly see the vessel on the sound. It was running with minimal lighting, just enough to let other craft know it was there. It moored at their parents' boat ramp. Their dad's missing boat was a reminder that things hadn't gone the way any of them had anticipated.

"Mom has company," Tripp said. "It appears to be a fishing trawler."

They watched the incoming vessel. From their vantage point, however, it had become partially hidden by their parents' house as it docked on the private pier of the canal that ran north and south. Carson waited a moment longer for the back security lights, which were motion triggered, to come on. They did after a few seconds. "Who the hell is that?" she said.

"Good question," Tripp said and headed for the door. Carson followed closely behind him.

Carson and Tripp hurried downstairs. Sanchez, who was scanning the surrounding area, turned suddenly as he heard their feet rushing down the old wooden steps. He instantly knew something was wrong and approached them. "What's up?"

"A boat just arrived at Mom and Dad's," Tripp said with noticeable concern.

Sanchez produced a two-way radio. He adjusted a knob or two to ensure it was working correctly, as if expecting to hear from someone about visitors. Soon he determined it was on. "Let's go check it out."

Sanchez led the way, with Tripp then Carson behind him. When he arrived at Jack's house, he made his way through the side gate and headed toward the back patio. Hugging the wall, he motioned for the others to do the same while he peered around the corner.

The back patio was roomy, with a Jacuzzi, two wicker couches, and several chairs surrounding a brick fire pit. Illuminated by the security light, the rear iron gate was open. Beyond it were stone steps, which led to the pier. Voices could be heard nearby and Sanchez moved his head farther around the corner to get a look at who was there. Then the light went out.

Sanchez retreated and bumped into Tripp. "Shit," he said softly and then wished he hadn't. They held their breath and listened. The talking ceased but started again, the voices still low. They all took a deep breath and sighed in relief.

"Who is it?" Carson whispered.

Sanchez wanted to shrug to show he had no idea, but the action was pointless in the dark. He moved his face closer to Tripp and Carson so he could speak softly. "Not sure, but I was hoping—"

"Don't move!" shouted the voice as bright lights hit them from both sides. The men who had flanked them were silent. Although blinded by the light, they all assumed guns were trained on them; three sets of hands went up.

After Sanchez was disarmed, they were corralled to the patio and escorted through the back door into Jack's private study and told to sit. The two men who had apprehended them were dressed in black and holding automatic rifles with flashlights under the barrels. Both had short hair and were clean-shaven, one dark skinned and the other with a lighter complexion. They each had an earpiece in their ears.

"Great, more professionals," Carson said a bit too loudly.

She looked surprised when one of the men, the darker one, smiled at this. He stood guard as the other went into their family's hallway. He came back with a much older scruffy-looking man with a salt-colored beard and hair. The man nodded to them.

"Poppy!" Carson yelled and scrambled to her feet. She was the only one who called him that.

Pops Page motioned to the two younger men to leave the room. He handed Sanchez back his weapon while Carson squeezed the air out of him from behind. He chuckled as he struggled to turn around and hug her back. "Baby girl, I hear you've had quite the adventure."

"You have no idea, Poppy." She held her embrace. "You scared the crap out of us."

Tripp also grabbed him from the other side and administered an awkward hug. He stood a few inches taller than the older man. "We're relieved it's you, Pops."

"I forget how big you are," Pops said.

Tripp looked at him curiously; he had been the same size for years. "It just makes me a conspicuous target, I suppose," he replied.

Pops gave his grandson a quick slap on the back.

"You gonna save the day, Poppy?" Carson asked.

"I am," Pops said. "Got your things?"

"We were interrupted when we saw your boat arrive. How did you get here so fast?"

"I took a seaplane over from the keys." He paused and put his hands on both of Carson's thin shoulders, locking his dark, steely eyes with hers. "Baby girl, I know you feel you're being kept in the dark. Trust me when I tell you that some things are better left unsaid."

Carson smiled weakly. "I wish there was more trust in this family, Poppy."

Pops cleared his throat. "I understand. One day, we'll be able to have a beer and talk about it."

"Is it the kind of thing that can get a person whacked?"

"It is, but you'll be safe with me." He winked and then walked to the door. "I'll have one of the boys take you back home to get packed." He turned his attention to Sanchez. "Rick, there's something we need to discuss."

Sanchez knew the tone of that voice. He left without another word, behind Pops.

Confused, the twins were left standing there.

"So," Tripp said hesitantly, "it seems Pops and Dad are in agreement when it comes to Page family secrets."

Carson wrinkled her nose. "So it seems. Guess we're about to take a journey of discovery."

"Perhaps we'll obtain a better understanding once we reach our destination," Tripp said.

"Oh sure." Carson rolled her eyes. "We'll be kept in the dark as we're herded off. Why should we expect anyone to tell us anything once we're locked safely away?"

Tripp had to admit this was a likely scenario but felt uneasy about where the conversation was headed. "Their priority is to protect the family."

"I'd suffocate under their protection. I'm not a scared little girl anymore."

"We're at a crossroads, sis. What are you suggesting we do?" Tripp asked, convinced his fears were grounded in truth.

She smiled thinly as she backed up toward the glass door. She slid it open along its track without looking behind her and stepped halfway through. Casually, as if for effect, she leaned on the door frame. "I suggest we go find answers."

"How do you suppose we can accomplish that?" Tripp said, more loudly than intended. "I recommend we get moving before more unscrupulous men with large caliber weapons show up."

"I agree."

"No," Tripp said and walked toward her. "I mean leave with the people who will get us out of the line of fire."

"That choice will never lead us to the truth," Carson said. She edged a bit farther out the door, as if teasing him.

"Let me suggest that ignorance might just be preferable to death."

"I'm tired of being ignorant, dear brother."

"You can't possibly be tired of it, Carson. You've only just realized how ignorant we are about our family's murky past."

"True, but think of how long we've already been kept in the dark. Do you want to go the rest of your life not knowing who you really are?"

Tripp paused. He knew his sister could find the courage to do just about anything. "I know who I am, Carson. I don't need to find a secret passage in the Page family history book to tell me that."

With a deflated look, Carson exhaled loudly. "Well, I thought I'd try. You take care of Mother while Daniel and I go find some answers."

The very thought terrified him. "Bad idea."

Carson held her hand up defiantly. "No, no, you stay if you want. The worst that can happen is I disappear. You'll grow old wondering what happened, wishing you'd been there for me."

Tripp stared at his sister in disbelief. He had to remind himself how effective she was at laying on the guilt. "Even for you, Carson, that's simply absurd."

"Dear brother, you have a choice to make. Either come with me on this voyage of discovery or stay behind. I'm leaving in two seconds."

Tripp put his hands over his face and fumed. He thought of all the times his sister had talked him into doing something he would later regret, including their adventure that day. He wanted to say no. He wanted to join his mom. He knew, however, he was going to do exactly what Carson wanted him to do.

FOLLOWING
BREADCRUMBS

Daniel searched Tripp's desk, a far easier task than trying to find something at his own workstation. He quickly located the burner phones in an entire drawer dedicated to phones and other electronic devices. He sifted through the assortment and chose two that would work. He pocketed them, along with their chargers, and headed back to his own desk to check on the progress of his application.

"Damn," he said as he read the screen. The graphical image of a laughing red skull and crossbones had but one meaning: his attempt to hack the phone had failed. He sat in the swiveling desk chair and growled at the image that taunted him. He chewed on the nail of his index finger, his eyes fixated on the screen and his mind wandering through various possibilities.

The sound of knuckles tapping against glass pulled him back to reality. Daniel peered around his monitor to see Carson standing at the front glass door. It typically wasn't locked, but because of recent events he was more cautious.

Opening the door, he stepped aside to avoid Carson and her stuffed backpack. He held it for a moment, waiting. When he realized Tripp wasn't there, he closed and secured it again.

"You locked us out," said Carson. She tossed her backpack on the small couch Daniel had acquired from a thrift store. It wasn't much, but it would comfortably sit a couple of potential clients—hypothetically anyway.

"Just you," said Daniel with a grin. "Your brother knows the code. Speaking of Tripp, where is he?"

"He's gathering his things. Dear brother first wanted to make sure I packed this time. Do you know how creepy it is to have your brother go through your underwear drawer?"

Daniel didn't answer at first, as he had drifted off into a fantasy. "Must've been rough," he said.

Carson punched his arm. "So whatever the plan is, it better be quick. Poppy's here and he'll be looking for us soon."

"Pops is here?" Daniel asked, his eyes widening.

"That's what I said. He reckons to take Tripp and me off somewhere safe. We'll call that plan A. I kind of like plan B."

"What's plan B?"

"That's where we go and discover a little Page family history."

"Oh, right," said Daniel, the reality of what she was saying hitting him. "So we're running from Pops?"

"Yep, it's called plan B."

"That's not wise, girlfriend."

"I told you never to call me that. And it's not supposed to be wise. We're going to use your geekiness, my brother's puzzle-solving skills, and my awesomeness at everything else to figure this crap out."

"I should run the other way now, but I'm somehow drawn to the idea."

"I do have that effect on you."

"Only problem is, I can't get into that Mark guy's phone. Without some clue to follow, we don't have any breadcrumbs."

"I thought you were good." Carson said with disappointment. "There has to be some other trail we can pick up."

"We can hope."

As Daniel spoke, he watched Tripp walk up, tap the code into the outside panel, and enter. He tossed an old green duffel bag on the couch next to Carson's backpack. "Did you get it?" Tripp asked.

"The phone? It may take more time, if it's even possible," Daniel said.

"We don't have time," Tripp replied.

"Then we might as well get going," Carson said as she picked up her pack and headed for the front door.

Tripp grabbed her arm. "Not that way," he said and pointed to the back of the office.

"There's a back door in this place?" She had been in the office many times and was unaware of a rear exit. Her own apartment had only one way in and out.

"Technically, there is a back door," said Daniel, "but it's been sealed up for years. We wouldn't want to use the front or back anyway, not if Pops is coming."

"So that leaves what?" Carson asked, confused.

"Another route." Tripp walked over to his desk and opened the top drawer. He had a curious look on his face, as if something seemed out of place. "Daniel, did you take the mad money?"

"Not from your desk. I grabbed it from behind the picture."

Tripp glanced up at the framed picture above Daniel's desk, the scaled-down reproduction movie poster of *Casablanca*. "Right—it's out of place." Daniel knew his own presence was always obvious from the chaos he left behind. Whoever had sifted through this desk drawer, however, had been careful to remove the money and leave everything else in its place. "Who's been in my desk?" asked Tripp.

"I was, but I went through the phone drawer." Daniel produced the two phones he had secured from Tripp's desk, tossing one to Carson and the other to her puzzled brother.

"Oh good, a phone!" exclaimed Carson. "What the hell is mad money?"

"It's a term Pops told us about. You hide money for a rainy day," said Tripp.

"Poppy used to hide money?" Carson snorted with laughter. "Probably from our crazy grandma."

"Really, guys, somebody went through my desk and liberated the mad money in it."

"Your dad drops by from time to time. Maybe he took out a loan. Even preachers need a drink every now and then," said Daniel.

"With the crap he's put up with lately, I wouldn't be surprised," Carson said.

"I assume you two are jesting," Tripp said. "Dad does own a bar—not to mention he has more money than I do."

"Our parents have money?" Carson asked.

"Seriously, Carson?" Tripp said. "A nice home on a canal, a bar, a boat, the building we work and live in . . . shall I go on?"

"I guess I figured Poppy bought all that for them. He's generous, while Mother's father would never part with any of his money."

Tripp looked irked by his sister's comments regarding their other grandfather but said nothing. He continued the search through his desk. "Hundreds of dollars are missing."

Daniel knew that once Tripp became obsessed with something, he'd never let it go. He was hesitant to mention the hidden camera in front of Carson, since she'd want to know how long it had been there. She had gotten drunk one night and decided it was closer to change her clothes in their office rather than climb the stairs to her apartment.

Time being of the essence, Daniel decided it was worth the risk of Carson's wrath in order to get Tripp moving again. "Let's just check the video footage, Tripp."

Tripp's head popped up. "Of course. Why didn't I think of that?" He promptly fired up his computer while the others gathered around the monitor as he searched through the approximate timeframe of footage. It took only a moment to find what he was looking for.

"It was Dad," Carson said as the image of Jack went straight for Tripp's desk and secured the money. "He must have come straight over here when he left the house earlier."

"I guess Dad didn't have time to run to an ATM," Tripp said. "I wonder what he needed it for at this time of night?"

"A vacation from mother," Carson said.

"Okay, mystery solved. We need to go," said Daniel, noticing someone through the glass coming their way.

Carson punched Daniel as he walked by her to grab his gear. "Anything else I need to know?"

Daniel knew better than to play dumb. "Nope," he said as he walked toward the back of the office.

Carson and Tripp grabbed their stuff and were right behind him. As they reached the back door, sealed shut, they stopped.

"Now what?" Carson asked.

"Now we take the low road," said Daniel as he lifted a panel on the wall to their right.

It slid upward with the sound of wood on wood. Beyond it was little more than a crawl space. Even Carson had to squeeze into the passageway as she toted her backpack. Tripp was the last one through and closed the hidden panel behind them. As they filed through, their eyes adjusted to the dim light from around a bend in the passage.

"What the hell is this doing here?" Carson asked.

"Don't know," said Daniel as he led onward. "Maybe it was a passage to an old speakeasy?"

Tripp groaned from behind him. "We've had this conversation, Daniel. Prohibition ended long before this building was constructed."

"I forgot we had that conversation."

As they made a sharp turn into a wider corridor, Carson suddenly stopped and looked down. While Daniel continued his journey toward a probable dead end, she stomped a few times, drawing him back to the spot. Something was bothering her about the floor. She dropped to her hands and knees and examined it further. "The floor is concrete, except for this one spot."

Tripp watched to see what she would do. Enclosed spaces bothered him, however, so soon he sped things along. "I believe you'll find what you're looking for to your left."

As Carson ran her hand along the baseboard, she found a piece of metal that moved. She lifted up on it and found it was some sort of handle. The sound of a latch giving way could be heard, but nothing happened.

"You'll have to move off the door," said Tripp.

"There's a door here?" Carson asked. "What's on the other side?"

"More darkness."

"You mean you haven't explored it?"

Tripp paused, as if thinking of what would sound like a good reason to his sister. With resignation, he said, "The passageway we're in is stuffy enough as it is. I never gathered enough curiosity, or courage, to travel deeper into the abyss."

"That's right—you hate being in stuffy places."

"It's called claustrophobia," Tripp said. "More accurately, I have an irrational fear of confined spaces."

"And I'm afraid of spiders," said Daniel. "There are plenty of spiderwebs to greet anyone who wants to go in. We did once try to send a small camera drone down there."

"What did you see?"

"Not much. It crashed, and neither of us really wanted to retrieve it."

"You're both sissies," Carson said as she moved, found the hidden latch again, and pulled. To her delight, about four feet of floor popped up like the hood of a car. The metal doorway even had hydraulics to keep it propped open. "We must go exploring."

"No way," said Daniel, shining his phone's flashlight into the opening. The light exposed a dirty concrete path that sloped downward gradually like a ramp, in the direction they had walked from, and disappeared into the unknown. The light exposed glistening white silk threads that stretched across their path. Daniel shuddered. "Too many webs for me."

"A bit too stuffy for my taste," added Tripp.

Carson tossed her pack into the darkness and let it roll down the ramp. She followed it down the walkway and lit her path with her phone's light, clearing the webs in front of her. The silk threads she touched were odd. As she brushed them, they fell and lay on one side of the wall or the other, the pattern a bit too uniform for natural webs. As she moved on, suddenly no webs blocked her path. They were fake webs.

Reluctantly, both Daniel and Tripp followed her. Their descent was equivalent to about a floor before it leveled off, and they found themselves in an underground basement where they could stand up and walk normally. Tripp located a hanging cord and pulled it, switching on a dim light above them. The room was mostly empty, save for some boxes in the corner and pipes that ran along the walls. What caught their attention was another door in the opposite corner. It was metal and secured with a keypad.

"I can't believe you guys were such little bitches that you missed finding this!" Carson exclaimed. The excitement of the discovery appeared to overwhelm her senses. "What's beyond this door?"

"The little bitches wouldn't know," said Daniel with a laugh.

"You do realize Pops will make his way into our office—if he hasn't already—locate the hidden passage, and find us down here, right?" Tripp said. reminding them there was little time for exploration.

"Did you close the hidden floor entry we came through?" Carson asked.

"No, I didn't. The thought of sealing ourselves into this tomb wasn't appealing."

Carson rolled her eyes. "Daniel, you work on the lock of that door," she said and pointed at it with her light. "I'll go back and shut us in. It might buy us some time to explore this place."

"I'm on it," Daniel said enthusiastically as he examined the keypad to the steel door.

Tripp wasn't as enthused as Daniel and shined his own light on Carson. "What about finding the truth?"

"Hello," she said and shielded her eyes. "Who owns this building? Who do you suppose used these secret passages?"

"I believe our great-grandfather Roy must have. I heard Pops tell stories of how he built a secret facility to run his illegal gambling operations." He paused. "Hmm, the technology on the door didn't exist at that time, though. Pops, maybe?"

"Even I can tell this place has been used since Poppy signed the building over to Dad years ago."

He seemed to acknowledge she was right. With all the talk about going off and finding a breadcrumb trail, they may have found one right under their noses. "I'll check those boxes in the corner while Daniel works on the lock," said Tripp.

"Great," said Carson. She stopped to closely inspect the walls in the room. "What are those things over there?"

Tripp's eyes traced where she pointed. "Those would be well points," he said matter-of-factly. "They're small pumps used to keep the water table lower than this room, so it doesn't flood."

"Is that because we're underground?"

"Yes, but not that far underground. This part of Viridian Square was built on a hill, a man-made one, it seems. I'd estimate that the upper two feet of that wall are above street level."

"Oh," Carson said and remembered she needed to go cover their tracks. She went back up the ramp and found a dangling chain that would allow her to pull the hidden panel shut. But before she did, a thought crossed her mind.

She exited and proceeded down the narrow hall to the apparent dead end. Daniel had started going that way for a reason, Carson thought. She ran her hands across the wooden wall, and it easily slid to reveal a brick enclosure with a metal door.

A light from the other side crept through the edges of the old door. She opened it and learned it only had a knob on the inside; it was used strictly as an exit.

The light turned out to be from a streetlamp on the road behind the square. Beyond the road was a small outside sitting area before the private parking for residents who lived on the canal just beyond it.

Carson realized she was at the far end of the building. She heard distant voices. They could be from anyone gathering on the square for a Saturday night, but she didn't want to take any chances. She ducked back in and left the door cracked open to make it appear they had exited the building.

Snickering like a mischievous child, she headed back to finish covering their tracks. That should throw Poppy off, she thought.

Carson found Tripp and Daniel at the locked door where she had left them, hovering around it as if some mystical force protected it. They failed to acknowledge her return as they discussed whether that particular model required a four- or eight-digit key code. On the surface, their chatter sounded like English but was a strange dialect to Carson's ears. They finally concluded it could be anything between four and eight digits.

"The door is secure," she said, then added, "the secret one."

"That took a while," Tripp said, not looking up from the phone he had decided to refer to. He had pulled up a map and was studying it. A puzzled look formed on his face. "I seriously doubt he used the zip code of his hometown."

"It was just a thought," Daniel said defensively. "Maybe it's the zip code of where your parents first met."

"Maybe it's not a zip code at all, geniuses," Carson said. "For all the brains you two supposedly have, you tend to miss the obvious. Did you try Mom's birthday?"

"We haven't tried anything yet," Daniel said. "We're still discussing this as a committee."

Carson started to push her way through to try something, but Tripp stopped her. He walked up to the panel and studied it a bit longer, then reached into a fanny pack hidden below his untucked shirt. He produced a short cylindrical jar half full of a fine gray powder. He then pulled out a small carbon fiber brush.

"What's that?" Carson asked.

"I'll assume you want to know what it's used for, not what it consists of."

"Try not to be a smart-ass."

"It's a fingerprint kit," Tripp said as he unscrewed the lid and dabbed the brush into the jar. Carefully, he dusted the keypad while Daniel held some light on the spot. "One, two, and nine are the prevalent button strikes," he said.

"Which tells us what?" Carson asked.

Tripp thought for a moment. "Assuming it's a four-digit year—and not a month, day, and year combination—I would suggest 1992."

"Which just happens to be the year we were born," Carson added.

"Let's try it," Daniel said, punching in the code. At first nothing happened. He stared at the doorknob, as if hoping he hadn't jumped the gun. Silently, a square panel next to the keypad sank in to reveal a fingerprint scanner.

"Now what?" Carson asked with frustration.

"Now, it's Daniel's turn," Tripp said.

Daniel looked perplexed by what Tripp was referring to. After the light came on in his head, he unlatched the magnetic clip on the leather satchel he wore and dug into the pack. He produced a cylindrical device with a cradle for a phone on one side and a thin slit that ran most of the length, about an inch below that. When Carson asked what it was, Daniel explained it was a special printer for his phone.

Tripp, knowing what to do next, rummaged through his fanny pack to retrieve materials for lifting a fingerprint with tape and placing it on special paper. He worked swiftly through the process and handed the lifted print to Daniel.

Using his phone's camera and a custom application, Daniel scanned the fingerprint, attached his phone to the miniature printer, and waited. Soon the fingerprint was duplicated on special paper coming from the cylinder printer. The image it printed produced the ridges and valleys of the human fingerprint. Carson watched, finding it magical.

"The image is sort of a cross between a 2-D and 3-D image," Daniel said to Carson. "When it dries in a few minutes, we'll find out if we have a copy of your dad's print that will fool the scanner."

"Cool," said Carson. "Can you do that for my fingerprint too?"

"Already have yours and Tripp's," Daniel said. His expression changed, and Carson knew he realized she had set him up.

She punched him in the left arm. "You do, eh?"

"I'll destroy it, of course," Daniel said as he rubbed his arm.

"You better," Carson said. "So why didn't you use this method to try to get into Mark's phone?"

"Good question," Daniel said. He turned and glared at Tripp.

"I sort of cleaned Mark's phone with hand sanitizer," Tripp admitted. "People carry a lot of germs on their hands."

"I'd assume that tends to destroy fingerprints left behind?" Carson said.

"Especially the way your brother cleans things," Daniel said with a laugh.

Tripp ignored their comments. After letting the fingerprint copy sit a moment longer, he retrieved it and carefully pressed it against the biometric reader. After a few tries, they finally heard the click of the lock.

Tripp turned the knob of the heavy metal door, which opened with surprising ease. A light automatically came on. Examining the door more closely revealed a watertight, sealed entryway. "Odd," he said, "But we are at least partially underground. This room appears to seal out water."

Carson and Daniel weren't as impressed by the door and started to push their way past him. As they all peered inside, the previously dark room came alive before them.

THE HIDDEN ROOM

At first they were hesitant to enter the room, which was slightly bigger but similarly proportioned to a train's boxcar. The medley of colors and sights, however, beckoned them onward. They passed various screen images that glowed from behind the smooth, dark glass walls that ran the length of the room on both sides. The floor, a glossy midnight blue stained concrete with a clear sealant, reflected the flickering images coming from the walls. At the end was a large screen on the wall hovering above a metal desktop that stretched the width of the narrow room.

Carson, Tripp, and Daniel took their time making their way to the end, studying the images embedded behind the glass. As they traveled along, they noticed the wall to their right was dedicated to family history; multiple, changing images of people and places appeared and dissolved. The opposite wall displayed current news channels, as well as text information that constantly updated or security camera feeds that monitored unfamiliar locations.

Carson paused on the history wall, noticing the changing images of her family throughout the years on one screen. Images of her mom's lovely face accounted for the lion's share of the pictures, but some showed her and Tripp at various points in their lives. She smiled at one: as a girl, she was boldly jumping off a rock into the water, while Tripp, beside her, hesitated to follow. The images cycled every few seconds. Then something stopped her in her tracks.

"Look at this," she said and hoped the others would catch a glimpse before it disappeared. Tripp and Daniel, who had been watching a webcam on the opposite wall from her, turned to see the picture. Two young men in their late teens were standing on a dock in front of a fishing trawler, each with an arm around the other. One had sandy-blond hair and vibrant blue eyes, while the other's hair and eyes were darker. The words, in red, at the bottom of the photo read "RIP, my brother."

"Dang, his eyes were as pretty as yours, Carson," Daniel observed of the bright-eyed man.

"Dad and Uncle Conner were both cute," Carson said, then thought it a strange thing to say. "That must be where I get my striking good looks from."

"From which one?" Daniel asked with a laugh as the image faded away.

Tripp shot a hateful look his way. "Please don't get her started on family conspiracy theories."

Another picture, a young Kate Page, appeared within the twenty-inch screen on the wall. She was standing beside someone, but the image had been cropped to a head and shoulders shot highlighting the planes of her beautiful face.

"Never mind, I got my looks from that hot mama," Carson said, impressed by how beautiful her mother had always been.

"She was definitely hot," Daniel said. "I've heard some refer to her as a milf," he added with a laugh, but he looked embarrassed when both Tripp and Carson shot warning glares.

"Try and remember who that woman is," Tripp said curtly and walked on.

Daniel muttered an apology as they reached the end of the room and examined the silver metal desk. They learned it was actually a framed dark glass top that stretched about six feet across and four feet deep. With a black border taking up the edges of the desk, the usable working area was equivalent to a sixty-inch monitor screen.

Carson reached out and touched the surface, then jumped back in surprise when it came alive with a shimmering blue image of water. She ran her hand across the surface and watched simulated ripple effects follow her touch.

"Way cool," said Daniel. "Your dad has a touchscreen table."

"An odd setup for a small-town preacher," Carson said, taking in the room around her. The ceiling above, made of tarnished old copper panels, was the only unreflective surface. She turned her attention back to the desk.

"I have to admit, Dad hardly seems the type to have such equipment," Tripp said. "We really should avoid disturbing anything."

Carson chose to ignore the warning. She had found a way to change the image to that of a glowing koi pond and amused herself by moving her finger across the simulated water's surface and watching the digital fish react. When she became bored with that, she began to touch random areas, which triggered a prompt for credentials.

"Oh crap," she said and tried to cancel the prompt. It persisted on the screen and she couldn't continue past it.

Daniel, seeing the request for authorization, fetched some hacking tools. He retrieved an ultrathin laptop and fired it up. He searched through his applications, which he had either obtained from hacking sites or crafted himself. After bringing up the one he wanted, he tapped away at a command prompt.

Carson soon became disinterested. She also needed to use the bathroom, but the closest one may have been back at Tripp's office. She turned to head out the door they had entered.

"Where are you going?" Daniel asked.

"To the bathroom. Is that okay with you?"

"I wouldn't. Odds are Pops is in our office by now."

Carson wasn't in the mood to argue. When a girl had to go, she had to go. She turned and gritted her teeth. "Oh, for the love of—"

"How may I assist?" A woman's voice echoed through the room.

Carson froze, as if not moving would prevent further detection, while Daniel jumped. The men started exchanging signals while Carson searched for the source of the voice. Daniel became confused by what Tripp was trying to direct him to do. Finally, the silence was too much for Carson.

"Who are you?" Carson demanded.

"I am Love, your personal assistant," the voice said.

"It's an AI assistant!" Daniel said, relieved it wasn't someone watching them. "Maybe she's like the holographic assistant in that game we play, Tripp."

"Would you be quiet? Geek," Carson said irritably.

"Okay, I will be silent," said the artificial voice. "Let me know if I may be of further assistance."

"Not you," said Carson. "I need to find a bathroom."

There was no response. She held out her hands in frustration. Tripp walked over and whispered instructions into her ear.

"Love, please tell me where the closest bathroom is."

"I will show you, Carson Page," said Love.

"Oh shit!" she exclaimed, "it knows who I am. This thing acts like my phone."

A green glow appeared around a section of the glass wall to her left. With the sound of hydraulics in motion, the glowing section of wall sank, slid sideways, and disappeared behind the rest of the wall. It exposed an opening to a hallway.

As Carson walked through the newly opened door, small LED lights on the edges of the hall lit up and stopped at another door to her right. Opening the door, she found a spacious bathroom. It too lit up as she entered.

The large bathroom was complete with a glassed-in shower, copper basin sink, and soft music emanating from an unseen source. The floor and walls of the entire room were gray sandstone. Carson made her way to the toilet. Afterward, she washed up at the sink, which was powered by motion sensors. Out of curiosity, she opened the medicine cabinet to see what was inside. It was much deeper than she anticipated and stocked with an assortment of toiletries for both genders.

Carson walked back into the hallway and turned to her right to explore further. As she moved forward, the rest of the short hall was lit for her, and at the end she had the option of going left or right. To her right was a roomy walk-in closet. It lit up as she entered.

The closet walls were hidden behind dozens of hanging clothes. There were suits, shirts, dresses, jackets, and other items. Below the wardrobe were containers filled with various items. Carson opened one near her and found hairpieces and fake beards and mustaches. Quickly, she went through one plastic tub after another and found items ranging from socks to jewelry to makeup. It was the wooden chest in the corner, however, that really caught her eye.

Inside, Carson found old pictures, high school awards, colored contact lenses, and even fake IDs. Several appeared to show her dad in various disguises, using aliases. A blonde woman's passport with the name "Diane Conner" grabbed her attention. She studied it and concluded it was her mother.

The shock of the discovery caused her to sit for a while before deciding she had seen enough. She took a picture of the passport with her phone and returned it to where it had been. Then she spotted a book.

Carson examined the little diary and realized she had seen it before—and recently. She picked the lock that bound it shut and read through some of its pages. "So, Mother, that's where you hid it," she said, referring the object that had started her and her mom's latest quarrel.

There was no time to go through the unread parts, and she debated whether to return it to its place or not. Finally, her curiosity won the internal struggle. Carson tucked the diary into her pants and pulled her shirt over it. She wondered what she might find next as she headed for the room across the hall.

The thick metal door had been left open. As she entered, the room lit up, revealing a much larger one than the one she had just left. Her eyes grew as big as saucers at what she saw. Guns, knives and a shooting range? What the hell? The newly acquired phone slipped from her hand and bounced on the floor. She retrieved it and found it had suffered a cracked screen from the fall. Cursing to herself, she snapped photos and headed back to the others.

Tripp looked at Daniel with uncertainty. "Are you sure about this?" He watched him remove a panel from underneath the touchscreen table.

"I told you, it's the only way to get a physical connection to this system," Daniel said, glancing up.

"I thought you said you'd hack in using Wi-Fi?"

"That was until I saw the encryption being used," Daniel replied. He looked for the connection that had been hidden behind the panel of the machine. "Whoever put this in here didn't want to make hacking it easy."

"Imagine that," Carson said as she entered the room. Quietly, she motioned for Tripp to follow her. He gave her a curious look as they walked to the room she had just come from.

"I was going to just show you a picture, but I thought you should see this for yourself," Carson said as they entered. "Not to mention, photos look like crap on a cracked screen."

Tripp surveyed a workout center, which was bigger than a three-car garage. As they walked across the stained concrete floor, he noticed the various workout machines, the punching bag that hung from a steel beam, and a small pistol range. On the wall was a paper target with several holes closely grouped in the center.

But it was the far corner of the room Carson wanted him to see. On one wall hung just about every melee weapon he could imagine. On the adjacent wall, recessed within a dimly lit shelf, was an extensive collection of pistols and rifles.

"I know Dad isn't a libtard, but did ya ever think he was the NRA's poster boy?" Carson asked.

"Although I don't subscribe to labels, he did give me some pointers when I was qualifying for my concealed weapons license," Tripp said.

"Okay, but did ya imagine this shit?"

"No," Tripp said and started to leave.

Carson hurried around him to block his exit. She held up the image of their mom's fake passport. "And how about this?"

Tripp studied the picture on the cracked screen, then put his hands on his sister's shoulders and looked straight down at her. "Carson, after what we just learned, this hardly comes as a shock."

Carson gave him an astonished look. "So this isn't beyond weird, huh, genius? They kinda forgot to tell us, didn't they? And what about the fake last name Mom used?"

"I saw it. She used Uncle Conner's first name as a faux surname. It's a common practice to choose an alias with some familiarity to it," Tripp said and moved her aside as he left the room.

"That's all you have to say?" Carson said.

"They're not secret agents, Carson." Tripp's voice echoed down the hall. She trailed after him. "You don't know that."

They entered the technology room and noticed Daniel was busy at the touchscreen table. From behind, they noticed he had accessed some type of files. Absorbed in his work, he failed to notice them at first.

"Any luck?" Carson asked.

"I was able to access one folder, but there's not much in it," Daniel said without looking away.

"You should make a copy so we can leave," Tripp said.

"Already done." Daniel dragged a file to the edge of the table with his finger. With another push, the virtual representation vanished and then reappeared above on the wall monitor. "I just wanted to see what this one was. It was recently viewed by someone else."

It turned out to be a satellite image of the southern coast of the country. A red pushpin icon marked one location. Glancing around for a way to manipulate the map, Tripp noticed a glowing pad appear on the touch desk. Using finger gestures for pinching and expanding, he was able to zoom outward.

It displayed the entire Emerald Coast, Mississippi, and parts of Louisiana. He had zoomed out a bit further than he intended. But because of this, they spotted more areas marked with the same red pushpin icons.

"More locations of interest," Tripp said and pointed. "I wonder if there's some sort of legend that tells us what these locations mean."

One marked area wasn't too far from their current location, while another two pointed to places in New Orleans. Scrolling to the west, they found two more spots flagged in Texas and one in Oklahoma. The last pin was out at sea, south of Louisiana. It was the oddest of the bunch. Not only did it pinpoint a location in the middle of the ocean, but it also wasn't red like the others. It was black.

"Whatever they mean, we need to investigate," Carson said. "The ones in Texas are places I've been near. That one's not far from Austin, or perhaps San Antonio. The other is north of Dallas where there are several possible towns. Those two are in New Orleans." She studied the remaining ones. "I have no idea what the black one stuck in the Gulf is, but this red one looks like a place near Perdido Key. The last is in Southeast Oklahoma near Broken Bow."

Nodding, Tripp confirmed what his sister said. He was impressed with her familiarity with various regions, although she did get around. While most of his knowledge came from books and the Internet, she loved to travel. "Daniel, can you find any clues to what significance these points on the map have?"

"Working on it," said Daniel as he fidgeted with the table display. He tried to find a menu listing but was thwarted by the roadblock of being prompted for authentication at every turn. "I can only get so far. If I fail to authenticate again, the whole thing might lock us out."

The room's lighting suddenly went red. Startled, everyone wondered aloud what they had done to set off an alarm.

"Warning, motion detected in the outer hall," came the synthetic female voice.

A video feed of the outer hall replaced the map on the big screen. The infrared camera, which they had missed seeing themselves, showed three figures making their way toward the floor panel Carson had sealed earlier.

"We need to leave, Carson," said Tripp, tugging at her arm. "Pops is on his way. Daniel, put this machine back together."

Daniel immediately got to work but Carson stood there, as if not wanting to leave.

"They may not know we're here," she said. "This place is well hidden."

"I must agree with Carson," said Daniel as he replaced the panel. "This place is great. Imagine the information we could access if given the time."

"Wishful thinking," Tripp said tersely. "We're likely being watched as we speak." They followed his extended finger to the upper corner, where they noticed the eye in the sky.

"Please—we may still have time to retrieve some more data," Daniel said.

"Cached memory flush completed per protocol," came Love's voice.

"Never mind."

"We have to believe Pops knows about this place," Tripp insisted.

As he said it, they witnessed on the video feed Pops opening the floor panel and stepping down into it. They had seconds before he reached the main entryway.

"Shit, you're right," said Carson. "Hey, Love, is there another way out of here?"

"In addition to the main entrance, there is an emergency exit," replied Love's voice.

"Love, show me the emergency exit."

A glass-covered panel on one of the walls behind Carson lit up in a blue glow. She stood by it and waited for something to happen, until the realization hit her. "Love, open the damn emergency exit."

The blue panel slid away to reveal a tunnel lit by white LED lights that formed a path on the ground.

Carson paused before she entered the newly exposed tunnel. "Love, did you also report an intrusion when we arrived?"

"All entries to this compound are logged."

"Just checking," she muttered and hurried away.

They followed the tunnel, which wound around to their left and then curved off to their right. It straightened out for another fifteen yards or so and ended at a steel ladder. Looking up, they could see a round hatch with a lever at the top.

Tripp took the lead and climbed the ladder, then opened the hatch. His head popped up in a small garden. Within seconds, he identified the place. "We're in the area between the canal and our street," he announced and climbed out. The other two followed.

"Who would've guessed this exit was here?" Carson said as she surfaced in the pocket park. Set on an irregular piece of land at the water's edge, it wasn't much—just a concrete bench, grassy walking area, an old iron grill on a concrete slab, and a single palm tree. It was dimly lit by a nearby streetlamp.

As Carson closed the hatch behind them, she pointed out a round, steel emblem in the concrete she had walked across many times. The parking lot for nearby residents was directly behind them, while the sidewalk that ran across the wooden bridge, leading to their parents' home, was in the other direction.

They all ducked as a flashlight appeared from the square, across the street from them. It moved away from them and traveled along the walls of the buildings that formed the back of Viridian Square. Whoever held it cast its beam upon Carson's and Tripp's apartment windows.

"They're looking for us. We need to get going," said Daniel. He led the way. They kept their distance from each other as they traveled a wide path around their building.

Carson looked puzzled when Daniel led her to her own vehicle. "What are you doing?" she whispered angrily.

"We need some wheels," said Daniel. "I don't have a car parked nearby and Tripp left his in Destin, remember?"

"Well, I don't have my keys. I wasn't exactly expecting to drive my own car tonight."

Daniel produced a key fob from the bag around his waist. He clicked a button and the lights on the Jeep Cherokee flashed, announcing it was unlocked. "Good thing I brought a spare."

"Where the hell did you get that?" Carson asked. "Only my parents have the spare."

"I keep a copy of both yours and Tripp's car keys," Daniel replied.

"For emergencies," Tripp added. "We need to go."

"Anything else I need to know?" Carson asked as she snatched the fob and climbed into the driver's seat.

Daniel waited until after she had closed the Jeep's door. "Should I tell her about having a key to her place?"

"No," Tripp said, moving to the other side of the Jeep. He climbed into the front passenger side, ignoring Daniel's call to ride shotgun.

Carson started the 4x4, manually turned off the automatic headlights, and slowly backed out. She made her way through the parking lot and headed toward the main road, where she turned the vehicle's lights back on.

"Carson, why are we sneaking around?" Tripp asked. "We're adults. It's not like Pops can make us go with them."

"Don't underestimate my Poppy," Carson said.

"Guys, you do realize your dad can track us by your watches," Daniel said.

Carson hit the brakes. She stared in her rearview mirror, as if waiting for something. Behind them was a group of motorcyclists who had been standing around talking in the parking lot. One of them put on his helmet, preparing to leave.

"Give me your watch, Tripp," Carson said hastily as she removed her own.

"Why?" Tripp asked, not thrilled with the thought of parting with his oversized custom chronometer. He slowly unfastened it anyway and handed it to her.

"I'll be right back," she said with a grin and exited the vehicle.

A MOMENT TOO LATE

Pops entered the narrow room, followed by his armed men. He glanced around and noted that the opened panels in the glass walls had begun to seal back up. His grandkids had likely vacated, but he knew he had to be thorough—that is, if he could remember how everything worked.

It had been a few years since Pops had been in the underground hideaway. Jack had shown him how he had renovated the once-illicit underground gambling establishment his grandfather, Roy Page, had made a small fortune on.

It looked nothing like the place Pops had known as a young man. Back then, the area had been sectioned off into two parts: one for cards and the other for slots. He still remembered the times the so-called waterproof place had flooded, until his dad finally found a way to seal it up. It was tricky enough to have any dwelling below the ground in Florida, but that was compounded by being so close to the sea.

In Roy Page's logic, the law would never think to look for his little gambling establishment there. As it turned out, he was right. Few living souls knew it was there, and fewer still remembered its existence. Those who did were probably too old and senile to remember its whereabouts. Pops really hadn't expected to ever walk into it again.

He examined the changes to the place; his son had made improvements. The electronics were certainly more advanced compared to the old slot machines that existed once upon a time. Pops was well aware of Tripp and Daniel's resourcefulness, as well as Carson's love of exploration. She was the one who worried him the most. His granddaughter, likely the leader, loved a good adventure.

Pops studied the room to get reacquainted with his surroundings. He knew the doors were labeled something, but his memory wasn't what it used to be. Hell, he thought, the damn artificial wench should understand what a door was. "Love, open all doors," he said, hoping it was the correct command.

"Voice recognition indicates you are Pops Page. Due to security lockdown, please enter biometric authentication on the panel in front of you."

He gave himself credit for remembering the name of what his son called the unholy machine. "Stupid name," Pops said as he placed his right hand on the designated area of the large desk display. Panels in opposite walls opened, and he motioned for his men to check both directions. They split up to do a sweep of the area.

"Love, show me what recently occurred in this room."

"What time frames would you like to see, Pops?"

"The last fifteen minutes should do," he said.

The big screen in front of him began playing back video of his grandkids and Daniel. He watched and listened to what had occurred. He allowed himself a chuckle as his granddaughter stumbled upon Love. He found equal amusement in his grandson's quest to be the voice of reason. Then there was the tinkerer, Daniel, who found every barrier an opportunity to breach it.

Pops's men returned from their search, but each signaled that the place was empty of anyone but them. With a sigh, he watched his grandkids' retreat as he had approached the room. "What are you lil' shits up to?" he said. The men behind him snickered as they watched Carson ask the AI if they had been reported and then quickly disappear. The recording stopped as it reached the present.

"Shall we follow them?" asked the darker one.

"No, Wes. I'm sure that intrepid bunch is long gone. We have other concerns right now. Wait for me outside." The two men exited the room. He turned his attention to the main screen. "Love, show me the map the others were viewing earlier."

Pops studied the map and noted all the locations. He had been to each of them. He was curious about the one near Denton, Texas, since he had some personal history there, but he couldn't think why Jack had marked it. He knew what the flagged location near San Antonio meant. That damn cavern, he thought. His grandkids might have figured it out as well had his arrival not cut short their efforts.

"Love, what security rights were on the recently accessed information?"

"All information is secured with authenticated user rights or higher."

Pops thought for a moment. He was no computer expert, but he had learned a thing or two in his time about securing assets. How strange that his son, one of the most careful people he knew, would allow such a lapse. For some reason, the machine knew who Carson was.

"Who all has those rights?"

"Current authenticated users are: Jack Page, Pops Page, and Kate Page."

"What are the rights of Carson Page and Tripp Page?"

"Limited users," Love replied.

Limited, Pops thought. Give those kids a brick and they'll build a wall. He pondered what his next move should be. Whatever damage was done was done, but he wasn't going to take any more chances of something more sensitive getting out. Rubbing his coarse chin hairs, he thought some more. "Remove all access to content for all users but myself," he said, rolling the dice that he could actually do this.

"Access denied," was the response.

"Damn," he said softly. He wasn't about to leave without doing something, even if that meant burning the place to the ground. "Love, can you delete all information stored here?"

He waited for the artificial brains of the place to think about his request. After a moment, Love came back and said, "All localized data was purged by security protocol."

"By whose authority?" Pops asked.

"Jack Page."

"Understood," Pops said and then remembered he was talking to a mindless computer.

He wandered over to a glass wall to review an image of his two sons from years past. He felt a little sentimental as he studied it. When the image cycled to another one, he glanced away and felt lost for a bit. The two of them were so different. The picture brought back memories of a time before all the madness had almost destroyed his entire family. No father wanted to outlive his children. He often wished he had been the one to leave such a wretched world instead of his lost son. He wasn't given the choice. That in itself angered him. At the same time, he knew he shared some of the blame.

"Love, locate Jack Page."

"Jack Page has shared his location with you. Please review the map displayed."

A map appeared on the big screen. A slow-moving red dot represented his son's location, somewhere on the water. By the look of things, Jack would probably be late for their meeting. He started to exit the room, then stopped. Knowing his son had tracked the twins earlier, he wondered if they still wore their watches.

"Love, locate Carson Page and Tripp Page."

"Locating . . ."

Pops saw another dot, a green one, appear on the map. It was headed north, just departing Viridian Square.

"Damn, just missed 'em," he said. Then he remembered something else he could do—that is, if the camera still worked in that location. After fidgeting a moment, he noticed a camera feed of the street just north of Viridian Cove appear. He waited for his granddaughter's Jeep to pass by.

The only thing that passed was a motorcycle with a single rider. Pops double-checked the map that was tracking the watches and shook his head as he realized what had happened. "Little shits got rid of their watches."

Pops locked the facility as he left and sent his men to assist with Kate's evacuation. He had given them strict instructions not to let her know her children had slipped away. It was something he would deal with later. One thing at a time, he thought.

He glanced around at the square, its buildings well-lit even though most were closed. The fountain in the center produced a sparkling display as floodlights shone blue and green brightly through it. The design of the square was his father's idea. The old gambler had left the remaining buildings that he owned to Pops, who in turn signed them over to Jack.

The night air was just the way Pops liked it, thick and warm. If it hadn't been for humidity, he doubted he could breathe at all. He started to make his way to Jack and Rick's bar and saw his son's red pickup parked nearby. He continued, thinking of the stiff drink he needed.

THE JITTERS

Carson's white Jeep traveled west on US 98, passing through Pensacola. She was still waiting for an answer about where they were headed from Daniel, who was in the backseat creating a travel itinerary. He was using the pictures he had snapped of the map before they hastily left, then entering locations into the GPS map on his phone.

"I'm really not thrilled about taping our Smartwatches to that motorcycle," Tripp told Carson.

"That big, ugly thing? I did you a favor, bro."

"Hey, that was a high-tech piece that allowed me to find you guys," Daniel said in protest.

"It was also crafted to look like a retro chronometer," Tripp added.

"Relax, steampunk nerds," said Carson. "I know the dude who owns that bike. He sells weed on the beach in Gulf Breeze."

"That's not comforting in the least." Tripp said. "Goodbye, watch. It's probably already in a pawn shop somewhere."

"You can wear mine until I make you another," Daniel said.

"No thank you. I seem to remember your last watch combusted."

"A minor glitch," Daniel said with assurance. "Besides, I wasn't wearing it when it burst into flames."

"Well, if Daniel doesn't come through for ya, maybe you can go kiss up to our rich grandfather in Texas," Carson said dryly. "He tends to buy you nice stuff."

Tripp didn't look amused. He had never understood Carson's perpetual animosity for the man. "Why are you so hard on him? I don't see the same acrimony directed at Pops."

"That's because Poppy is cool. The guy from Mother's side is a smug prick." Before Tripp could give a rebuttal, Carson said, "Daniel, do you have an address or not?"

"Sheesh, Carson, you should stop somewhere to get a bite to eat," Daniel said. "You get cranky when you're hungry."

"And when she's sleep deprived or going through long periods of abstinence," Tripp added.

Daniel laughed loudly from the backseat. Even Carson had to fight off a grin as she flipped Tripp off. Her brother wasn't typically combative, but he had been known to become irritable after being around her for a while.

"I am getting hungry," Carson admitted. It had been quite a while since anyone had eaten anything. Still, she had a one-track mind. "We can stop in a bit. For now, make your best guess about location."

"It's not exact," said Daniel.

"What do you mean?"

"I think Daniel's saying that we were viewing a static map with points signifying approximate locations," Tripp said.

"Well, what good does that do?" Carson asked with a scowl.

"I don't believe the map was intended for anyone but its creator, meaning our dad," Tripp said. "Had he left it for our personal use, he would have been clearer."

"I think I've got it," Carson said, annoyed at Tripp's condescending tone. "Daniel should've hacked us a better map."

"How is this my fault?" Daniel asked defensively.

While Carson was capable of being reasonable when she wanted to be, she was in no mood to be now.

"I suppose I'll have to resign myself to the fact that we'll be making the drive to Perdido Key. We'll manage with the breadcrumbs we have and hope luck is in our favor," said Tripp.

"I believe in destiny, not luck," Carson said. "Where are we going, Daniel?"

"Uh, here." Daniel scribbled an address on a piece of paper, handed it to Tripp, and winked. Tripp returned a wary look before he punched it into the navigation console.

Following the new route, Carson guided them to Perdido Key, a barrier island. She was forced to endure her brother's and Daniel's insatiable need to discuss trivia involving their destination. Tripp had a penchant for being a walking encyclopedia of useless information. Geeks, she thought, learning that *perdido* in Spanish meant "lost," and that the key used to be a peninsula and later became an island during construction of the Intracoastal Waterway, and so on.

The sight of sandy white beaches and sun-bleached resorts couldn't come soon enough. But the address Tripp typed in brought them straight to a local burger joint right off Highway 292. Carson realized she had been duped as she pulled into the parking lot. "Jerks," she muttered, too weak from hunger to protest further.

It was an older building that needed some exterior touch-up work but seemed clean on the inside. They purchased their food and were about to settle into seats near the large front window of the little restaurant when Carson noticed something outside.

An ugly brown pickup pulled into the gas station next door. Carson knew that truck. She walked closer to the window and confirmed what she suspected. She returned to the table, grabbed her food from the tray, and fumbled in her jean shorts pocket to find the key fob.

Daniel ignored her and took a big bite out of his burger. Tripp, on the other hand, stared in curiosity at her. Madly hunting for her fob, she almost dropped her food. Carson caught Daniel's attention as she cursed, but his mouth was full so he kept silent.

"What are you doing, sis?" Tripp finally asked as she gained control of the fob.

"Come on, we're leaving."

"We just arrived."

Daniel, after taking another bite, grabbed his food and followed her without a word. Tripp, looking unsure about why they were leaving, gathered his own meal and chased after them. Carson went straight to her Jeep and closed her eyes, as if this would make her less visible to the man at the pump.

Tripp paused long enough to identify the man putting gas into his old Chevy pickup. "Is that Sanchez?"

Carson turned around and pushed Tripp from behind toward the back driver's-side door. Daniel had already grabbed the shotgun position up front.

"Yes, now let's go," she whispered.

Tripp turned his head and watched out the back window. "I wonder what he's doing here."

"I don't know," Carson replied as she climbed into the driver's seat and started the engine. "He's driving his personal truck, so it can't be official police business. Let's find out."

They waited as Sanchez finished getting gas. He pulled out and returned to the highway, and Carson tailed him from a short distance. No one said much, as they were too busy inhaling their dinner.

They traveled across the island. After a while, Carson wondered if they were going to cross the Alabama–Florida state line. However, Sanchez finally did turn off the highway, toward the bayside. She slowed down as he pulled into a community of colorful condos; she cautiously turned in, hoping he didn't notice he was being tailed.

Carson parked her Jeep near the entrance to the community and turned the lights off but left the vehicle running. They all watched as Sanchez exited his truck, glanced around, then headed to one of the condos. It was pink, although the yellow streetlamp gave it more of a salmon look. He knocked on the front door and waited.

"See," said Carson with a smirk, "destiny."

"I certainly hope so. I'd hate to think we just caught him cheating on Mrs. Sanchez," said Tripp.

"You would worry about such things. This is a sign. We find a map with this area marked, and Sanchez shows up here. It's just meant to be," she said and lowered her voice. "I hope."

"I won't even try and guess the odds," Tripp said.

"Save your brain for more important tasks. Let's go," said Carson as Sanchez disappeared into the small condo.

"Exactly where are we going?"

"We're exactly going to that pink condo and looking in the windows. Where's your sense of adventure, Detective?"

Begrudgingly, Tripp followed. Daniel, eyeing Carson's fries, decided to stay back in the Jeep as a lookout. He said that the more bodies that hovered around the house, the better the chance they had of getting caught.

Carson and Tripp maneuvered around parked cars, under the cover of night. As they crept up to the closest window near the corner of the condo, a shadow approached the door and opened it for Sanchez. Soon the door closed again.

"Did you catch a glimpse of who opened the door?" asked Tripp as they knelt down near the window.

"No," said Carson, peering into the window and then ducking down again. The room was dimly lit. "I do see an old man standing there. He's talking to somebody, probably Sanchez."

"What does he look like?"

"Well, he's Hispanic, has an old pickup—"

"That's cute. I'm familiar with what Mr. Sanchez looks like."

Carson chuckled at her own joke and stuck out her tongue. "Oh, you mean the other guy. Well, he's old, has some white fuzz on his pasty head. His face is pitted and he's as thin as a rail. I think he's wearing pajamas. Why don't you get up and look for yourself?"

"Nice description, and no, I'm fine where I am. Can you hear anything?"

"Yeah, my brother's blather. It would be nice if I could hear the conversation inside, though."

Tripp said, "Okay, I get the hint. I wished I'd brought along some additional gear. My sound amplification equipment from the office would have been ideal."

Carson suddenly ducked down. Instinctively, he lowered himself beside her.

They peered up as the window opened slowly. Over the windowsill hung bony fingers. They dared not move for fear of being spotted. Soon the hands disappeared.

"Dat better?" came the raspy voice. "Da cleanin' lady was sick dis week."

As they heard the words, the stench coming from the window hit their olfactory nerves. It reminded Carson of the time she tagged along with her dad, as part of his church duties, to visit an old sick woman in hospice. She pinched her nostrils and made a gagging gesture. It wasn't the worst smell she had ever been subjected too, but it did seem excessive for someone who had just missed a single week's worth of cleaning. At least now they could hear the conversation in the room better.

"Yes, thanks," came Sanchez's voice. "Jitters, I need to go into the attic."

"I already told ya," said Jitters, who had to cough before continuing. After he hacked up whatever was in his lungs, he wheezed. "Dere's nuttin' in da attic ya need, cop."

"Look, Pops sent me and I know what I'm looking for. You don't, old man. I'm going up there."

The sound of Sanchez's boots on a wooden floor echoed throughout the house, followed by the distinct creak of stairs being climbed. Tripp took his turn peering into the window. He whispered a report to Carson. "Sanchez is already up the stairs, and Jitters is sitting in a chair near the window."

The man hacked and then cleared his throat. "Dat briefcase is gone," he yelled in a high-pitched nasal tone. Then he said under his breath, "Stupid wetback."

They heard the sound of Sanchez's rapid descent down the stairs. Tripp ducked down again.

"What did you say, old man?" said Sanchez.

"Nuttin'."

"Know what? Pops has been good to you. He saved your worthless butt and let you stay in this nice place. You owe him a lot. Now you say the briefcase is gone."

Tripp gave a puzzled glance to Carson. She mouthed the question "Pops's condo?" He shrugged.

"Oh dat," said Jitters, sounding relieved he didn't hear the wetback remark.

"How did you know there was a briefcase up there? It was well hidden." Sanchez's voice had more than a hint of concern in it.

"Pops' boy came n' got it."

"Jack retrieved it? That sounds like bullshit to me."

Carson had to risk a peek, even though Tripp was silently trying to dissuade her from it. She rose cautiously until her left eye could see in. Sanchez, looking down at the phone in his hand, was about to call someone. She ducked again as he raised the phone to his ear.

"Pops, I'm here. The old man claims Jack already collected the briefcase."

"Not Jack, ya idiot." Jitters's words were accompanied by a spray of spittle.

"Wait, you just said Pops's son, you old fart. Now which is it?"

The old man coughed. "Da odah one—da lil' wetback."

"Joe?"

"Yup."

Sanchez relayed to Pops that Joe had picked it up and swore as he hung up. "Looks like I'm heading to New Orleans now."

Jitters said something inaudible as Sanchez walked toward the door.

Carson and Tripp headed for the nearest vehicle they could find in the parking lot, a gray Acura, and hid behind it. The Jeep would be too far away to get to before Sanchez walked out the door.

As he left, Sanchez turned back to Jitters. "I better not ever hear you call anyone a wetback again, ya crusty Cajun bastard." He shut the door abruptly and walked right past where Carson and Tripp were hiding. After he got into his truck, he called his wife to let her know he wouldn't be home for dinner. He crossed himself, started the old pickup, and left.

As Sanchez drove away, Jitters stuck his head out the window and yelled to the departing truck. It was unintelligible and full of profanity. When Sanchez kept going, the old man made a frustrated sound, waved a dismissive hand, and closed his window.

"What form of dialect was that?" asked Tripp.

"Bad Cajun, I guess--don't really care. C'mon," said Carson excitedly as she pulled him toward the Jeep.

"I assume we're going to New Orleans," Tripp said, trying to keep up with her fast pace. Her lack of response made him nod; clearly it was the only confirmation he needed.

Carson yanked the Jeep's door open. "Let's go. We have to beat Sanchez to Uncle Joe's."

Daniel jumped at her abrupt entry. He was studying what little data he had found from their dad's computer. "Where are we going?"

She and Tripp were seated with their belts fastened before she answered. "New Orleans. Plot me a course to Uncle Joe's house," she said as the Jeep bolted off.

"I don't know where your uncle Joe lives," Daniel said.

"It's saved in my navigation," Carson replied. "I found the address and went to see him last year."

"Right. I vaguely remember Tripp mentioning that."

"I'm surprised you don't have a copy of my navigation entries, like you did my key fob," Carson said, her eyes narrowing as she glanced back. "Do you have a dupe to my apartment too?"

Before Daniel could try to avoid the question, a car pulled out in front of them, making Carson swerve. After they avoided the accident, as well as survived Carson's road rage moment, Daniel mumbled something about being grateful to the car for providing a distraction.

"How about we just get there in one piece?" Tripp said.

Daniel avoided any further questions that might have incriminating answers. "We can do trivia."

At that, Carson reached over and turned the radio on. She searched for a rock station and turned the volume up loud enough to drown out any conversation. Daniel and Tripp got comfortable with the noise and tried to nap, while Carson plotted her own course and set the cruise control about ten miles per hour higher than the posted speed limit. The radio drowned out her sudden cursing as she realized she should have used the bathroom before they left.

THE POKER ROOM

The bar was located on the other side of the square, almost directly across from the old post office. It wasn't particularly large, but it had three levels. The lower level included a pool table, some dartboards, a few round tables, and a jukebox. The second level housed the main bar and several tables for eating. Its weathered wooden interior was meant to resemble an old ship. The walls were covered with various pictures and decor that reflected life at sea during the heyday of piracy in the Caribbean. The top floor had a similar theme to the one below it but with a smaller bar and an open smoking area.

After finishing a phone call with Sanchez, Pops ascended to the top patio where he was met with the scent of cigar smoke and humid night air. As he reached the last of the wooden steps, he searched for a cigar in his pocket but couldn't find one. With everything going on, maybe he had already smoked it.

He figured on seeing Jack, but instead there was only Shelby, dressed in his typical fedora and jacket. A faint rise of cigar smoke came from the ashtray on the table, probably from where a stogie had just been extinguished. The man sat with his back to the railing and spotted Pops right away. He raised a whiskey glass as Pops approached.

Pops grumbled to himself as he reached the table that sat off by itself. Shelby was hardly someone he wanted to partner with, but it seemed circumstance had brought them together.

"Good to see you, Pops," Shelby said as he stood and extended a hand.

Pops shook his hand briefly. "Glad you decided against a dress, Shelby." He sat down across from him.

Shelby motioned for the bartender, a young woman with blonde hair and pink highlights. "This gentleman will take your best Scotch on the rocks and a cigar. Oh darlin', this also goes on Jack's tab."

The young woman nodded and smiled as she glanced over at Pops. "You're Carson's grandpa, right?"

"I am, young lady."

"I've seen a picture of you and her. I took her shift tonight. She was a no-show."

"So I've heard," Pops said. He focused on Shelby when the young bartender wandered off to fill his order. "I have Sanchez on assignment, so don't expect him anytime soon. Where the hell is Jack?"

"Maybe he's chasing down your grandkids."

"That would be a pointless endeavor. Besides, I saw his truck outside."

"Then you know as much as I do," Shelby said and took a drink.

Pops growled in frustration. "Apparently, neither of us knows a whole lot of anything."

Shelby nodded as he reached into his jacket pocket and produced a Zippo lighter. As if on cue, the bartender arrived and served Pops his drink and cigar. Shelby intercepted the cigar and examined it. He put it in one of his jacket pockets and then reached into the other to produce two others. "Cuban?" He cut both and lit one for Pops.

Pops lost his scowl and nodded as he took a drag from the long stogie. "Don't mind if I do."

"How was your meeting with Fumi?" Shelby asked, smoking.

Pops eyed him suspiciously and exhaled an almost perfect ring of smoke. "You seem to have a knack for knowing other people's business."

"I never figured that trick out," Shelby said, watching the smoke ring rise and dissipate. "It's my job to know things."

"In addition to leaving messes in your wake, it seems."

"I love you too, Pops. By the way, you're welcome for rescuing your daughter-in-law."

Pops mumbled, "Thank you, Shelby."

Shelby leaned over the table, holding his cigar in one hand while giving Pops a half-crazed look. "What?"

"Thank you, Shelby," Pops repeated, more audibly the second time.

Shelby sat up straight and took a deep drag from the cigar, extended his hands, and looked at the ceiling. "And there were angels singing in the heavens at the miracle they had witnessed." His tune was off-key and white puffs of smoke danced out of his mouth with each word.

"We might as well talk shop while we wait," Pops said.

Shelby tried to put on a serious face. "Okay, what shall we talk about?"

Pops cleared his throat as he thought about how to approach it. "To start with, Fumi seems to value your opinion."

"He should. I do quality work."

Pops ignored Shelby's self-congratulatory words. "He wasn't quite himself. It seemed he was trying to say more than his words alone conveyed."

Shelby pursed his lips as he considered Pops's statement. "Maybe he just used good English, something you're not used to."

Pops wasn't amused. "Are we going to do this or not?"

"Okay, sorry," Shelby said with a chuckle. "I couldn't help myself. Look, Fumi is under a lot of pressure since accepting that chamber position. It requires him to filter everything he says to you."

"I'd expect that for anyone except me," Pops said skeptically. "He also had some new faces surrounding him."

"Probably guild-appointed lackeys."

Pops leaned into the conversation. "Why would they appoint Fumi to the chamber, knowing his relationship to me? Particularly with everything that has happened."

Shelby considered it. "That's a good question, Pops. They must be desperate."

"Fumi spoke of some new organization. What have you heard?"

Shelby stared at his drink and shook his head. When he looked up, he was almost somber. He lowered his voice. "There's nothing new or mysterious about this organization, Pops—not to the discerning observer."

"You sound like Fumi. Just spit it out."

"There are no outside forces at play here."

"Fumi seemed inclined to share that opinion."

"And you have a hard time with that?"

Pops thought about it. "The last time the guild turned on itself was in response to an outside stimulus that affected its core."

"If I recall my guild history, your own father took part in the solution to that problem. You also seem to forget that you too had to deal with internal struggles during the Cold War."

This confirmed his suspicions that Shelby knew far more about the Guild of Libra than any outsider should. "Your point?"

"What if this time around it's something different? In nature, things sometimes have to evolve or die out."

"Thanks for the biology lesson. What's the guild evolving into?"

"Good question," Shelby said, then hesitated before he continued. "Perhaps a question best saved for Fumi himself. After all, he'd have to be part of such an evolution."

Pops glared at Shelby in warning. "Be careful with your theories, Shelby. It was Fumi, after all, who suggested we work together. I doubt he would have done so knowing you'd use it as a conspiracist platform."

"That's where you're wrong. It's precisely why he wanted us together on this one."

Pops was skeptical but decided to move the conversation in a different direction. "Let's talk about these hired guns who gave you and my family trouble today."

"Remember your old buddy Alan?" asked Shelby. "Of course you do. Apparently, someone tapped Daddy's little bastard to give the Page clan a fit."

"Victor, I would assume," Pops said. "So Alan's reaching from beyond the grave through his son. That doesn't explain why now. I can't help but think Fumi's surprise visit and this are connected."

"Of course they're connected. But there are some missing pieces. Maybe it's time you helped fill in the blanks."

"Me? You apparently know a hell of a lot more about what's been going on around here than I do."

"Around here, yes," Shelby said. "Beyond that, I'm still trying to figure out how it all fits together."

Pops finished off his drink. "That makes two of us."

"Look, I was doing some research for Fumi when Victor's goons started popping up on my radar. I don't believe in coincidence. Whatever Fumi got himself into followed him here."

"But Victor? If that's the best they can do, then this will all be a done deal by next week."

"Don't underestimate a bastard who takes himself too seriously. He may not be as formidable a foe as you're used to, but he was brought in for a reason, perhaps to keep you busy. Let's also not forget you're no spring chicken."

"I can still raise some hell," Pops said, snorting. "What's my son's take on all of this?"

"As you know, Jack doesn't typically share what's on his mind."

The bartender brought another round and quickly departed. Shelby retrieved his stogie, while Pops dipped the end of his in the Scotch.

"There are times I miss who he was before he became a saint," Pops said, allowing himself a slight grin. "He was more predictable back then."

"Hell, we can both drink to that," Shelby said with a chuckle.

Pops's phone rang. The caller was the captain of the *Abril*. "Whatcha got, Ed?"

The way his old friend sighed before he spoke told Pops it wasn't good news. "Pops, the Coast Guard found Fumi's yacht burning, east of Miami. At this time, word is that there's no survivors."

Pops was stunned. "Let me know the minute you have more." He was clearly distraught as he hung up and sat quietly.

Shelby sensed the bad news. "What's wrong?"

Pops downed his freshly poured drink and sat back in his chair. He took a long drag from the cigar and held it. After exhaling, he struggled to find the words. "Fumi's yacht was found by the Coast Guard, drifting and scorched." He tried to shake off the shock. "Apparently all aboard were lost."

"Oh shit," Shelby said, processing the news. "You realize what this means, right?"

"I do," Pops said solemnly. "We have a lot more to worry about than Victor Lloyd."

THE BIG EASY WAY

Joe Page looked at his watch. It was neither fancy nor high-tech. His mother had probably paid very little for it, but it was one of the few things he had left to remember her by—and the last thing she had given him before she died. He missed her.

Memories of his mother were not, however, why he was checking the watch. He wondered why his half-brother's friend was calling him so late. He had met Rick Sanchez when he had accompanied him and Jack to a Saints game a couple of years before. They had gotten along okay and exchanged numbers.

He let the call go to voice mail, debating whether to listen to it now or wait until morning. Joe decided to wait. He owed that side of the family nothing—except his current business, the place he lived, the car he drove. Hell, he thought. For someone who cared so little for Pops, the bastard who had donated sperm to bring about his existence, he sure had accepted a lot of things from him over the years. Setting the phone down on his coffee table, he headed to the kitchen to grab a beer.

The phone rang again.

Swearing under his breath, he scooped it off the coffee table and answered it. *"Hola,"* he said. "Sanchez, what's up?"

Balancing the phone between his ear and shoulder, Joe walked back into the kitchen. He twisted the lid off the cold brew and took a big swig while Sanchez spoke.

"Hey, Joe. Sorry to bother ya so late, but Pops wants me to grab the suitcase from ya," said Sanchez.

"Sure bro, I can fetch it," said Joe. "Come by tomorrow to get it."

"I'm actually on my way there now."

"Tonight? No, dude, my girl's coming back over. She's already pissed that I worked all day and missed dinner." He started pacing as Sanchez continued speaking.

"I hear ya, man, but it's important I grab this tonight."

"Well, it's important I get laid tonight too, man," Joe said irritated.

"Sorry, Joe."

"Shit. Okay, come on over. Bye."

Joe wasn't in the mood for company, except that of the curvaceous, bleached blonde Wanda that he'd been dating off and on for the past couple of years. Between his busy schedule and her need for constant attention, their relationship never seemed to move forward. That, and she was a nut. He figured his lady would probably be gone by the time Jack's friend arrived. She rarely stayed the night anymore. He was thankful for small favors.

Joe sat on his green fabric couch, drinking beer. His home wasn't large, but it was in a nice neighborhood—and it was his, though he had accepted it from Pops. The man's attempt to make good for not being in his life had its benefits. Still, gifts aside, he really didn't care for Pops to be part of his life.

His half-brother Jack, on the other hand, was different. Initially, he hadn't cared to get to know him either, but the guy was just a cool person to talk to. He had never approached Joe with anything but a desire to connect with his brother. He was also a good listener. Besides, he thought, nobody chooses their parents.

Jack had reached out years ago when he learned he had another brother. Joe remembered his surprise that a preacher actually drank, much less joined him at the casino once. The man listened to Joe vent about their dad and seemed to understand his anger with Pops for not attending his mother's funeral. Their talks were actually therapeutic.

A knock on the door snapped him back to reality. He wasn't expecting Wanda yet, but perhaps she decided to arrive early. Opening the door, he saw nothing. He stepped out and looked both ways. Did I imagine it? he thought.

Closing the door, he walked back to the living room. His back porch light came on and he could see a shadow in the window.

Retrieving a revolver, another gift from his estranged dad, he opened the back door and stepped out. The source of the shadow was the lawn umbrella, which typically stood between two lounge chairs but was leaning against the window. It had been in its place earlier that morning. Someone was playing games with him.

"Who's there?" he said and listened. His backyard was mostly a green-stained concrete deck surrounded by a cedar privacy fence. He was rather fond of the color green, as his house and car would attest. The gate was still latched and there was nowhere to hide, except behind his large grill. He crept over and peered around it.

Nothing.

After a moment of hearing nothing but a neighbor's music seeping out of their walls, Joe went back inside. He tucked the pistol into the back of his blue jeans, concealing it under his black T-shirt. He headed back to his living room to finish his beer.

In his peripheral vision, he caught the movement—something coming at him. He instinctively turned, but the knife came at him fast. He felt it hit his stomach as he staggered backward and fell to the floor. The figure hovered over him.

Joe let out a yell, holding his hands up defensively. The white mask was something from a horror movie. The large knife was a dull gray with red covering its blade. He frantically felt for a wound. Surely being stabbed should hurt more, he thought.

Then he saw the person remove the mask. He noticed the blonde hair first, followed by those hazel eyes, and finally that familiar laugh. "What the hell!" he yelled.

Wanda was cackling with laughter as she tossed the mask and fake knife on top of his chest. They landed with a thud, making him flinch. He lay there, staring at the ceiling and trying to collect himself. "Crazy bitch," he said, slowly sitting up. "What's wrong with you? I could've shot you!"

Wanda took off the black apron that concealed her curves. Tossing it aside nonchalantly, she squatted down to look at him, her eyes ablaze with mischief. "Need to go change your shorts?" she asked with a wicked grin.

"Not funny. Help me up."

"Sure," she said, standing and unbuttoning her blue blouse. She bent down to show off her cleavage. "How's this?"

"Cute," Joe said, sweeping the mask and fake knife off himself before standing. "You change your hair?" It did look shorter, but mostly he just wanted to talk about something other than what a coward she had made him feel like.

"Like it?" she said, striking a model's pose and running her hand through her thick hair.

Shaking his head and straightening himself, he pulled the pistol from behind him and started for the living room. "It's nice."

Wanda looked surprised, her mouth agape. "You really had a gun? Shit."

Joe stopped and turned. "And now you see why pulling a stunt like that was stupid."

"No, owning a gun is stupid," she said, still stunned. "Where'd you get that?"

Joe tried to retrieve the much-needed beer and didn't bother to turn as he spoke. "Pops," he answered. He set the firearm down and traded it for the beer. He took a long drink and tried to ignore Wanda's glare.

"So you'll accept a gun but turn down money from your old man?"

"It's none of your business," Joe said after finishing the beer. He walked past her, tossed the empty bottle in the trash, and grabbed another one. The hiss of the carbonation escaping and the click of the lid on the counter was music to his ears. "I've accepted enough. I don't need anything else from him."

"If you hate the bastard so much, take him for whatever he's worth. We can milk him for money, trips to Europe, cars, whatever you want." She followed him back into the living room.

It wasn't the first time the subject had come up.

Her list reminded him of a sales pitch he was duped into listening to in Vegas from one of those time-share people. At least he got a free show for that one. He turned suddenly, causing Wanda to stop in her tracks. "I don't hate the man—I just don't care for him either. If you want to go milk someone's family, go bother your own daddy. Last I heard, he wanted to make amends."

"Screw that! The monster who donated a sperm for my existence doesn't have money like your donor does. If he did, I'd make him pay for all those years. "

"Well, I don't want to be like you."

The words seemed to sting at first, but she quickly shook them off. "Maybe you should be. It's not like he worked hard for it. He's a drug smuggler."

Joe laughed at her words. "I never said he smuggled drugs. I once said the guy could be a smuggler for all I knew. Stop making shit up. I don't want anything else from the man. It's not like it would change the past anyway."

"Well, if you don't take advantage of it, you'll never be anything more than his half-breed bastard." Her cruel stare was unwavering.

Angrily, Joe pointed a warning finger at Wanda but said nothing. He wanted to kick her to the curb, but he knew makeup sex was the best, if not only, sex worth having with the woman. She could be quite selfish. But every time he wondered why he put up with the abuse, all he had to do was take one look at her. She might have been a spawn of hell, but the fiery pits had passed along primo genes.

Sitting down to enjoy his next beer, he decided the best thing to do was ignore her. She would hate that. True enough, she eventually tired of picking at him and disappeared into the kitchen to get a drink. Joe could hear her mumbling but chose not to pay attention. He turned on the fifty-inch television to check the news, ensuring the volume would drown out Wanda's grumblings. Flipping through the various local and cable channels, he only saw the same polarizing garbage that everyone was typically subjected to. He clicked it back off again.

Wanda stayed in the kitchen for quite a while. When she returned to the living room, she was no longer wearing pants or underwear. Drifting quietly by Joe, she sat beside him on the couch and let him get a good look at what was beneath her open blouse.

This he did notice.

After plenty of foreplay and arguably some of the best sex they'd had in a while, they both drifted off to sleep on his couch.

In the back of his mind, Joe thought he heard knocking. He drifted back into consciousness and sat up, listening. He heard nothing; it must have been his imagination. He looked at his watch and figured he had been asleep a couple of hours. Damn, he thought, trying to disentangle himself from Wanda's limbs. He quickly got dressed in boxers and a T-shirt.

The back porch light came on. Instead of going to the back door, which hadn't turned out well the last time, he peeked out the closest window. Walking past his window were three figures. They went straight to his patio door. The girl in the group knocked. The two men stood behind her and waited.

Retrieving his gun, he waited to see what they would do. After a moment, the knocking grew louder. Joe sat there, watching through the blinds. Wanda sat straight up on the couch, still waking up.

"Joe?" she called.

"By the window," Joe said in a low voice.

"Is somebody knocking?"

"Yes," Joe said, watching the group.

Wanda found her own window and peered out. "Who's the blonde? You expecting another plaything?"

Her jealousy was amusing to Joe, since he was certain she dated other men behind his back. Glancing over at her, he said, "Yeah, I thought I'd do her and the two dudes standing behind her," he said. Wanda flipped him the bird and curled her upper lip into a snarl. As he turned back toward the window, he was startled to see piercing blue eyes staring back, just a few inches away.

"Hi," said the girl through the window.

Joe jumped back and stumbled. Wanda giggled at the sight of him trying to regain his balance. After cursing a bit, he opened the blinds again. "Come to the front," he said loudly.

Throwing on some pants, he met the three at the front door, the gun tucked behind him. They're not much more than kids, he thought. Opening the door, he was greeted by a chorus of different salutations.

"What do you want?" Joe asked.

"Uncle Joe, it's me, Carson."

"Who?"

"Your niece," Carson said, sounding offended he didn't remember. "You know, your brother Jack's daughter?"

"Oh, right. I hadn't seen you since you were, like, a teenager."

"I was twenty-three when I came to visit last year," she said and walked past him. "You'd know that had you been listening to me instead of watching my boobs."

"Really?" Joe said, feeling he had been abused enough for one night. He turned back to the two men who were still waiting to be asked in. "Who are these guys?"

"That's Tripp, my brother and your nephew," Carson called back from the other room. "You've never met him because he's a homebody. The other guy is Daniel, his best friend."

Joe followed Carson into the living room, where Wanda was sitting and glaring at her. Carson smiled and nodded at the woman, who was barely covered by the crumpled blouse she tried to hide her nakedness with.

"Oh hi," said Carson. "You are?"

"Trying to sleep," Wanda snapped.

Joe moaned. "Shit. Come on in," he said, turning to Daniel and Tripp and motioning for them to come in.

"Who's this?" Wanda demanded.

Tripp and Daniel appeared behind Joe.

"Whoa," said Tripp, turning around in embarrassment as he spotted the woman's partially uncovered breast. "Sorry, ma'am."

"Ma'am? Do I look like some old lady to you?"

"Chill, Wanda. The boy's just trying to be polite," said Joe.

"We're family," said Carson. Her hands moved to her hips as her eyes narrowed on the other woman.

"That's nice," Wanda said sarcastically. "More of the Page clan, I suppose? Did your dad screw a Chinese whore too?" She looked straight at Daniel.

Daniel looked taken aback by the comment. "I'm actually not related," he said. "Also, I'm about a third Japanese."

"Please tell me this isn't my aunt," Carson said.

"No, she's not." Joe said, and Wanda sneered. He had spoken too assuredly for her taste. "It's late. I was expecting a dude named Sanchez to drop by, not you three."

"Relax, Uncle Joe. He'll be here. We passed him after crossing into Alabama. His truck is old and slow."

"Then why are you here?" Joe said, irritated.

"Answers. We know something's going on that involves this family. Since nobody else will tell us, I thought I'd introduce my brother to his uncle."

Tripp offered a hand while using the other to shield his eyes from the sight of Wanda. Joe shook it and turned his attention back to Carson.

"I don't know what the hell you're talking about. If you came all the way from Florida to get answers from me, lil' niece, you've wasted your time."

"Yet Sanchez is coming here to pick up a briefcase. Look, I was kidnapped and held at gunpoint this morning—well, technically yesterday now—and I want some answers. What does Dad have in that case?"

Joe was still trying to determine if he had heard the part about kidnapping correctly when Wanda, suddenly interested, positioned herself between him and Carson.

"Yeah, Joe. What's in the case?" said Wanda.

"I didn't bother to look," Joe said. "My brother asked me for a favor. I obliged."

"Is it money? Let's have a look-see," said Wanda, excitement in her widening eyes.

"I'll second that," said Carson. She looked both unsure and glad someone else wanted what she did.

"It's not here," said Joe, repulsed at Wanda's greed. "Even if it were, none of you would have a vote on the matter. As soon as this Sanchez gets his ass here, that thing will be gone forever, out of my life."

"You really didn't look inside this briefcase, Joey?" Wanda asked, unconvinced. Her tone had become sultry. She stood up and pressed herself against him, running her hand from his chest to his belt. "Let's go have a look-see. Your little niece wants to see it too."

"I said it's not here," Joe said, growing annoyed. "I seriously doubt it's money."

"I sure hope not," Carson said. "I'd prefer deep, dark family secrets."

"Steamy ones," added Wanda. "Something we can blackmail your bastard father with."

"Really?" asked Carson and Joe in unison. Both folded their arms and glared at the woman.

"Oh, you two are definitely related. Where's the case, Joe?"

"None of your damn business, Wanda. Get dressed so I can kick everyone out together."

Wanda huffed as she grabbed the rest of her clothes and headed for the bathroom. She made sure to slam the door. Joe didn't flinch; he had grown used to her tantrums over the past two years.

After he was sure Wanda wasn't going to come flying back out of the bathroom, Joe turned to his visitors. "I'd like to say she's not usually like this."

"Sir," came Tripp's voice, "we're sincerely sorry for interrupting your evening and causing a ruckus. We wouldn't have done it if it weren't for what happened to us yesterday–that and my sister's insatiable need to know everything."

"It's okay, kid," said Joe, relieved for the break from the Carson and Wanda duo. "You guys were kidnapped?"

Carson started to answer, but Tripp abruptly held a finger across her lips, as if to suggest that she really needed to let him do the talking. Joe was impressed anyone could silence the fiery blonde. He knew of no force in the universe that could do the same to Wanda.

Tripp told a short version of the story, about how their lives went from routine, if not mundane, to more adrenaline charged than they bargained for. He explained how they tried to get answers from their dad, which only produced more questions. He mentioned the secret rooms they found but didn't go into detail. When the part about Jitters came up, Joe only rolled his eyes.

"Someone needs to put that poor bastard in a padded room," Joe said. "So you're worried about your dad?" Joe asked. "Is that the gist of the story?"

"Yes, sir."

"Very worried," Carson added quickly, then fell silent again.

"Okay, I can call your dad. But I'll only give the briefcase to this guy Sanchez. I don't want my only brother to be pissed at me."

"Understood, sir. We don't intend to disturb the contents of the briefcase—only to look them over for any clues that may shed some light, if you will."

"Dude, stop calling me sir. It's either Joe or, in your case, Uncle Joe." He glanced over at Carson. "How can you two be related, much less twins?"

"It's a mystery," Carson said.

"As for the briefcase, it's well hidden. You'd be crazy to want to grab it at this time of night anyway. I wouldn't. I'll give Sanchez directions and he can go retrieve the damn thing. If you want to follow him out there, you're more than welcome to."

"We had to try, Uncle Joe," said Tripp, as if in surrender. He glanced over at Carson, who, arms folded, was tapping her foot in an annoying manner, clearly unimpressed with his efforts. "I'm sure it's a bad part of New Orleans to be in at this time of night anyway."

"It's not really the part of town, kid. It's just not a place I'd go at night."

"Some areas can be eerie after the sun sets."

"You can say that again," Joe replied.

"Daylight is usually a better time to stray from the land of the living," Tripp continued.

"Right," Joe said, then realized he was being interrogated. "Okay, clever nephew, no more hints for you."

"Thanks, Uncle Joe," Tripp said. He would have to be content with not getting any further details.

"Uncle Joe, can you tell us anything about our uncle Conner?" Carson asked. "People typically avoid talking about him."

"Aside from he's dead?"

"Right—that's about the extent of our knowledge. It just seems strange how he died, don't you think?"

Joe shifted his gaze between Tripp and Carson. "There's a lot of strange crap about this family, kiddos. I'm happy to say I'm oblivious to most of it."

"But not all of it, right?" Carson said.

"Look, when your uncle died, the shit hit the fan. My mom told me she'd never seen Pops like that. He went from charming to spooky. She said he became obsessed with some plan to make things right."

"Make what right? How?" Carson asked.

"I don't know."

"Does your mom know?"

"She knew more than me, but you won't get anything from her. She died many years ago."

The three expressed their condolences. Carson hesitated, as if thinking something through. "Daniel, pull up that map on your phone. Let's show Uncle Joe and see what he thinks."

Daniel brought up the information, including the map they'd obtained. They crowded around his coffee table and went over it. Joe indicated he was unsure what most of the points on the map were but became interested in the one near Denton, Texas.

"That one," said Joe, pointing, "is where my mom lived. This one, of course, is where I live. As for the others, you'll have to ask your dad."

"What happened to your mom?" asked Carson.

"She died from cancer about a decade ago. She tried reaching out to Pops before she left this earth, but he didn't bother showing up until after her funeral. When he did pop in out of the blue, he started giving me things—I mean, lots of stuff. Sure, he always sent my mother money, but I guess it was his way of trying to prove he was more than a sperm donor." Joe realized his tone had soured a bit with the last statement and decided to change it. "Look, my mother was a good woman. Whatever her reason, she loved the guy. She was never really capable of having another relationship after him. I tried to tell myself he must have had some redeeming value, but the only thing I ever saw was his ability to make you feel guilty for despising him."

"Sounds like a talent I wish I had," Carson said with a smile. Tripp nudged her in the ribs. "You know what I mean."

"Right," said Joe. He noticed Wanda was dressed and standing behind him, rolling her eyes. "Looks like it's time to kick everyone out. I'll pass along your concerns to your dad. Go home and get some sleep, or go chase some ghosts."

"Uncle Joe, is there anyone else who could shed some light on the events of long ago?" asked Tripp, inching toward the door.

"You mean aside from your parents or Pops?" Joe paused to think about his next words and just laughed. "You could always try the Wicked Witch of the Midwest," he said. "On second thought, stay away from that crazy old hag."

"Who's that?" asked Carson.

"I would guess that would be our grandmother, who lives somewhere in the southeast corner of Oklahoma," Tripp said. "Pops once used similar if less colorful words to describe her."

"He would know," said Joe. "She was probably what drove him out to sea. Really, guys, forget I said anything. I'd stay far away from her."

"We don't know her," Carson said. "How do you?"

"She paid a couple of visits to my mom when I was a boy—the first time being when she learned of Pops's affair with my mom. She was sticky nice at first, but then she launched into some insane stories."

"What kind of stories?" Carson asked.

"It's not important," Joe said dismissively.

"Please," Carson said.

Joe gave a deep sigh. "I don't really remember the details. Her second and last visit, after your uncle died, she said something about your grandpa being a leader of some dark cult, which had his own son killed. She rattled on about her dead son being caught up in another world or some other batshit crazy stuff like that. When my mother questioned the stories, your grandmother became this vile, hateful creature. She's a scary woman."

"We'll keep that in mind," Carson said, following Tripp and Daniel to the door. She stopped and went back to give Joe a hug. As she wrapped her arms around him, she whispered in his ear, "Good luck with your own batshit crazy woman."

Joe laughed. "Thanks. Good luck on your quest." He walked them to the door and then decided he couldn't just send them off into the night on an aimless search. He knew they would strike out whether he said anything else or not. One more hint won't hurt, he told himself. It's not like Sanchez wouldn't catch up to them and find it first anyway. "If you do insist on visiting our local tombs, you might try the ones north of here—toward the lake."

"Thanks Uncle Joe," said Tripp.

"You didn't hear it from me. Now get outta here," Joe said. He closed the door and turned to face Wanda, who seemed ready for a fight.

After the door shut, Tripp, Daniel, and Carson walked to her Jeep.

"Now what?" she asked.

"Now we find the cemetery Uncle Conner was buried in," Tripp replied.

"Why the hell would we do something like that at this hour?"

"Because, dear sister, that's where Uncle Joe will be sending Sanchez to retrieve the briefcase."

"Why don't we just wait for Sanchez and follow him there?" Carson asked. She wondered how her brother could actually be more in favor of going to a place with dead people than she was.

"Spooked are you, Carson?" Daniel asked, ribbing her.

"A little," she admitted.

"It is not the dead we should be worried about—it's the living that are armed with guns," Tripp said. "As to why we shouldn't just follow Detective Sanchez, I'll simply ask you this: Do you want to actually examine the contents of the briefcase or simply admire its exterior from a distance as it's taken back to Pops?"

Carson's adventurous spirit came alive again. "Good point. Let's do this."

TOMB RAIDERS

They left the Lower Garden District and headed northward—per Uncle Joe's hint—and searched for some sites closer to the Lake Pontchatrain area. Daniel had created a list from his web search of the area. They would split up and search each cemetery quickly and then move on to the next one. They were making reasonable time, all things considered, until Carson was pulled over for speeding. To the others' relief, she managed to talk her way out of it—proof she could be charming when it suited her.

At one of the larger cemeteries, Carson's frustration had started to tax her spirits. To lift them, she hid in the darkest, most foreboding spot she could find and waited for her brother and Daniel to come near. She caught them both together as they searched for her. She started by making her best eerie sounds and threw small stones in different directions, then jumped out at the most opportune moment. The startled looks on their faces was her reward.

They scolded her and moved on. As more time passed, however, any hope of finding the gravesite before Sanchez arrived started to fade. They decided to refuel their bodies and relieve their bladders at a twenty-four-hour convenience store. Tripp struck up a conversation with the Indian clerk. After telling the man he was a private investigator searching for a particular gravesite, at night no less, the man gave him a few leads to follow. Tripp wrote them down and thanked him.

After using the bathroom, Carson decided to call her uncle to find out how long ago Sanchez had arrived and departed to the place they searched for. To her surprise, he had been delayed due to both a flat tire and a rusty lug nut that refused to come off. He had left Joe's place only moments before she called. When she told them about this lucky break, the others regained a sliver of hope.

As they set out with renewed vigor, Tripp shared the short list of local cemeteries. One that wasn't on Daniel's list and was much smaller than the others caught their interest, so they headed to Lazarus Tombs. Carson noticed it was protected by a locked iron gate. She, Tripp, and Daniel quickly scaled it and, with flashlights out, began their search. Winding their way around the impressive stone monuments, they noticed a circular pattern to the place.

Strangely, some tombs were not marked, while others had names they were unfamiliar with. Less than a minute after starting, Daniel called for the others. As they approached, the light from his flashlight illuminated a stone sepulcher.

"That's it!" Carson shouted, running her hand across the engraved lettering. Her flashlight traveled down to the engraved words "Conner Page" and "October 17, 1991." It continued to a scripture reference, Luke 17:33, followed by an inscription below that. She felt puzzled as she read it.

> *a Time for a son to exit*
> *a loss to father and mother*
> *death found but One*
> *life hid the other*

"What the hell does that mean?" asked Carson.

"Poetic," Tripp said.

"It must be a code for something," Daniel said excitedly. He and Tripp stood there and studied the words.

Carson read it again to herself but found nothing useful. It sounded like gibberish. Getting impatient, she started pacing in a circle around the sepulcher. On the second pass around, Tripp and Daniel were still going over the possible meaning of the epitaph. They agreed it referred to the death of one brother and the survival of the other. What puzzled them, though, was the capitalization of the words "Time" and "One."

"Maybe we should look for a clock," Carson said, wanting to move on with finding the briefcase. She shone her flashlight around the area. "No clock," she said and started to search the rest of the grounds.

"Where are you going?" Tripp, looking suddenly inspired, asked.

"To search for clues," Carson said, flashing her light on the next gravestone. "Or maybe I'll just walk in circles."

"Circles," Tripp repeated pensively. He walked to the center of the graveyard where there stood a tall stone fountain with two cherubs, one above the other, pointing in different directions. He held out his flashlight, turned slowly, and counted. "Carson, I believe you're correct. There is a clock of sorts."

Carson, whose patience had grown thin, joined her brother near the fountain. She watched him turn on one heel a full 360 degrees. "Or maybe it's just a stupid poem meant to make people waste their time," she said.

"Right," said Tripp. "There's no time to waste. Let me give you a boost."

"Boost? To where?"

"The top of this fountain," Tripp said.

"Why?"

"I've a theory I need you to confirm," Tripp said. He cupped his hands and waited for her to put her foot on them so she could begin her climb.

After a brief hesitation, Carson used her brother's support to lift her high enough to grab the first stone cherub. She climbed it to the point where her head was the highest point in the cemetery. "Now what?" she asked.

"Shine your light on the top of each sepulcher and tell me what you see," Tripp said.

At first, Carson simply guided the beam of light across the tops, but after scanning about three gravestones she noticed the obvious pattern.

"What do you see?" asked Daniel.

"Would you believe a clock?" Carson shined her light at the other structures. Each had a Roman numeral engraved on top.

"Where's the one o'clock position?" asked Tripp. "I'm betting that the capitalized word, *One*, from the inscription on Conner's tomb has some reference here."

"There," Carson said, pointing opposite to where Conner's tomb was. "Uncle Conner's tomb is at the seven o'clock position."

"Excellent," said Tripp. He headed to the tomb Carson had identified as one o'clock and began searching around the dark stone structure. At the base of the rear side, he noticed a glint as his light passed over the spot. Looking closer, he found a brass lever. He pulled it toward him. It was difficult to move at first but started to give as he tugged harder. Gurgling, like water traveling through a pipe, could be heard.

"Something just happened," Daniel called out from the other side, still shining his own light on Conner's tomb.

Tripp headed back and stopped to help Carson, who had started her climb down from the fountain. They joined Daniel back at the original gravestone.

"The water valve I just opened must have triggered the mechanism to unlock the tomb door." Tripp shined a light in the new hole that formed when a circular stone panel moved aside. He stuck his hand in the hole and pulled a handle he found. With the sound of metal sliding within the stone walls, the entire bottom half of the tomb was freed and swung on hidden hinges. Tripp opened the concrete door and peered inside.

Carson was squeezed tightly next to him, trying not to miss anything he might find. "Is there a body?" she asked.

"No, but there's something inside." Checking the cramped surroundings, he cautiously leaned in and produced a dark brown leather briefcase. Judging from how Tripp heaved it, it was heavier than it looked. "I believe this is what we're looking for."

"Oh! Oh! Oh!" said Carson, dancing in one spot. She wanted to grab it from her brother but forced herself to wait. "C'mon, let's open it!" she sang.

Carefully setting it down, he examined the case. It was aged but seemed sturdy. The locking mechanism consisted of a series of four dials, numbered zero through nine.

"This should be easy," Daniel said. He produced a stethoscope from the pack he wore across his body. He listened while Tripp carefully went through the numbers, signaling when the correct one was hit. After a moment, they heard the click of the lock as it released.

"Good job, boys," said Carson. She rubbed her hands together in anticipation. Cautiously, Tripp opened the briefcase and they all hovered over its contents.

"What is that thing?" Carson asked.

"Some type of computer?" Tripp said.

"Actually, I think it's some sort of player device. Look, a single disc in that glass window in the base of the case, and the lid contains the monitor screen. Probably a simple old CD or DVD player. Here's the plug," Daniel said, pulling the cord out a corner that had been covered with a flap.

"Great," said Carson. "Where do we plug the damn thing in?"

"We can take it with us," said Daniel.

"No," Tripp said. "We have to glean what we can from looking it over and put it back for Sanchez to retrieve later."

"Forget it," Carson said. "I say we take it with us. That way we have all the time we need to see what's on that player thingy."

"Lest we forget, Detective Sanchez is retrieving this for a reason," said Tripp. "Aside from his being very upset if we were to take it, we might also be obstructing him from using it for whatever good he intends."

"Damn," said Carson, conceding her brother's point. "Then we need to find a plug somewhere so we can power this baby up. Daniel, got anything in that pouch of yours?"

"I don't for this old dinosaur. You should have a standard plug in the back of your Jeep that would work off the vehicle's battery."

"I do. C'mon, let's hook this baby up." Carson was over the gate at once and reached through the bars to accept the briefcase from Tripp. He handed it to her while Daniel climbed over.

Daniel stopped when he realized Tripp wasn't following. "You coming?"

"No," Tripp said, pointing back to the cemetery. "There are a couple of things I need to check." Something seemed to be eating at him.

"Don't be long," Carson said.

Carson and Daniel revved up her vehicle, opened the back hatch, and plugged the device into the available standard socket. Holding their breath, they found the power button and waited. Slowly, the old screen started to light up.

"Ancient technology," said Daniel.

"As long as it works," said Carson with renewed optimism. "Don't forget to record this."

"Right." Daniel pulled out his Smartphone and started the video recorder.

As they watched, the black screen displayed the words

"Dream Stream Proof of Concept
Project: Echo"

After a moment, two men in white coats appeared on the screen. One was tall and thin, the other a bit shorter and stockier. The taller man had a confident manner, while the shorter one smiled pleasantly.

"I am Dr. Erich Dasinger, and this is my assistant, and brother, Dr. Albert Dasinger. We are excited to be working with our partners to bring about this proof of concept. While this wasn't the original intention of our experiments, other benefits seem of interest to certain parties. Let me state that Project Echo represents a smaller piece of a much bigger picture, something we like to call Dream Stream. Along with the exciting transdimensional discovery my brother and I made a few years ago, we are taking a side step, if you will, to explore a security mechanism that was but a small part of the aforementioned larger project . . ."

While he spoke, various images and video clips appeared of what they were referring to. The format looked like that of an amateur documentary, without the CGI enhancements of modern-day efforts.

One frame showed a cavern with strange equipment all around, along with wires and hoses hanging almost haphazardly. While the large computer towers and CRT monitors were witness to a time past, other equipment looked like something from a retro sci-fi movie.

A silent video then showed a platform set within a chamber in a cavern. Several bland-colored objects sat on the platform, including a boxy armchair, a stack of blocks, and other geometric objects. Gradually, a warm glow from an unseen source saturated the area. The light was multicolored but bled into a sea foam-green haze.

Daniel and Carson watched as things became even stranger. The haze moved not just over and around the objects but through them. The simple objects morphed into things more complex and abstract. The chair, for example, went from dull with well-defined edges to something colorful with smoother corners. A male in a gray bodysuit, wearing some type of face shield, entered the frame. He sat in the chair, and soon the bland bodysuit began to take on the chair's colors. As he leaned back, the armchair contorted around him until it no longer looked anything like a chair. Then, as the man suddenly stood up, he just vanished. Afterward, the room returned to reality.

Carson and Daniel exchanged confused glances and kept recording. Footsteps came up behind them, and Carson assumed Tripp had finally decided to catch up.

"You've got to see this, bro. You're missing out," she said.

"Oh, I think I got here just in time," came Sanchez's voice.

They jumped and scrambled to regain their composure.

Daniel turned to face Sanchez but kept his phone camera pointed at the video. "Oh hi, Detective Sanchez."

"You kids really shouldn't be messing with this," Sanchez said sternly.

"It's part of our family history," said Carson.

"No, Carson, it's part of your family's curse," Sanchez said, looking beside himself. He must have been wondering how they even knew of the briefcase, much less found it. "I don't even know what's on that thing."

"Then you need to come watch it with us."

Sanchez stepped closer. "I don't want to know, Carson. People have disappeared for knowing less than what you'll learn from that disc."

Carson moved away a bit from Daniel, so as not to disturb his efforts to record the material. She stood in front of Sanchez. "But we knew nothing and people still came for us. I don't know about you, but since I'm a target, I'd like to know why."

Sanchez looked as if he wanted to argue the point, but maybe he realized she was making sense. "This stuff is going to get me killed," he said as they made room for him.

They watched as images of strange experiments filled the small screen. Then, it switched to a ship being loaded. The name on the bow was *Dream Stream*. One of the scientists, the taller one introduced as Albert Dasinger, shook hands with his brother Erich and walked up the ramp of the ship. Erich stayed behind, waving as the ship left dock. It was obviously staged, a form of low-budget narrative. A map showed the ship's path from Galveston, Texas, to New Orleans, Louisiana, and then to some location south, at sea.

This transitioned to a black screen with white words: "Project Echo." A split screen showed two different rooms. Both had platforms. The right side was empty, while the left showed a volleyball sitting. The left frame filled with that strange glow as before. However, something new happened. With a flash, the ball disappeared and suddenly reappeared in the right side of the screen, a few inches above the floor. It bounced a bit before rolling to one side.

"Whoa," said Daniel, looking at the others. "Tripp is gonna love this stuff."

Carson was unimpressed. "Looks like cheap special effects to me."

"Do you kids really need to record this?" asked Sanchez. "It's probably a bad idea."

"It's for posterity, Mr. Sanchez," Carson said.

After he watched a moment longer, Sanchez seemed to lose interest. He positioned his hands in front of Daniel's camera. "Let's get this thing to Pops and get out of here. It's not safe."

As he said it, footsteps came up from behind them. They turned and saw Tripp emerge from the shadows. But they froze as he entered the light of the streetlamp. His hands were raised in the air. Someone was holding a gun at his back.

"Hands where I can see them," Mark said and shoved Tripp toward the others. "You . . . cop . . . nothing funny or I'll find you a permanent resting spot in a tomb back there," he said, gesturing toward the cemetery.

"This doesn't have to go down like this, man," said Sanchez as he raised his hands slowly.

"You can thank the lil' bitch and her pals for bringing me here." Mark drew closer and a bandage wrapped around his head became visible. "I wouldn't have found you or this place if I hadn't been following this group." He stared straight at Carson. "Miss me, sweetheart?"

"Leave her alone, Mark," Tripp said as he faced the man, hands still in the air. "You've done quite enough today, including injuring the security guard I found on the far side. He'll need medical attention." He turned to the others. "That was one of the things I went back to check for. I couldn't quite grasp why a place that held valuable secrets didn't have someone guarding it. I discovered the unconscious guard a moment before Mark found me."

Mark raised the pistol, seemingly more for effect than to get a better aim. "I'll be sure to finish him off after I'm done with all of you."

Carson felt herself going back into a panic mode. She struggled with it briefly but then resolved not to be petrified again. "You can go straight to hell."

Mark looked surprised that she had found such courage, but his expression soon turned to anger. He started toward her but then noticed the briefcase open in the back of her Jeep. "What's that?"

"We were watching a movie," Daniel said and tried to move in front of it.

"Step aside, Chink," Mark said.

Daniel complied. Carson, to everyone's surprise, including her own, moved into his former spot and stared defiantly at Mark.

He trained his pistol on her, but she didn't flinch. "Crazy bitch."

"Go ahead, Mark. I'm done being afraid of you," she said, trying to sound calmer than she felt. "If you're going to shoot me, just get it over with."

Mark simply laughed. "I'm not going to shoot you, sweet thing. I need you." He casually waved the gun around at the others. "I don't need any of them, though. Maybe you can watch me shoot them, one by one. You know, like I shot down that stupid Derrick."

"I've got a better idea," Carson said as she took a step toward Mark. "How about another concussion?"

Mark snorted. "You wanna take another shot at me, bitch?"

She smirked as she looked beyond the man to a figure in the shadows. "No, but he will."

Mark barely had time to turn his head before the wooden bat caught him solidly. The gun went off right before he hit the ground with a thud. Time slowed down when the pistol discharged. Carson and Sanchez hit the ground. Tripp and Daniel staggered backward. Joe Page stood over Mark for a moment, ready to strike again if he tried to get back up. Joe glanced around to check on the others. "You guys okay?"

Carson and Sanchez checked themselves for bullet holes, while Tripp and Daniel confirmed they were fine.

Joe kicked the crumpled Mark where he lay. The man didn't move. "Who's the bitch now?"

"Uncle Joe!" Carson exclaimed as she jumped up and hugged him. "That was a home run!"

"I guess you changed your mind about coming," Sanchez said as he patted Joe on the shoulder.

"Well"—Joe tried to breathe while Carson squeezed him—"Wanda wouldn't shut up about wanting to follow you. She still thought the briefcase was full of money."

"Greed can be good," Carson said, smiling.

"Well, is it money?" came Wanda's voice from behind Joe. She scurried as fast as her stilettos would allow.

"I told you to stay in the car, Wanda," Joe said.

"Yeah, and I told you where I'd stick that bat if you gave me orders again," Wanda said. "So, where's this briefcase everyone's so eager to find?" She stepped over Mark's body, unconcerned by the fate he had met.

"Over here," said Daniel. "It's an old video player, not money."

Wanda's face dropped. "Shit."

"Actually, it's no longer even that," said Tripp as he handed it to Sanchez. Everyone eyed the dark, shattered screen the bullet had struck. Sanchez cursed as he took it, while Daniel peered around him to inspect it.

"Can you fix it, Daniel?" Tripp asked.

"No. But it's just the screen that was hit. Pops can take the inner media and play it on another device. I doubt it's been damaged."

"Well, I'm taking what's left of it, along with this guy, to Pops," Sanchez said. He cuffed Mark's hands behind his back and checked his vital signs to ensure it wasn't a wasted effort. "Afterward, I'll turn him over to the authorities for the murder of Derrick. Someone help me carry him to my truck."

"I'll help you, Mr. Sanchez," said Tripp, and they both dragged the man across the street. Daniel followed them as he dug into his pouch for something.

Carson had released the grip on her uncle, to his relief. He patted her on the shoulder. "You're one tough gal," he said.

"Thanks," she replied with a confident smile. "I was just tired of being afraid of that prick."

Wanda laughed. "Hell, girlfriend, maybe we'll get along after all." She turned to Joe and smacked her gum. "So is there a reward for this?"

MISS DIRECTION

Sanchez, unable to persuade Carson and Tripp to join him, drove off into the night, taking Mark with him.

Soon afterward, the ambulance arrived. The security guard, a retired police officer, had awakened just before it came and was greeted by a concerned Carson. "Are you an angel sent to take me to heaven?" he said.

As Carson looked on, the man was treated by paramedics, while the police questioned Joe and Tripp. Daniel had gone off by himself to fidget with a phone of Mark's he had gained access to. After the police had taken statements, the group converged again.

Joe warned Tripp he'd better not give Wanda any reward money. Tripp put his wallet away and Wanda turned aggressively toward Joe, mouthing something that would have burned Tripp's sensitive ears.

Carson found Daniel, who sat in a spot lit up by an old streetlamp. "Uncle Joe can sure pick 'em," Carson said and chuckled at the sight of her uncle arguing with his girlfriend. "What are you doing?"

"Going through Mark's cell phones, compliments of his providing me, while he was unconscious, with his fingerprint to open it," Daniel replied with a grin.

"He had two?"

"Yep, the one he left on the boat, which I couldn't get into. The other one's a new replacement, which I was also happy to liberate from his person."

"Good man," Carson said, giving him a hearty pat on his back. "Let's find those breadcrumbs."

"You got it, boss lady."

Tripp approached them, silently watching Daniel work. He placed a hand on Carson's shoulder to get her attention. "We should keep moving."

"Soon," Carson said. "We'll just let Daniel find those breadcrumbs and we'll be off."

"Now would be better," said Tripp sternly. His voice didn't leave much room for negotiation. "Daniel can work on his hacking skills as we travel north."

Carson was impressed with Tripp's sudden attempt to assume a leadership role, but she wasn't ready to hand him the reins just yet. "Where do you suggest we head next?"

"Denton."

She wrinkled her nose. "Why there? Do we know what we're looking for?"

"Not yet," Tripp replied. "But we have a good place to start. Uncle Joe was telling me he has a place across from the old Denton County Courthouse-on-the-Square. It was his mom's apartment before she died. I got the impression he held on to it for sentimental value. Our dad seems to have found a use for it."

"Dad? What does he use it for?" Carson asked.

"Uncle Joe seems to neither know nor care, since Pops is the one who's always paid for it," Tripp replied. "If you want me to continue on this quest of yours, we need to keep moving."

As Tripp headed toward their vehicle, Joe stepped away from the angry Wanda to intercept him. "Where ya going, kid? You guys had enough adventure for one day?"

"I have," said Tripp. He gestured at Carson and Daniel. "But I have a feeling those two wish to continue. I'll concede to the will of the majority."

Carson glanced up at them, pulled herself away from Daniel, and joined her brother and uncle.

"There's safety in numbers," Joe said. "But I suggest we update your dad on what's happened, and then you guys can come stay with me for a bit."

"Good luck with getting ahold of Dad. Why don't you come with us?" Carson asked.

This brought a guffaw from Wanda. "Sure, let's all get our asses shot off so we can learn a little Page family history."

"We've done just fine so far," Carson shot back.

"You've been lucky so far, girlfriend," Wanda said, then turned to Joe. She folded her arms and smacked her gum. "So, you want to bring 'em to your place and make targets of us all?"

"You didn't seem to mind so much when you thought there was money involved."

"At least money's worth sticking your neck out for."

"No, *family* is worth sticking your neck out for," Joe said.

"You don't have one of those," Wanda retorted with a laugh.

Joe threw up his arms in frustration and started to retreat but turned back to her. "You'll never understand the importance of family, Wanda. Though it's no surprise when your father was never around and your mother was a drug addict. Furthermore, sex with you is great, but hardly worth the frustrations that come with it."

While Joe and Wanda had their next standoff, Tripp took the others aside to discuss their next move. Once they came to a decision, he cleared his throat loudly, apparently to get Wanda's attention. "We agree we should all stick together, but taking multiple paths to the same destination may make tracking us harder for our pursuers."

Joe and Wanda seemed confused at what he was suggesting. "Are you saying we should split up or stay together?" Joe finally asked.

"Both, obviously," said Tripp. "We take two different routes and then all meet in Denton. If either group finds they're being tailed, they alert the others and make adjustments as needed."

"We're going to chase this thing either way, Uncle Joe," Carson said. "You might as well join the party."

"Aha!" Daniel said, doing a little victory dance. After a few corny moves, he realized all eyes were upon him and ceased his gyrations. "I went through the numbers on Mark's phone. I've traced one to a landline in Atlanta. After cross-checking that—not easy since the number's unlisted—I think it's some private security outfit."

"Are they the ones trying to kill us?" Carson asked.

"Probably," Daniel said. "There's another number I found more interesting. It appears to be from a payphone near San Antonio."

"Why is that interesting?"

"Because it is near one of the marked points on our map."

"That could be a coincidence," Tripp said. "We should investigate Denton but also consider what might be in San Antonio that's of interest."

"How about a cavern?" Carson said. "The video Daniel and I watched had cavern chambers in it. There are caverns in that part of Texas."

"That's not a bad theory," Tripp admitted.

Wanda and Joe listened to the discussion but looked lost since they hadn't been privy to the details around the map or video. Wanda obviously didn't like what she heard. "You fools keep forgetting that these pricks have guns."

"Relax, Wanda. You weren't even invited," Joe said and was met by her glare.

"There may be something you can do, Wanda," Daniel said. "It wouldn't require you to travel far and involves money."

"Really?" said Wanda with sudden interest. "Continue then."

After some discussion and a bit of debate, the group decided to split into three. Carson and Tripp would head to Denton via a route through Shreveport. Daniel and Joe would take a different route west through Houston, then cut north to Denton. Wanda, much to her chagrin, would serve as a decoy by driving around in Mark's car before ditching it somewhere in New Orleans.

She resisted until Daniel handed her five one-hundred-dollar bills as a down payment for her services. Her acceptance confirmed everyone's opinion that money was the most effective means of negotiating with her.

Daniel wanted to find the server that hosted the information Jack's secret room tapped into. The Denton apartment seemed the logical place to start, but Joe lacked a key to it. Possibly Jack had the only one. They would figure out how to get in later.

If they didn't find anything useful there, they could always journey to San Antonio. Carson suggested they split up and hit both areas at the same time, but Joe insisted they not be split up for too long. Both Tripp and Daniel sided with Joe's wisdom.

Daniel used Mark's key fob to search the dark streets until he spotted the flashing lights of Mark's Ford Mustang. He, along with Tripp and Joe, inspected the car, but it was clean. On their return, Daniel handed Wanda the key and Mark's two phones.

"Don't answer either phone," Daniel said. "Just drive around town, Wanda. Let us know if anyone follows you. If so, ditch the car and get out of there."

"Like hell," Wanda said, grabbing the key from his hand. "I might as well keep that baby."

"Lady, don't let your greed get you killed. You're driving around in Mark's car with his phones. Anyone tracking him will actually be tracking you."

"Please try to buy us some time without putting yourself in harm's way," Tripp said. "It's enough to simply confuse any pursuers."

After hugs and goodbyes, three cars left the dimly lit street in front of the cemetery. Joe's green Camaro headed west on Highway 10, taking them through Houston first. Carson's white Jeep also headed west on Highway 10 but would cut north on Highway 49 once she and Tripp reached Lafayette. Wanda took Mark's car.

Wanda begrudgingly decided to head south until she grew tired or bored, whichever came first. Soon after she began her journey, fatigue set in. She needed something with caffeine to stay awake. She finally decided on a place she could go at that hour and still find a friendly face. She plotted a course to the French Quarter.

She searched her phone's contact list, selected the name "Jake," and waited for an answer. Instead, she received the man's voice mail.

"Jake, it's Wanda. I'm heading your way, assuming you work tonight. I thought you'd enjoy a little company."

Wanda hung up and continued. A casino in the French Quarter was the perfect place to hide out. There were a lot of people around, including cops. She didn't particularly like the police but figured they might come in handy should any unsavory characters show up. Jake worked the graveyard shift, so she wouldn't be bored all night. He might even offer her a place to stay. His gain and Joe's loss, she thought.

As she arrived, she picked the best parking she could find. It was no skin off her teeth, since any parking charges she racked up wouldn't come back on her. The more she stiffed someone, the happier she felt. Bastards deserved what they got.

As she walked toward the tall, brightly lit casino, she was vaguely aware of a vehicle rolling up behind her. Crossing the street, she glanced back. The black SUV stopped and a big man with small eyes, a broad forehead, and no neck, dressed in a black shirt and pants, exited briskly. Wanda picked up her pace.

She continued to glance back. He was gaining ground. Her adrenaline kicked in and she ran for the casino's main entrance. Had she bothered to take her heels off, she might have easily outrun him. She spotted a couple of uniformed officers within a few feet of her destination and ran right up to the closest one.

The black policeman was startled by her approach and turned, clutching his sidearm. His white partner also readied himself. Looking her up and down appreciatively, they eased up.

Out of breath, Wanda simply pointed behind her. The big man had stopped at the valet area. He stood and watched her from a distance, apparently talking into an earpiece.

"That creep's following me," Wanda said between breaths.

The second officer stepped past his partner and looked around, but there was only an old lady being helped to her car by a large gentleman.

"Where?" the officer asked, not convinced.

"You just wanting some attention?" the other asked flirtatiously.

Wanda watched as the man, who had grabbed a random stranger so he could play the Good Samaritan role, taunted her with a wicked grin. Slowly, she turned to the policemen. She smiled sweetly, drew back a left fist, and decked the one closest to her. The other cop brought her down hard on the concrete and arrested her.

REALITY CHECK

Through the rising cigar smoke, Pops stared blankly. The possibility that he'd lost his longtime friend Fumi hadn't yet sunk in. He held the whiskey glass loosely; only a single, partially melted ball of ice remained. Even as a somber feeling washed over him, he still held out hope.

Hours had passed and Shelby sat silently. Each time he looked as if he wanted to say something encouraging, he couldn't get the words out. Finally, he started to speak.

Before he could, however, Pops grumbled, stood up, and walked over to the bar. He felt Shelby watching him as he sat down and signaled the bartender for another drink. The young blonde was still there, far beyond her normal shift--and past closing hours. She knew something bad had happened, so she had kept her bar talk to simple pleasantries.

Pops zoned out and replayed in his head the last time he had seen Fumi alive. He kept searching for some clue that the man was in more danger than he let on. How someone could get the drop on his friend continued to eat at him. Fumi was very careful.

Shelby gracefully slipped into the bar stool next to Pops and raised his glass. "A toast to Fumi. May that flamboyant Oriental be gliding around in satin robes in whatever plane of existence he finds himself."

Pops raised his own glass briefly and they drank. "Someone needs to let Daniel know what happened."

"There will be time for that later. Right now, we need to confirm the worst, find the bastards who did it, and eliminate 'em before they can strike again."

Pops silently agreed. He felt ready to doze off but turned to Shelby. "What do you make of all this?"

Shelby looked as if he was trying to shake off the shock of actually being asked. "Well, sir," he began as he sat the drink on the table and turned to make eye contact, "I really don't think this is about you or Fumi."

"What's that supposed to mean? Who is it about?"

"I'd like nothing more than for him to be alive and well, but we must be prepared for the worst."

Pops didn't like to make assumptions, but he understood Shelby's reasoning. "All right, then. Why was Alan's bastard drawn into this?"

"I'm telling you, Pops, there's more here than you or I know. Let's first think of the right questions before we can speculate on the right answers," Shelby said and took a drink.

"What the hell does that mean, Shelby? I asked for your advice, not for you to spit riddles at me." Pops said it more loudly than he intended.

Shelby gestured to Pops to keep it down but was met with a fiery gaze. He tried to explain himself. "Let me give you an example. They're not trying to kill anyone with the last name Page, at least not yet. Why?"

Pops's was tempted to grumble that he had no idea, but he forced himself to consider the question. "It would have been easier than going after someone like Fumi."

"Exactly."

"So they want something from me. Going after Fumi was meant to clearly demonstrate their reach."

Shelby nodded, took a drag from his cigar, and exhaled a cloud. "Go on."

"I have a feeling Victor's more of a distraction than anything."

"I can't argue with that," Shelby said. "They didn't hesitate to take out a powerful guild member."

Pops considered it. "I can only imagine what they'd want."

"A good question might be this: What connection is there between you and Fumi that requires only you to be alive?"

"Question, questions," Pops said, frustrated. "I need answers."

"We're asking the right questions, Pops. There is, of course, another possibility. One that requires an answer from someone else."

"Who, pray tell, would that be?"

"Jack, of course," Shelby said matter-of-factly.

"Jack? He should be on no one's radar."

"Not everyone's radar works off the same band."

"If you have something to say, just spit it out."

"Where is Jack?"

"Not here," Pops said angrily.

"Right, so what does that tell you?"

Pops took a sip of his drink and decided to not even consider that something bad had happened to him. The thought hadn't crossed his mind before. Jack was hours late. Pops told himself his son was simply distracted with something else. He just wished he had answered his phone. "Jack needs to wear a damn watch."

"He was wearing a smartwatch. Those things tell the time, the weather, and maybe the future."

For the first time, Pops understood something as he glanced over at Shelby: the man knew more than he let on. Not only that, but he loved to play games. He never once questioned where Jack was until that moment.

"Are we going to sit here all night, Pops, or do something useful?" asked Shelby.

Pops nodded. "Okay, let's do something. Have you ever seen the Page family cellar?"

"That structure built into the hill that half of Viridian Square sits on?"

"Aye, that's the one."

"I found my way down there a couple times before Jack had the whole thing renovated. It's secured now with more than a deadbolt. I was never really good with the high-tech stuff."

Pops rose from his seat and stretched. He took several hundred-dollar bills out and dropped them on the table. "Let's go."

Shelby's eyes lit up. "You mean I'm invited to Jack's secret lair?"

"If you can keep up."

Shelby turned to the bartender. "Close out our tab, darlin'." He started after Pops, who was already at the stairs.

DON'T KNOW JACK

Pops led Shelby to Jack's underground abode. The light that glowed from the walls had turned a soft red color.

"This is like the set of an old war movie where the crew's on emergency alert. All it needs is a Klaxon alarm to complete the effect. I like what Jack's done with the place," Shelby said. "Tell me it has a pisser."

"Love, allow access to the bathroom," Pops said. The computer chirped an acknowledgement.

"That's an odd name. Is Jack having a fling with a cyber-wench?"

"Speaking of Jack, make sure he's not back there sleeping."

The panel along the red wall turned blue just before it opened. Shelby seemed impressed with the technology. He started to enter but popped his head back in briefly. "What are you looking for?"

Pops merely grunted as he swept his hands across the desk monitor. The occasional prompt for authentication irritated him. He started a search through the files and folders but saw nothing of interest.

"You don't know, do you?"

Pops grunted again, but then paused his search. "You ever hear of the word 'doppelgänger'?"

"Sure. It's German for orgy, isn't it?"

"Is it even possible for you to be serious?"

"It refers to a ghost that resembles a living human. Why?"

Pops's frustration showed. "Fumi leaves me a single clue and then dies. What the hell am I supposed to do with that?"

"Fumi said something about a ghost?"

"Not exactly," Pops said as he retrieved the piece of paper, walked over, and handed it to Shelby, who was still halfway out of the room.

Shelby glanced at it and noted the numbers on the other side of the paper. After he snapped a picture of both sides with his phone, he handed it back to Pops. "Maybe you should have Jack do some research. He apparently likes that sort of thing."

"No, my son has been acting like a flake. If I don't find anything, I'll have my grandson or Daniel get on it."

"Probably a better idea," Shelby said and then disappeared into the next room.

Pops continued his search but found no references in Jack's archive either. However, something else grabbed his attention. He launched the video and watched it; as he suspected, he had been right about what Jack was up to, though he didn't know his reasons. His next endeavor was to figure out how to get the video to display on the wall monitor before him.

After a few minutes, Shelby returned just as Pops had solved the problem. The wall lit up with a splash screen that displayed an image of the platform in the Gulf—before it was swept away years before.

"Can you play video games on that thing?" Shelby asked as he placed a hand on the surface of the table's screen. He seemed intrigued by the glow that appeared around his finger when he touched it and the trail he left as he swept his hand across its glass.

"I suppose, if you enjoy wasting your time. Stop messing with it. I just got the damn thing to do what I wanted."

"It took ya that long, you old artifact?"

"I have people who do this sort of crap for me," Pops said in his defense.

The presentation started. While Shelby seemed completely in the dark about what he was about to watch, Pops had an inkling. They listened to a voice explain what was being shown on the screen. It wasn't Jack speaking, but an older gentleman who was a very familiar to Pops. Dr. Eriks, he thought.

On October 14, 1991, a gathering of scientists, engineers, and representatives from various military and intelligence agencies of the US government witnessed an experiment with profound implications. The project was known as Echo. Its purpose was to transport an object, a volleyball in this case, from one location underground to another on a floating platform at sea.

The mechanism behind this feat was a complex machine that could breach the fabric of our universe, creating an ephemeral tear in space-time. The government's immediate interest was in one particular aspect of the experiment called the Trapdoor, originally intended as a fail-safe. It had already been tested successfully, albeit on a much smaller scale.

The two scientists involved, the Dasinger brothers, held differing opinions regarding the scope of the test. While Dr. Albert Dasinger believed he could achieve the results sought by the US government, his brother, Dr. Erich Dasinger, preferred more testing. The former's opinion won out and Project Echo was given the green light, although weather conditions were not ideal—

Pops abruptly stopped the video when Shelby asked a question. "What?"

"I asked if Sanchez has checked in again?"

"No, but he will any moment, I imagine. What the hell has that got to do with what we're watching on the screen?"

"Not a darn thing. I guess my mind wanders."

"Try and stay focused."

"Okay, let's discuss some related material. Why am I living through this nightmare all over again? Why would Jack make a presentation about it? Is he hoping to sell the movie rights?"

"You know as much as I do."

"That says a lot of nothing, except maybe neither of us really knows Jack." Shelby looked pleased with his play on words.

"Can we continue?" Pops asked. He resumed the video when Shelby motioned for him to continue. Seconds later, he paused it again to take a call.

Shelby went back to playing with the desk monitor's light effects. He accidentally turned off the presentation and fumbled to get it back on the main screen again.

Pops tried to ignore Shelby's antics and focus on the call from Sanchez. "Whatcha got for me, Rick?"

"Pops, I've got the briefcase and a prisoner. This was anything but a midnight run," said Sanchez.

"A prisoner? Who? What happened?"

"Some thug named Mark had followed your grandkids to Lazarus. Please don't ask how they got on the trail and beat me there. Shortly after I arrived, this dude emerges from the shadows with a gun and starts making threats. Your youngest boy, Joe, shows up out of nowhere and clubs the bastard pretty good."

"Is everyone okay?"

"Yep, even ol' Mark is still breathing—though, I wouldn't attest to what condition his brain is in. Joe tagged him pretty good. That was on top of the head wound that he received from Carson earlier. This was the same guy who had tried to grab the kids in the bay. Talk about persistence."

"Glad he's the only one with a headache," Pops said with relief. "Let me know the minute you're within sight of Viridian Square."

"You got it, Pops."

Pops hung up and started to relay the conversation to Shelby.

"Mark? I know that scumbag," said Shelby. "He and his barbecued buddy, Matt, were working together. So ol' Sanchez rode to the rescue?"

"Not exactly. While he did show up, it was my other son, Joe, who saved the day," Pops replied.

"The little bastard ya had with what's-her-name? How'd he get involved?"

Pops ignored the bastard comment. "Her name was Alejandra. As for how Joe got suckered into this, that's beyond me. My grandchildren seem to have recruited him for their quest."

"The more the merrier, I suppose."

"Did you miss the part where I said my grandkids found their way to Lazarus and were followed?"

"It's odd they'd go there, particularly at night. I'm hoping ol' Mark is dead this time."

"He's not, but Sanchez has him. You know what else he has? The briefcase he was sent to retrieve."

"The briefcase you kept around as insurance? Sounds like all good news to me."

"Except that Carson and Tripp found it first."

Shelby seemed confused. "Wait—at Lazarus? I thought Jitters, that crazy old fart, had the briefcase. By the way, bad idea trusting a drug-crazed zombie with it."

"Apparently, Jack felt the same way and had Joe move it to the crypts."

"So glad the left hand knows what the right hand is doing. So Sanchez has both a prisoner and the briefcase. What else could Jack's kiddos possibly get into?"

"With what you know about this family, do you really have to ask that question?"

"That's a good point. As impressed as I am, though, they've just scratched the surface. Maybe it's time to give 'em what they want. We could certainly use all the help we can get."

The idea had occurred to Pops, though he was still resistant. "One step at a time. Let's finish up here, find Jack, and then go after them."

"Sounds fun. Well, at least more fun that watching this crappy documentary."

Without hesitating, Pops started the video again before Shelby could find something else to talk about.

SEVERED RELATIONS

The dusty brown Chevy pickup made its way east on Interstate 10. Sanchez had just gotten off the phone as he entered Biloxi, Mississippi. After briefing Pops on what had transpired, he called his wife to assure her he'd be home soon and reminded her to have a big hug and kiss for him. Mrs. Sanchez had informed him she would likely be sound asleep, but his cold dinner would be sitting in the microwave. He didn't have the heart to tell her he had grabbed a burger, as he couldn't wait any longer to eat something. He promised not to stop at the casinos, as he often did when he passed through that area.

Shortly after entering Biloxi, Sanchez noticed the headlights behind him. That in itself wasn't noteworthy. However, something else about the vehicle bothered him. If he sped up, the dark SUV behind him did too. If he slowed down, it matched his speed. Sanchez performed one last test to confirm he was being followed.

As he approached an exit leading to several casinos, he moved to the left lane and passed a red minivan. He waited. Like clockwork, the SUV also changed lanes. The exit was just ahead of him. He decided to time his next move.

As Sanchez was right on top of the next exit, he turned the wheel hard right and crossed to the other lane, barely catching it. He slowed down as he entered the off-ramp to avoid overshooting the sharp turn. The driver of the SUV couldn't react fast enough and missed the exit. They immediately pulled off onto the shoulder and backed up. He noted it was black and its windows were tinted to conceal its occupants.

Sanchez hit the gas and headed for the back roads along the coast. His old truck couldn't outrun the other vehicle, but he'd be damned before he let anyone outmaneuver him. He was a betting man, and the odds were in his favor that he knew the back roads better than his pursuers. Several large casinos were found along the coastal area and he'd been to all of them over the years. Only the locals would be more familiar with the region.

After he had changed course and followed the twisting and winding roads for a while, he noticed he was no longer being followed. He made his way along the back streets of the Mississippi coast until he hit Highway 90, then followed it east for a short while. The road closely paralleled the interstate he'd been following; it was just farther south. Sanchez began to feel paranoid about being on a major road, however, so he headed farther south until he was on the parallel route closest to the shoreline. He called and left a voice mail for Pops to give him an update.

From behind him, he heard Mark stir. The man moaned for a bit before he sat up and realized he was someone's captive. Sanchez glanced back at the mirror to see Mark's bloodied head.

"Good morning," Sanchez said.

"Where the hell am I?"

"In the backseat of my pickup," Sanchez said. "Just sit back and be a good boy so I don't have to sedate you again."

"Sedate? You knocked me out, you bastard." Mark, his arms behind him and handcuffed, leaned forward and used his knee to stop the blood from trickling down the side of his face. A jolt of pain shot through him as he touched the spot where Joe's bat had struck.

"I can't take credit for the bump on your head. That was someone else's work. Serves you right, though. You were threatening to shoot us. After two attempts, you're lucky to be breathing, bud."

"I need something for the pain."

"When we get back to civilization," Sanchez said. "Thanks to your buddies, we're taking the longer route."

"Buddies? What happened?" Mark asked, nervously looking out the back windows on either side of him.

"Don't act so surprised, dude. Your friends caught up to us. I had to give them the slip."

Mark laughed, but it wasn't the funny kind. "They're not my friends, cop. I can only hope you lost them."

Sanchez glanced at him again in the mirror. "We seem to have lost them so far."

"Just wait. They'll find us."

"You seem so sure," Sanchez said curiously. "Your employer hasn't exactly sent the brightest bulbs our way."

"The people who will be following us don't work for my employer. I was told that if I missed my target again, I'd be marked myself—no pun on my name intended."

Sanchez smiled at this, then decided it was wise to press on with his questions. "Well, if they're not working for your boss, who are they?"

"Who knows?" said Mark. "My team lead told me some black ops types were coming on board. You know, the type of guys who help topple governments. It would be wise to avoid them."

"They sound spooky," Sanchez said, trying not to convey how concerned he really was.

"They are," Mark said. "That's why I took a chance to grab the girl again. I figured if I got her, I had some insurance to get the hell out of this mess."

Sanchez determined he sounded sincere. He had his phone ready to call Pops again, but he wanted to see if he could get anything else out of Mark first. The man angered him with his talk about taking Carson. He'd known her most of her life. She was almost like one of his own kids. "Glad you didn't get her. She's a good kid. But you wouldn't know about that, would you?"

"Oh, I used to be the good soldier boy once. I learned you don't get anywhere being the nice guy. I wanted to get out of this shithole job but needed one good score to do so. This was my chance." Mark's voice trailed off, as if some sad reality had set in.

"Well, people aren't objects you can use for your own benefit. They have lives and dreams too."

"Shit, dude, you sound like my old man. I don't need the lecture."

"Maybe you should've listened to your father, son. It might have made a difference."

"Yeah, sure."

"Tell me again why you're so sure these spooky fellas are going to find us. They have access to some government satellites or something?" Sanchez cocked his head to look out and up, thinking he might actually catch a drone circling.

"Well, my car and phone could be tracked by GPS. I guess I must've come off as a real screwup because the guy who picked me up even made me wear this tracker around my ankle too."

"Shit," Sanchez said as he realized what Mark was saying. He figured on the car and phone, but he didn't think to check for any other devices on the man. He fumbled for his phone and began madly pressing buttons.

From the corner of his eye, Sanchez saw the headlights to his left. It was too late to do anything but brace for the impact. As they passed a cross street, the SUV struck the driver's side door and sent the truck spinning off the road. It finally came to a stop in a sandy area less than a hundred yards from the water. It was well planned—no houses or other structures to get in the way.

Sanchez's head lay on his steering wheel, bleeding. He was barely conscious as men surrounded his pickup. They came in from the back passenger side, since the driver's side was smashed in. In a swift, businesslike way, they yanked Mark from the back of the cab and moved him to the front of the truck. They tossed him on the hood, and he was too injured to even beg for his life. He merely repeated, "I don't know," to whatever they asked.

There were four of them, all dressed in black. One of the men, the leader, walked up to the driver's side window. He brushed some shattered glass aside and poked Sanchez with the silencer attached to his pistol. "Wakey, wakey, mate," he said, his accent clearly Australian.

Sanchez flinched and tried to raise himself up. It took a moment for the ringing in his ears to abate. He reached up and wiped the blood that was flowing over his left eye. He could make out the face of a man—a square jaw, and intent eyes meeting his. The man said something else, but Sanchez had to fight to return to reality. "What?" he asked, still groggy.

"Your name's Rick Sanchez, mate." The man pointed to the name plate above his badge. "It says it right there."

"My friends call me Rick. Sanchez will do. You are?"

"Everyone just calls me Ryder. You're in possession of something we need, mate."

Sanchez brought up a blood-covered hand and waved it toward Mark, who was being questioned in the headlights. "He's all yours, man."

Ryder stopped just short of laughing as he slapped the door. "Nah, that's not what we came for. Sure, we'll settle unfinished business with ol' Mark. No, we took your briefcase. I bet you're glad you had it and not those kids. Tragic when the young get involved in this business."

Sanchez tried to focus on the man. "Yeah, lucky me. I'll let you settle your business and be on my way."

Ryder seemed amused, but his manner soon turned sober. "Truth is, I've got another purpose for you. First, tell me what you know about the whereabouts of the Page clan."

"You'd be wise to avoid them. They're good folk, but I doubt they'd like you much."

"Fair enough, mate. Just tell me where Jack Page is."

"I don't know."

"And if ya did?"

"I'd still tell you I didn't know."

Ryder laughed and shook his head. He glanced at the front of the truck, where Mark was pleading for his life. One of his associates, done with his questioning, raised a silenced pistol and pulled the trigger.

Sanchez saw the blood from Mark's head splatter across the truck's hood. He glimpsed the dead man's eyes as his body slid off and hit the ground. Mark's executioner gazed at Sanchez, leaving little doubt there would be more than one casualty that night.

"I have a family."

"We all have family, mate. It's a brutal business."

Sanchez's thoughts turned to his wife. His grown children would be fine, but he wondered how she would fare without him. He always knew such a day might come. He could accept his fate but felt terrible for the missus. "I'm going to miss them."

"I'm sure the feeling is mutual," Ryder said and gripped his pistol tighter. "One more question before we part ways. I hear you were once mates with Conner Page. What was is like knowing a bloke like that?"

The question surprised Sanchez, who laughed out loud. When he finished, he stared straight into the night. He could hear the ocean surf in the distance; it had always been music to his ears. "You've heard of Conner?"

Ryder looked a little impatient, as if time was short. "Didn't know him personally, but there were stories. For what little time he had, his training was put to good use. We had a common mentor, he and I."

Sanchez was curious what sort of a man had been sent after his friends. He apparently knew about the secret world from which they came. "He died in a car accident."

Ryder grinned. "A cover story to avoid too many questions, but you knew that already." He patted Sanchez on his mangled shoulder. "I hear he got good odds before the government assassins caught up. I'm glad all I have to worry about is an old man and a preacher nowadays."

"You should worry," Sanchez said as he strayed closer to unconsciousness.

Ryder caught one of his men pointing to his watch, a reminder it was time to go. "You referring to the old bloke, Pops? He was good in his day, but he's ready to be put out to pasture. His hired hands are no more of a threat than Victor's toy soldiers. Those two can kill each other for all I care. This time next week, I'll be on a beach somewhere back home."

Sanchez took a deep breath, as if it were his last. He could taste salt, unsure if it was the sea air or the blood in his mouth. "Around here, we take care of our own. You have a best friend, Ryder?"

"Archer, the one who just relieved ol' Mark of his worries, is about as close to a cobber as I care to have." As he said it, a glow appeared from Sanchez's half-buttoned shirt. "Someone's calling, mate."

Ryder reached into his shirt and retrieved the phone that had somehow found its way there during the crash. "Give me your hand."

As Sanchez complied, Ryder wiped the blood off of it and used his thumbprint to unlock the phone. He went through the phone quickly, looking for anything useful. He noted the missed call was from Jack Page and wondered if the man was close by. That would be the real prize, he thought. He typed a message on the phone, but there was one last thing to do before he hit send.

Sanchez had closed his eyes and seemed to have drifted to some magical place. He hummed an unfamiliar tune.

Must be a religious song, Ryder thought. "Need a moment to make good with your maker?"

"Did that long ago," Sanchez murmured.

"Then give my regards to Conner when you see 'im, mate."

Just before Ryder pulled the trigger, he could have sworn he heard, "Tell 'im yourself."

He snapped a picture of Sanchez's lifeless body and, along with the text he had written, sent it. He tossed the phone into the cab of the truck and motioned to his men.

As he walked up to the newly arrived SUV, his associates finished torching the one they had crashed. They approached the pickup that held Sanchez's body to do the same.

"Get anything?" one asked.

It took Ryder a moment to say anything. "That was the most relaxed bloke I've ever killed," he finally said.

The other man snickered, but Ryder didn't share in the humor. He tried to shake off the feeling that something wasn't quite right. A chill ran down him as he watched the flames dance and the thick smoke rise high into the night sky.

GAME CHANGER

The video presentation wasn't as boring as Shelby had thought. Not only had he managed to stay awake, but he also had feedback and questions for Pops afterward. While the feedback included the suggestion that popcorn would have made it a better feature, the questions indicated a man who appreciated good research.

"I'm impressed," Shelby said afterward. "I'm also a bit disappointed there was only a single frame with me in it."

"I'm sure Jack will include more in the deleted scenes for the Blu-ray edition," Pops said sarcastically.

"I do have to wonder about something, though. Jack rescued that mad scientist and you hid him away? All those people died, including your son, and you saved one of the bastards responsible for it all."

"It wasn't his fault that certain parties sent in saboteurs."

"Of course not. He and his brother just built something that made Oppenheimer's project look like a science fair exhibit."

"My son initially vouched for Dr. Eriks when he brought him to me. I've found him to be a good man."

"Dr. Eriks? Is that what Erich Dasinger calls himself nowadays? You know, I met his brother briefly—before he got sucked into another dimension. That old fart has to be about a hundred years old now."

"He's a few years older than I am."

Shelby stretched his arms and yawned. "Like I said, Pops, he's ancient. Hey, why do you think Jack made that documentary? I doubt anyone's going to let him run it on the History Channel."

"I wish I could tell you what goes through my son's mind."

"He seems to be a man of many thoughts but few words."

Their thoughts were interrupted by a perimeter alarm. Both Pops and Shelby looked at the main monitor, which showed Jack heading toward the entrance.

"Speak of the devil," Shelby said.

Pops noted the look on Jack's face as he approached the door. "Something's wrong."

Jack entered the room and stopped just past the doorway. He had the lost look of a man who had seen death. Pops was sure he himself must have looked the same when he heard about Fumi.

Shelby walked past Pops and closed the space between himself and Jack. "Who is it this time?"

Jack struggled to find the words. "They got to Sanchez."

"Oh hell," Shelby said, taking his hat off and throwing it across the room. He kicked one of the walls. The thick glass managed to absorb the blow without cracking.

As Pops walked over to the other two, he saw the phone in Jack's hand. He retrieved it and grimaced at the picture of Sanchez, slumped in the cab of his truck. The bloody hole in his temple left no doubt he'd been murdered. He read the accompanying message aloud. "G'day, Jack. Tell Pops we need to catch up. Cheers."

Pops tossed the phone back to Jack in disgust. "I can think of a couple of Aussies who might have done this, but one of them's been dead for years. I don't remember the other's name, but the other guy did some contract work for the guild."

"One of yours?" Shelby asked.

"No, one of Stella's last projects."

"Just great—one of the witch's flying monkeys. You still wonder how involved the guild is?"

"The evidence is mounting," Pops admitted. "Whoever they are, they also have the briefcase."

Jack's eyes narrowed. Was he thinking about his children and where they were going next? He walked over to the computer table and displayed a map on the main screen. Two places were marked. "The device in the briefcase will purge most of its data after being played once. The new owners will find a few files on it, should they look hard enough. One is this map that shows the locations of both Echo and Source. However, if they do have connections in the guild, they already know what's there." He brought up a satellite image and zoomed into what appeared to be dirt and trees.

"The cavern?" Shelby asked.

"The cavern."

"What are they going to find there, son?" asked Pops.

"Possibly my children, if we don't warn them."

"I'll get on that," Pops said. "What else is there?"

Jack looked torn, as if fighting some internal battle. The tears welled in his eyes. He looked away and walked to the nearest door before he stopped. There was an eeriness to his silence.

"Son?"

Jack turned and stared blankly for a second; then his mouth formed just one word. "Regret," he whispered. He retreated through the open doorway to the back.

Shelby and Pops exchanged confused glances.

"Son, what's in that cave?" Pops called after him.

"Did he mean *we* would regret what they'd find, or are *they* going to regret it?" Shelby asked.

Pops merely shook his head and grumbled to himself.

Shelby retrieved his hat. He used the reflective walls as a mirror to ensure it was on straight. "I think we need a new plan, Pops. Jack seems to be checking out." Shelby didn't wait for a response as he too disappeared through the open panel.

Pops stood for a while in silence. With Sanchez murdered, the game had changed. He cursed softly and pondered his next move when a thought struck him: Not only was he asking the wrong questions, but he was also asking the wrong people.

"You have any C4 in there?" Pops yelled into the next room. Within seconds, a case full of what appeared to be taffy came sliding out. As Pops examined it, he confirmed it was only meant to look like candy. "C4—oh yeah, this will do."

"Don't eat it, Pops," Shelby called from the next room.

Pops made his way into Jack's workout room. He saw nothing of interest so he proceeded to the walk-in closet where he found Shelby going through various outfits.

"Can you believe Jack has a dress in here?" Shelby said as he held it up.

"Unlike you, I doubt he actually wears it," Pops said with a sneer.

"Don't be so sure," Shelby said with wink. He went back to going through the collection.

"Where's Jack?"

Shelby's head popped up long enough to say he didn't know, and then he went back to checking out the Kevlar vests. As Pops left, he could hear the man mutter something about getting a hard-on.

Pops passed the bathroom but stopped and circled back. He walked inside the dimly lit room and found his son sitting on the bench built into the shower stall. Jack had his head down in his hands, but raised himself up as he heard him enter.

"Permission to sit?" Pops asked.

"Granted," Jack said and let out a frustrated sigh. "This is all my fault."

Pops grunted as his old rump found a resting spot on the seat. "I know." Surprising himself, he put an arm around his son's neck. "It's your fault Sanchez loved you so much, he was willing to take part in something he knew might end like this. It's your fault I'm here, sitting in a shower stall in Viridian Cove knowing that, at any time, someone might come looking for my ass. It's also your fault your children turned out to be stubborn and reckless like their old man." He paused and watched a teardrop travel down the bridge of Jack's nose and drip onto the tiled floor.

"You have to take some of the blame for your grandkids, Pops," Jack said and wiped his eyes with his shirt. "They have your DNA and loved the adventures you took them on."

"Okay, we'll share that one." Pops smiled. "Let me tell you what isn't your fault, though. You had no control over who your parents were nor the organization they were a part of. You certainly didn't force your brother to make the decisions he made."

"This helps how?"

Pops chuckled. "I was never good at this type of speech. Go join your wife, son. Let ol' Shelby and me take care of this."

"I need him to find the twins. These people are dangerous. Once all my family is safe, I'll have the luxury of looking for answers."

"Why does it all have to be your burden?"

Jack paused before answering, as if unsure how Pops would take what he was going to say. Then he just spit it out. "I haven't been very forthcoming. The good doctor and I have been working in secret on a project at Source. I was late because I had to gather a piece that was needed."

Pops patted him on the shoulder and then stood up. He had recognized Dr. Eriks' voice. "We saw your documentary. To be honest, I knew the old man was up to something. I had both his offices bugged but figured I'd already missed the good stuff. As for the cavern, let's leave that nightmare in the past where it belongs."

"It may become our problem again," Jack said. "Somebody's been disturbing the skies around Echo."

Pops thought it curious but brushed it off. "Anything else?"

Jack looked frustrated, as if he thought Pops had failed to understand the magnitude of what he was saying. "Someone with very intimate knowledge of this family is involved in this. I believe that person is my mother."

Pops didn't flinch. "Of course she's involved."

"Do you know to what extent?"

"We both do, but I'm not wearing blinders like you are. Look, years ago, around the time she was expelled from her last assignment, she resorted to trying to brainwash you and your brother. Our separation from her was ugly, as you probably remember."

"She did leave some scars," Jack said. "Look, I know Mother has her demons and carries a grudge, but I find it hard to believe she'd put her family at risk."

"She's merely a shell of the woman she once was. Your mother was never the most stable person in the world, but the years haven't been kind to her mind."

"Do you think she knows?"

Pops understood that Jack referred to the fate of Conner. He considered it before he responded. "She has always suspected. In her world reality and fiction collide, so it probably doesn't really matter what she thinks anymore. Who would listen to her?"

Jack seemed skeptical. "I should still dig further into it, Pops. There's something I need from her anyway."

"Perhaps when things settle down, you can travel down that road. For now, I fully expect to see you and Kate on the deck of the *Abril* when I return to her. Speaking of ships, I've recently acquired a vessel unlike anything in my collection. I'll give you a tour when we rendezvous with her."

Jack nodded. "Okay, Pops, but I need to synch with Kate about an item or two. I'll also need to visit Maria. Rick's loss will be devastating to her."

"Of course," Pops said, relieved. "I'll let Captain Ed know to provide you with whatever you need."

"I'll be sure to take advantage of that."

Pops's bones crackled as he rose and stretched. "Now if you'll excuse me, I have a date with an old acquaintance."

SQUARE ROUTE

The sun was still high in the Shreveport, Louisiana, sky, sending rays through the window. As it started its slow descent, the light pierced the half glass of water sitting beside Carson and rippling light danced across her face.

Carson had awakened with the pounding head of a hangover, and nature's strobe light wasn't helping. She hadn't planned on drinking so much the night before; nor had she wanted to sleep until mid-afternoon on a Sunday. She sat up suddenly, grabbed the water, and downed a couple of aspirins her brother had been gracious enough to fetch from the casino gift shop.

Tripp had just gone out to grab some late lunch. Before he left, he had recapped last night's events. He had only allowed himself a couple of light beers and had made it his duty to ensure his inebriated sister got to her bed safely, as well as alone. He had to sternly warn one anxious and drunken fellow from following them up to the room.

As Carson was lying back down on the bed, a knock came at the door. She cautiously got up and peered through the peephole to discover Tripp standing there. She wondered why he didn't let himself in. The reason became clear when she opened the door and saw his hands full of food and beverages.

"What did you get us?" she asked, her stomach growling as if on cue.

"Cheeseburgers and, for your hangover, an electrolyte-enriched sports drink," he said as he handed her the simple meal.

A scowl formed on her face. "Cheeseburgers again?"

He had just walked by her and stopped to turn. "Well, if you hadn't spent so much at the card tables last night, I might have sprung for a steak. I also had to pay for another night, since your recovery time exceeded the eleven o'clock checkout time."

"That's what ATMs are for, bro. Are we staying another night?"

"No, we're not. As for ATM usage, that's for people who don't care to keep a low profile."

Carson curled her lip at her brother's patronizing tone but ultimately understood he was upset by her earlier behavior. Being a drunk, loud attention whore was her trademark. She hung her head low as she started into the burger. "What time are we heading to Denton?" she asked between bites.

"As soon as I'm reasonably certain you can hold down your food," he answered, then took a bite from his own cheeseburger.

Carson looked around as if something were missing. "No fries?" The glare he shot back made her return to her burger. "Just asking. Did you hear from Uncle Joe or Daniel?"

"Yes, I received a text from Daniel. They were tired out after hitting Houston, so they stopped off at a place near Galveston Bay and got some rest. They were going to hit the road again after lunch."

"If they've already started out, it'll be a close race to see who gets to Denton first."

Tripp hesitated and looked uneasy. "With recent developments, they may be delayed."

"What's wrong?"

"Pops called Daniel last night. It seems his uncle Fumi has died suddenly."

"Suddenly?" Carson gasped and put down her sandwich. "As in he was killed in an accident? Or murdered?"

"The jury is still out, but from the way he spoke, foul play is a possibility."

"Oh shit," Carson said. "Is Daniel okay?"

"Physically, he's fine."

"I know he's okay *physically*, dumbass. I was referring to his emotional state. Does he want to forget about this whole thing and go to a funeral or something?"

"I can only speculate, but he gave no indication of not seeing this through."

"Good man," said Carson proudly. "I'll make swashbucklers out of you two yet. Well, you still need some work."

"I look to your wisdom," Tripp said sarcastically. "Daniel also mentioned he's awaiting another update from Pops. I'm unclear about its nature, but we can call on the road to find out."

"More bad news?" Carson asked.

"We shall see," Tripp said softly, as if unsure. "Oh, Pops sent a number for any of us to call should we decide to give up on our adventure or find ourselves in a difficult situation."

"I can tell you which one of those won't happen," Carson said as she entered the number into her cracked phone. "These don't look like his normal digits."

"They're not. If I understood correctly, we'd reach some type of assistant of Pops's who would engage whatever resources we need."

"No shit," Carson said. "You mean like our own lifeline? What if I need to ditch my Jeep and get . . . what does James Bond drive?"

"Aston Martin," Tripp answered. "Don't even think about abusing the hospitality."

"Hospitality is what you do for strangers. We're family." As Tripp started to protest, she added, "We'll be discreet, of course."

"Of course," Tripp repeated, looking unconvinced. "Finish your food and get dressed. It would be nice to be to our destination by nightfall."

After finishing their "lupper," a word Carson used to describe a meal that fell somewhere between lunch and supper, they hit the road again, Tripp driving this time. Heading west on I-20 took them most of the way to Dallas, where they turned north onto I-35.

Tripp had looked up the address of their destination, an apartment located in the old downtown area and known by the locals as Denton Square. It was already plotted into Carson's navigation.

"I think I've passed through there on the way to one of my storm chases in Oklahoma," Carson said.

They continued on their journey northward, passing through North Dallas, Coppell, Lewisville, and finally to Denton. Carson tried to call Daniel a couple of times along the way but received his voice mail. Tripp tried to entertain her with trivia about the places they would be passing, but she opted to take a nap.

In Denton, they navigated to a local motel Tripp had found while searching online. They checked in and stood briefly by the door of the small room. It wasn't much, but it was close to their destination. Carson wanted to go straight over to the apartment and check it out, but Tripp nixed the idea. "It would be better to go during the day when we can blend in with the locals," he said.

He looked surprised when she didn't argue but instead embraced him. "I'm so proud of you," she said.

He stood there awkwardly for a moment, as if wondering what he had done to deserve it, but then accepted the hug.

"No, really," Carson said, unsure whether he understood. "You've embraced your adventurous spirit and taken on a leadership role."

Tripp returned the hug. "I'm proud of you too, sis."

"Me? Why?"

"Well, you haven't gotten us killed yet," Tripp said with a smile.

Carson scowled. He had ruined the moment. "Really?"

"Okay, you're also learning to be a team player."

"Aw," she said and hugged him again. "Let's go find a place to grab a drink."

"Really? You've recovered from last night that fast?"

"That was hours ago." She waved it off as if it were nothing. "Let's go."

They left together and Tripp drove. Carson fidgeted with the radio, and not satisfied with the song selections, switched it off. She gazed out the window. "I wonder how far out the others are?"

Tripp had stopped listening to her. Something had caught his attention. He had a reputation for not noticing things, but that was because he usually wasn't looking. But she noticed he had been doing a lot of paying attention lately, putting some of that PI training to use.

She glanced back to see what was bothering her brother. She spotted a dark sedan just as its lights went out.

"Are we sure they're following us?" she asked and immediately dreaded the answer.

"One way to find out," Tripp said, pushing the gas to accelerate. The headlights reappeared as the sedan pursued them.

"Shit. Now what?"

"We lose them," Tripp said.

"How did they find us? We were very careful."

"I have a theory about that," Tripp said as he made a sharp turn. "I should have thought of it before."

"What?"

He shook his head. "I believe they're tracking us, probably with a small GPS device somewhere on your Jeep," he said, taking another corner faster than he should have. He barely missed the minivan coming from the other direction.

"Let's ditch it and find another ride," Carson said, holding on for dear life.

"Agreed. But we'll need to lose these people first."

He drove until they reached an intersection. Off to their right was a parking lot with two police cars beside one another, facing opposite ways. Tripp pulled up beside one of the cars. He watched as the dark sedan slowed down, then took off into the night.

"They'll be back," he said.

The officer in the squad car next to him rolled down his passenger side window. "Can I help you?"

"Uh, we're just lost, Officer," Tripp said. "Can you tell me where old Denton Square is?"

The officer gave them directions and went back to talking to the policeman in the other car. After thinking something over, Tripp drove off. "It won't be easy for the driver of the sedan to predict where we're going or to catch up," he said.

He started toward Denton Square but turned off on a street several blocks from it. He pulled into a back alley behind an old building, just past some railroad tracks. Jumping out, he checked the vehicle, found the device, and ran off around the corner. Carson got out and looked around nervously. After a couple of minutes, Tripp came trotting back.

"Where'd you go?" Carson asked.

"I pulled a Carson." He tried to catch his breath while she stared blankly. He explained that he had found another vehicle to plant the GPS device onto, as she had done the night before with their watches. It was moving in the opposite direction they needed to go.

"Great. What are we waiting for?" She started toward her Jeep.

"By foot," Tripp said as he grabbed her arm and reeled her back in.

"Why? You got rid of the GPS device."

"Right, but they still know your vehicle. We need to leave it hidden here. We can take the slow route now and find another mode of transportation later."

"Where are we going?"

"Oh, I changed my mind. It makes sense to do this Denton Square adventure tonight. We may not get a chance tomorrow."

"Now you're talking. Let me get some things."

After Carson grabbed her gear, both kept off the main roads as they made their way toward Denton Square. When they arrived, people were still walking around, although not as many as Tripp would have liked. He could only hope the people following them were distracted long enough for them to finish what they needed to do—whatever that was.

They found the right apartment, a loft sitting above a music store, and walked up the two dozen or so steps that went straight to the door. Tripp examined the lock and was hardly surprised when the key his uncle had given him didn't work. With his lock pick set in hand, he went to work on the deadbolt.

Carson kept glancing down the long staircase to ensure nobody was coming. A sidewalk was visible through the glass door at the bottom of the steps below. Occasionally, a pair of feet would pass by.

"This place is fairly active for a late Sunday," she said. "Too bad it's not Saturday. I bet we'd have a crowd to blend into."

"I hear this area is known for its music culture," Tripp said as he continued working on the lock.

"That's some trivia I don't mind hearing. Some music and a cold beer would be nice right about now. You got that lock yet, bro?" As she said it, the deadbolt clicked and the door opened. "Oh, good." Carson turned around and stopped in surprise.

"Can I help you?" asked the young man curtly from behind the door. He pushed the glasses up his broad nose and glared at Tripp with magnified eyes.

Tripp froze in his hunched-over position. Glancing up and feeling terribly awkward, he read the word "Dentonite" on the man's stained white T-shirt. "Sorry, we were told we could find something of our father's here." It was all he could think to say.

The man eyed him suspiciously. "There's nothing here for you. You should go." He started to close the door.

"Wait," said Carson before the door completely shut. "Our dad is Jack Page. I believe our uncle Joe actually owns this place."

The man didn't seem to hear what Carson had said as he stared at her for the first time. He seemed suddenly enchanted with her and hesitant. Unconsciously, he started combing his unkempt hair with his hand while scanning every part of her body. "Who are you?" he asked. It was as if Tripp wasn't even there.

"I'm Carson Page," she said and extended a hand.

The man, his eyes glued on her, shook it. Gradually, he snapped out of his daze. "Page, huh? I guess you can come in, for a moment anyway."

Carson walked past Tripp and winked. She swayed her hips as she walked past their host, whose eyes were on autopilot as they traced her steps. Feeling he might as well be invisible, Tripp shook his head and followed her inside.

The loft was much longer than it was wide. Carson continued her swaying down the hall and entered a living room. She was met by Daniel and Joe, who sat on the sofa and cheered.

"What did I tell you, Daniel? Carson worked an angle to get in."

Daniel laughed. "Wow, Carson, you really put on the moves."

She looked embarrassed at first but shook it off as if it were nothing. "When did you guys get here?"

"Before you," Daniel said, laughing.

"I see you've met Putter," said Joe, who introduced him to Carson and Tripp.

"I call myself that because I like to putter around with everything from cars to computers."

"That's nice." Carson glanced at him and turned back to the others. There was no longer any need to act interested in the man.

"Putter is the administrator of your dad's server room," Joe said.

Tripp and Daniel exchanged glances; both knew where Daniel would be later. Putter stood around for another moment, then found a reason to excuse himself for the night.

After he left, the others crowded together on the sofa. Carson told of how she and Tripp had to outrun some more bad guys. Joe was concerned and agreed with Tripp that her vehicle was probably no longer safe to drive around. They would use Joe's car the next day.

"Anyone hungry?" Joe asked.

Carson was the first to confirm that food was the next order of business. They all left the apartment and began their hunt for a place to eat on the square.

TO ERR IS DEADLY

From the thirteenth floor of the Lloyd Tactical Forces Tower, Victor would be sitting in the tall mahogany and leather chair behind his massive oval desk, staring at the twenty-seven-inch monitor. The back of his seat would rise high above his head, as if some medieval throne was its inspiration. His office was roomy, but it was tough to grasp its size since he kept it dark. There were no windows in the circular room within the center of the cylindrical office tower his father had built years before. Even if Victor did have a window, Carl thought, he wouldn't care for the view of metropolitan Atlanta, Georgia.

The walls had dim red and orange lights that changed patterns, giving the impression you had walked into the devil's den. Wrought iron and stone furniture accentuated the motif. His desk, a solid surface made of obsidian, was raised above the rest of the floor. When people paid him a visit, they would be looking up at him. In addition, a motion-activated floodlight would temporarily blind the visitor.

Carl hated walking into his boss's office. He was used to the whole Hades theme, but Monday mornings were bad enough without it. If only people referred to the place as a hellhole because of the decor, but he was well aware that its occupant had more to do with the label than anything.

As he walked through the double doors, that infernal light hit him at precisely the moment he reached the middle of the room. It was expected that visitors would stand there and wait for Victor to take his time finishing whatever he was working on before he acknowledged them. Carl's tapping foot was unlikely to annoy his boss, so he allowed himself the impatient habit.

After another moment of studying his monitor, Victor glanced down at him, a trusted lieutenant. "Thanks for coming."

"You mentioned we have a new development?"

"We do. Joshua, the esteemed rep of our highest-paying customer, has a new concern."

"You mean beyond the mess we created Saturday?"

Victor hesitated uneasily before answering. "Yes, although I get the feeling they may be somehow connected. First, the young Page twins are on the move. I figured they'd be well hidden from us by now, but apparently they have different plans."

"Plans? That's unlike Pops to not move everything out to sea."

"I'd tend to agree. The parents allegedly transferred to a ship called the *Abril*. Curiously, the children have gone a different route. This is a concern to our customer."

"Concern? What did they expect? We were instructed to monitor only."

"True, but that brings us to point number two. Did you see the reports of the yacht that caught fire off the coast of Miami?"

"I saw something on the news yesterday. How's that connected?"

"I'll tell you," Victor said, pointing to the report he had just read. "The yacht was owned by one Fumi Yoshida. Ring any bells?"

"He's a member of the guild and a close friend of Pops Page."

"He *was* a member," Victor said, jubilant. "Now he's dead. That's one less ally for our quarry to use against us."

Carl knew his boss had a terrible case of tunnel vision. "Victor, this may not be a good thing. Fumi was an important, if not infamous, member of the guild. These are powerful people. If they even suspect we had anything to do with this, we'll have far more to worry about than Pops coming at us." He was apprehensive about his next question. "We didn't have a hand in this, did we?"

Victor laughed. "No, Carl, this wasn't our work. Which brings me to my point. Not only is our client bold, but they also must have impressive resources at their disposal."

"And here I thought Joshua was discreet."

"That's a term used for those too afraid to act. In any case, Joshua informed me not to be alarmed by any new developments. We're to focus on a new mission. It will require more resources, which equates to more billing on our end. We must now monitor the Page twins and also be ready to move in when the time comes."

"Move in and do what?"

"Apprehend, kill, tickle, or invite for tea. I didn't ask, nor do I really care about the minutiae. As long as this ends in a fat paycheck and I get the bonus of seeing Pops Page suffer."

"The details may indeed matter, Victor. The messier this gets, the more likely someone will be marked the patsy. It took us years to rebuild this empire but only seconds to watch it crumble. Your father learned that lesson the hard way."

"My father is dead," Victor snapped. "If not for Pops Page, we wouldn't need to rebuild it." He lowered his voice. "For now, we'll simply do as we're instructed. Any questions?"

"No," Carl said as he started to leave, but he stopped halfway to the door. "There is one more thing. I hear Steve caught up to that screwup, Mark, and then sent him out again. He was supposed to track the Page twins."

"So?"

"Well, he went silent again."

"Tell me he at least put a tracking device on the girl's vehicle before he disappeared?"

"Surprisingly, he managed to get that accomplished. I can only wonder what happened after that. As you know, to err is deadly in this business." Carl gave a salute with his index finger as he headed for the door.

Victor caught the veiled warning. "Do let me know if you're not totally on board with this, Carl."

"I have a lot invested in this company, Victor. I'll have a team follow whatever GPS trackers are active."

"You do that," Victor said as he departed.

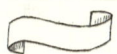

Victor sat for a while, tapping the black desk. "June?" he said, which triggered a voice-activated call to his secretary. After a few seconds, she responded. "Tell my newly demoted projects lead, Steve, that I want him in my office right away."

Soon June's voice returned. "He seems to be off campus right now, Mr. Lloyd."

"I don't care where he is."

"I'll bring him in, sir," she said indifferently.

Victor leaned back in his chair and cracked his knuckles. Although he hadn't slept much over the weekend, he fought the urge to take a nap. There will be time to sleep when I'm dead, he thought.

Carl continued down the hall and entered the elevator. Once he reached the ground floor, he checked his watch and headed toward the door. Strangely, the main lobby was more crowded with people than normal. He even saw a woman pushing a stroller. As he passed a man on one of the couches reading a newspaper, he thought he heard his name. He paused but continued onward. He heard it more clearly the second time.

"Carl."

He didn't recognize anyone in the lobby, just a few people waiting here and there. The man reading the newspaper shifted his body, but his face was still hidden. Carl approached with caution.

"You talking to me?"

The paper lowered and the man rose. It was an old associate. Known for being fearless, Carl nonetheless almost jumped as he came face to face with Pops Page.

"Got a hug for an old friend?" Pops asked, and he raised a hand that had been concealed by the newspaper. Obviously a weapon lurked beneath the headline news.

"Sure," Carl said and closed the gap, giving Pops a quick but careful hug. Pops let the barrel of the pistol poke Carl's protruding belly. Stepping back, the men eyed one another. "What do you want?"

"Two things," Pops began, his steely gaze piercing Carl. "One, leave my family alone. Two, I want Victor's head for what he did to my friend."

Carl swallowed hard as he mustered the will to maintain his fortitude. "You'll have to take up the first request with Victor. As for the second, we had nothing to do with Fumi's death. We heard it on the news."

"Unlike your boss, I know you're not deranged enough to start a war with me. Still, time and age can cloud a man's judgment."

"You listen to me, you old sea gypsy. I warned Victor about coming for you. He wasn't supposed to harm anyone, just get your attention. As for Fumi, you're right—I wouldn't be dumb enough to be standing here if Victor had given that order."

"You may not, but I never gave that little bastard much credit. I warned his old man about breeding with the whores he kept company with. Now you have to deal with the consequences."

Anger swelled up in Carl. "You'd do well to leave Alan Lloyd out of this. He was your friend, and you stabbed him in the back."

"Ruining him financially was an act of mercy, particularly after what he did."

"You can drop the self-righteous act. Alan made a mistake, and you made it a personal quest to destroy him for it."

Pops got straight to the point. "Who's pulling Victor's strings on this? I know the man's ego exceeds the size of his gonads. When I check my list of enemies, who shall I include and who can be crossed off?"

Carl said nothing but glared, his jaw locked. He wasn't showing defiance; he was just going over the possibilities, the reality of consequences he had already thought about.

Pops clenched his teeth and a vein surfaced on his forehead. He pressed the gun harder into Carl's gut, producing a painful grunt from him. "Who gave you the false courage to come gunning for me?"

A bead of sweat formed across Carl's brow. "Neither Victor nor I know their identity, but it's a shrouded entity with abundant resources at their disposal. They seem to have no fear of the guild, much less you. We figure they had Fumi killed to get your attention."

"Your mysterious client will regret not sending a subtler message."

"As you well know, we all have our regrets." Carl contemplated whether he should continue and decided he had nothing to lose. "They knew of Victor's venom for you and even offered your head as a final bonus."

Pops pulled away from him. "I'm not the only one they'll use to get what they want. Your client may not fear me or the guild, but they were reckless to engage on multiple fronts. The irony is, Fumi's death may not be the worst of the two messages they sent."

This piqued Carl's curiosity. "I assumed the cop was collateral damage. You must know something I don't."

Pops lowered the pistol. "I know Victor's nothing more than someone's marionette. He's also too stupid to realize he's currently the only target presenting itself."

It was an understatement, but Carl found no value in discussing it further. Instead, he rolled the dice. "Your son the preacher seems to have a considerable value to our client. As hard as I've tried, I can't imagine why that could be."

Pops looked satisfied, as if that affirmation alone was worth the visit. "Well, they have a funny way of showing how much they value Jack—they attacked him near his home with automatic weapons."

"That misstep was with quality control, not our client's directive. Heads will roll for that one. You're avoiding the subject, old man. That tells me more than any words could."

Pops looked at him cautiously. "It boggles the mind as to why someone would be that interested in my son. I guess we're both missing something."

Carl straightened his jacket and took a deep breath. "We can agree on that. Look, there's no lost love between us, ya salty bastard. Still, I don't want a war either. Regardless of what happens to Victor, I'll always protect what Alan built. I owe him that."

"Victor won't be running board meetings much longer. Who will take the reins after he's gone?"

It was a threat and a choice rolled into one. "I'll cross that bridge when I come to it."

Pops put away his pistol and tossed the newspaper on the nearby couch. He stood, shoulder to shoulder with Carl, facing the opposite direction. "You may want to cast your vote while you still have time. Do I go after the head of the serpent or the entire beast?"

Carl said nothing as Pops sauntered to the entrance and left. He felt a chill as he witnessed everyone in the lobby suddenly stop what they were doing and depart as well. The woman pushing the stroller was the last to leave. He'd bet good money there was no baby in there.

Carl shuddered at how many enemies had occupied the lobby. How many more were outside, or worse, still in the building? Going forward, he would need either more daytime security or an extended vacation.

He went outside and scanned the area. None of the people who had exited just moments before were in sight. His limo was close by, but the journey seemed longer than normal. Something arrested his attention in the parking garage across the street, but it was only Victor's Porsche sitting in its private spot. The sun's rays sparkled off the metallic silver paint.

Convinced that the blinding light had played tricks on his eyes, Carl stepped into the limo after the driver opened the door. He started down the road and called June's desk. She had just answered when a fireball erupted behind him. The limo driver slammed on the breaks, jolting him forward.

"What was that?" came June's voice.

Carl collected himself and peered back, though he already knew the answer. "That, my dear, was Victor's prized car being engulfed in a fireball. Please be sure you're done laughing before you remind him he was warned."

June giggled. "You can tell him that last part yourself. I'll just say his car overheated."

MORNING MOURNING

Carson and Tripp awoke on the stiff leather sofa. It looked far more comfortable than it really was. At least it was a roomy sectional that easily fit the two of them. Regardless, Carson had a tendency to flop around during the night, awakening Tripp a couple of times by striking him.

She studied the room around her, trying to get her bearings. The decor seemed out of place for something her uncle owned. Paintings of prairies, deserts, and other landscapes adorned the walls. It was probably still decorated exactly the way her uncle Joe's mom had left it over a decade ago.

Carson stretched as she glanced over at Tripp, who rubbed his eyes. "Morning, sunshine," she said.

"That's actually your nickname, sis," Tripp said as he tried to fully wake up.

"Only Mother really calls me that." As Carson tried to stand, her mother's diary dropped to the floor.

Tripp reached for the small book. "What's this?"

"Nothing," Carson replied as she tried to scoop it up. She retrieved it first, but Tripp seized it from her hand.

He examined it. "Where did you get this?"

"That closet in Dad's hideaway. I wanted some history, so I borrowed it." She lunged for it but missed.

"Borrowing requires permission. This is of a very personal nature and it destroys your integrity if you read it."

"Wrong." Carson grabbed it on the second try. "Everyone knows I'd read it, therefore my integrity is intact."

"You've read it before, haven't you?"

Carson decided it was time to confess. "Okay, Mother caught me reading it a couple of months ago, after I returned from my last storm chase. I was looking for a pair of shoes to borrow and came across it."

"She let you read it?"

"No, of course not. She was pissed. I only read some of it before she snatched it and hid it in a better place. I guess she figured I'd never find it in their secret underground lair." Carson laughed as she said it.

Tripp looked at her disapprovingly. "So that's the reason you and Mom have been at odds. You invaded her personal thoughts, so naturally she's been upset. Which makes me wonder about your anger issues. I'll assume you read something in those pages that sparked some animosity toward her."

"Do we really want to go into this?"

"No, there's a more pressing matter to discuss." Tripp closed his eyes as though debating how to proceed. With a deep breath, he took the plunge. "Pops called Uncle Joe with news last night. You were already asleep, so we agreed not to wake you."

Carson's heart went into her throat. "What happened?" She braced herself for the answer.

Tripp found it difficult to say the words. "Mr. Sanchez is dead."

Carson gasped as the words came out. She neither spoke nor moved as she absorbed their impact. The tears snaked down her cheeks. She finally sat on the couch, her head in her hands, and cried.

Tripp put his arm around her. Their uncle and Daniel appeared from a back room. No words were needed to tell them what was wrong. They all gathered around Carson and mourned the loss of their dear friend. Although Joe barely knew Sanchez, he understood the pain of losing someone much loved.

Carson slowly pulled away and wiped her eyes. She allowed anger to replace her sorrow. "If that bastard Mark did this, he's going to pay. Do you hear me, Tripp?"

"I hear you, sis."

"Daniel, when we catch up to him, you hold that little prick while I beat him to death. You got that?"

"Carson," Joe said firmly. "It wasn't Mark who did this. I believe he's dead as well."

"Then who did?"

"Pops believes very dangerous people are on our trail."

Carson stood up and took a couple of steps back. "This is all my fault. I insisted we do this. He'd be alive today if I weren't such a selfish bitch." The tears streamed down.

"It's not your fault," Daniel said.

"Shut up. Don't be nice to me. I deserve the guilt."

"Nonsense," Tripp said. "Your actions had nothing to do with Mr. Sanchez's death. His own involvement put us on the same trail he was on. The only thing our choices could have affected was ourselves."

Was it true, or was he was just saying what he thought she needed to hear? The others waited while she considered his words. Before long, she reached a conclusion.

"You're right, Tripp. Thank you."

"We can head back home and offer our condolences. I'm sure after everything settles down, we can revisit any unanswered questions."

"No."

Tripp started to speak but was silenced by Carson's raised hand.

"You listen to me, all of you," she said, emphasizing each word. "Whoever murdered our friend may come for us. That won't change, regardless of what we do next. Poppy is welcome to send whatever resources he sees fit to aid us, but I'll finish what we started. I won't live in fear of whatever assholes may come our way. That would only dishonor Mr. Sanchez's sacrifice."

The three men looked at one another and nodded. She had rapidly switched gears. Daniel was the first to get up and return to the server room. Tripp hugged Carson and followed.

Joe sat, a grin forming. "We expected the resistance, but that was a damn fine speech."

"You just like tough girls."

"If you're referring to Wanda, I only wish she had the heart my niece does."

Carson smiled but moved past the compliment. "Somehow, these people will pay, Uncle Joe."

"I know," he said and stood up. "I'm going to go fetch us some lunch while the geeks work on that computer. Want to join me?"

"Thanks, but I'm going to check every inch of this place."

The server room turned out to be little more than a study. They found an older PC tower locked behind a glass cabinet. Tripp easily picked the simple lock. As for breaking into the secured machine, it would take more work.

While Daniel got to work on the task, Tripp left the room to check on his sister. He found her headfirst in a closet. She had already pulled out most of the contents and stacked them in the hall. "Anything of interest?"

Carson paused when she heard his voice. "Not in the closet itself, but have a look-see at what was behind all this junk."

"Are you okay, sis? You probably need more time to process what's happened."

"Are you going to look or not?"

Tripp peered inside and saw a safe painted to match the white concrete wall it was embedded into. It had a peculiar lock mechanism. He moved closer and studied it. "I won't be able to pick this lock," he said. "I'm guessing, but what unlocks this is likely a disc-shaped object, similar to a hockey puck but slightly smaller. It should have several teeth or pins, ranging in number from a few to many."

They searched for such an object but couldn't find it. As they started to clean up their mess, Putter walked in. He lingered, as though wondering what they had been up to. Carson walked up to him as Tripp finished putting things back in their place.

"Hi, Putter," she said and slapped him on the shoulder.

He adjusted his glasses as he surveyed the mess. "What are you guys doing in here?"

"Did you know there's a hidden safe in that closet?"

"No," he said. "I don't mess with things that don't belong to me."

"You haven't seen a hockey puck with teeth, have you?"

Putter looked at her in confusion. "A what?"

Tripp and Putter discussed what she was referring to. Carson retreated, shaking her head. "At least there's one other human in the world who can communicate with you," she said, eyeing Tripp.

She wandered over to the wall across from the hall closet and noticed a picture of a clock tower. "I've seen this picture somewhere before." Then it came to her. "Dad has this exact same picture in his study at home."

Carson removed the picture from the wall, but she found nothing behind it—no hidden safe. She started to replace the picture but felt something in the back of it. She turned it over and found an old key embedded in the cardboard backing. She pried it out and showed it to Tripp.

It was long with an engraved round bow on one end and a single wavy bit on the other. "Cast iron," Tripp said as he examined it. "Nice weight. Whatever lock this fits would be easy to pick."

"My grandmother has a clock with a key kinda like that," said Putter.

"Clock!" exclaimed Carson as she retrieved the key and put the picture back on the wall. "There's a clock tower across the street."

"Of course. It's a famous landmark around here."

"That's where we're going."

"What do you hope to find in the museum?"

"It's a museum?" Carson's enthusiasm only increased. "So there isn't a bunch of cops over there?"

"Just one near the entrance," Putter answered, looking unsure.

"Good—we can work with those odds. Come on," she said and tugged at Tripp's arm.

"Wait," said Putter, confused. "That clock is far too big for a key of that size. Also, you can't tour the clock tower, only the lower levels."

"I'm aware of that, nerdling, but I'm betting this key being hidden behind a picture of the same clock tower isn't a coincidence. This may be the key, in the literal sense, to finding whatever unlocks that safe in the closet." Carson took her phone out and made a call as she headed for the door.

Tripp believed it was a long shot but still feasible. "Who are you calling?"

"The Pops emergency service. We're going to need a new ride once we find what we're looking for."

"We can all travel together in Uncle Joe's car."

"I like to control my own destiny, thank you." She walked out the door.

Tripp gave a deep sigh as his sister stood outside the doorway and waited. "Let me apprise Daniel of our plans." He found his friend in the server room and updated him. Daniel chose to stay and work on the machine. As Tripp rejoined Carson, he passed by Putter and thanked him.

"Good luck, whatever it is you guys are chasing," the man said with a wave.

"Oh, my sister will tell you that luck has nothing to do with it," Tripp said. He closed the door and followed her down the steep staircase.

LIKE CLOCKWORK

The old Denton courthouse sat on a courtyard surrounded by four streets that formed a perfect square. Built over a century before, the structure, with its limestone walls and sandstone-capped columns, rose above the several oak trees that dotted the well-kept lawn. The clock tower, its highest point, had four faces. The historical building had been converted into a museum years before and was a popular hangout for families and local college students. All around were shops, eateries, and, of course, bars.

Carson and Tripp stepped through the glass door, crossed the street, then skirted a yoga class on the courthouse lawn. They went around to the southern entrance of the building, and once inside, passed a single guard, who also happened to be a Denton police officer.

Tripp had to wait while his sister flirted with the young policeman. The officer smiled as Carson, feigning bashfulness, walked on. Quickly but gently, she elbowed Tripp's rib cage. "We're not going to have any problems in here," she said, smirking.

"Don't mistake a man's flirtatious gestures for a sign he'd hesitate to carry out his duties," Tripp said.

"You really do underestimate the power of a woman," Carson said with a hint of haughtiness. She swayed her hips as she walked, knowing the policeman's eyes were glued to her.

"I await the day that routine backfires."

"Not today, little brother."

From the floors to the custom wood-paneled walls, everything about the multistory courthouse breathed its history. The twins started at the center of the first level, peering up into the open rotunda that cut through the floors above them. There were many things to see, which meant as many places to investigate. They started with the exhibits on the first floor and moved along to the offices still used by city employees. On the next level, there was an old courtroom, complete with a surrounding galley. Along the walls was a visual history of the judges who had presided in the chamber.

After about half an hour of exploring each exhibit and room on the floors accessible to the public, they were still no closer to finding the elusive key. Carson wanted to go up into the clock tower, but it was gated and tourists weren't allowed in.

"Why can't we just pry the damn safe open?" Carson asked in frustration.

Amazed, Tripp said, "You saw it. It's solid steel and built into a concrete wall. Besides, we don't know if some mechanism would set off an alarm or even destroy its contents if we tried."

"This seems like a dead end." Carson rolled her eyes and walked up to the black metal spiral staircase. "Give me a boost," she said, glancing back.

"If memory serves, this was your suggestion," Tripp reminded her. He lifted his sister's thin frame over the rail of the staircase, bypassing the gate that blocked their path at the bottom. It took him a bit longer to climb over, even with Carson's help.

Climbing the tight, spiral staircase, they headed up the first two levels of the tower—which were empty—before coming to a room that housed the inner workings of the clock itself. Tripp had to stop and investigate the gears while Carson decided to open the nearest window.

She stepped out onto a veranda that provided a nice view of the Denton courthouse square. After surveying the area, she returned inside to find Tripp staring straight up. Their remaining journey required a climb up two more flights by ladder. They proceeded to the next level which housed a large bell.

"I don't want to be anywhere near that thing when it goes off," Carson said.

Tripp nodded his agreement and they continued up until they reached the top and found they were behind the clock facing itself. There were four different clock faces—one for each direction.

Tripp and Carson examined the room carefully. Aside from old brick walls that the large clock faces were embedded into, there was little else to look at. As they resigned themselves to starting their journey back down, something caught Tripp's eye.

Reaching up, he examined some scratches on a brick in the corner. "It looks like a shield or banner, perhaps. These marks may represent three birds," he said pointing.

"How did you get all that from that terrible drawing?" Carson asked, unimpressed by the discovery.

"If I'm not mistaken, this is a rudimentary drawing of the Page family crest," Tripp said, but then grinned. "Or it could just be what's engraved on the iron key's bow."

"Smart-ass."

Running his hand over the spot again and again, he confirmed what he had hoped. "This appears to be a colored plaster meant to match the bricks around it." He pounded his fist into the wall, making Carson jump. After a few more hits, he was able to brush away the damaged plaster.

Carson tried to figure out what he was doing and stood on her tippy-toes. "Well?"

Tripp pulled out a pocketknife and began clearing the area around a keyhole. "You were correct."

"I was?"

"Indeed," Tripp said as he inserted the iron key in the keyhole. With a little effort, it turned and locked into place. He used it as a handle and pulled outward. Dust and plaster rained down, revealing a short drawer in the wall. He reached into it and triumphantly handed Carson a round metallic object.

Carson cupped it in her hands as if it were a delicate treasure. It was heavier than it looked, and one side was smooth, while the other had several points sticking up.

She counted the points. "Eleven teeth," she said, smiling, and handed it back to him.

Tripp took it, raised his shirt to expose a fanny pack, and tucked the object inside. "Let's get back to the loft."

They descended the tall ladder and reached the level with the veranda. This time, however, they had company—two bald men dressed in dark slacks and jackets. The taller one had a long face, while the shorter one was round from head to toe. The men stood silently, gazing at them from behind the sunglasses they wore.

"Not again," Tripp said with a sigh.

Carson tried to appear oblivious to the fact that the men didn't work for the museum. She smiled as she tried to walk around them. "I know we're not supposed to be up here."

The men blocked her path to the spiral staircase. One pushed her backward as she tried to move past him.

"We'll pay the fine and be on our way."

Tripp knew the men weren't buying it. They obviously were the ones who had been tracking them. "It seems warm for jackets."

"It is," said the shorter one as he produced a gun. Carson and Tripp stepped back with their hands up.

"Did you find what you were looking for?" the taller one asked. His partner gave a grin that showed off his gold tooth.

Tripp stalled, trying to think of a way out of their predicament. "We did enjoy the historical and architectural aspects of the building. Plus, exploring the clock tower was almost like hunting for treasure."

The shorter one addressed his colleague. "Paul, what should we do with our young explorer?"

"He seems like a smart-ass, James. Maybe we just grab the girl and throw this one away."

James peered over the guardrail, through the octagonal hole that exposed the floors below. It was several stories straight to the bottom. "We can let him explore gravity." Both snickered.

Tripp sensed Carson's anger, but she was forcing herself to be cool and sultry. "I've got a better idea. Maybe we can work something else out," she said as she ran her hand down James's arm.

"Sis, what are you doing?" Tripp said through his teeth.

James looked at her and laughed. "You're not my type."

Carson seemed confused by her total lack of appeal to the man. She backed up to the window behind her and climbed out onto the veranda before either of the men could react. "I'll scream, you pricks," she yelled. "Then I'll jump!"

"Go get her, James," Paul said as he grabbed Tripp, pushed him against the wall, and poked a revolver in his midsection.

James crawled halfway out the window, one foot still inside. Carson stood up on the ledge and almost lost her balance. The man froze as if uncertain what would happen if he continued outside.

"Not another step," she said.

James looked back to his partner, who seemed equally confused.

"Tell her I'll throw her brother to his death," Paul said.

"She might jump if I say that," James whispered. "Bad things will result if something happens to either of 'em."

Paul slapped his own forehead in frustration.

Tripp observed that this kidnapping attempt differed from the first one. He had been convinced Mark would have shot him. These men, however, had been bluffing, undoubtedly to get them to cooperate.

Knowing this, Tripp found the courage to roll the dice. "Sir, you should allow me to go out there and retrieve her."

Paul studied Tripp with a skeptical look. He raised the pistol and held it to Tripp's chin. He drew closer, his breath pungent. "And why would you do that?"

Glancing down, Tripp noticed the man's finger never touched the trigger. "Because she's my sister, and I can't bear the thought of anything happening to her."

The man didn't have a better play. "Go, boy. No funny business."

"Understood." Tripp crept out the window while the two men watched. Carson stared at him, puzzled at first as she saw him unwinding a cord he had hidden under his shirt.

She gave him an amused look. "What's this?" she asked softly and took the hooked end he handed to her.

"It's a self-repelling device."

"Please don't tell me this is another of Daniel's flawed inventions."

Tripp thought it wise to refrain from admitting just that. "Allegedly, it should hold both our weights."

Carson looked worried. "What the hell has happened to you? You're acting crazier than me."

"Desperate times." He calculated the rate of their descent with the extra weight. "We'll need some dramatics on your part to secure it to the stone railing down there."

Dramatics she could do. "No, you're on their side," she said loudly. "They've brainwashed you. Come with me, brother. Let's jump to our destiny." Carson turned and looked about to dive over.

"Sister, please contain these irrational passions," Tripp said and instantly wished he'd taken more of an interest in theater.

Carson groaned. Their acting was worse than what you'd see in an elementary school play. "Think of something," she whispered.

While not the brightest bulbs, the men in the window were convinced something was up. They decided to take the risk and climb out.

The danger of what he and his sister were about to do hit Tripp and he hesitated. Carson grabbed him and dove over the stone railing. They missed the shocked expressions of the men.

Carson and Tripp hit the slanted roof—that was mere feet below them—and slid down where it ended at more stone railing. Carson, not waiting for the two men to figure out what had happened, hopped to her feet and quickly fastened the hooked end of the rope around the railing. Tripp had just stood when she grabbed him and pulled him over once again.

At first they dropped a couple of stories slowly, but as with most of Daniel's devices, something went wrong. The rope tightened and then abruptly loosened. They plummeted to the ground, Carson landing on top of Tripp.

Her drop cushioned by her brother, Carson sprang to her feet. Tripp, however, wasn't ready to rise. He waited until he could breathe again.

The men above them, surprised by the plunge, yelled down and waved their pistols. But a few people on the courthouse lawn had witnessed the stunt, and realizing it was a bad time to flash guns around, James and Paul cursed and ducked back into the tower.

Carson motioned for Tripp to follow her and tugged on his sleeve. He yelled to alert her he was sore from their landing. He also had to remove the hidden harness that housed the repelling device.

"We have to get back to the apartment before those guys can catch up," she said.

Tripp followed her around the courthouse and back across the street. As they reached the top of the stairs, Carson pounded on the door.

"C'mon, Daniel, open up!" she yelled, just before the deadbolt was unlatched.

The door opened, and Tripp and Carson took a startled step backward. It wasn't who they had expected.

The man tipped his fedora and nodded. "I'm not buying cookies this year." They stared at him, baffled. "Girl Scouts? Oh, never mind," he said, pulling them inside.

While Tripp had no idea who the man was, Carson soon figured it out. "Shelby? Without a dress?"

"In both spirit and flesh."

"What are you doing here?"

"You called for a ride, didn't you?" He started toward the kitchen. "I was just finishing the lunch your uncle Joe provided."

Carson followed Shelby into the kitchen. "That was supposed to be our lunch. Speaking of Uncle Joe, where is he? And Daniel?"

"Well, let me see if I can repeat what the nerdy one said. The computer at this place is merely blah, it points to some other blah, and they'll call when they find what they're looking for near San Antonio."

Tripp tried to translate the terribly conveyed message. "So this location isn't the server room we're looking for. I'm guessing the machine here acts as some sort of proxy server, perhaps to throw off anyone trying to trace the IP address of the actual server. That means Daniel accessed the machine here and determined it communicates with another server near San Antonio."

Shelby was impressed. "You have a strange magic, kiddo. Glad I could help."

Carson looked less impressed. "I'm used to you taking something vague and making it overly complicated, Tripp. We'll retrieve our treasure and head that way."

She went to the closet and began to remove things. Tripp assisted her while Shelby looked on disapprovingly.

"No more treasure hunting, kiddos. Pops sent me to retrieve you guys."

After everything they had been through, Carson was hardly ready to give up. Even Tripp protested. At first, Shelby would hear none of it, but Carson in her stubborn fashion wore the man down. Banging his head against a Carson-shaped wall only prolonged things.

"Fine. Go get your treasure," Shelby said, gesturing for them to proceed.

Tripp retrieved the round device from his pack while his sister haphazardly threw the contents of the closet out into the hall. Once he had a clear path, he dived into the closet and carefully inserted the disc-shaped key into the safe door. He tried to turn it clockwise first, but it wouldn't budge. He then tried counterclockwise, and it eventually began to rotate.

With a metallic click and a brief hiss of escaping air, the door to the safe popped out. Tripp pulled on it the rest of the way to reveal an airtight, sealed drawer. A light in the drawer came on, illuminating the inside.

Carson's and Shelby's heads poked into the closet. Tripp reached into the drawer and lifted out the single item it contained. He carefully backed out, turned, and displayed the object.

"What in the hell is that?" Shelby asked and touched it. "It feels cold."

"I was hoping you could shed some light on the subject," said Tripp.

It was about a meter long, roughly four inches in diameter and tubular. Although metal, it wasn't as heavy as it looked. Lighter than steel but heavier than aluminum. Tripp concluded it was titanium.

It was far from being a perfect cylinder—slightly thinner on one end than the other. All sorts of engraved patterns decorated it, and holes of various sizes appeared throughout the structure. It was neither solid metal nor hollow but contained some sort of material. There were no discernible buttons or switches on it, but Tripp figured it had to be an electrical device.

Carson ran her hands across it as she examined the many grooves and engravings. "It's pretty, in a Gothic sort of way."

Shelby's phone rang. He glanced at the number calling and muttered, "Thank goodness," before he answered. "Hey, Jack."

Carson's eyes lit up. "Dad!"

"Yes, that was your daughter. And thank you, Shelby, for going all the way to Texas to get your kids." He paused to listen to Jack.

"Tell Dad we found this cool device," Carson said, but Shelby hushed her so Jack wouldn't know what they had been up to. It was too late.

"Uh, you mean that weird tube hidden in the closet?" Shelby asked, speaking to Jack on the other line. "Sure, we can retrieve that. No, I think we can figure it out."

Tripp studied Shelby's expressions as the man listened. He looked puzzled, then surprised. Noticing he was being watched, Shelby turned his back to them. "Okay, just to confirm I'm not insane, you want us to go where?"

Carson and Tripp were straining to hear their father's voice. They tried to follow Shelby, but their efforts were in vain, as he disappeared into a room and locked the door.

"Dammit," Carson said and put her ear to the door.

Most of what Shelby said on the other side of the door was muffled. He sounded resistant to some request. The one thing they made out clearly, when Shelby raised his voice: "Because that woman scares the bejeebers out of me."

A siren could be heard in the distance. Tripp wondered if someone had seen the two men in the tower with guns. Carson pulled herself away from the door and went to a back window. She watched as two police cars passed the street behind them, headed for the square.

"Shit," she said as she went back to the door and knocked to get Shelby's attention.

He finally came out of the room, no longer on the phone with their dad. Carson opened her mouth to start questioning him about the call, but he held up a hand for silence. It sounded as if the police cars had stopped nearby.

"What did you kiddos do?" Shelby asked. "What part of the story did you leave out?"

"Nothing," Carson said.

"Someone might have seen our attackers holding weapons and called the police," Tripp said.

"Attackers?"

"We escaped by plunging off a veranda. They've almost certainly searched for us outside."

"Well, we shouldn't go out the front, then. Is there a back exit?" Shelby asked.

"Just the window in the back server room. There's a steel ladder on the side of the building, but I don't think it goes all the way to the ground."

"Just how far does it go?" Shelby asked.

"Roughly twelve feet, give or take, short of the pavement," Tripp said. "But if you were to hang down from the bottom rung, the drop should be about half that."

Shelby studied the window and contemplated the drop. "That's just lovely."

"Hey, Shelby," Carson said, "what the hell is that contraption in my brother's hand?"

"Something I wish we'd never seen."

"I hope it doesn't have radioactive isotopes within its components," Tripp said with concern.

"Damn, that would suck," Shelby said.

Carson disappeared and came back with two pillowcases, which she and Tripp wrapped around the mysterious device. They tied it snuggly with a computer cord they had salvaged. Tripp found another, longer cable, an RJ-45 connector for a router, in a drawer. He tied it to the device so they could lower it out the window.

Shelby made on his way down the ladder. As he reached the end of it, he hung as close to the ground as he could and dropped the rest of the way. His feet hit the pavement and he rolled backward, down the three steps that led into the street. Carson and Tripp watched as he slowly got up, in obvious pain, and motioned to them to lower the device.

After doing so, Carson went next. She made the drop look easy. She slapped Shelby on the shoulder as she passed by him—a mild taunt. Tripp followed. The gracefulness of his effort was somewhere between Carson's and Shelby's.

"Where are you parked?" Carson asked as she looked around for Shelby. He had quietly disappeared as Tripp came down. "Where'd he go?"

Tripp dusted himself off, then froze at what he saw just beyond Carson. She looked alarmed as he raised his hands.

"Did you miss us?" came the voice from behind her.

Carson whirled around to see the thugs from the clock tower. She backed up until she was almost even with Tripp. The two men followed, their pistols aimed at them.

"Oh look, Paul, they actually thought they'd given us the slip," James said. "I guess they thought they were smarter than we are."

The other man grinned briefly but lost the smile as he lowered his weapon, dropped it to the ground, and raised his own hands. "James," he said and pointed at Shelby.

James looked dumbfounded until he saw the silenced pistol pointing at them. He followed Paul's lead, and soon both men had their hands up.

Shelby emerged fully from behind the large steel Dumpster he had ducked behind. He motioned to Carson and Tripp to join him, then waited as they moved out of the line of fire. "Would you gentlemen prefer the head or the chest?"

Paul swallowed hard. "What do you mean?"

"I mean to shoot both of you. Where would you like the bullet?"

"Uh, sir, do we have another choice?" James asked. "I mean, people don't really walk away from being shot in either of those spots."

Shelby eyed him curiously. "Your scrotum, perhaps? Look, I have to shoot you somewhere. It's your fault I had to climb out of a four-story window when there was a perfectly good front door."

Both men followed Shelby's finger as he pointed at the window. Paul said nothing, while James looked as if he was thinking.

"Maybe if you just winged us in the leg, we'd be even."

"James, is it?" Shelby asked and the man nodded. "Tell me why Lloyd Security wants these two so badly and I promise to shoot just one of your nuts off."

The two looked horrified at the prospect. They both said, one right after the other, "Who?"

"Really, jackasses?" Carson said angrily. "They're the same pricks who hired your buddy Mark. You know, the guy who tried to kidnap us and murdered at least one person."

"We really don't know what you're talking about, little lady," Paul said.

"Oh, so now I'm a lady. Mr. Shelby, maybe if you shot one of them the other would start talking."

"I like your style, lil' darlin'," Shelby said as he aimed at Paul.

Tripp was alarmed. "Hold on," he said as he moved between Shelby and the two men. "I don't think these men came with the same intentions as Mark."

Shelby lowered his pistol halfway. "Get out of the way, Tripp."

"Hear me out," Tripp said. "They never even placed a finger on the trigger of their guns when pointing them at us. And they gave up easily when you pointed your gun at them. They hardly strike me as professional at anything, except perhaps lying."

"That's all true," James said. "Paul and I are just security guards. We wouldn't really hurt anybody."

"I have a wife and two kids," Paul said. "And James has an ex-hubby who ran off, but he still gives him money."

James flashed an irritated look at his colleague. "You could've just stopped with your wife and two kids, Paul."

"Well, at least I didn't tell 'em your hubby ran off with a woman."

"You just did, asshole."

Carson laughed. "Oh, so that's why my charm didn't work on ya."

"No offense," James said.

"Enough," Shelby said. "Okay, Tripp, you win. I won't shoot these pathetic bastards if they tell me what I want to know."

"Thank you, Mr. Shelby," Tripp said with relief.

"You're welcome, softie. Okay, bastards, who hired you?"

"We honestly don't know who he is, sir," said James.

"He was a young black fella with a lot of cash. He visited us at work," said Paul.

"In McAlester," James added.

"Where?" Tripp asked.

"There are several prisons in McAlester, Oklahoma," Carson said. "I've passed through that town a few times."

The men confirmed she was correct. Shelby questioned them further but learned little. They had been given a sizable down payment to make the trip down to Texas, with the promise of even more upon delivery of the twins. The men had no idea where the drop-off would be since they were supposed to call when they were on their way.

Shelby used one of their phones to call the number, but it went to voice mail. Whoever would be listening to the message would call back with instructions. Typically, that would be when to set a trap for the party responsible, but Shelby was pressed for time.

Carson felt the men were getting off way too easy and wanted to teach them a lesson. Reluctantly, Shelby disappeared and then returned with a roll of duct tape. "Get creative," he told her. Tripp and he tossed them in the Dumpster once she had finished her work.

"The van is this way." Shelby pointed to the vehicle parked on the other side of the dumpster.

"You're disturbed," Tripp told his sister as he entered the back of the van and found a spot to secure the long metal object. He climbed over the seat to sit behind Shelby.

"I'm an artist," Carson replied, clearly proud of her work with the tape. She took the shotgun seat, and immediately her face expressed her disdain for the vehicle's interior.

"I like old vans," said Shelby, as if reading her mind. "They're very useful."

"I'm sure," Carson said, cringing at the dingy smell. "I hope you don't mind if I puke in here."

"Here," Shelby said as he handed her a paper bag. He started the van and carefully guided them away from the square to the highway. They turned north onto I-35. Shelby plotted a course on his phone's GPS map.

"Where are we heading, sir?" asked Tripp.

"You can call me Shelby, and we're heading north." He paused as he altered the final coordinates. "To Grandma's house we go."

"Whose grandma?" asked Carson.

"Yours, of course." But Carson merely looked puzzled. "The crazy one," he added.

"The witch?"

Shelby laughed. "Right, the Wicked Witch of Southeast Oklahoma."

"Why?"

"Because your dad wants us to retrieve something."

"How about you go get it and we'll head south."

The look on Shelby's round face said more than his words. "If I showed up without you guys, I wouldn't make it through the front door. Even If I did make it through, I'd never be seen again."

WITCH WAY

Over the river and through the woods to Grandmother's house they went. The area was alive with campers, kayakers, and fisherman. It had been years since Tripp had been to this or any part of Oklahoma, although Carson had traveled to the state whenever conditions were ripe for storm adventures.

The white van, windowless in the back, made its way along the route. Shelby was ready for a drink and cigar but figured it better to wait. In the backseat, Tripp was still fidgeting with his phone. In the front passenger seat, Carson had been flipping through some pages of her mother's diary but grew tired and decided to take a nap.

When she awoke, Shelby had to endure countless questions from her. At first, they were of the type he didn't want to answer. He tried to give her a subtle hint by turning up the radio.

"What was Dad doing?"

Radio turned up.

"What in the world is a preacher going to do with the items we're collecting?"

Radio turned up louder.

"Why are you not answering me?"

And so on, until Carson ripped off the knob from the radio. Shelby had witnessed the pretty little human morph into a Tasmanian devil right before his eyes. He'd always wondered what a female version of Pops would look like.

Carson needed to vent. "We were supposed to catch up to Uncle Joe and Daniel."

"That would have been preferable," Shelby said, regretting he had agreed to this task.

"Why would our dad want us to steal from our grandmother?"

"Steal? No. We're reclaiming something your dad hid there years ago. It's probably the last place anyone would look for it. I know I sure as hell wouldn't."

"Well, I don't care to go either," Carson said with a groan.

Shelby glanced at Tripp, who looked unnerved that his sister was resistant to the idea. She typically didn't avoid challenging scenarios. Had recent events taken their toll on her?

"Carson mentioned that Grandma Page believes she can speak with the dead," said Tripp.

"Would that be the ones buried in her backyard?" Shelby quipped.

"You seem apprehensive when it comes to Grandma Page. Did you two have an unpleasant relationship?"

"Thankfully, I've never met Stella, but I've seen her from a distance more than once. Her reputation alone is a powerful repellent."

"Dad's also avoided her over the years. Still, she *is* family."

"Tripp, were you dropped on your head as a child?"

Carson spoke up. "When we were in the womb, I probably kicked him a few too many times."

"Boy, I believe that," Shelby said.

To change the subject, Shelby went over the plan once they got to their grandmother's house. It involved Carson distracting her while they searched for the item Jack wanted, supposedly hidden in a compartment behind a china cabinet.

Carson disliked the idea and introduced plan B, which was just the opposite of what Shelby wanted to do. She would find the item while the men provided the distraction. Shelby conceded to the possibility of her plan B but informed her that plan A was still the main objective.

"What exactly is this thing we're looking for?" Carson asked.

"I don't remember your dad's exact description, but for some reason I imagined a soccer ball made of crystal, but not much bigger than a golf ball."

After a pause, Tripp said, "It sounds like a polyhedron."

"Polly who?" asked Shelby.

"A polyhedron. Think of it as a sphere made up of hexagons and polygons."

"Sure, let's just go with that."

"I wonder what this particular object is for," said Tripp.

"Well, young professor, if we actually find it and take it away with us, you can analyze it all you want,"

Carson mouthed the word "nerd," then closed her eyes to take another nap. They drove for a while longer until the phone's GPS indicated they were almost there.

Shelby checked the sky to see if any vultures were circling near their destination. He didn't spot any, though he told himself that might change if things didn't go well.

Carson started to say something almost as soon as her eyes opened, but Shelby made it clear his ears were still on break. With a grunt, Carson turned her attention to the world they passed through.

At least the drive through that part of the state was lovely. The surrounding trees, lake, streams, and hills took some of the gloom out of where they were headed. Broken Bow, a quaint town in Southeastern Oklahoma of just over four thousand residents, was a popular spot for campers and kayakers.

It was hard for Shelby to understand why Pops's former wife had chosen such a pleasant place to reside. He imagined her living in a gingerbread house in some dark, shadowy forest. "There it is, kiddos," he said as they turned off the road and headed up the heavily graveled drive.

Tripp stopped what he was doing, and he and Carson looked at the small home on the hill in front of them. The yellow house wasn't much to look at, though it sat on a nice plot of land.

"Don't let the appearance of this place fool you," Shelby said. "The woman who resides in that humble abode is loaded."

"Maybe she enjoys the simpler things in life," Tripp said.

"Trust me, there's nothing simple about that woman."

Carson took a deep breath and exhaled in preparation for the encounter. "Okay, I need to put on my game face. I can handle a few minutes of crazy to get what we need."

"Remember, lil' darlin', we're here to obtain an item for your old man, not grill Broom-Hilda about family history."

"We'll just call that that *plan C*."

"I'm definitely gonna need a drink," Shelby mumbled as he parked the van and looked around.

The place wasn't exactly a shanty, but it could have used a fresh coat of paint. It sat on roughly two acres of land, with smaller trees dotting the homestead area. The rest of the property disappeared into the woods behind it. The front yard seemed well kept, with a little fish pond and various statues of pixies and angels frozen in a dance around a garden.

"You kiddos ready for this?"

"As ready as we're going to be," Carson replied.

They exited the van and noted that the backyard, mostly hidden by a weathered privacy fence, was less inviting. The gate was open, allowing a narrow view of it. Junked appliances were stacked beside a shed and a sinister gargoyle statue was partially hidden by a shrub. Traveling along the side yard and attached to a steel rod in the ground was a chain. It wound through the gate and vanished around the house.

"Chains like that usually mean one thing," Carson said, just as a mean pit bull came racing around the corner.

Instinctively, they all took several steps backward. The dog almost choked itself when the chain ran out, mere feet from them.

"Whoa there, big fella." Shelby reached into his pocket to retrieve some beef jerky and tossed it to the dog. "Never leave home without it."

The snarling dog paused long enough to sniff it but seemed determined to tear some flesh off his new guests. The barking and growling continued.

Carson drew closer and squatted, then held out her hand and spoke softly to the animal. He seemed curious at first but lunged for her. Shelby snickered as she fell backward. Tripp helped his sister to her feet.

"Go lie down, King David!" came the raspy voice from the raised front porch. Following the voice, they saw the thin frame of a gray-haired woman in a dark purple dress. Her hair was windblown and her bleached skin blotched with age. It was her emerald eyes, however, that were her most noticeable feature. They seemed to glow as they focused on everyone.

King David ceased his lunging and withdrew to the backyard. The woman studied them one by one. Tripp seemed as hesitant as Shelby to approach the old woman.

Carson decided to greet her first. "Hi, Grandma, it's me, your granddaughter."

"I know who you are," the woman said. "What do you want?"

"I thought you'd like a visit," Carson said, attempting to be convincing. "It's been too long."

Her grandmother seemed troubled by her words at first but regained her composure. After she further scrutinized Carson, her frown transformed into a strange, uneasy smile. "Yes, it has, dearie. I've missed you. Won't you come in?"

Carson glanced back at the others as the crazy-haired woman went inside. She gave the thumbs-up gesture and trotted after her. Tripp and Shelby looked to one another for support and followed gingerly.

Inside, the elder Page woman was already in the kitchen preparing something for her guests to drink, her hospitality embedded in Southern traditions. They could hear the clinking of glasses as Tripp and Shelby sat at the round wooden table in the dining room.

Carson, always the explorer, wandered around the living room and examined everything she could find. The house was neat but cluttered. Three china cabinets were full of antique cups, saucers, and other items. Two large baker's racks were stacked with various pots and pans. Then there were the gnomes. Big and small, wooden and porcelain, they were everywhere throughout the house. Some were happy little critters, while others were unsightly monsters.

"You sure collect a lot of stuff, Grandma," Carson said.

"Oh yes, dearie," came the woman's voice from the kitchen. "I do love my little treasures."

Shelby leaned over to Tripp and whispered in his ear. "Only bona fide witches use that lingo."

Tripp's brow wrinkled and he turned his attention to his grandmother. "Grandma," he called, "do you have a bathroom?"

Hesitating, she directed him to go down the hall and to the right. As he headed that way, she called out again, "Don't go anywhere else."

Walking into the dining room, she set a tray down with four glasses of sweet iced tea. Carson joined them and took a drink. She grimaced as the sweetness overwhelmed her.

"Too sweet, dearie?" asked Grandma Page as she handed Shelby his drink.

"It's fine, Grandma." Carson forced a polite smile.

"None for me, ma'am," said Shelby, holding up a hand. "My diabetes won't allow it."

"Who's your friend, dearie?" she asked Carson, not addressing Shelby directly.

"Folks just call me Shelby, Ms. Page," he said, ignoring her indirect approach.

"And folks know not to use the name 'Page' around me," the woman shot back, her green eyes practically burning a hole through him. She observed Carson's concerned look and smiled uneasily. "You may call me Stella."

"As you wish, Stella," Shelby said. He was tempted to check his torso to ensure there were no new holes in it.

"Shelby," Stella said as she took a seat near Carson. "I once knew of someone by that name. Is your family from Arkansas?"

"Louisiana, ma'am," Shelby said, concerned where the questioning would lead. "Shelby is actually my surname, but everyone just calls me that." Usually, he'd create an elaborate story, but he feared the woman could somehow read his mind.

"I'm sure," Stella said, no longer interested. She turned back to Carson. "Did you know that the name 'Stella' means star?"

"I didn't," admitted Carson, apparently fascinated by the fact. "It's a very pretty name."

"Thank you," Stella said. Her smile revealed her small yellowing teeth for the first time. "I'm curious, though, why your father gave you a boy's name."

Carson looked unsure about how to answer that one. She took another drink of the overly sweet liquid and thought for a while. "I suppose he somehow knew I'd grow up to be tough."

"My Bradley would never have chosen such a name," Stella said, sipping her tea. "Did you need a straw, dearie?"

"No, I'm fine," Carson said. Her grandma clearly thought her mother had come up with the name. "Dad prefers to be called Jack."

Stella ignored her last comment. "Where's your brother?" she asked, looking around.

"I'll get him." Shelby abruptly stood up. "I need to use the pisser anyway." He tipped his hat and started walking.

Stella Page watched Shelby suspiciously as he disappeared down the hall. "What a queer person he is. How did you meet him?"

"Oh, he's one of Dad's old friends," Carson said, waving her hand to minimize his importance. "We broke down in Texas, so he gave us a ride."

"Texas? Were you visiting your other grandparents? I'm sure those Germans miss their daughter and grandkids. I can certainly relate to that." Stella leaned back and glared.

"No, we broke down in Denton," Carson said.

"Denton? The devil's den," she blurted out. "So I hear."

Carson hesitated in her response. "Why would you say that, Grandma?"

"Oh, that's where your grandfather was seduced by dark magic. He had orgies there, you know. Many a woman lost her virtue to that pirate. He fathered at least one bastard that I know of."

"Okay," said Carson, not sure what else to say. She desperately wanted to change the subject and hoped to get some information in the process. "Can I ask you some questions about Dad?"

Stella looked down as if sad. "Of course, dearie, though I barely remember what he looks like."

"He stays quite busy with church work, Grandma. He says he misses you." She hoped the fib would make the old woman feel better.

Stella took a moment to consider Carson's words. Her forced smile returned. "I miss all of you," she finally said. "What's your question, dearie?"

"I hope it's okay to ask this," Carson said. "How did Uncle Conner really die? I mean, was Dad there when it happened?"

Stella looked straight at Carson and cackled loudly. It sent chills down Carson's spine and seemed to shake the windows. When she was done, she gazed at a wall and took a sip of sweet tea. "My dearie is so confused. My Conner isn't dead."

"He's not? Well, wait, Grandma. Everyone says he died long ago in a car accident, but Tripp and I found something that suggested he was involved in some super-secret stuff. And these guys, out of nowhere, started chasing us. It's been a crazy week so far." Carson paused to gauge her grandmother's reaction. She hadn't meant to pour it all out at once, but there it was. "Also, Dad won't talk about it."

Stella rose a bit and leaned across the table. As she spoke in a low, raspy voice, Carson was hopeful she was about to get some answers. "My Conner occasionally talks to me, you know, but I don't see him. He's not quite himself anymore."

"That's weird!" Carson then remembered she was trying not to offend the woman. Their mission required more self-control than she was used to.

A lower, softer laugh came from the older woman. She sat up straight, as if composing herself. "I know. Life can be so strange, cruel even to the righteous. I didn't lose just one son that day." She took another sip of tea. "Let me ask you something, dearie."

"Sure, Grandma." Carson tried to smooth the fine, thin hairs that stood up on her arms.

"Which brother do you think Kate loved more?"

"Kate? My mother?" Carson asked in surprise. "I would hope my dad. Why?"

"You would think," Stella said as she leaned in. "But you never know what one brother would do for the woman he loves. My Bradley loved Kate so much, but his little brother was a thief of hearts. You know how boys can be."

I knew it, Carson thought, but she didn't want to reveal her suspicions and decided to play ignorant. "Why, Grandma, what are you saying?"

The old woman seemed to study her every word. "Fret not, dearie. It's just an old woman's blather." She scooted her chair closer to Carson's and whispered in her ear. "I hope you take more after your father and not that harlot who spit you out of her loins."

Gaping in shock, Carson leaned away. She bit her tongue at first. She and her mother had their problems, but to hear her grandmother speak as if she were some slut burned at her. If anyone was going to accuse her mother of such things, it would be Carson herself. "Grandma!" she finally said.

Stella seemed to take delight in the reaction. Her stare pierced through Carson. "You have such beautiful eyes, my dear. Just like my Conner." Stella looked around the room and suddenly realized both men were still missing. "Where's your brother and that ugly man?"

In the hallway, Shelby paced. Tripp had been exploring the next room. He came out of the dimly lit space and softly closed the door so as not to be heard.

"That is one bizarre place," Tripp said.

Shelby had been trying to listen to the conversation in the other room, shuddering every time the old lady cackled. "The witch just said you were ugly," he lied. "She should be in here soon. Looks like it's plan B after all. What did you find?"

"I don't really know," Tripp said, confused. "It appears to be some sort of shrine. I took some pictures."

Shelby felt a shiver. "Let's hope it's not dedicated to us," he said as he felt the woman approach behind him.

"What are you two up to?" Stella demanded.

"Oh, just guy talk," Shelby said. Something dropped in the dining room. "So how's the girl talk?"

"We wanted to give you ladies some time to yourselves," Tripp said. He glanced at Shelby who nodded, affirming it was a good lie.

Stella said nothing but turned to go back into the dining room. As she did, Shelby motioned for Tripp to do something to stall her.

"Uh, Grandma?"

Stella's face was stony as she pivoted around.

"What's in the room behind us?" Tripp asked, pointing.

"That's my meditation room," she said. "Don't go in there."

"Okay," Tripp said.

They both watched Stella disappear around the corner, her long dress dusting the floor. A few seconds later, she called out to them. "Get in here, boys."

"That has got to be the worst attempt at a distraction I've ever seen," Shelby whispered.

"Sorry," Tripp said sheepishly. He headed back to where the women were.

As they entered the dining room, Carson was still in the same place they had left her. Stella had gone into the kitchen for something.

Tripp started to sit down but stopped when he heard a car door. "I believe Grandma has company."

Shelby was already at the window and the twins joined him. A dark blue sedan was parked behind their van. Two men in black shirts and pants had already gotten out. A third man— black, bald, and wearing a suit threaded with silver— exited and then leaned back into the vehicle to retrieve something. As they approached the steps, Shelby hoped it wasn't a really big gun.

"Check out the threads on that guy," Shelby said, referring to the one in the suit. "That's quite the pimpin' outfit."

"You need to leave," Stella said curtly from behind them. Her voice made them jump.

"Some men just arrived at your house, Grandma," Tripp said.

"Do you know these people?" Carson asked as she put a hand on the frail little woman's shoulder. Her grandmother stared and said nothing. Carson looked unsure of what her silence meant.

Shelby went to search for a back door. He opened it to reveal the junked appliances, and beyond it, a maze of shrubs guarded by gargoyles. The dog was nowhere in sight, but Shelby could hear him announcing the arrival of the strangers. Soon the pit bull stopped barking.

Shelby motioned for the twins to join him. "I'm sure they're nice people. We should leave your lovely granny to her guests."

There was a knock on the door.

"We could stay if you wish, Grandma," Tripp said.

"That won't be necessary," Stella replied. "They're just neighbors from down the road."

Carson looked alarmed. Perhaps she'd also noticed the dog had stopped barking. "Are you sure, Grandma?"

"Oh dearie, Grandma will be just fine. Now, let's go out the back since those big dummies are already blocking the stairs," Stella said, guiding them to the back door where Shelby was. "I'll make sure King David doesn't bother you."

"Okay," Carson said.

Stella opened the back door and commanded her dog to heel. Shelby was the first one out, and he kept a careful watch on the pit bull. It lay obediently with its chin resting on its front paws.

Tripp said nothing as he hugged his grandma goodbye.

Carson looked tall next to the woman as she embraced her lightly. "Love ya."

As she started to walk off, Stella grabbed her arm and pushed a manila envelope into her hand. "Something for you, dearie," she said, mischief written on her face. She closed the door.

On the front porch, the three men waited. One grew impatient and started to go around the back of the house. A snap of the fingers from the one in the silver-threaded suit, however, stopped him in his tracks and he lined himself up beside the other man.

The door opened and the bodyguards moved aside to allow their boss to walk up the steps. He had something hidden behind his back as he closed in on Stella and revealed the item once he stood before her.

Stella's eyes grew large at the sight. "For me?" she said as she accepted the yellow rose. She had to stand on her toes in order to kiss the young man on the cheek. "A charmer, just like your father."

A warm smile formed on his dark, handsome face as she took his arm and escorted him through the door.

Just before they entered, she turned to the men standing guard. "You two, inside as well," she snapped.

They promptly did as they were told.

POLYHEDRON

Shelby waited for the door to close, then quietly moved into the driver's side of the van and fired up the engine. He looked relieved that no one ran out of the house shooting. Carson and Tripp climbed into the boxy vehicle and Shelby maneuvered his way around the sedan. They drove off and kept watch behind them.

"Odd encounter," Tripp said.

"Very," said Shelby. "I'm just glad to be out of there."

As they drove, Carson examined the large envelope her grandmother had handed her. She slid the picture out; something was familiar about it. It took her a moment to realize she had seen this picture of her mom before, only this version hadn't been cropped to just include her—it was the original.

Kate Page stood on the far right of the frame beside a young man with sandy-blond hair and eyes eerily similar to Carson's. Beside him was another man, slightly shorter and with dark hair and eyes—her dad. She assumed the one on the right was her uncle. To his left was another woman who resembled her mom but wasn't as attractive. Her aunt, she guessed.

Carson's eyes widened as she realized what the photo meant. It was proof that her dad was not originally with her mom but her mom's sister. More importantly—and this supported Carson's conspiracy theory—her mom and uncle had once been a couple. No wonder the picture had been cropped. She turned it over to find four handwritten names.

She read them to herself, from left to right: Rebecca, Bradley Jr., Conner, and Kate.

Carson was so absorbed in the picture that she was hardly aware Tripp had spoken. She returned to reality when he nudged her. "What?"

"I said it would have been nice had our plan actually worked out," Tripp said. "At least I took some interesting pictures on my phone in Grandma's so-called meditation room."

"That's nice," Carson finally said, her mind still elsewhere.

Shelby said, "Next time, we go with my plan and encyclopedia boy back there learns some better stalling tactics."

"Why?" asked Carson as she put down the manila envelope. "My plan worked just fine."

From her shorts pocket she produced an object wrapped in old newspaper, several layers of aged packing tape around it.

Shelby hesitantly accepted the crudely wrapped gift. "Is this it?"

"The only thing hidden in a compartment behind an old china cabinet," Carson said with pride.

"You little shit," said Shelby. "I thought we did all that for nothing."

"Sorry, I was distracted by this," she said as she handed the envelope to Tripp.

Tripp inspected the photo but didn't comment on it. "How did you know which china cabinet to search?"

"I'm just that good," Carson said. She turned her attention to a river they were crossing over. Several kayakers were about to pass under the bridge they were traveling on. She wished she were with them instead of riding in the smelly van.

"You mean you were lucky," Shelby said as he checked his phone for a new GPS route.

"I don't believe in luck," Carson said. "Only destiny."

"Whatever," Shelby said with a laugh. He punched in a new route while he drove. "Nice work."

Tripp leaned in between the two front seats. "Sir, I believe you agreed to let me see the object we retrieved."

"Did I? Okay, but hand it back after your superior brain is done analyzing it," Shelby said and handed it to him.

Tripp eagerly accepted the wrapped treasure. As he removed years of old tape and newspaper, a round object emerged. When it was completely unwrapped, he held it up to the light. The sun's rays danced off its surface, reflecting different colors, as he turned it in his hand.

"Definitely a polyhedron," he said. "Not translucent, at least as far as I can tell. Then again, the reflective properties could offset any perceivable light that might refract through it. It's some type of polished crystal."

"How does it work with the device we found?" Carson asked.

"Any hypothesis would require the support of further investigation."

"Just saying, 'I don't know,' would be a lot quicker, ya geek."

Shelby laughed. "Okay, geek, hand it back and settle in. Back to Denton we go."

"Denton?" Carson said.

"Yeah, I'm going to drop you kiddos off wherever you left your Jeep. I'll escort you back to Florida, where Pops will arrange for you to join your parents."

"And if I decide I'm not going back to Florida just yet?"

"Look, you get kudos for your spirit. I wish I worked with more folks like you. However, I wasn't given a vote. So, if you give me any crap, I'll stick you in a box and ship you back home via FedEx."

Carson started to protest but suddenly stopped. "Okay, you win. Drop us off and we'll tuck tail and run for safety."

Shelby swore under his breath. "If you get yourselves killed, I'm leaving the country."

DOWN UNDER

Ryder held the binoculars to his eyes, watching the green muscle car drive up and stop. From about a hundred yards away, he saw the two men exit and begin searching the area. Soon they would find the cave entrance. He and his team were resigned to waiting behind the sparse layer of oak trees, until they were ready to move in.

Sure enough, the men, one Asian, the other Hispanic, found the slope in the earth and walked down and disappeared into it. They weren't who Ryder had hoped they would be. He glanced around as he pressed a button on his earpiece mic. "On me, move in slowly."

Eleven men in woodland camo and Kevlar vests, armed with bullpup assault rifles, emerged from their cover and formed a broad semicircle as they moved toward the cavern entrance. They held their preselected positions and awaited further orders. Ryder, the only member wearing a boonie hat, wasn't crazy about his team being in the open, but they needed to be closer to make their move.

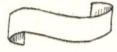

Beyond the line of trees where Ryder and his team had left their vehicles, another figure watched and waited from some brush. A military cap hid most of his blond hair, while a balaclava shrouded the lower part of his face. From behind yellow shooting glasses, he counted heads and identified the team leader. Hunched down in a patch baked golden by the Texas sun, he blended in well into his surroundings. He took particular interest in the sniper, who seemed chummy with the leader.

After the group of soldiers for hire moved out, the masked man glided across the terrain and hid between two black SUVs. The mercenary never saw or heard his stalker, nor did he have time to react as the hand slipped around his face and covered his mouth. A thin blade entered the side of his neck.

As the life left his victim, the man dragged him through the brush until he reached the edge of the open field. As if for some predetermined purpose, he left the body there.

He took the variable-scoped AR-15 off his shoulder and switched to the magnified setting. Peering through it, he surveyed the area around the cavern and made a mental note of where Ryder's team had set up.

Daniel and Joe walked down the slope into the earth. The path they took started as rock and dirt but became a man-made stone walkway as they approached the cavern entrance. The walkway was in disrepair but still useful; what used to be more hospitable was now overgrown. Reaching the entrance, they were met with a solid wall erected to seal it off. In the center of the wall was a narrow steel door. It should have been locked, but someone had taken bolt cutters to the thick chain that once secured it.

The door's rusted hinges creaked as Joe carefully opened it. He turned on his flashlight as he entered the unknown.

Daniel grabbed his arm. "You sure about this, Joe?"

"Really, dude? You were the one who insisted we do this, even after Tripp called and warned us that bad people may be looking for the same thing we are."

"I know," Daniel said as he released Joe's arm. "It's just that I've heard about strange species of spiders that live in caves."

Joe paused and looked surprised. "Spiders are the least of our worries, buddy. Let's find this underworld server room and then get the hell out of here."

"That part excites me. I just hope no undesirables are lying in wait." Daniel's words echoed through the narrow passageway.

"If there are, your chatter is sure to announce our arrival," Joe whispered.

They continued on the journey downward, passing a salamander creeping along the wet wall. Its red gills and lack of eyes gave Daniel the shivers. "Tripp wouldn't have done well down here," he whispered.

"He afraid of critters too?"

"No, enclosed spaces."

Steps had been carved years before to aid whoever had last used the cavern. They traveled down a spiral passage, their lights guiding their path. The sound of dripping water bounced off the walls. Joe paused to study their texture as they descended deeper; there was something strange, even unique, about their patterns and color.

Daniel went around the bend while Joe checked out the area around him. Daniel's light was a flickering glow as he moved ahead of and below Joe.

The slope in the cavern floor leveled off and Daniel noticed the remnants of a man-made wall in an open chamber. Stalactites tapered from above, while stalagmites rose up along the perimeter. As he approached the wall, Daniel wondered what had ripped most of it away. He had a feeling of déjà vu; he had seen this place somewhere before. Yet it was somehow different.

As he stepped forward, Daniel kept his light on the wall and could sense the emptiness beyond the ruined structure. He took his phone out and replayed the recording of the video from the briefcase. He fast-forwarded until he found the section he was searching for.

Comparing it to the area around him, he finally reached a conclusion. Yes, it was the same place, but a chill ran down him. He stood where something terrible had happened years before.

Daniel took another step forward to get a look around the wall. After another step, there was no longer a floor beneath his feet. He lost his balance and fell forward. The light tumbled from his hand as he hung in the air. Below him, the light bounced around and plopped into a previously unseen pool of water below him. The light cast an eerie glow as it sunk and then flickered out.

At first, Daniel wasn't sure why he had not followed the flashlight into the depths below, but then he felt a tug on the back of his shirt. He heard Joe grunt from behind him as the man—who had obviously caught him before he could go over—pulled him back to level ground.

"You really have to be more careful, dude," Joe said.

Daniel collected himself and grabbed Joe in a bear hug. "Thanks, Uncle Joe!" His voice bounced around the massive chamber.

"No problem, and it's just Joe. Knock off the uncle crap." Joe freed himself from Daniel's embrace and shined his light downward. He whistled at what he saw. "What the hell happened here?"

"It's a crater." Daniel spoke in a low voice to minimize the echo. "This must be the final results of what happened in that video we watched."

Joe moved his light around and noticed something odd when the beam tracked across the center of the crater. "Do you see that?"

"Do it again."

As he did, they watched the beam refract near the center of the crater and then vanish. "What the hell?"

"There's something there, a distortion of some type. I wish Tripp would hurry and get here. He's good at making hypotheses about the unknown." Daniel pulled out his cell phone and recorded the strange effect of Joe's flashlight beam striking the spot.

"You can show it to him later," Joe said with a chuckle.

"Why the laugh?" Daniel asked.

"You two seem an odd couple. When we first met, I thought you and Tripp might have been an item—that is, until I saw the way you looked at Carson."

"We've always been good friends," Daniel said, avoiding the subject of Carson. "He's upset with me right now."

"Oh? For what?" Joe asked while his light still danced around the distortion.

"He learned I was paid by my uncle to watch over him and his sister," Daniel said.

Joe stopped and turned his light on Daniel. "You were paid by your uncle? The one who died?"

"Yes," Daniel said, shielding his eyes from Joe's flashlight. "My uncle was very good friends with Pops. He felt it was his duty to help protect Pops's family."

Joe shook his head in disbelief. "So you became friends with Tripp because you were paid to? I guess I'd be pissed too, dude."

"It wasn't like that," Daniel said defensively. "Years ago, I was paid to stay close and watch over them, not be friends. Friendship was something that just happened. I tried explaining that to Tripp."

"What about your family? I mean, aside from your Uncle Fumi, where are your folks at?"

"My father died years ago when I was very young. My mother lives in one of my uncle's penthouses in Hong Kong. I go see her every now and then. Aside from her and my uncle Fumi, the Pages are really my only family."

Joe lowered his light and gazed at him, as if recognizing something familiar. "Man, we have such a dysfunctional family."

Daniel laughed. "At least we have a family."

"True," Joe said, sounding impressed. "When I first met Jack, he told me some things about our dad. I'm sure there's more, but he probably shared more than he had to. He avoided talking about our brother's death, at least in the beginning. As we discussed my own pain around my mother's death, he eventually opened up a bit. Definitely some unresolved issues there."

"Maybe it's just survivor's guilt."

"There seems to be more to it," Joe said. "How much were my two brothers alike?"

"They were polar opposites, according to Mrs. Page. I once asked her questions about Conner. I was, you know, curious."

"What did you learn?"

"She described him as very smart and bold," Daniel said. "She spoke of him very fondly."

"Uh-oh. Sounds like she liked the guy," Joe said. "I get the impression Jack and Kate's relationship is a complicated one."

"Want to hear something really strange?" Daniel asked. "Carson once told me that her mom wanted to name Tripp after his dead uncle."

"No shit? She wanted to call him Conner Jr.?"

"I guess," Daniel said and giggled. "Isn't that weird?"

"That and your laugh. How did Jack feel about it?"

"I guess it didn't go over so well with him. So we now have Bradley Jack Page III, known as just Tripp. Tripp won't talk about it, but Carson, as you've seen, says what she thinks."

"I noticed. What did she think?"

"She figures her mom was banging her uncle before he died."

Surprised, Joe laughed. "That's weird." He started back in the other direction.

"Wait for me," Daniel said. "I don't have a light anymore."

"You have your phone's light," Joe said as he continued walking.

"I need to conserve battery power," Daniel said, catching up to the man.

They backtracked to a point where Joe noticed another path going into a different branch of the cavern. As they followed it, they could see scorched walls and burned-out equipment from years past. Shells of computers and monitors, relics by current standards, and other older equipment had been destroyed in a blaze.

"Looks like things got pretty hot in here," Joe said. "Strangely, this seems to be the only part affected by fire. The other areas were . . . well, I don't know what the hell happened out there. That bizarre distortion in the crater room still gives me the creeps. Did your video turn out?"

Daniel hadn't checked. He pulled out his phone and watched the short video. When he started to comment on it, Joe shushed him.

Joe stood silently, listening. "Someone's in here with us," he finally whispered. "Let's get moving."

He used his flashlight just long enough to find the path that led back up and out. He turned it off while he and Daniel hugged the wall, using it to guide them. When Daniel quietly chanted, "No spiders . . . no spiders . . . no spiders," he elbowed him.

As they headed back up, footsteps echoed and a light appeared up ahead. Joe and Daniel hurried back down and hid behind a colonnade of stalagmites. Hopefully, whoever it was would pass by without searching too thoroughly.

They held their breath as the light came around the bend. Its beam flickered all around them as a figure passed by. To their relief, the person moved on.

After they waited another moment, they zigzagged around rocks and stalagmites in the direction that led back to the surface.

As they drew closer to the entrance, natural light poured in like a beacon of hope. Joe, however, stopped in his tracks. Daniel almost tripped as he tried to do the same.

"What?" Daniel whispered.

Joe, dimly lit by the light just ahead, had the look of a man undergoing an epiphany. Daniel waited as he stood briefly, apparently calculating something in his head.

Joe didn't have to say anything. "There are more out there, waiting for us," Daniel said.

"I'm afraid so."

"What should we do?"

"Either try to find a hiding spot in here somewhere or make a run for it."

"There should be plenty of places to hide. Let's find a good one and wait this out."

"That may work, unless they saw us enter. In that case, they'll eventually find us."

"Right," Daniel said, trying to calculate the odds. He reached the same conclusion as Joe.

They prepared to make a run for it.

UNDERGROUND REUNION

Tripp awoke first, his back stiff from sleeping in a reclined seat. The twilit sky was the first indication he hadn't had a full night's sleep. The second was he was still tired. His sister slept on her side in the front passenger seat. He envied her size, knowing he would never have been able to fit as snugly in the cramped quarters.

They had been dropped off at Carson's Jeep in Denton the evening before. Then, after they lied about heading straight to either Shreveport or Houston after they ate, Shelby took off to eventually rendezvous with Pops in Florida.

They kept in contact with Daniel and their uncle Joe while on their way to Austin. They were still an hour from the Live Music Capital of the World when they received the update that Joe and Daniel had already found the place they were looking for. It was in close proximity to both San Antonio and Austin, but Tripp and Carson were worn out and opted to stop in Austin. The others, however, already had a hotel in San Antonio. The coordinates were sent and they would meet up in the morning.

Tripp wished they had sprung for a cheap hotel, but Carson had assured him she had slept comfortably in her vehicle before while chasing storms. From the peaceful sound of her light snoring, he was certain she had. He, on the other hand, had to get out and stretch.

The parking lot of the truck stop was more active than when they had first arrived late in the night. Tripp went inside to grab coffee and donuts.

When he returned, he witnessed the miracle of his sister coming to life suddenly at the smell of the day's first cup of java.

"Morning, sunshine," Carson said as she struggled to raise her eyelids.

"As I've pointed out, that's your nickname," Tripp replied. "Good morning."

"Oh, yummy—donuts." She examined the coffee cups. "And look at you, paper instead of Styrofoam."

"I'm just doing my part to save the planet, one coffee at a time."

"They probably didn't even have Styrofoam cups."

"No," Tripp admitted. "Let's eat and hit the road, shall we?"

"Let's." She then answered her phone.

It was Daniel. Her chat with him was brief, as he had called to let them know they were on their way to the mysterious cavern. They were eager to get started on the day's adventure. Carson checked her navigation system to gauge the distance.

The sun peeked above the horizon and cast an orange glow across the eastern sky as they gassed up and headed out to meet Daniel and Joe. Carson took her turn at the wheel since Tripp had driven the night before. It had given her time to finishing reading through her mother's diary. She thought back to what she had learned.

Most of its secrets were boring things she and her mother had already argued about. Her mother loved Conner but married Brad, and so on. As she got to the end, however, it became a far more interesting read.

The last handwritten page started to detail a disaster that had befallen her dad and his brother in some underground structure. She wondered if referred to the cavern they headed toward. Unfortunately, the entries abruptly ended before anything significant was revealed. Why? she wondered.

She took a careful sip of coffee since it was still too hot to gulp down. After a nibble of her donut, stale by her standards, she decided to take another look.

Tripp noticed her studying the book as she drove. "Carson, you can either read or drive—you can't do both at the same time."

Something had caught Carson's eye and she remained fixated on it. "I know why Mother's diary ended so abruptly," she said finally. "I must have been tired last night and I missed it."

"I still have no interest in knowing the private thoughts of my mother."

"Geez, it was from long ago, when she was younger than we are now."

"That changes nothing."

"Then let me introduce a fact you may find more interesting." She held up the book.

Tripp looked worried. "I told you I won't read it. Please keep your eyes forward."

"You don't need to read anything. I'm trying to show you that a page is missing. It's been torn out."

Tripp took the diary and examined it. At least one page had been carefully removed. "The care in removing the page may show a desire to preserve it."

"I knew you'd find that fascinating."

"Interesting is a better word. A missing page from a diary, particularly when you expect a revealing moment, does have a certain intrigue to it."

"I know, right?"

Against his better judgment, Tripp went ahead and read the last page. "This ends with Mom waiting to find out what happened to Brad and Conner. The next page, the missing one, might have revealed something both important and sensitive."

Carson loved both a good mystery and a challenge. "See, it's like a cliffhanger, daring us to discover what happened next."

"Possibly, although the truth may not be earthshaking. We know our dad survived the incident, but our uncle presents a mystery. The date in the diary indicates the tragedy occurred three days before our uncle officially died. That leaves a couple of possibilities—at least. One would be that he must have made it back, only to be involved in a fatal car accident three days later."

"Not likely," said Carson, who felt it was too coincidental. "I prefer the theory that he made it back and faked his own death."

"Perhaps, but that means he would've lied to everyone who loved him—and remained hidden for years. If we're going to be conspiracy theorists, it would make more sense that he died in a bizarre manner and the government tried to cover it up with a staged car accident three days later. It wouldn't be the first time I've heard of a cover story being used to explain a death resulting from something that officially didn't occur."

Carson considered it. "If so, don't you find it odd that our mother would remove a diary page? It's not like she would want to help the government cover up a covert operation."

"That *is* a curious thing."

"It's more than curious," Carson said "Whatever really happened must've been why our parents were so paranoid for years. We also moved around a lot before settling in Florida."

Tripp nodded.

Carson could feel the adrenaline kick in. "All this talking about it just makes me more excited to get where we're going. How much longer?"

"We're getting close.," Tripp replied.

They followed their navigation system and turned off on a paved road that had seen better days. It curved around until they arrived at their destination. It was easy to spot their uncle Joe's bright car. Once parked, they looked for any sign of a cavern. Tripp spotted what he believed was the place and they headed for it.

As they passed through the cavern entrance, they almost ran right into Daniel and Joe.

"Hey, guys," Carson said with enthusiasm.

"Crap," Daniel said. "I meant to tell you not to come."

"That's a lousy welcome."

Joe quieted them both down and pointed to where they had just come from. "There's someone in here looking for us," he whispered.

"He's heavily armed," Daniel added.

"We need a new plan, then," Carson said and started to leave.

Her uncle stopped her. "Did you see anyone out there?"

"No. Why?"

"Because Daniel and I think there are more people out there, watching."

"With guns?"

"Yes."

Carson grumbled and tried to think of a plan. "Are you armed, Uncle Joe?"

Joe hesitated, as if he'd almost forgotten he was. He reached behind himself and produced the revolver. He held it for a moment. "Yes, but there's no way I'm going to get into a firefight."

Carson went to the entrance and hugged the edge as she peered out. She watched as the others behind her whispered among themselves. There was not much of a line of sight since the entrance was basically in a huge hole. She figured the place must flood during every good rain.

"So you really have no evidence that more people are waiting outside to ambush us?" Tripp asked.

"Not really," Daniel said. "It's just a gut feeling."

Tripp suddenly lowered his voice as he stared beyond them. "Then I suggest we take our chances. There's a light coming from the recesses of this place."

Daniel and Joe saw it too.

"That settles it, then," Joe whispered as Carson brushed passed him.

"Where are you going, sis?" Tripp asked.

Carson stopped and spun around. "I just saw a head pop over the hill. I'll take my chances in the dark."

She started to trek down into the cavern, but Tripp stopped her. He watched as the light grew brighter; the intruder would be upon them soon.

"If you really want to take a risk, then I have an idea," he whispered. He quickly explained it.

Carson thought it was nuts, but it was so unusual, especially coming from her brother, that she reluctantly went along with it. She walked down the winding path toward the growing light and was blinded by it as she rounded the corner.

The man's voice ordered her to stop, but she hugged the outer wall and pushed onward. She somehow found it within herself to hum a tune.

The man repeated his order as she passed right by him. Confused, he hesitated and looked around, as if to make sure no one else was following her, before he turned to catch up.

He had to chase after her, as she had picked up her pace. When he caught up, he abruptly spun her around to face him. "I told you to stop, bitch. Where the hell do you think you're going?"

Carson stared blankly at him and pointed. "Down there."

The man gritted his teeth, which contrasted with his dark skin. "No, you're not. You're coming up that way with me."

"No, bitch, you're coming down this way with me."

Looking bewildered by her resolve, he attempted to force Carson to go with him. He suddenly froze at the touch of the cold metal at the back of his neck.

"We'll take those weapons, dude," Joe said from behind as Daniel and Tripp each grabbed an arm.

The man seemed to realize he had fallen for a trap and complied. They escorted him into the chamber and told him to sit. Tripp had their prisoner's rifle slung over his shoulder, while Daniel had taken a large knife, his communication headset, and a Glock pistol.

Joe approached their new prisoner, intent on gathering information. "How many more of you are out there?" he demanded.

"You'll find out soon enough," the man replied.

"That doesn't help much," Daniel said, then stared down at his phone. "Someone just texted me and said to stay put and wait for further instruction."

"Who?" Joe asked. "How do they know where we're at?"

"I don't know who. The number is blocked."

They all used their lights to search the cavern until Tripp spotted the camera above them, in the shadows.

"We have an audience," Tripp said.

"Find out who it is, Daniel," Carson said.

Daniel texted the unknown number back and waited. He soon received a response and read it aloud. "It says, 'I'm on your side.'"

"A mysterious friend or a trick?" Joe asked.

"I think a bad guy would just come in here and shoot us all," Carson said. "Whoever they are, they're obviously watching us."

Daniel looked less confident. "What if that's the idea? They tell us to stay in one spot so they can come for us?"

Tripp said, "I agree with Carson. No one would alert us that they're watching us if they intend to do us harm. Whoever it is has Daniel's number, so that favors the ally theory."

Carson agreed but still didn't like to leave anything unsolved. She shined her light on the camera. "I wonder why you don't tell us who you are," she called out.

"I'll assume they'll reveal themselves when the time is right," said Tripp. "Until then, we've little choice but to wait."

"I hate waiting," Carson said with a moan.

Daniel nodded in agreement. While they waited for whatever was to happen next, he showed Carson and Tripp the strange anomaly in the center of the chamber.

Tripp did several tests with light similar to what the others told him they had done earlier. He wanted to climb down into the chamber to investigate further, but Joe stopped him. A light was shined down to illuminate the pool of water that lay below the anomaly.

Tripp didn't feel like swimming so decided on a new test. He threw a rock at the exact spot where the light disappeared. The others were perplexed when the rock didn't pass through it but diverted at an angle.

"That's crazy," Carson said. "Do it again."

Tripp did so several more times. Each time, it did the same thing—until the last try. The stone simply vanished.

"Now that was fascinating," Tripp said.

"What could cause that?" Daniel asked.

"I'd be guessing at this point."

Joe, distracted by Tripp's experiments, had taken his eyes off the man he was watching. "Shit. Guys, we have a problem. Our guest is gone."

They beamed their flashlights around the cavern in an attempt to find him, but to no avail. The mercenary had clearly made a run for the exit.

"He'll be back with reinforcements. We can't stay here," Daniel said.

"Where do you suggest we go?" Carson asked.

"What in the world could your purpose be?" Tripp's voice echoed from near the crumbled wall.

"Did you find him?" Joe asked.

"No, but I did find an unusual man-made structure on the far side of the cavern wall. It resembles scaffolding that rises toward the ceiling, with a catwalk situated over the anomaly."

"Hello? We're trying to find a safe way out of here," Carson said with a moan.

"What about that other chamber?" asked Tripp.

"It's a dead end full of junk," Daniel replied. "I would think—" He stopped as his phone vibrated. He read the new text. "New message from our mysterious friend," he announced.

"What does it say?" Carson asked as she drew closer to him.

Daniel read it verbatim. "Your prisoner exited the cavern. Proceed to the next chamber."

"We just established it was a dead end. We should probably stay here, in this larger chamber. There are more places to hide and set up an ambush if need be."

"Carson, we should go into the other chamber," said Daniel.

"Why, because some mysterious person says so?"

"Well," said Daniel with a chuckle. "Our mysterious friend says, 'Tell Carson to quit being a pain in the butt.'"

"If it's my mother, tell 'er we're fine where we're at," Carson said.

"What if it's your dad?" asked Daniel.

Carson muttered something and stomped off. The rest of the group followed her to the next chamber. It was much smaller than the one they had left and was probably used as a control center at one time. Just as Daniel had said, it was full of burned-up old equipment. Sure enough, a dead end.

Daniel sat on the floor, using his cell phone for light, and took out the tactical headset he had taken from the man they captured. He began to fiddle with it.

"What are you doing?" Carson asked.

"I'm going to try to listen in to see who's out there. Maybe we can stay one step ahead of them."

"You gonna share the experience?"

Daniel searched through his pack. "If I can get it to work. Something's interfering with the signal."

"Please hurry. We don't need any more surprises."

AVENGING SPIRIT

Ryder had watched the white Jeep park close to the green Camaro. He tried to verify who they were but couldn't be certain. The two, a male and female, were definitely not professionals. He informed his team to avoid engagement, just in case they were unacceptable casualties.

After they had disappeared into the cavern, his team began to materialize, as if by magic, from their hiding places and resume their positions. Archer moved to a small hill on the far end of the bowl-shaped form above the entrance to the cavern. He took a prone position, his sniper rifle ready, and blended in as best he could.

Ryder found a dent in the field and burrowed into it. He hadn't heard back from Rogers, who was supposed to be scouting the cavern. He radioed him again but got no response.

"That's what ya get for sending in a green Yank," said Archer over their channel.

"It'll be the last time I send a muppet to do a man's job," Ryder replied.

A shot rang out.

"All positions report," Ryder commanded. He turned around toward general direction the shot had come from. Another one went off. A team member flanking him, less than ten yards away, fell backward.

Multiple reports came in; the shooter was in the line of trees behind them, the direction they had come from. Ryder ordered his team to change their firing positions to compensate. He burrowed back into his crevice and radioed the man he had left back at the vehicles.

"Leader to base camp, what's your status?" Ryder said into the mic attached to his earpiece. He waited for a couple of seconds. "Repeat, base what is your status?" He swore as he concluded two of his team were out of commission. "Spencer is down," he announced in his comm.

Ryder pulled up the binoculars to check the area where Spencer was supposed to be. As he scanned the copse, he spotted something. "Archer, I need a scope on that underbrush, one o'clock."

The seconds ticked away until a single sniper shot rang out and Archer's voice came back. "Got 'im."

As Ryder stood up to get a better angle to verify this, he heard someone approach behind him. Instinctively, he lowered the glasses, drew his sidearm, and turned.

The black man held his hands up. "It's me, chief."

"Rogers, where the hell have you been?" Ryder noticed something missing. "And where's your rifle?"

Rogers shrugged as if he could hardly explain it. He simply pointed back toward the cavern.

"Bloody muppet," Ryder swore as he tossed him his spare pistol. "Watch that entrance and let no one leave."

As Ryder turned, another shot pierced the silence. He dived for cover amid the confused chatter from his men that flooded his ear. He promptly ordered silence so he could give direction. "Archer, we have another shooter."

Archer's French accent came back, cursing. "No, not a new one. I apparently shot Spencer, or at least his lifeless body. That son of a bitch set him up to look like the shooter."

From his position, Ryder could barely see the glint of Archer's scope over the hill he was using for cover. Archer seemed absorbed in spotting their opponent.

Ryder used his binoculars to scan the area. "Clever bastard," he said. Their opponent, he surmised, had drawn them into a firefight so his compatriots could flee. He set himself up between them and their own vehicles to deny them an exit. A nice plan, he thought. "Rogers, watch that cave entrance. Archer, look for return fire."

"Roger that," Archer replied.

Again, Rogers failed to respond. Reluctantly, Ryder moved his attention back to the entrance and found what he expected.

Not far from where he had last seen him lay Rogers. The last shot that rang out was meant for the man, and their opponent's aim was true.

Another shot pierced the silence.

From various positions, Ryder's team opened fire into the copse of trees. After saturating the area, he called a ceasefire. Silence, for the moment, returned.

Ryder glimpsed Archer, who still hunted for a target. The man shook his head in frustration. He was one of the few who had worn a combat helmet. On its side, he kept a miniature video camera that recorded the entire mission.

"Status?" Ryder said. One by one, his team reported back that all was quiet. Their adversary had either retreated or was hit, Ryder thought. "All units, close in on that position. Archer, hold back for a moment, mate. Let's see what our shooter does."

"Roger that."

Ryder waited as his men crept across a mostly open field of dirt, rock, and scrub toward a clump of sparse trees. Ryder knew he might lose one or two before Archer could get a bead on the other sniper, but it was a risk he had to take. As they came within about ten yards of it, the team set up on the border of the area they believed the shooter was in.

Ryder waited for news. As the group held their new position, he rose and started in that direction. "Two men move up," Ryder said.

As he carefully yet briskly cut across the open area, two of his men entered the trees. A couple of seconds later, an explosion erupted. Everyone hit the ground.

As the smoke and dust settled, Ryder raised his head. "Booby trap," he said. The man must have left them a gift as he retreated. "Report," he said into the mic.

One of his men reported that Buck, the other Yank on the team, had been hit by the concussion but survived. His partner, who had been behind him, was more fortunate and tended to his teammate's wounds.

The distinct sound of a motorcycle engine revving up was heard. Archer instinctively stood, hoping to get off a shot before their opponent could flee. The rest of the squad looked hesitant to do the same.

Ryder listened to gauge the direction the motorcycle had taken, but something wasn't quite right. It didn't retreat but circled around them.

He's not done with us, Ryder thought. "Archer, stay alert. He's coming around for another pass."

"I'll be ready," the man said as he changed position. He waited for a clear shot while the unseen rider circled them in the distance, hidden by hills and trees. At last the engine went silent. Everyone on the team waited, their rifles readied.

"He's out there," came Archer's voice.

Ryder knew the man on the motorcycle wouldn't leave until his companions were free. An uneasy feeling came over him. He wasn't one to wait for another ambush. "Someone get down there and check the vehicles," he ordered. "Archer, hold position. We need to ensure we own the high ground, mate. Everyone else on me."

"Already on it," said Serge, an Italian and newest member of his team.

"Roger that," Archer replied and returned to a prone position.

It didn't take long to assess the status of the vehicles. "Ryder, we have a problem. Vehicles are disabled," said Serge.

"What about the briefcase in the boot?"

A moment later, he had his answer. "It's gone."

"Shit." Ryder kicked the dirt. He knew his opponent was good, but he couldn't escape the feeling that he and his team were sloppy. After cursing repeatedly, he was suddenly struck by a thought. "Serge, check Spencer's body. Let me know if anything's missing."

Promptly, Serge came back and said, "Spencer's headset is gone." It was just as Ryder had feared.

"Radio silence," Ryder ordered. He removed his earpiece and put it away. From that point on, they would use hand signals or talk in person. They had backup systems, but those were likely compromised as well. He turned and walked toward Archer to discuss strategy.

Archer was standing on the hill, facing the opposite direction. After a few more steps, Ryder realized the man wasn't following his normal routine. He just stood there. A chill ran down Ryder's back. He was still at least seventy yards away, so he peered into his binoculars.

Archer's hands moved in gestures, as if he was speaking to someone. He was looking down toward the other side of the hill, where Ryder had no line of sight. His weapon wasn't in his hand nor across his shoulder.

As Ryder scanned the ground around Archer's feet, he saw the sniper rifle lying there. He placed the earpiece back in his ear. "Archer."

"Ryder." Archer's tone all but confirmed his situation. "Our guest wishes to speak with you."

Ryder took a deep breath as he stared at the back of his longtime friend and teammate. "This is Ryder," he finally said.

The man's voice was calm. "I would have left you in peace, but unfortunately there's one more matter we need to address."

"We may be able to work out a deal that allows your friends in the cave to leave unscathed."

"That's going to happen either way. I refer to another matter. Rick Sanchez was a good man."

Ryder realized it was more than a rescue mission; the man had vengeance on his mind. "Let's discuss this, mate," he said quickly, unsure of what else to say. "I'm sure we can find a reasonable solution, one professional to another."

Ryder, his rifle ready, continued toward Archer as he awaited a response. He stopped suddenly as his opponent's voice returned.

"If you wanted professionalism, you shouldn't have murdered my friend."

"If you play the avenging angel, the devil will find you," Ryder said with a snarl just before a single shot went off. He cried out as Archer fell limp.

Had Ryder not been running at full speed, his aim might have been better. The man came over the hill and dove into the sunken earth by the cave entrance. Ryder's shots missed and Archer's killer disappeared into the cavern entrance.

Damn, Ryder thought as he ran faster. "Everyone on my position," he ordered. He knew the mysterious man was listening, but he no longer cared. He wanted him to know he was coming for him.

Ryder reached the top of the hill while his men edged up into positions around the cavern entrance. He examined Archer's body and found the bullet hole in the middle of his forehead. The blood streamed down between Archer's open gray eyes. With his free hand, he closed them gently. "Sorry, mate," he said. He knew his men were watching, so he kept his goodbye brief.

As he stood and turned, he heard one of his men announce that the briefcase was sitting in the cavern entrance. Ryder instantly realized the man hadn't lost it or decided to give it back. "Take cover!"

The briefcase exploded as his team scrambled for safety. Soon Ryder emerged from the orange cloud and assessed the damage. His team had been pummeled with dirt and rocks, but those who remained gradually appeared. Serge looked dazed by the concussion of the blast and struggled to clear his senses.

The entrance had partially collapsed. Momentarily, the armed men took up position again around it. They waited as the dust slowly cleared and must have wondered if their opponent was done with them.

Ryder returned to Archer's lifeless, debris-covered body to retrieve an item he needed. He reached over and unfastened the military-grade camera from Archer's helmet. He wiped off the dirt caked on it, and figuring out how to open the device, retrieved the micro-SD chip inside.

Ryder placed the chip in his shirt pocket and made his way to the outside of the cavern. A wall of rock about waist high had formed in the entrance and gave him shelter to crouch behind. He dared to be much closer than any of his men were willing to be. He rinsed his mouth with water from his canteen and took a drink.

"If your little explosion was supposed to kill us or seal you inside, I'm afraid it came up short on both counts." Ryder said, unsure of whether the man was close enough to hear and would answer through the missing headset. "Are you coming out or am I going in after you?" He listened but heard only his own words echo through the darkness.

Then Ryder heard the static, followed by the voice in his ear.

"How does it feel?"

"Come back and I'll show you," Ryder replied.

His remaining men stared curiously at him until they realized he was talking into his headset. They scrambled to put their own communication pieces back in their ears.

"I think there's been enough bloodshed for one day, don't you?" said the man.

"Not until I see your blood."

"You may get your chance. Be better prepared next time."

"I promise," Ryder said and spat more dirt from his mouth. "How will I know you when we meet again?"

"Ask Archer."

Ryder's eyes narrowed. "Bloody bastard."

"I'll see you soon."

"Damn right you will." Ryder removed his earpiece and tossed it aside in disgust. He stood for a bit longer.

Serge walked up and extended his arms in a frustrated gesture. "What the hell was that, chief?" he asked, dumbfounded. "Four dead and several wounded."

Ryder shook his head. "Payback."

"For what you did to that cop?"

"The cop," Ryder repeated. "Serge, patch me through to Joshua. I want video so he sees our situation."

"On it," Serge said as he retrieved the system from one of the packs. He set up a small dish, monitor, and camera.

While Ryder waited, he reviewed the conversation he had with their opponent. "Ask Archer," he said. He walked over to the pile of packs his men had gathered from their disabled vehicles. After sifting through them, he found Archer's duffel bag. Inside was the deceased man's tablet, which he used to play back missions.

Ryder slid the SD chip into place and searched through the footage Archer had recorded. He found what he wanted a moment before Serge informed him he had reached Joshua. He brought the tablet with him as he sat in front of a monitor set up for the video conference.

The young black man stared back at him. "Ryder, you look the worse for wear."

"I've had better days."

"So I see. You ran into resistance at the cavern?"

"You could say that, Joshua. Some pissed-off bloke indicated he was friends with the dead cop."

"What's your status?"

"Four confirmed dead, a few banged up. Our opponent retreated into the cavern, along with four noncombatants. Two of them are non-engagement—Stella's, I believe."

"You're not to proceed where collateral damage is even remotely possible."

Ryder knew that was coming. "Understood."

"What do you know of the team that hit you?"

Ryder felt as if Joshua hadn't heard him the first time. "It wasn't a team. As far as I could tell, it was a single bloke." He produced the tablet, the relevant footage paused on it. "Let me just show you, mate."

He turned up the device and pushed Play. He held it so Joshua could see the playback. The image of a man came into view. Archer's camera pointed to the man as he spoke into his earpiece, talking to Ryder. He then looked straight into the camera, addressed Archer, aimed his pistol, and fired.

"Play that last part again," Joshua said. Ryder did so.

Joshua strained to hear the words through the conferencing connection.

"Whoever tries to keep their life will lose it."

"Pause there," Joshua said. He studied the image of the man peering over his sunglasses just before he had fired the deadly shot. Those eyes were like sapphires. "Ryder, this operation is over. Make damn sure your team engages no one else. Clean up your mess and prepare for emergency evacuation. A helo is en route."

The communication ended before Ryder could respond, not that there was anything left to say. The man had spoken.

"We're done here," Ryder said to the others. "You know the drill."

A LIGHT FROM THE SHADOWS

They were scattered throughout the dimly lit chamber, having turned off all but one of their lights. When the shooting had started outside, Joe insisted they not present themselves as targets. Every now and then, Daniel would catch something coming over the tactical headset he had liberated from their former prisoner. Reception was spotty, due to interference likely caused by being underground, if not the anomaly in the adjacent chamber. Still, he relayed whatever he did manage to hear.

A massive explosion was followed by silence. They waited for something to happen. The distant dripping of water was the only answer they received.

Daniel strained to listen into the receiver. He had meant to rig something so everyone could listen, but time wasn't on his side. The seconds ticked by and occasional static teased him into thinking something was about to come through. Finally, he heard a conversation.

Two men were in a terse exchange. At first, he caught only parts of it, then, complete sentences. Daniel made out two distinct voices. One threatened the other. He heard the words "I'll see you soon."

"What's happening?" came Carson's impatient voice from her dark corner.

"It may be over with," Daniel replied.

"Great. Who won?"

"To answer that, we'd probably need to know more about the opposing forces," Tripp said.

"Thanks, oh wise one. What about that mysterious friend we're supposed to have?"

"Nothing yet," Daniel said after he checked his messages.

"We can't just sit here and wonder," Carson said. "How about if I sneak back the way we came and see what's happening?"

"A poor plan," Tripp replied from the shadows.

"Do you have a better one, Tripp?"

Chatter erupted briefly. Outside the small chamber they occupied, a hoarse whisper echoed. They couldn't make out the words. After an eerie pause, Carson finally spoke up.

"Be quiet, everyone," she whispered. "Hello?"

"Enter the next chamber and wait until it's safe to leave," the male voice said.

"Uh, no, we're not coming to you so you can kill us."

"Not this chamber," the voice echoed back.

"Sir, where's this next chamber located?" Tripp asked.

On cue, the sound of rock grinding against rock came from the corner where Carson sat, startling her. She spun to see a soft blue glow coming from just beyond the false cave wall as it opened. Soon a new entryway exposed a dimly lit tunnel that led somewhere else.

"What's in there?" Carson asked.

"Safety," the voice said. "And the knowledge you seek."

"Are you disguising your voice?" Daniel asked. "You sound a lot like Christian Bale's version of Batman when you talk."

There was no response.

"Why should we trust you?" Carson demanded.

Daniel glanced at his phone. "Because our mysterious friend says, 'Trust him.'"

For a group with few options, it was good enough. One by one, they stepped into the tunnel, with Carson the last to enter. Before doing so, she turned back into the darkness. "Who are you?"

"One of the good guys," the voice answered.

"Come on, sis," Tripp called from somewhere within the curved tunnel.

Carson stepped in and the wall began to close. Before it did, she shined her flashlight in the direction she thought the voice had come from, which was difficult to discern from the acoustics of the cavern.

Just outside of the entrance to the smaller chamber, she spotted a pair of sapphire-blue eyes between a cap and a balaclava, staring back at her.

With a screech reminiscent of fingernails on a chalkboard, the door sealed itself.

RETRO CHAMBER

The air in the tunnel had a mustier scent than that of the other chambers they had visited. The dim lighting revealed walls of natural rock, although the tunnel itself hadn't been naturally formed. This was obvious to Tripp, who was anxious to escape the enclosed space. To his relief, the journey to the new entryway was short.

Daniel joined Tripp in examining a new obstacle. A stone archway had been built into the rock. Within it was a steel cage that housed an old wooden elevator. Locating the latch that secured it, they slid open the rusty cage, which screeched in resistance.

The wooden door, with its small window, wouldn't open. Tripp spotted the call button on the brass panel. After he had pressed it, the door unlatched. It slid more easily than the cage had, and a florescent bulb flickered to life inside it.

Carson had been watching and stepped through before the others had a chance. She discovered the old round crank and ran her hand across its handle. The temptation to play with it subsided and she waited for Tripp to examine it.

"An antique brass crank." Tripp determined it would rotate clockwise or counterclockwise to three choices that were engraved into the metal.

To the far left was Exit, while the one to the far right read Control. The middle choice, and where the crank was turned to, read Main. As Daniel and Joe entered the cramped elevator, the door slid shut. The majority decided that Control sounded more appealing than Exit.

Joe was the only one ready to go. "After you guys get to this control place, I'll be heading up to the exit."

Carson tried to intervene. "We need to stick together, Uncle Joe. What if I need you later?"

Joe laughed. "I feel sorry for anyone who messes with you. Besides, you have plenty of help now. I need to head home and get Wanda out of jail."

"Can't you just leave her there another day or two?"

"It's tempting, but she did end up there because she was helping us. It's been a couple of days, and I fear for the cops if I leave her there much longer."

Tripp, who waited by the antique elevator crank, said, "Uncle Joe, it may still be dangerous aboveground. It was you who said there's safety in numbers."

"There's also the danger of pissing Wanda off. Now let's get moving, assuming this thing even works."

Tripp wound the handle of the crank clockwise before releasing it. "We'll soon find out."

With a jolt, they began their descent. The elevator was slow but still arrived soon at its destination, indicating they hadn't traveled much deeper into the earth. Tripp was eager to exit, as being in cramped quarters was making him anxious. The others got out of his way as he slid the door open.

After they stepped out, each hugged Joe goodbye and watched him until the wooden door closed. The old mechanism started up again and the elevator began its journey upward. They continued into the new chamber.

It was a larger space than the one they had left, but still much smaller than the first. Green light flooded the area. While the cavern had been formed naturally, it had also been modified for some purpose. Stalactites hung down and clusters of stalagmites rose from the floor, but some had been left in patterns, while the rest had been cleared for floor space.

They passed a trickling waterfall that pooled locally and disappeared into the unknown. Tripp speculated that the water had come from a chamber above, likely the pool below the anomaly. He further suggested there was another chamber below them where the water traveled to, if not an underground stream or river.

The purpose of the place became clear as they crossed its center and spotted a glistening metallic object in the corner. As they approached, the floor rose two feet by way of steps and became a raised concrete floor.

Before them was a long brass console that merged with the natural rock. It was dotted with knobs, levers, and buttons. On the wall just beyond it was the largest round monitor they had ever seen, framed in brass. It was a retro sci-fi fan's dream.

"It's like something from a Jules Verne novel," Tripp said in awe.

"It's beautiful," said Daniel and wiped a tear of joy from his eye.

"It's a geek's wet dream." Carson wasn't as impressed. "What is it?"

Tripp wasted no time in examining it. "The control center."

Daniel had his own theory. "I'm betting it's our elusive server."

"We may both be correct."

"Whatever it is, does it come with power or do I need to find the bike and start peddling?" Carson said impatiently.

Daniel walked up to the brass console and touched the metal qwerty keyboard. With a hum, various lights came to life and two smaller built-in round monitors displayed amber text. The bigger screen mounted to the wall came alive with static electricity but displayed nothing.

Tripp was the first to spot the tray as it slid out to reveal a biometric reader. Without thinking, he placed his right hand over the pattern before Daniel could object. Both waited with apprehension to see what would happen.

Carson wandered off to find a bathroom. She spotted a door across the stained concrete stage and headed for it. She found herself in a short hallway. Unlike in the rest of the chamber, someone had built plaster walls. At the end was a dark room with no door. To her right, about halfway down, was a closed door—the bathroom.

After she completed her business, Carson proceeded to the room at the end of the hall. She used her flashlight to find the light switch and flipped it on, revealing a sink, coffeepot, small table, and boxes of rations stacked in the corner. "So, this is what an off-the-grid break room looks like," she said before deciding to head back to the others.

Carson spotted Tripp approaching; he had come in search of her. "You really need to see the information Daniel's bringing up over there," he said.

She lit up with anticipation. "Information? How did he hack into that old relic so fast?"

"It's not old at all—only meant to look retro. This equipment is, in Daniel's words, pretty beefy. Also, he didn't hack into anything. I was granted full access."

Carson smiled. "You see, this must be a family affair."

"It would be difficult to argue with that now," Tripp said.

When they got back to the console, Tripp turned his attention to the large round screen. An image of three items was being displayed.

"Recognize anything?" Daniel asked.

"Besides the fact that using round monitors is dumb? Sure, those are the things we found in Denton and at our crazy granny's house," Carson replied.

"Exactly."

"What's that third item?" Tripp asked. The last one they had never seen before—a thin rod with some sort of bracket on the end.

"Watch this," Daniel said as he pressed a button that started an animation sequence.

The three items moved across the screen and lined up in the order in which they were designed to fit. First the long tube with engravings, followed by the rod that fit into one end, and finally the polyhedron that fit into the bracket. The animation then showed how the newly assembled device was attached to a robotic arm, which pointed at a glowing object that grew in intensity. Rings of energy formed around the device just before it shot the polyhedron into the radiating center, which rapidly dissipated.

"What just happened?" Carson asked.

Tripp stepped forward. "Would you agree it represents the anomaly in the other chamber?"

"It just might," Daniel said. He typed something and the screen showed a camera view of a catwalk with a robotic arm attached to one side.

Tripp said, "So that device is a stimulus to open or close a wormhole?"

"I'm not certain about the wormhole part. I just discovered the device's name: the Trapdoor Key."

"Trapdoor Key?" Tripp repeated. "What would our dad be doing with it?"

"Maybe he was holding it for someone else?"

"Perhaps," Tripp replied. He reviewed a cascade of possibilities. "Can you download all relevant information? I'd like to review as much data as we can later."

Daniel produced a thin laptop from his backpack. "I can connect using a standard USB cable and start the transfer. There's a lot of data here. What shall I grab?"

"I suppose whatever my credentials will allow access to."

"That's my point—you have access to several terabytes of information. I have no idea what's the most interesting without reviewing it. I do know I only have space to grab a fraction of it."

"Best guess," Tripp replied.

While Daniel went to work transferring data to his laptop, Tripp went through several folders until he spotted something intriguing. He brought it up on the screen for the others to see.

A drawing of a pyramid with the words "Guild of Libra" over it came into view. It depicted several layers of an organization. The top layer was labeled "Guild Master," followed by "Chamber," "Divisional Captains," "Members," and finally, "Casuals." A legend on the page confirmed that this was some sort of secret organization.

"Was Uncle Conner a member?" Carson asked.

Tripp, annoyed by his sister's obsession with their dead uncle, checked anyway. The others waited as he searched a membership list. He stopped his search and simply stared at the smaller monitor.

Carson was the first to notice he'd stopped. "Are you going to tell us or paste it on the main screen?"

"No, Uncle Conner doesn't seem to have been a member." He turned to his sister. "However, Pops and Dad are listed."

Carson did a double take. "What? Dad belongs to a secret organization?"

Tripp was uncertain about his findings. "Both he and Pops are considered Casuals. Before you ask what that means, realize that I may be telling you more than I know. Casuals seem to be a label for either neophytes, some form of asset, or those with emeritus—or inactive—status."

"So is our dad still active?"

"I'm just conveying what I see here, but I believe both he and Pops are inactive members."

"That's so weird that Dad belonged to this organization but not our uncle Conner."

A light seemed to come on in Daniel's head. "I'd think my uncle Fumi would have also belonged to this guild."

Tripp reviewed the membership list. "He appeared to have been an active member. Judging from the time stamp, this list was updated several months ago."

"No way," said Daniel. "Have you learned what it is they do?"

Tripp's speed-reading skills got a full workout. After scanning through several pages, he found something. "Their motto is *Statera Mundi.*"

Daniel already had his phone out to translate and had the answer before Tripp could bring up his own browser. "It's Latin for either 'world balance' or 'the balance of the world.'"

Tripp, noting he had no bars on his own phone, was curious how Daniel could use his. "You have access down here?"

"Dude, it's called joining the local network."

"How silly of me to not have looked for an unsecured cave hotspot."

Daniel laughed. "Never judge a cave by its—uh, whatever."

Carson jumped in before they got off on a tangent. "These people wanted to bring balance to the world? Is that like world peace?"

Tripp read further but came to no conclusion. "I'd need more time to research what their goals were."

"Well, we seem to have plenty of that," Carson said.

A flash and a pop came from above and startled them. The data that had once been on the screen was replaced by a lovely and familiar face. Kate Page stared down at them as if taking a silent roll call. "Where's Joe?"

"H-he just left." Tripp stammered with surprise at seeing his mother's image on the screen.

"Did you find what you were looking for?" she asked.

"Mother?" was all Carson could manage, her mouth agape.

"I believe we have," Tripp said, still perplexed.

Daniel held up and waved his phone. "Are you the mysterious friend that has been texting me?"

"I am," Kate replied.

"And you couldn't have just said it was you?" Carson asked.

"Had you known it was me, Carson, you would've argued about everything I asked you to do." Kate replied. "Besides, I know you love a good mystery."

Carson's silence acknowledged that Kate's points were valid.

"What's your part in all of this, Mom?" Tripp asked.

"That's a long story, and I don't have time to explain." She shook her head like she used to do when they were young and she had caught them doing something wrong. "I warned your father this might happen."

"Men do tend to have selective hearing, Mother," Carson said.

"He's not the only one," Kate fired back. "I knew you two couldn't stay ignorant of your family history forever."

Carson scoffed. "We'd still be ignorant if you and Dad had your way."

"There's still so much you don't understand."

Carson pulled out her mother's diary and flashed it at her. "I'm starting to catch up, though the page you ripped out might've made that easier. Who walked out of this cavern twenty-five years ago, Mother?"

Surprisingly, their mother didn't seem upset by the sight of her diary. "Oh, sunshine, I knew when I hid that book from you that it was only a matter of time. When you were young, you'd search endlessly for your Christmas gifts and peek at them. It's always been in your nature."

"I'm well aware that I'm notorious for hating surprises, but I'm not about to get distracted. Who all survived, Mother?"

"Be careful about opening doors that can never be closed."

"I think the hinges have already been blown off. Uncle Conner seems to be doing well for a dead guy. I recognized him despite the disguise."

Both Daniel and Tripp turned to her as if she were crazy.

Kate looked a shade paler but recovered at once. "What are you talking about?"

"Please stop blowing smoke up our asses. You coordinated with him to help us. I know I saw him in the shadows. If I have to search this entire cavern, I will."

"It's far more complicated than you realize."

"Give it a shot, anyway."

There was uncertainty in their mother's expression, but she seemed to shake it off as she came to her decision. "No, Carson, it's time for quid pro quo. If you want to learn about the Page family ghost, you need to come join us on Pops's ship. Once you're safely here, we can talk."

Carson took on her signature defiant stance. "It wasn't a ghost who helped us, Mother."

"There's just no reasoning with you, young lady. Go waste all the time you want on your ghost hunt."

Carson looked taken aback. "But I saw something."

"You've no idea what you've seen. The three of you shouldn't be in that cavern. If you knew how dangerous it was, you'd run out of there screaming."

"Right, and then get shot by the assholes who tracked us here."

Their mom changed her tune. "I didn't mean you should run out this very minute. Still, you should know that some secrets there that have gotten many people killed."

"About that," Tripp said. "Why would we be granted access to such potentially dangerous material?"

Their mother groaned. "Pops and your dad are obsessed with keeping sensitive information around as insurance. Your dad decided you both needed access, in case something happened to us. Someday you'll need to carry the burden, though you weren't supposed to find it so soon."

"It's so weird when the truth is even crazier than any theories I could have come up with," Carson said.

Daniel nodded.

"Even with everything we've learned, Dad just doesn't seem a likely covert operative," Tripp said, lacking the same conviction he had before.

"You said that about Shelby too." Carson playfully poked him in his side.

Their mother had turned to her left, as if speaking to someone off-screen. She listened to whoever it was and returned her attention to them. "We'll have to talk later. Right now, I'm needed elsewhere on the *Abril*. Pops is on his way to your location. He says he has a task for you three. Please stay put until he arrives."

"We will," Tripp assured her.

"Unless we find another breadcrumb trail that entices us to follow it," Carson said.

"Try to make adult decisions," their mom snapped, then softened her tone. "Please be safe and know that I love you. Also, welcome to my world."

Her image disappeared. They silently absorbed what they had heard. The sound of trickling water and the hum of the nearby machinery softly echoed throughout the cavern.

It was Carson who finally broke the silence. "We've come a long way, boys."

"And found a trove of information," Tripp added.

Carson grinned as she slapped him on the back. "Isn't it great?"

Daniel smiled as well but with an air of uncertainty. "What's next, guys?"

Carson pointed to the dark screen on the wall where her mother had just appeared. "You heard the lady. Pops is on his way and he has something for us to do. You two continue your techie stuff until he arrives."

Tripp wanted to believe his sister was willing to wait for their grandfather, but he took nothing for granted. "Just to clarify, we are heading back with Pops and will join our parents on the *Abril*?"

"Yes, and eventually," Carson replied.

"Mom did seem willing to be forthcoming," Tripp said, trying to entice her to stay.

Carson walked over to him, smiled, and hugged him. "I do want to hear what Mother has to say. But I'm not going to promise that, should a shiny object catch my attention, I won't go chasing it." She released him, turned, and went in the other direction.

"I'd expect no less. Where are you wandering off to now?" Tripp asked as she headed to the other side of the chamber.

"This girl needs a snack. I'm wondering what rations taste like."

CHANGE OF PLANS

To Stella's delight, the blue sedan returned sooner than she had expected. Two times in as many days. She greeted the young man with a kiss. His dark pants and shirt contrasted with a white jacket. He didn't bring a flower this time and was more sedate than the day before. Still, it was a personal visit instead of a phone call. Something had happened.

The man was no older than his late twenties, yet he had an aura of wisdom and leadership. He took a seat at the little table, while the two men who had accompanied him stood silently a few feet away. Stella poured a glass of the iced tea and set it in front of him. He gave the typical polite smile as he took a sip of the sweet liquid, only grimacing when he thought she had looked away. She took a seat across from him.

"So soon? And you just get better looking all the time, Joshua," Stella said.

"You're biased," Joshua replied as he ran his hand over his waxed bald head. "I hadn't planned on intruding so soon."

With a thin pale hand, she reached over and patted his darker one. "Your presence is never an intrusion."

Joshua smiled pleasantly, then turned to business. "I have news."

"Good news, I hope."

"That remains to be seen. There's a developing situation."

"Do tell, Joshua."

"Before I do, I wanted you to know that your suspicions were correct. The man who visited you yesterday was the same Cornelius Shelby you remembered."

"His visit was unexpected," Stella said with a scowl. "I would have thought Albert's boy was long dead, particularly with his family history. Like an infestation, the man keeps returning."

"Yet he brought you the very grandkids you were looking for. I suppose the men you had me hire weren't up to the task."

"I wanted men who weren't trigger-happy, not fools."

"Those fools, as you say, were found climbing out of a Dumpster, half-naked and taped together in a compromising fashion. They told the local authorities that a young woman was responsible."

"Grandma's baby girl has spunk."

Joshua forced a thin smile. "Indeed." He motioned for his men to leave. After they had stepped outside, he continued. "This is a good segue into another topic I wanted to discuss. While Shelby's presence does complicate things, it also builds a narrative," he said as he rubbed his dark whiskers.

Stella shifted in her seat. She could tell something was eating at him. "Oh?"

"Word about Rick Sanchez has made the rounds of the guild. There's concern from various parties about poking the old bear twice."

"I couldn't possibly care less what certain parties think. After everything Pops has done, he deserves whatever he gets."

"Still, our own colleagues have questioned the wisdom of it. They sent a warning with Fumi, but this latest jab caught more than Pops's attention. Now with Shelby in the picture, they fear our enemies are gathering."

"I'm not concerned with that ugly man."

"He's not the only concern. They fear the mission has been compromised. I tried to convey confidence, but I was at a loss as to how to mitigate their fears."

Stella managed a hint of remorse. "Oh, dearie, I'm sorry you weren't consulted before the decision to kill the cop was made. Timing was everything."

Joshua looked skeptical. "Or was it the possibility that I would have advised against it? It was you who had taught me to remove emotion from such things. A subtler message would have been preferred. This, of course, was in addition to you placing your personal stamp on the removal of the guild's internal investigator. As you know, we cannot afford to let such passions cloud our judgments."

Stella's demeanor turned icy. Who and how she removed someone was her own business. "For all those years Gayla batted those eyes at my ex-husband—the bitch had it coming. So what if I enjoyed the methods used? What's done is done. The damage should be negligible."

"Time will tell. But these actions seem to have caused a ripple effect."

Stella's eyes narrowed as she realized she hadn't heard the real news yet. "What's happened?"

"Earlier, Ryder went to the cavern in the southeastern part of Texas. He was supposed to assess the work being done there and eliminate any hostiles not on our exemption list."

"What did he find?"

"Among other things, your grandchildren. They wasted no time traveling south after leaving here. They met up with two others. Early reports indicated Fumi's nephew and a Hispanic male. It's unconfirmed, but the latter may be Pops's other son Joe."

"I would've removed that blight from existence long ago if I thought killing him wouldn't garner his deadbeat father's attention," Stella said. As much as she hated Pops, she was also keen not to place a target on herself—at least not for that reason. "What were they snooping around there for?"

"It's unclear. Ryder took measures to avoid them but found himself in the crosshairs."

"From my grandchildren?" she asked.

Joshua got up and paced before he continued. "No, of course not. Ryder's team ran into a well-trained operative. He lost several of his team before I pulled him out."

"That bastard somehow fielded a team, one that could take on Ryder, much quicker than I thought possible."

"It's unlikely Pops would have sent this particular man."

Stella's curiosity was piqued. "You say just one man—an asset from the guild?"

"Not from the guild, though you'd probably be familiar with his training."

Her mind wandered. "This was revenge for the cop?" she asked, her voice cracking slightly.

"Yes. That was conveyed to Ryder in no uncertain terms." Joshua waited for her reaction.

Stella rose from her seat and made her way to the dining room window. She watched as King David sniffed around the edge of the front garden. It was about as far as his leash would allow him to go. She had intentionally shortened the chain since her dog tended to chew on the pixie figurines.

Joshua approached and stopped just behind her. "I can't be certain of the man's identity at this time. But I'll pass along a clue he left."

Stella barely blinked as she gazed at her reflection in the window. "Please continue," she finally said.

"Before this individual killed Ryder's best man, Archer, he made a statement. I believe it was a message meant for you." Joshua played the audio sound bite that Ryder had sent from Archer's camera.

"Whoever tries to keep their life will lose it."

Stella was as still as a statue for what seemed an eternity. Finally, with teary eyes, she turned and buried her face in Joshua's chest. An odd, sobbing noise came from her and soon morphed into something else. Still tearing up, she threw her head back suddenly and cackled.

"Whoever tries to keep their life will lose it, and whoever loses their life will preserve it. Luke 17:33." She stepped away, retrieved a handkerchief, and dried her eyes.

"A subtle message few would understand."

"A mother knows the scripture engraved on her own son's tomb," Stella said, then came to a realization. "He knows, Joshua. He knows I sent Ryder."

"Which means we have much to do and little time in which to do it. To make matters worse, we lost the briefcase."

Stella seemed unconcerned. "I already told you it was nothing more than a red herring. At most, it was some form of insurance."

"We may never know. Either way, without some blueprint, we need to go with an alternate plan. Ryder and Victor must combine forces for a swift and unexpected mission into the dragon's lair."

Anger flashed across Stella's face. "Victor can't be trusted. He had one simple job and couldn't even manage to grab my son's whore. He's a tiny man with a simple agenda."

"Time is of the essence. Let's gather our resources while we still can. I don't know how much longer our allies will protect us," Joshua said.

Stella's mind raced through the various outcomes. "There's still collateral damage I can't accept. Victor's an accident waiting to happen and Ryder will want blood."

Joshua held up a hand. "Ryder's a professional. He'll do exactly what he's told. If Victor steps out of line again, Ryder will remove him from the equation. I'll coordinate this dance, if you'll allow me."

"Of course. I won't interfere this time." Stella's thoughts drifted to an old concern that nagged at her. "Be careful, Joshua. I don't want to lose what family I have left."

"We're certainly on the same page," Joshua said, then smiled. "No pun intended."

Stella felt calmer. "You do excellent work." She walked over, stood on her toes, and kissed his chin. "Use whatever resources are necessary. There's still one last mystery to solve."

Joshua placed his arms around her and hugged her. "One way or another, Grandmother, we'll put that subject to rest."

INCOMING

Pops sat in the leather chair and held his Scotch. He didn't care for being trapped in the vacuum-sealed coffin, doing over five hundred knots. The things I do for my family, he thought. The private jet he had chartered would soon arrive in San Antonio. Then he'd find out if his friend and ship's captain, Ed, had secured him a helo to retrieve his grandchildren. He liked helicopters only slightly less than jets.

Given the choice, he would have used his own plane, a prop-engine amphibious aircraft. However, Captain Ed needed it, and it didn't have the range or capabilities he required. He had one of those new tiltrotor aircraft on backorder, but it was still a ways off from being delivered. The tiltrotor was an expensive investment, but Pops liked the idea of having the best of both worlds—an airplane that took off and landed like a helo. Someday, he thought.

Pops was taking another drink when his phone rang. A glance showed it was video call from Shelby. On a hunch, he had sent the man to watch Jitters's place. Shelby hadn't had much rest when Pops gave him the the assignment. If he had to work with the crazy son of a gun, he might as well take advantage of his talents.

"What do you have?" Pops said.

Shelby's face appeared. He was dimly lit and appeared to be in his van. He took a drag from his cigar and blew the smoke toward his own phone, making himself vanish in a white cloud briefly. This taunted Pops, who couldn't smoke—probably Shelby's real goal. "Just checking in, Pops."

"I never said you needed to do a check-in."

"I know, but I was bored. Have any anxiety attacks yet being stuck on that small plane?"

"It's a jet, and yes, if that makes you feel any better."

"It really does."

"Ok, goodbye, you son of a—"

"Whoa, I was just kidding. I do have a couple of updates."

Pops grumbled as he held his glass up for a refill. The attractive flight attendant, in her white blouse and black skirt, smiled as she poured the amber liquid. He waited for her to move on before he continued. "Proceed."

"For one, ol' Jitters just had a visitor. Some Oriental woman stopped by for less than ten minutes. The conversation was cryptic at best, but I'm certain there was a threat in there somewhere. I had a few problems listening because of static, but I distinctly heard a word mentioned that you'll find interesting."

"Do tell."

"Doppelgänger."

Pops sat up from his relaxed position. "In reference to what?"

"Well, that was one of the static-laden parts. It might have been a message or threat from someone or something called Doppelgänger."

"That's vague, but still interesting," Pops said and settled back into his chair. "Anything else?"

"You bet. Speaking of ghosts, my second item is a question. What the hell just happened at the cavern?"

"You know as much as I do."

"Is this a good thing?"

"Do you really think any good can come of this?" Pops said.

"You're probably asking the wrong guy. Maybe you should talk to the Secret Page when ya get there."

"I'm sure he'll vanish just before I arrive."

"He can be so weird," Shelby said and took another drag from his cigar. "Still, this little reaction must have sent a ripple back to those interested parties."

"No doubt they'll change their strategy moving forward. We need to be ready."

"Roger that. I'll keep watching from my post."

"You do that," Pops said. He started to end the video conference but realized he had one more request. "Shelby, next time please just call me. I'd rather not have to look at that mug of yours unless I have to."

Shelby saluted. "Aye-aye, El Capitan, audio not video." He blew another cloud of cigar smoke at the camera and then his image disappeared.

Pops inhaled deeply and let his mind drift. He knew the game had just begun. Once upon a time, he relished the challenge. Now he felt like a tired old man. It was tough enough trying to figure out what the enemy's next move was without trying to keep up with what his own family was going to do next.

The flight attendant returned, smiled, and placed a delicate hand on his shoulder. "We'll be landing soon, Mr. Page. Someone will be waiting to guide you to the next leg of your journey."

"Thank you," Pops replied. He took her update to mean that his helo would be waiting for him.

As he tried to relax in preparation for the landing, he let his thoughts go to his grandkids. They had shown themselves to be resourceful and persistent. While he was proud of them, he knew they had just entered a world where they'd always be looking over their shoulders. That alone saddened him. There was a certain comfort in ignorance—a comfort they no longer had.

NEW RECRUITS

The noise bounced off the cavern walls and resonated throughout the chamber. Carson couldn't decide whether it sounded more like a cow in labor or her brother making a new discovery. Since she knew of no cave-dwelling cattle, she assumed it was Tripp.

The decision about which MREs, or Meals Ready to Eat, to take a chance on boiled down to two choices. However, her curiosity as to what all the excitement was about finally got the better of her. She grunted as she tossed the packages aside and headed out of the small kitchen.

Whatever Tripp was on to, Daniel seemed equally excited by it. They both urged her to come closer as she approached the retro control station they had been tirelessly working at.

"Did you find Mother's missing diary page?" Carson asked.

Tripp said, "You've got a one-track mind. I neither searched nor expected to find it."

"I think it's important."

"Then you're going to love this," Daniel said.

"I better. I was just about to decide between chicken or spaghetti."

"They have spaghetti rations?"

"Who knew, right?"

Tripp cleared his throat as he finished bringing up the data. On the large monitor above them, a split screen appeared. The paused presentation on the left seemed familiar; it resembled the cavern video they had watched part of in New Orleans. But the one on the right was new.

Water droplets must have been on the lens when the video was shot. The camera was pointed toward a platform resembling something oil companies used, with a menacing sky above and an angry sea around it.

Tripp explained. "On the left is the cavern chamber we passed through earlier, somewhere a level above us now. On the right is a platform at sea. The camera must have been on a ship nearby. The two videos are synchronized to precisely the same time frames, twenty-five years ago, and represent two sides of the same experiment."

"What are those numbers above each window?" Carson asked.

"Ah, good catch, sis. Those would be location coordinates."

"So we know the first one shows our location, but did you look up the second?"

"You know I did. It's in the Gulf of Mexico, south of Louisiana."

That prompted Daniel to retrieve his phone. He found the image of the map, the one that had started them off on their adventure, and zoomed in on the marked location. "I bet that's the black pushpin on our map."

"Without a doubt," Tripp said. "Now let's all watch this before we continue our discussion."

He began the presentation and they stared in wonder. Tripp and Daniel had already seen it, but they eagerly watched it again. The left side of the screen showed the cavern, a man-made wall in the background.

As the video played, the wall bowed inward, imploding from some unseen force on the other side. Concrete blocks were ripped away until a gaping hole formed. They watched in horror as a man in a white coat, his arms flailing, was dragged away into the unknown.

Simultaneously, in the right frame, a vortex formed in the heavens and pulled the floating platform into it. The implosion had occurred just as the violent sky abated and what was left of the platform fell back into the ocean.

"That's crazy!" exclaimed Daniel.

"What in the hell was that?" asked Carson.

Tripp said, "My theory is based solely on the data before us, but I believe this was an experiment involving opening a doorway from one location to another. Obviously, something went terribly wrong."

"No shit," Carson said.

Daniel's eyes lit up. "So it was a wormhole?"

"That's the best explanation I can think of. So yes, it would appear so."

Carson seemed puzzled. "So this wormhole is like something from a sci-fi flick?"

"Yes, except it's more than science fiction. It's consistent with Einstein's general theory of relativity. Think of it as a conduit through space–time that creates a shortcut between two points distant from one another."

"Sounds like science fiction to me," Carson replied.

Daniel could hardly contain his excitement. "Do you know what this means? We could cross immense distances in space in the blink of an eye."

"If we could stabilize such a connection," Tripp said. "But what we've just seen shows what happens when an experiment of that magnitude collapses. I find it hard to believe anyone would attempt it anywhere near our planet, much less on its surface."

"You give people too much credit." Carson laughed. "Do you suppose Dad was there that day? If so, why? Was he on the platform or in the cavern?"

"All good questions. I have no idea, but—" It was as if he was mentally connecting the dots. "Of course, it would make sense."

This aroused Carson's interest. "What makes sense?"

"Let's assume Dad, for whatever reason, is more than the custodian of family secrets. What if he's one of the few survivors of this catastrophe who knows the science involved?"

Daniel had his reservations. "He's a preacher, dude. Creationist theory might be the closest he's ever gotten to science."

"But it was Dad who built that complex under our building." He turned to Carson. "Remember when Mom used to help us with our homework? When would she send us to Dad for assistance?"

Carson felt it was a curious question and thought back. "He always helped us with the hard science stuff. So what? He was good at it."

"He was more than good. He had a depth of knowledge that could make your head spin."

Carson was usually the one with crazy conspiracy theories, not her brother. She felt odd suddenly playing the skeptic. "So did my physics teacher in high school. I doubt he has mercenaries chasing him. Are you actually suggesting that a preacher holds the key to some sci-fi mumbo jumbo?"

"Key!" Tripp shouted. "Dad had the key—though scattered abroad—all along. It's likely—forgive the term—a key ingredient that someone would need to reproduce the experiment that failed long ago."

Carson thought it made sense. "They tried to grab us so Dad would have to give them the key. When that failed, they killed his best friend."

"It's a theory."

"Something doesn't quite add up. If this key was well hidden, why would Dad want us to gather up the pieces?"

"We'd have to ask him that question."

"Just another item to add to the ol' list."

Daniel had something on his mind. "Tripp, do you suppose your uncle died in that experiment?" It seemed a serious question at first—that is, until he grinned. "Or has he just been hanging out in the chamber above us for the past twenty-five years?"

"Not funny," said Carson.

Tripp tried in vain to hide his amusement. "Let's not speak of the dead—or the undead, for that matter."

Daniel burst into laughter, while Carson's sour expression suggested she found the subject anything but humorous.

"Screw both of you," she said and flipped them the bird.

Daniel tried to slap her shoulder the way she typically did to them, but she dodged it. "C'mon, Carson, you're usually the morbid one."

"Not when it comes to family, dipshit."

Daniel poked at her again to put her in a better mood. "Maybe we can ask Pops his theory when he gets here."

An image appeared on the large monitor above them. Pops glared down at them. "Is that before or after I put my foot up each of your shafts?"

"Hey, Poppy!" Carson exclaimed as she spun around. "Are you here yet?"

"I'm landing now. Stay put."

"Pops, we've made some stunning discoveries," Tripp said proudly.

"You've also placed me in a tough spot. As guardian of those secrets, I'm sworn to protect them."

"Yet I was given full access to them," Tripp blurted out.

"That's something I'll be taking up with your dad."

Carson came to her dad's defense. "It's not his fault we're so curious."

She detected a flicker of amusement, but Pops reverted to a sober expression. "Baby girl, your actions will have consequences."

His tone and words concerned Carson. "Poppy? We're family."

"You're more than that now. Each of you, willing or not, will help shoulder this burden."

"Burden?" Carson asked.

"Playtime is over. Your initiation starts the moment I arrive. Prepare to be boarded." With that, Pops's image disappeared from the screen and they all stood around silently for several seconds and stared at one another.

"That was even eerier than what your mom said before she signed off," Daniel said.

"Yes," Tripp said. "We may have crossed the point of no return and inadvertently brought about our conscription into this secret organization."

Daniel and Carson considered the potential ramifications, and a broad smile formed across Carson's face. "Damn skippy. This shit is just beginning, folks. Maybe now we'll learn some kick-ass dark secrets."

"That or we'll be subjected to a life of servitude under the mysterious syndicate."

"Nah, Poppy has our backs. What's the worst that can happen?"

Tripp looked incredulous. "I think you're underestimating the gravity of what we've discovered. Pops isn't taking it lightly—nor should you."

Carson considered it. "Okay, we'll see what Poppy has for us." She turned and headed back to the other side of the chamber. "I plan on asking about that missing page."

"The diary or the uncle?"

Carson kept walking. "One probably leads to the other."

Daniel called to her. "Now where are you going? Pops is almost here."

As his voice echoed across the chamber, another sound emerged from the other side—the old machinery coming to life. The elevator was on its way down.

"Poppy's already here," Carson said from the hallway she had entered. "Tell him I'll be in the kitchen trying out the spaghetti."

Pops waited for the slow elevator to grind to a stop before he opened the antique door and stepped into the dimly lit cavern. He shuddered at the thought of even being in the place. The sooner he got back to the sea, the better. He was glad he had worn the thin brown jacket—though once he returned to the surface, he'd regret it once the Texas heat hit him. At least it did allow him to conceal more than just a pistol.

Pops's old eyes struggled to adjust to the low light and focus on who was at the control center as he approached. He ignored the trickling water to his left, as it reminded him he was basically walking through an underground riverbed. With a grunt, he climbed the few steps up to the platform.

Tripp was the first one he spotted. His grandson turned to greet him, smiling. That, at least, was a good sign—he hoped so, anyway.

Pops opened his arms and embraced Tripp with a hearty hug. "Good to see you, boy. Where's Daniel and your sister?"

Tripp moved aside to reveal Daniel rising from the floor, where he'd been trying to plug into something underneath the console. "Daniel is right behind me, while Carson is in the kitchen eating some form of ration she found."

Pops grunted at the thought. "The food is a lot better on the jet we'll be taking home."

"Good food sounds awesome, Pops," Daniel said, and he put his arms around the old man.

"You've been busy, Danny boy," said Pops. He grabbed Daniel by both shoulders. "Should the worst-case scenario occur, know that Fumi was a good friend to me. His family is my family."

"Thanks, Pops."

Pops reached into his shirt pocket and produced a piece of paper and handed it to Daniel. "Now I have something else for you guys. Since you both like to discover new things, tell me what the hell this means."

Daniel read both sides of the paper. "'Doppelgänger' and a bunch of numbers on the back. Where did it come from?"

"It was the last thing I received from your Uncle Fumi before the—uh, incident with his yacht."

Tripp took the paper from Daniel. "The term itself means an apparition that represents or is a counterpart to a living being. The numbers could be coordinates of whatever Mr. Fumi was trying to show you."

Tripp handed the paper back to Daniel, who scowled as he tried to make sense of the numbers. Then his eyebrows rose as if another thought had entered his mind. "I've got another theory."

Daniel walked over to the console and typed away on the metal keyboard. The large round monitor above came alive, and he brought up an Internet browser and tested adding periods after every third number. After a moment, a dark screen appeared with a single text box and a red button labeled SUBMIT.

"What exactly am I looking at, boys?" Pops asked.

Tripp offered his explanation first. "Those numbers must represent an IP address, the numeric, raw form that points to a device on the Internet."

Pops eyed his grandson. "You found a website?"

"Yes, a darknet website, to be precise."

"A dark what? What the hell am I supposed to type into this box thingy?"

"I'm guessing that the password is 'Doppelgänger,'" said Daniel. He typed the word in and hit SUBMIT. They waited for something to happen. It took several seconds, but the screen finally changed and a video slowly loaded. It automatically began to play, Fumi's face appearing on the screen. He was wearing a white satin robe and reclining casually on a comfortable chair. The recording was directed to Pops.

Hello, Bradley. Since you're seeing this message, some ill fate has likely befallen me. I hope my death was a good one. If not, please be sure to tell anyone who cares that it was a gorgeous demise. I know you remember how to lie.

I apologize for not being able to tell you this in person. It would have been wonderful to see your expression. You see, the guild is in peril and it needs one of its most famous sons back. That's right, Bradley, we feel only you can make things right again.

I'll give you a moment to allow the shock to wear off. Better now? Anyway, I was supposed to appeal to you to assist us personally, but I apparently failed to convince you, or something didn't allow that to happen. Perhaps it was my death at such a young age. In either case, you're needed, my old friend.

You see, the guild is very sick. A darkness has grown from within her and threatens everything we, and the fore-families, have ever stood for. It's probably been festering for some time, but within the last few years has begun to manifest itself more openly and aggressively.

A powerful faction feels it's time to be more than the silent mediators we've been for decades. They believe that only through more aggressive means can human beings be given a reason not to make themselves extinct.

On the surface, that may not sound like such a bad thing, except the reality is more frightening. If you haven't figured it out, allow me to enlighten you. They want Project Dream Stream, and they'll do whatever they must to get it. That, unfortunately, means removing any obstacle in their way.

You, like me, are an obstacle. If you're still alive to see this, it means my message isn't too late. You must stop them, Bradley. If anyone obtains the secrets of Dream Stream, they'll wield such power that there will never be balance in the world again.

I've already put some things in motion that should assist you. Your part will be to stop any immediate threats to those secrets and then contact an old friend. You know to who I speak of.

One more thing. Please tell Daniel that I'm very proud of him. He has exceeded my every expectation and brought honor to himself and his family. He will soon be rewarded for his services.

Goodbye, my friend. I miss you already.

The transmission ended just as Carson returned from the kitchen with spaghetti sauce on the corner of her mouth. "That stuff was meant to be fully cooked before eating it." She grabbed Pops and hugged him. "What's going on, Poppy?"

"Trying to solve a mystery, baby girl," Pops said.

"We just watched a message from Daniel's uncle Fumi," Tripp said.

"No way. He's alive?" Carson asked.

Daniel's face fell and he wiped his eyes. "It was a recorded message. It pretty much confirms he's gone."

Carson embraced her friend and held him for a moment while he gathered himself.

Pops, too, needed a moment. He stared at the blank screen before deciding to hear the message again, in case there was some subtlety he needed to remember. "Play it again, Daniel."

Daniel tried but couldn't get it to work. After fidgeting with it briefly, he turned to Pops. "I believe the message was meant to be seen only once and likely removed itself from the server that housed it."

"That sounds about right," Pops said and then addressed all of them. "I was wrong to think you three weren't ready for what lies ahead. Before you get too tickled by that, understand that our journey will be fraught with peril."

"We understand, Poppy," said Carson.

"I look forward to stopping my uncle's killers," Daniel said.

Pops turned his attention to Tripp, who seemed deep in thought.

"I accept the task of trying to keep those two alive," he finally said.

Pops switched the control center's computers off and headed back toward the elevator. "Good. You'll all accompany me back to Florida and we'll get started."

THE LID REMOVED

Pops was halfway to the elevator when he realized no one was following him. He stopped in his tracks and turned back toward the control center, more than a little irritated with the delay. He found his grandkids and Daniel still standing there—Carson, arms folded, in her typical defiant posture.

Cursing, Pops wandered back to the raised area, climbed the steps, and stood a few feet from the group. "What?"

"We have questions that need to be answered," Carson said.

"Not until we're far away from this cursed place," said Pops.

"I love ya, Poppy, but I'm not going anywhere until I get what I came for." She then gestured to the others. "And neither are they."

Pops vigorously rubbed his gray beard, then shook his head slowly. "Damn, you're stubborn. What do ya wanna know?"

Carson unfolded her arms and relaxed her posture. "Everything—but for starters, let's talk about a missing diary page and Uncle Conner."

"I don't know anything about a diary page," said Pops.

"Okay . . . why's my uncle, who supposedly died long ago, sitting in a dark cavern above us?" Carson asked.

Pops knew that one was coming. Right before he had landed, Kate warned him the lid on Pandora's box had been loosened. "Oh, hell's bells," he said with gritted teeth. "Okay, ya lil' shits, this isn't my story to tell, but I'll see what I can do. Let's get this over with—gather 'round."

The others gathered in front of Pops as he found a seat on the top step of the platform. Daniel sat on the floor, Tripp knelt on one knee, and Carson paced. The cavern grew still, the distant trickle of water the only sound to be heard. Pops surveyed his audience before he began. The hunger for the truth was most noticeable in his granddaughter. This was hardly surprising.

"First, this Uncle Conner crap is nothing more than a distraction," said Pops.

"I know what I saw, Poppy," Carson said, quite sure of herself.

"No, you don't. There is no Uncle Conner. Let's be clear about that," Pops said and held up a hand before Carson could protest further. "Next, you need to understand the past before you can possibly grasp where we find ourselves today."

Pops waited for each one to nod that they understood.

"Both my sons were in this very cavern about twenty-five years ago when the proverbial shit hit the fan. Conner had been invited, but Brad should never have even been here."

"How could a preacher even be involved in this?" Tripp asked.

Pops was keenly aware it was a good question. "Because not everything is what it seems, Tripp. Now shut up and listen."

He waited until he was sure of no further interruptions.

"Two insanely smart guys, the Dasinger brothers, were known through the scientific community for their work in physics. They invented some method to cross into another dimension or something like that. Don't ask me how it worked, because that shit is far beyond my comprehension."

Pops sighed as Tripp's hand immediately went up. "Yes, Tripp?"

"Would that be the Trapdoor Key—the device for opening a wormhole?"

"Okay, I see you've absorbed the science mumbo jumbo, so I won't sound stupid trying to repeat it," Pops said with some relief. "Aye, that's basically it. Although, that wasn't their big project—it just so happened to be what caught everyone's attention."

"What was the big project, then?" Tripp asked.

"Who cares," Carson said with annoyance. "Let's get to the good stuff."

"Right. It's outside the scope of this tale. Now no more interruptions," Pops said.

Before continuing, he reached into his brown jacket and produced a flask. After a quick drink of whiskey, he cleared his throat. He spotted

Carson's interest in the flask and tossed it to her. She downed a swig before returning it to him.

"Okay, so the good doctors had found a way to rip open a hole and shoot stuff through it. This represented some serious potential for whoever might get their hands on it. Naturally, the US government was ready to apprehend the two men and seize all their work. The guild had learned about it from our intelligence sources in the CIA. We, the Guild of Libra, had an emergency meeting—the Chamber of Ten, plus two captains—and decided the discovery was far too dangerous for one government to control. The only problem was, as with earlier decisions, the guild was of two minds on how to proceed. Many, like Fumi and I, wanted to follow tradition and monitor what happened first. Our usual method was to monitor and mold the outcome behind the scenes. However, some felt a more radical approach was needed."

Pops paused to take another drink. He quickly regretted it, as Carson stopped pacing and took the opportunity to pounce with her next question.

"No offense, Poppy, but what's this got to do with our dad and uncle?"

"I'm getting to that point. It helps to have some background, don't ya think?" Pops said hoarsely. He had to take another shot from his flask.

"Gotcha . . . sorry."

"Anyway, blah . . . blah . . . blah, the guild was divided about what to do next. Fumi and I decided to monitor the Echo platform in the Gulf. It was a good thing we did too, as I ended up rescuing the crew of the Dream Stream—including Shelby's dad and ol' Jitters. It was the vessel used to transport equipment to the Echo platform. Fumi arrived shortly afterward and dragged a single survivor out of the water. Shelby had fallen off the rig and managed to avoid getting sucked into the unknown. After that, he left the CIA and worked as a freelancer."

"That crazy dude Shelby was there?" asked Carson.

"He was."

"Is that how he knew Dad? How did Dad get into the cavern?"

"Patience. I'm getting to that part," Pops said.

"Oh, good." Carson sat on the floor beside Daniel.

Pops was getting to the tough part and needed another dose of liquid courage. "We got lucky, or so we thought, in that the CIA already had operatives in place—and the guy in charge of that operation was a member of the guild. On Echo, Shelby was assigned to monitor the results. For the cavern, the CIA had borrowed a young naval intelligence officer for the task. Imagine my surprise when I learned his name was Conner Page."

Pops waited for "No shit" and other comments to die down before he continued.

"Conner was skilled and intelligent. He had tested off the charts and could've done anything he desired. But for his own reasons, he joined the military," Pops said. "Our guild operative in the CIA figured that Conner, being my son, would certainly do the guild's bidding. He was wrong. Conner hadn't joined the Navy so he could serve the guild."

"He wanted the US government to have those secrets?" asked Tripp.

"That's right. It was the last thing the upper echelon of the guild wanted to hear," said Pops.

"Did you feel betrayed?"

Pops looked away, conscious that the others could see the emotion in his eyes. He decided to continue so he didn't reveal more pain. "I did, but not by Conner. I already knew he hated the guild. He felt it was an old solution that had become the current problem. It didn't help that Conner had adamantly turned down two offers to join the guild. His hatred for his mother, the embodiment of all things wrong with that secret organization, was just too great."

"He hated her?" Carson asked sadly.

"For good reason," Pops said. "Stella had tried to break him, just as she did his older brother. The witch had made Brad her own brainwashed meat puppet. Conner and he were very close, so naturally the more self-absorbed of the two set out to prove he was smarter and stronger willed than the woman who bore him. Stella had met her match in her own child. Conner was both her greatest student and biggest disappointment."

"How old was he at the time?" asked Tripp.

"He was fourteen before I got my head outta my ass and rescued both boys from that insane bitch," said Pops, the bitterness swelling within him. "Stella and I had been separated for some time. I guess it never occurred to me that the mother of my boys would bring her work home and practice on them."

"How did Conner endure while his brother was broken?" Daniel asked.

Pops smiled as he thought back. "Stella had a wicked brilliance about her, which is what made her so effective for the guild. But Conner was as stubborn as a mule. He endured her abuse, learned everything she had taught him, and then used it against her. She wasn't accustomed to having the same mind games she played herself turned on her. After I took the two away from that nightmare, Stella soon had a nervous breakdown."

"I bet it took a while to deprogram him," Daniel said.

"It was a challenge, Daniel, but Conner really wanted to return to reality. Brad, however, was never the same," Pops said with melancholy in his voice.

"Just to be clear." Carson rose to her feet, her fists clenched. "Dad was our crazy grandma's—What did you call it?—meat puppet?"

"I think Pops is saying that she was an overbearing control freak who made it her mission to mold her own children into subservient drones," said Tripp.

"I know what Poppy meant by the term, dipshit," replied Carson. "But it's just stupid. Dad is one of the kindest, most rational people I've ever met. He's thoughtful in everything he does."

"You're right, baby girl. I've been trying to spoon-feed this story to you, but the reality is dysfunctional."

"That's bullshit," said Carson. "Just spit it out, Poppy."

Pops watched his granddaughter start to pace again. "If you're willing to listen, I'll explain."

"Please proceed, Pops," said Tripp. "And if you'd be so kind, please clarify exactly what our grandmother did for the guild."

"She created monsters," Pops said. "The man who killed Sanchez was a product of that woman's programming."

Carson turned pale. "Really? Then I need to pay that old bitch a visit. First, tell me something. For a monster, my dad seems to be a pretty good fella. How is that?"

Almost there, Pops told himself. "I'm getting to that. Remember, you asked for it."

Carson rolled her eyes, then bowed to encourage him to continue.

"Back to the disaster," said Pops. "Our guy in the CIA had to send a new operative in once he realized Conner wasn't his man. He couldn't remove Conner, though he tried, because my clever son had got in good with both scientists. Once they understood how gifted he really was, they insisted he stay on the project. Another operative was brought in, a young man who was also a guild member, unlike Conner. More importantly, this man was sympathetic to the more radical elements of the guild. There was no way he was going to allow that experiment to happen. As a bonus, he used Conner to get his foot in the door. He was quite good at manipulation. It was the ultimate betrayal."

Daniel was intrigued. "How could anyone use Conner?"

Pops took one more drink and swallowed hard. "Only Brad could've pulled that one off. Conner had a soft spot for him. Even though their relationship had been strained, Conner wanted nothing more than to reconnect with his big brother. Brad used that to his advantage. He was the perfect choice."

"How did that even come about?" Tripp asked, perplexed.

"My old friend, Alan Lloyd, recruited Brad for the job—behind my back, of course," Pops replied. "He and I settled things later when the dust cleared. It's his son, Victor, who wants to return the favor."

"I'm hearing nothing more than that Dad was a brainwashed puppet, while Conner was so cool," said Carson. She started to stomp off but suddenly turned. "I'm done with this. Does my dad even know you think so little of him?"

"Young lady, I have the utmost respect for him," said Pops.

"Then why do you say these things about him, Poppy? Carson asked.

Even with his poor vision, Pops could see the tears in her eyes. "I've said all along that your dad survived his personal nightmare. His brother Brad wasn't so fortunate."

Carson's jaw dropped. "What are you saying?"

"If you haven't figured out by now that Conner's your dad, then you've got tunnel vision, baby girl."

Carson screamed in horror at the revelation, her cries echoing throughout the cavern. She turned and retreated into the darkness.

Pops rose to follow her, but Tripp blocked his path.

Tripp turned to Daniel. "Go after her," he said to his friend.

Daniel rose and followed Carson.

Pops studied his grandson. "You, of course, understand what I'm saying."

"Even though I suspected, the confirmation is dizzying," Tripp replied, visibly shaken.

"When did you start to figure it out?" Pops asked.

"Grandma Stella handed Carson a picture of our parents when they were young. I noted how tall each brother was in comparison to Mom."

Pops nodded. "Conner ended up being the tallest of all my sons."

"Dad is five inches taller than Mom."

Pops wiped a tear that insisted on forming in his right eye. If anyone had asked, he would have said it was allergies. "Young Tripp, your sister needs to come to grips with this."

"She just needs to overcome her preconceived notions, Pops," Tripp said.

"I fear there's only one person who can help her do that," Pops said.

THE SECRET PAGE

Silently, in the cavern located above where the others were, he watched what had unfolded via the camera feed sent to his phone. It broke his heart to see Carson learn the truth so abruptly. Tripp and Daniel could resort to logic and reason, but Carson was an emotional powder keg. He wished Pops had taken the time to deliver the truth in smaller doses.

Lifting the balaclava up to conceal all but his eyes again, he headed for the elevator. The old lift groaned as it made its way down to the lower level. As it reached the bottom with a thud, he opened the antiquated door and cage—which screeched and announced his arrival.

Taking his phone out again, he accessed an app that adjusted the lights to allow a glow to form in the center of the cavern's chamber. He proceeded to that spot, listening as he quietly reached the lit-up area. In the shadows to his left, he could hear Carson's soft wailing. She had decided to kick a rock and cursed from the pain that ensued.

He watched as Pops spotted him and drew his .45 caliber pistol. The old man approached with caution. "You kids stay back," he called out.

He raised his hands when Pops closed in. "This isn't exactly how I imagined this would play out."

Pops holstered his weapon and stepped into the illuminated area. "It's about damn time you showed up."

Wearing combat fatigues, his face still hidden, he lowered his hands. He stared out from the balaclava, looking for the others. His rifle was slung over his shoulder and his pistol stayed holstered. He took a few steps toward Pops, then stopped. "I've been busy."

"So I've heard." Pops glanced back at the others approaching from different directions. "Thanks for getting your little brother, Joe, safely off."

"Of course. He's a good man."

"Indeed," said Pops.

"Ryder and his team left shortly before you arrived."

"Ryder," said Pops. "We owe that bastard and whoever sent him."

"He received a down payment today. I'm hoping he leads us to whoever his masters are."

"We've a pretty damn good idea where to start, son."

Tripp had come in from behind Pops, while Carson and Daniel emerged from where they had disappeared earlier. Carson was having trouble walking on her own.

"Son?" Carson asked as she hobbled into the light. "You're Uncle Conner. You must be our dad's brother—you even sound like him."

"Carson Ann Page, your grandfather's already pointed out that there's no Uncle Conner." He removed the cap and balaclava, revealing his clean-shaven face, sandy-blond hair, and, of course, those eyes. "Your uncle Brad died before you were born."

"Dad?" Carson's voice trembled and she staggered backwards. "What the shit happened to your beard? . . . your eyes . . . that hair!"

Jack moved farther into the light so the others could see him better. "This is what I look like when I'm not hiding from the world." He tossed something to the group, which Daniel caught.

After examining the contents of the small case, Daniel said, "Colored contacts."

"I—I don't get it, Dad. Why?" Carson asked.

Jack slowly closed the distance between himself and Carson, then gently placed a hand on her shoulder. He struggled with where to start. "It was far too dangerous to be Conner Page," he said.

At that, Tripp and Daniel moved in around Jack and Carson.

"So, you're actually Conner Page?" Daniel asked, visibly stunned. "The legendary, badass Page himself?"

"My suspicions were correct, but it's still hard to comprehend," Tripp said. "You must explain, sir."

"First, call me Dad like you've always done," Jack said. "Next, it would take more time than we have to explain everything. You'll have to accept the condensed version."

Carson pulled back from him. "Dad, you're Jack Page, right?"

Jack looked at his daughter with empathy. "For most of my life, I've been Jack Page," he said. "It's a lot to take in, sweetie. I had to assume my dead brother's identity or I, too, would have been killed. I couldn't bring myself to go by Brad's first name, so I adopted his middle name."

"But why?" Carson asked.

"Because I extinguished the lives of several people—ones with powerful connections."

Carson started to shake. Jack knew she was fighting a panic attack and quickly grabbed both her hands. "Remember your breathing," he said calmly.

"Okay," she said and practiced slow, deep breaths. After a moment, she continued her questioning. "Did ya get your vengeance?"

"That was my intent, but I soon realized that revenge was just an emotional, knee-jerk reaction on my part. My brother made his own decisions. My rage was simply a way to blame someone else."

"Then why have you always acted like you have survivor's guilt?"

Jack's eyes immediately teared up. He didn't want to say it but knew he had to get it off of his chest. "It is guilt, but not for the reason you may think. In this cavern that day, while things were falling apart, Brad admitted he was responsible for what was happening. My words to him were quite harsh, to say the least."

"Well, duh," said Carson. "He got everyone killed."

"I guess he figured we were all dead anyway. It was his final confession, I suppose," said Jack. "But I wasn't one to give up. We found a way to avert complete disaster, but it came at a cost."

The others stood silently as Carson tried to ease her dad's conscience. "But you saved the ones you could."

Jack gave a feeble smile. "Actually, the ones in the cavern were the least of our concern. This thing had the potential to kill far more people. No, my daughter, I don't regret any of that. What haunts me is, I knowingly sent my brother to his death. I used him to buy Dr. Dasinger and I the time to find another solution, knowing he'd die the instant we tried it."

Everyone silently processed what they had heard.

It was Pops' brusque voice that broke the silence. "You did what you had to do, son."

"It doesn't make it all better, Pops," said Jack.

"I know that as well as anyone," Pops said.

Jack decided to change the direction of the conversation as Carson hugged him. "I have to finish what I've started. If I don't, things will get much uglier," said Jack.

"Let 'em get ugly." Carson pulled away so she could wipe her runny nose. "It's more important that you're safe."

Jack appreciated the gesture but knew there was a bigger picture. "There's far more at stake here than just me or this family."

"We'll take care of ol' Victor and Stella's cronies," Pops said.

"Pops, this isn't just about cleaning house. Those people are after us for a reason. That reason is this cavern and what it holds."

"Not a problem, son." Pops reached into his coat pocket and produced some of the C4 he'd taken from Jack's secret room. "I can fix that problem real quick."

"No, sir, you can't," Jack said sternly. "You could blow this place to pieces all day long and that anomaly will still be there."

"So? I bet Poppy can bury it so nobody ever finds it," Carson said, starting to return to her normal self.

"That's not the point, sis," Tripp said, seeming to understand what Jack was saying. "There must be a purpose to that anomaly—and I'm guessing it's related to why the one over the Gulf waters is being kept in check."

Jack was impressed with his son's quick grasp of matters. "Tripp is absolutely correct. You see, there are two ends to this wormhole. When the guild had my brother sabotage the device, those of us left alive had to quickly slap a bandage on the situation. Dr. Dasinger, without a working Trapdoor Key to stabilize the rupture, had to reverse the parameters of the experiment, thus holding both ends of the wormhole in stasis."

"That's fascinating," said Tripp.

"No, that's some other language," Carson said. "Really, Dad? I'm used to Tripp speaking geek, not you."

Jack started to explain, but soon Tripp took over. "The rift, or whatever you want to call it, never closed," he said. "It's being held in a state that requires perpetual balance on both ends. Disrupt one end, and what started years ago will come back with a fury."

"Yes," said Jack. "If we don't close it permanently, we risk the lives of every being on this planet. I've been working on doing this for years—with Dr. Eriks's help, of course."

"Dr. Eriks?" asked Daniel.

"Dr. Erich Dasinger took on the pseudonym of Dr. Eriks when I hid him away from the world," said Pops. "Son, are you saying you never really closed that hellhole?"

"We did the best we could at the time, Pops," Jack replied.

"Ah, dammit," said Pops. "Okay, so how do you propose we fix the problem while taking on the forces coming after us?"

"I've already got things in motion," said Jack. "I had to play devil's advocate, but we should be able to kill two birds with one stone."

"And just how did you manage this? Which devil are we dealing with?" asked Pops.

"The one you recently scared the hell out of."

"Carl?" exclaimed Pops. "Getting that ol' bastard to betray Victor is a tall order."

"True, but if Mother taught me anything valuable, it was that human beings tend to look out for themselves first. I convinced Carl, with your help, that it was in his best interest that we both get what we want."

"And Victor?"

"Carl reluctantly agreed that Victor is doing more harm than good to Alan's legacy."

Pops seemed to have trouble accepting that one. "What does Carl want out of this?"

"To complete the project he's being paid to do."

The surprise on Pops's face was instant. "How does this help us?"

"Lloyd Security was paid to bring me out in the open and get me to agree to open the rift over the old Echo coordinates—as some proof of concept. This is exactly what I want to do. Before you ask why, understand that we can't close the wormhole properly without reopening it first."

"That's a batshit-crazy idea, son!" Pops said loudly.

"I'm gonna have to agree with Poppy on this one, Dad," said Carson.

"Dad's right," Tripp said, to everyone else's disbelief. "To close the wormhole properly this time, you must first return it to its former state."

"Whoa—wait a minute," said Carson. "Aren't we trying to keep people from doing just that?"

"It feels really strange that we're taking the opposite roles here," said Tripp. "Look, if someone else breaches the rift, we're all doomed—because they don't have the means to close it again."

Jack was greatly relieved to have someone else on his side. "That's exactly right," he said. "We're the only ones who should ever do this, because we're the only ones with the knowledge and the Trapdoor Key itself. It's not an option. We must do this—and soon."

"Just curious, but what the hell's the rush after all these years?" Pops asked.

"Last week, someone in the Gulf tried to open the rift themselves," Jack said. "When I checked the anomaly in the cavern above, I noticed it had become unstable."

"Just great," said Pops. "How long do we have?"

"At best estimate, perhaps days."

"Well, we have our work cut out for us. Where are you off to next?" asked Pops.

"I have to synch up with Kate to coordinate our next steps. She can fill you in once we have a solid action plan," said Jack.

"Wait a minute, Dad," said Carson. "Are you telling me my mother's part of all this?"

"Sweetie, I couldn't do this without your mom," Jack replied.

"This shit keeps getting crazier and crazier," Carson said. "Okay, I'm in."

Daniel and Tripp spoke among themselves before agreeing to do whatever was needed to assist the cause. Jack said his goodbyes and prepared to depart on a separate path. Pops had offered him a lift, but he had already arranged his own means of travel. Carson insisted on leaving with her dad, but he was equally adamant she was needed elsewhere. It was an awkward farewell.

As Jack entered the elevator, Carson called to him with one last question. "Dad, did you just pretend to be a preacher all those years?"

He took his time in responding, as he had asked himself that same question more than once. "At first I did. As the years went on, however, it was my faith that allowed the healing to begin. I'm more Jack Page today than I was ever Conner Page."

Carson's nod indicated she accepted that. "Be safe, Dad."

"You guys be careful as well," said Jack with a quick wave. "We'll get through this."

As the elevator shut, Carson ensured she got the last word. "No promises, but I'll try to be a good team player."

Once Jack departed, Pops gathered his new troops before they headed for the surface themselves. "Okay, folks, I'm heading to Florida to meet up with Shelby. I'll drop you guys off in Biloxi. When we're ready for the next phase, I'll call."

"Biloxi? What are we supposed to do there, Poppy?" Carson asked.

"Take a day off to absorb everything you've been through. There are some nice casinos, as you know. Drink and unwind. It'll be back to work soon enough."

"Aren't we forgetting that there are dangerous people out there, Pops?" Tripp asked.

"I'm not forgetting," Pops said. "You'll obviously need to be careful— and I'll have people watching. That said, this is your new reality, kids. You've proven you're not helpless victims. You asked for this, so now you must learn to live with it."

"Shouldn't you train us to be badasses?" Carson asked.

"You're already more capable than most veterans I've worked with," said Pops with a hint of pride. "Besides, if your dad's right about Carl, you guys won't be the targets. I'll know more after I catch up to Shelby."

Carson seemed to fully bounce back to being herself. "Well, ya don't have to tell us twice," she said and turned to Tripp and Daniel. "You heard the man—let's get moving."

ACKNOWLEDGMENTS

First, I'd like to thank everyone – family and friends – who supported me in my endeavors to write this novel. You know who you are.

Next, to my readers who provided valuable feedback…
Mel, for questioning the little things and putting up with my deadlines.
Ed, for his efforts and feedback – though he prefers stories set in the wild west.
Eric, whose favorite chapter only took me thirty minutes to write.
Cyn, for reading and reading and reading…then reading some more.

To the fine folks at Denton Square Courthouse Museum – particularly Kelsey, who took me on a tour of the clock tower. I appreciate not having to climb that last ladder (it's really tall).

Thanks to Caroline for doing a fine job editing this book. Please note that any changes – or potential mistakes – I made at the last minute are all on me, not her.

Thanks to Scarlett and Jason for their design work.

To the state of Florida for being a fun place to run off to and do research – and drink at the bars along the coast.

And to my Creator….for everything else.